PRAISE FOR KRISTY CAMBRON

"Enchanting and mesmerizing! *Castle on the Rise* enters an alluring land and time with a tale to be treasured. Ireland comes to life with as much vivid light as the characters of this dual-timeline tale of redemption and love. For those of us who love Ireland and its misty shores, its myths, and its mysteries, Kristy Cambron brings it all to life. More than once I wished to walk through the pages of *Castle on the Rise* and join Cambron's magnificent women on a quest for the truth, and for love."

—Patti Callahan, *New York Times* bestselling author of *Becoming Mrs. Lewis*

"*Castle on the Rise* perfectly showcases rising star Kristy Cambron's amazing talent! Perfect pacing, lovely prose, and an intricate plot blend together in a delightful novel I couldn't put down. Highly recommended!"

—Colleen Coble, *USA TODAY* bestselling author of *Secrets at Cedar Cabin* and the Rock Harbor series

"Cambron's latest is one of her best. Gripping and epic, this intricately woven tale of three generations seeking truth and justice will stay with you long after the last page."

—Rachel Hauck, *New York Times* besselling author

"Vivid visual descriptions will make readers want to linger in the character and time period of each chapter, but they will become quickly immersed soon after starting the next. Romance fans will appreciate how Cambron builds multiple love stories within this richly historical, faith-based tale."

—*Booklist* for *The Lost Castle*

"Cambron once again makes smart use of multiple eras in her latest time-jumping romance. Cambron spins tales of resiliency, compassion, and courage."

—*Publishers Weekly* for *The Los*

"Cambron does it again. However, this
Take a family legacy spanning three era
and you have the latest split-time romance from Cambron."

—*RT Book Reviews*, 4 stars, for *The Lost Castle*

"Set in three different time periods—the French Revolution, World War II, and present day—[*The Lost Castle*] untangles threads of history to reveal a continuous theme of love, heartache, and restoration . . . Cambron slips deftly through generations, weaving tales of romance and intrigue . . . Readers of contemporary and historical fiction will find this book captivating."

—*CBA Market*

"As intricate as a French tapestry, as lush as the Loire Valley, and as rich as heroine Ellie's favorite pain au chocolat, *The Lost Castle* satisfies on every level. The three time lines weave and build upon each other as the three heroines navigate dangerous times and unravel ancient secrets. Kristy Cambron's writing evokes each era in loving detail, and the romances are touching and poignant. *C'est bon!*"

—Sarah Sundin, award-winning author of *The Sea Before Us* and the Waves of Freedom series

"It's been a long time since I've been so thoroughly engrossed in a novel. Kristy Cambron grabs you from the start and weaves a fabulously intricate and intoxicating tale of love and loss. Her settings are breathtaking, her historical detail impeccable, and her characters now dear friends. *The Lost Castle* kept me spellbound!"

—Tamera Alexander, *USA TODAY* bestselling author of *To Whisper Her Name* and *Christmas at Carnton*

"An absolutely lovely read! Cambron weaves an enchanting story of love, loss, war, and hope in *The Lost Castle*. Spanning the French Revolution, World War II, and today, she masterfully carries us into each period with all the romance and danger of the best fairy tale."

—Katherine Reay, award-winning author of *Dear Mr. Knightley* and *A Portrait of Emily Price*

"Readers will be caught up in themes of family, loyalty, and courage—as well as a mystery and even a bit of a fairy-tale romance—in Kristy Cambron's *The Lost Castle*. Cambron weaves together the lives of three very different women with vivid emotion against the lush backdrop of France."

—Beth K. Vogt, Christy Award–winning author

"Cambron's lithe prose pulls together past and present and her attention to historical detail grounds the narrative to the last breathtaking moments."

—*Publishers Weekly*, starred review, for *The Illusionist's Apprentice*

"Cambron has written a gripping tale of suspense that will please her growing fan base."

—*Library Journal* for *The Illusionist's Apprentice*

"At once a love story and a mystery, *The Illusionist's Apprentice* will appeal to anyone who likes novels about strong, enigmatic women, as well as to those curious about what goes on behind the curtains on a magician's stage."

—Historical Novel Society

"Cambron takes readers on an amazing journey into the world of vaudeville illusionists during the Roaring Twenties."

—*RT Book Reviews*, 4½ stars, TOP PICK! for *The Illusionist's Apprentice*

"Prepare to be amazed by *The Illusionist's Apprentice*. This novel will have your pulse pounding and your mind racing to keep up with reversals, betrayals, and surprises from the first page to the last. Like her characters, Cambron works magic so compelling and persuasive, she deserves a standing ovation."

—Greer Macallister, bestselling author of *The Magician's Lie* and *Girl in Disguise*

"With rich descriptions, attention to detail, mesmerizing characters, and an understated current of faith, this work evokes writers such as Kim Vogel Sawyer, Francine Rivers, and Sara Gruen."

—*Library Journal*, starred review, for *The Ringmaster's Wife*

"Historical fiction lovers will adore this novel! *The Ringmaster's Wife* features two rich love stories and a glimpse into our nation's live entertainment history. Highly recommended!"

—*USA TODAY*, *Happy Ever After*

"Cambron takes a real person, Mable Ringling, and breathes fictional life into her while staying true to what is known about this compelling woman. The novel is an intriguing look into circus life in the 1920s."

—*RT Book Reviews*, 4 stars, for *The Ringmaster's Wife*

"Cambron vividly depicts circus life during the 1920s. With a strong supporting cast of friends and family—including a nemesis or two—the women experience heartbreak, loss, hope, and triumph, all set against the colorful backdrop of the 'Greatest Show on Earth.'"

—*Publishers Weekly* for *The Ringmaster's Wife*

"A soaring love story! Vibrant with the glamour and awe that flourished under the Big Top in the 1920s, *The Ringmaster's Wife* invites the reader to meet the very people whose unique lives brought the Greatest Show on Earth down those rattling tracks."

—Joanne Bischof, award-winning author of *The Lady and the Lionheart*

"The second installment of Cambron's Hidden Masterpiece series is as stunning as the first. Though heartbreaking in many places, this novel never fails to show hope despite dire circumstances. God's love shines even in the dark."

—*RT Book Reviews*, 4½ stars, TOP PICK! for *A Sparrow in Terezin*

"Well-researched yet heartbreaking scenes shed light on the horrors of concentration camps, as well as the contrasting beauty behind the prisoners' artwork."

—*RT Book Reviews*, 4½ stars, TOP PICK! for *The Butterfly and the Violin*

"Cambron expertly weaves together multiple plotlines, time lines, and perspectives to produce a poignant tale of the power of love and faith in difficult circumstances. Those interested in stories of survival and the Holocaust, such as Elie Wiesel's 'Night,' will want to read."

—*Library Journal* for *The Butterfly and the Violin*

CASTLE *on the* RISE

BOOKS BY KRISTY CAMBRON

The Lost Castle Novels

The Lost Castle

Castle on the Rise

The Painted Castle (available October 2019)

Stand-Alone Novels

The Ringmaster's Wife

The Illusionist's Apprentice

The Hidden Masterpiece Novels

The Butterfly and the Violin

A Sparrow in Terezin

CASTLE
on the
RISE

A
LOST CASTLE
NOVEL

KRISTY CAMBRON

THOMAS NELSON
Since 1798

Castle on the Rise

Published in Nashville, Tennessee, by Thomas Nelson. Thomas Nelson is a registered trademark of HarperCollins Christian Publishing, Inc.

Published in association with Books & Such Literary Management, 52 Mission Circle, Suite 122, PMB 170, Santa Rosa, California 95409–5370, www.booksandsuch.com.

Interior design by Emily Ghattas.

Thomas Nelson titles may be purchased in bulk for educational, business, fund-raising, or sales promotional use. For information, please e-mail SpecialMarkets@ThomasNelson.com.

Library of Congress Cataloging-in-Publication Data

Names: Cambron, Kristy, author.
Title: Castle on the rise : a Lost Castle novel / Kristy Cambron.
Description: Nashville, Tennessee : Thomas Nelson, [2019] | Includes bibliographical references and index.
Identifiers: LCCN 2018040686 (print) | LCCN 2018042597 (ebook) | ISBN 9780718095505 (epub) | ISBN 9780718095499 (tp : alk. paper)
Subjects: | GSAFD: Christian fiction. | Love stories.
Classification: LCC PS3603.A4468 (ebook) | LCC PS3603.A4468 C37 2019 (print) | DDC 813/.6--dc23
LC record available at https://lccn.loc.gov/2018040686

Printed in the United States of America

For Jeannie and Richard,
because dear friends should have
a castle of their very own.

God spoke to you by so many voices, but you would not hear.

—James Joyce

ONE

When you pass through the waters, I will be with you;
And through the rivers, they shall not overflow you.
When you walk through the fire, you shall not be burned,
Nor shall the flame scorch you.

—ISAIAH 43:2

PRESENT DAY
LES TROIS-MOUTIERS
LOIRE VALLEY, FRANCE

Fairy-tale weddings never included rain on the guest list.

Or snow—and they had both.

November possessed an obstinate will, and Laine Forrester defied every raindrop that dared linger upon the leaded-glass windows on her best friend's wedding day. Misty hollows clung to the autumn landscape outside the estate house at the Domaine du Renard vineyards and shadowed corners of the guest suite inside. Even as the clock nudged toward evening and they'd begun fitting Ellie in her bridal gown, the sky refused to relent.

By the time Laine escorted Ellie along the road to Château des Doux-Rêves—"The Sleeping Beauty," as the castle was affectionately known—a thin layer of white frosted the limbs of the wild plums that lined the road on both sides. Snowflakes drifted down to greet them against a palette of winter grays and violets.

Even with a stunning landscape, Laine now wished they'd thought better of the walk beforehand, as a tea-length bridesmaid dress of satin and lace was not winter's favorite companion. Each time the wind shifted, it sent those pretty little flakes straight down her bodice, and she was forced to reconsider the whole *France is romantic* notion she'd built up in her mind.

"Ellie—you're sure you don't want the driver to take us to the chapel steps? I'd hate for you to have to walk all this way."

"And miss this view? Never. I told the man to drop us off at the front gate or I'd refuse to pay him. And I meant it."

Laine had to admit her friend was wearing the bride image well.

The glow. The confident smile. The little kick in her step as they walked . . . all of it, down to the vintage 1930s bridal gown they'd found just days before, waiting in a shop window in Village Saint-Paul—the eclectic block that was home to some of Paris's best tucked-away treasures. Ellie had paired it with a loose-braided chignon at her nape in twists of ebony. It was in deep contrast to Laine's shorn and newly platinum style, but an equal complement to the wine and deep plums in their bouquets.

The bride draped a lavender-gray stole across her shoulders—the *something old* and *something borrowed* from her husband-to-be's grandmother. And despite a few noticeable shivers shared with Laine, Ellie seemed at peace—very unbridelike.

Even un-Ellie-like, come to think of it.

It seemed they'd flipped personalities, and Laine's usual steadiness had been replaced with a skittishness in every second breath. She trailed behind, ready to save the bride from falling into a snowbank.

"I still think Quinn would take issue with this. Does he know you opted for a hike through the forest before exchanging vows?"

"Who's going to tell him now?" Ellie challenged, angling her heel around a tiny patch of ice.

"Of course I wouldn't say a word. But it doesn't feel the least bit honorable to make you hike in those shoes—or in the snow, for that matter. We'll be the traditional *something blue* when we do get you to the chapel. Wraps only cover so much, you know."

"It's just a dusting." Ellie smiled one of those knowing grins that said she was listening, but just. "And you're not complaining. I can take it if you can."

"I know you, Ellison Carver. You're being gracious like your grandma Vi taught you, but then you'll do exactly what you want to anyway."

"And I know *you*, Laine. You're as enchanted with this walk as I am. Admit it. All those years spent haunting the back rooms of your grandfather's antique shop mean your imagination is waking up again. And for a self-proclaimed history buff, a castle has to be the ultimate temptation. You're just mother-henning me, but we're almost there. See?"

Laine lifted her gaze to the ghostly cutout of stone through twilight and trees. She exhaled low—like she'd held that breath for too long and the shock of beauty finally drew it out.

It did remind her of the vintage shop.

Of books that told stories . . . instruments that played melodies . . . They were no less an art form than an ages-old castle whose spires touched the sky.

Ancient walls seemed to climb and crumble at the same time, six stories against the clouds. A moat surrounded the ruins, its waters still as glass. Tree limbs waved and creaked with the toying wind. And at the grove's edge stood a tiny chapel, with cobblestones leading to an open door, its candlelight inside glowing warm and inviting behind stained glass.

"I know what you're thinking," Ellie whispered. "It's freezing.

I'm Ms. Clumsy, and the heels are a few inches too high for anything good to come of it. But I need to stand up next to Quinn. You know—tall versus petite-ish genes and all. I want to look that boy in the eye when I say 'I do.'"

"Actually . . . I was going to agree with you. How many times in life does a girl get to live a magical moment like this?"

Laine paused, the kiss of candlelight through the trees making rhetorical questions sink deeper into her heart than they should. She bounced back a smile that wouldn't be questioned, no matter what was silently fracturing her on the inside.

"I'm defenseless with this view."

"You and me both. I remember the first time I saw it, and it felt the same." Merlot lips spreading a soft smile across her profile, Ellie hooked her elbow around Laine's and leaned into her shoulder. "I just realized . . . this is the last time we'll be together before I step through that door and become a Mrs. too. Any final advice?"

Laine accepted a wedding in France, though beautiful, for what it was: an escape from the life crumbling back home.

Now was not the time to share her brand of advice. Or brutal honesty. The story of a broken marriage and uncertain future would have to wait its turn. Maybe she could come clean when Ellie and Quinn returned from their honeymoon. Or in the spring, when life had settled down. By then, Laine and Cassie would be back home—in a *new* home.

She could face the truth when it felt safe to pick up the pieces and start again.

It was a battle, but Laine shoved the ache away. She held on to her smile with everything she possessed and stood back, marveling as Ellie dropped her train—satin and lace absorbing the glow of light from the chapel door. They paused together, the snow drifting in a dance around them.

"Live every moment," Laine whispered into the twilight. "That's what you said to me when I walked down the aisle, remember? I gift it back to you. Fix every second of this night in your heart. Protect it, and visit it often."

"Live every moment. Yes." Ellie half laughed, then paused and cast her gaze off in the distance. She creased her brow. Deep. Like she was lost somewhere else for a breath.

Funny, she always did that just before she . . .

"Oh—no tears!"

Laine rushed forward a step and dotted impending tears with her gloved pinkie before Ellie could ruin her wedding photos with mascara tracks. "I'm so sorry. What did I say?"

"Nothing!" Ellie blinked, turning her face up to the night air as Laine continued patting and fanning. "It's nothing. I'm just so glad you're here, that's all. With everything moving so fast and getting married without Grandma Vi . . . It's a lot to manage on my own."

"Well, you're not on your own. You have Quinn. You have me and Cassie—that little flower girl in there who loves her honorary Auntie Ellie more than anything. And there's a chapel full of guests who are probably wondering where in the world we are. All that love makes me sure Grandma Vi's watching over you right this minute. So no tears, darling. At least not until after Quinn sees you, heels and mascara intact."

"You're right. No tears now. Not even the happy ones." Ellie inhaled deep, then let it out in a fog of frozen breath.

Being a head taller and a shade older, Laine couldn't help it; she had everything necessary to give her friend an effective maternal glare. And she did. Staring down her nose with just enough pertness to warrant her concern. "Are you sure you're okay? I want this to be perfect for you."

"It already is perfect. His family is here and so is mine. And I get to become his wife. What else could I need?" Ellie bit the corner of her bottom lip, alerting Laine that a sweet little request from her best friend was likely to follow. "Except maybe to get on your good side so I can convince you and Cassie to stay a bit longer?"

"How long is a bit?"

"Oh, up to Christmas? Or a couple of weeks at least? It seems like such a long trip to stay only a few days. And I know you're still looking for a new job, so there's no vacation days to request. Don't answer now—just think about it. It can be your wedding present to us. Quinn knows I'll want my best friend and her daughter here as long as possible. And he has an almost-niece now too, so I'm sure I can convince him with that angle."

Ellie had said it tongue in cheek, but she didn't know how right she was. Staying through Christmas wouldn't be a problem. As far as home was concerned, Laine and Cassie could stay on forever. It was everything after the staying that had her chewing her thumbnail these days.

"We can talk about all that later. Right now you have an appointment I won't dare let you miss." Holding out the bridal bouquet put an end to it. "Let's go get you married."

Laine winked as Ellie took the flowers in hand, nudging a little spring back in her blushing-bride status. They eased into step with one another as they neared the chapel stairs, where Quinn's grandfather—the enigmatic estate winemaker, Titus—would be waiting to walk her down the aisle, despite blindness having taken hold. Laine paused and tugged Ellie's elbow as movement at the side of the castle ruins caught her attention.

A man in a sharp-cut black suit stood out against the backdrop of silver and stone. He cut a path through the trees, until she had a clean view of his profile. There was something familiar but still foreign about him. Coal-black hair. Tall. Broad shouldered . . . Like she'd seen him before somehow but still knew she'd not.

"Ellie, who's that? Another wedding guest?"

"Who?"

"Him." Laine pointed out the figure coming their way. "If we're late, then he really is. He's headed for the chapel too—like he's here for a wedding but just decided to take a stroll through the snow."

"That must be Cormac."

"Who's Cormac?"

"Quinn's older brother, from the side of the family I haven't met. I've only seen photos. He lives with their father in Dublin. They have a younger sister too—Keira—but all I know is she's in London and rarely visits . . . I never dreamed he'd come all this way."

"Is it that surprising he would come to his brother's wedding?"

"It is if they haven't seen each other but a time or two in years. When we moved up the wedding date, Quinn and I just decided to keep it simple—family and friends on the estate, and some from the village in Loudun. And you, of course. But Quinn must have invited him."

The man strolled through the snow at an even pace, scanning the envelope of woods on all sides. Until he caught sight of them shivering in evening gowns, with bouquets that had taken to trembling in their hands, and quickstepped in their direction.

He stopped before them, the glow from the chapel resting upon his shoulders.

There was no doubt in the light: He was every bit a Foley in the eyes and face, but in his mannerisms was clearly a walking opposite. Where Quinn was laid back—wearing worn-in pub tees and lugging around a beat-up guitar case—Cormac appeared buttoned up. Clean cut. Musicless. As frozen as the evening air around them.

"Ye must be Ellie." He stepped forward, tall like his brother but with a much deeper brogue, and clasped the bride's free hand in both of his. Ellie tried and failed to cover what must have shocked her speechless.

"Um . . . yes. Cormac, is it?" She nodded, her sweet smile dwarfed by the nervous bobbing motion of her chin that didn't stop right away.

"Nice to finally meet ye." He offered the slightest shadow of a smile to Laine as he released the bride's hand. "I hope 'tis alright I came without the RSVP. 'Twas last minute, an' the flight was delayed 'cause o' this weather. But by the looks o' things, I see I made it just in time."

"Yes, of course . . . Quinn will be so happy you're here."

"Welcome to the family," he added, with an artful deflection of the groom, and what Ellie inferred may signal family troubles. "I'll just see ye inside then." He tipped his head in a respectful nod to them both, then stepped into the chapel without another word.

"Well, if married life brings surprises," Ellie said, smiling, "I suppose we're starting right now."

"You'll have to tell me what that was later."

"If I even know myself."

A raised bouquet and a groom's grandfather later, the bride was ready. And in a tiny chapel with candles flickering, Laine's four-year-old twirling as a fairy flower girl, guests standing in a semicircle, and a besotted groom grinning his life away at the altar, Laine watched as two people united their tomorrows.

It was hushed and hopeful—every bit the fairy tale that had nothing to do with a storybook castle looming in the background and everything to do with the surrendering of one heart to the other. No matter what stories and secrets tomorrow held, Laine knew one thing for sure.

She wanted to believe in love again. *Needed* to believe in it.

Even as candles flickered low and a newly married couple kissed at the altar with loved ones gathered around. And an estranged brother of the groom, brooding in the back, seemed to usher in a host of questions about Quinn and Ellie's potential for a fairy-tale future.

In the midst of all that mattered for those dear to her, Laine could have sworn Cormac's hallmark Foley greens dared to glance her way—more than once.

What in the world could she make of that?

TWO

DECEMBER 27, 1915
26/27 ABBEY STREET LOWER
DUBLIN, IRELAND

"Are these seats taken?"

It was the Abbey Theatre's opening night performance of *A Minute's Wait*—anyone with a ticket must have known all seats were occupied for a sold-out show. But Issy knew that voice too well to overlook it. She'd been attempting to tuck back a wisp of cinnamon hair that had escaped the pins at her nape but abandoned it and looked up instead.

Sean O'Connell.

Standing in the aisle of the U-shaped balcony. The electric lights cast a glow on the clerical dress of a vicar instead of the customary white tie the other gentlemen wore. So the rumors they'd heard about the elder O'Connell brother were true. In the many months Sean had retreated from Dublin's social circles, he'd stepped headlong into the role of clergy.

Problem was, he resembled anything but the guilelessness of the uniform.

His hair was quite smart, the burnished brown combed back off his brow in a more mature style like he'd decided to take life with a more deliberate manner, beginning with the comb. With eyes the cool sea blue he shared with his brother so direct in focus on her, it seemed they were alone in a crowded room. Seemingly indifferent to the high spirits around them, Sean ignored the sniggering of ladies in opera dresses who eyed him from a row in front. And though Issy hadn't expected to see it again—maybe not ever—he gifted her with a smile she could only read as genuine.

The entire portrait smacked of forgiveness, and surprise triggered a flutter in her midsection.

"'Tis the first time I do believe I've ever caught Lady Isolde Byrne without a reply."

"I've never been Lady Isolde to you, and I don't mean to start accepting a title now."

"Who would dare leave ye alone at the theater?"

"No one with intention of harm, I assure you." Issy recovered, patting a gloved hand on the velvet seat back of the aisle-side chair. "This one is Honor's, but she's been detained for the moment. And the other was to be Rory's, but I daresay my brother's meeting has run late on Dame Street, so it appears we've lost our escort. Won't we be the scandal of the ladies' parlors tomorrow?"

"Well, we can' be havin' that, can we now? I could be persuaded to abandon my seat all the way in the back an' join ye up here."

"Please." She pulled her knees back so he could scoot by her.

Sean slipped into the inner seat. And before Issy could fret over finding some measure of polite conversation, he leaned close, engaged her without a veil of awkwardness between them. Like they'd last seen each other the day before instead of six months prior.

He rolled his show program and pointed across the balcony, in the direction of a man with prominent seating in the front row. "'Tis him over there—Pádraig Pearse."

"The leader of the Irish Citizen Army is actually here?"

Issy leaned past a lady's voluminous coiffure in front of them, eager to catch a glimpse of the schoolmaster–turned–rebel leader whose spirited, *"Ireland unfree shall never be at peace!"* had impassioned masses of Irishmen at Fenian leader O'Donovan Rossa's eulogy that summer. His words had been all over the newspapers in August, igniting a spark of energy throughout the country. Controversial or not, he was a real-life news headline in that very theater.

Pearse boasted a reserved presence that lent much more to his past as the schoolmaster of St. Enda's boys' school—not a fiery leader who inspired the hearts of Irishmen and -women across the country. A clean-shaven jaw and thick brow appeared as if rarely animated. He sat up straight, attentive to a lady with a remarkable lace evening gown and Gibson-girl pompadour seated next to him. As she chatted he nodded, pensive in taking in the sights while they awaited the curtain to be drawn back.

"You're certain that's Pearse?" Issy whispered, completely taken in.

"In the flesh." Sean nodded. "Special guest o' the Countess Markievicz. The older gentleman on his left is the socialist James Connolly. After him, Michael Mallin—wit' the impressive mustache. An' Seán Connolly will be onstage tonight—bein' an actor with the ICA Liberty Players. Revolutionary company for our audience, I'd say. Though the unionists here would call them rebels, as they advocate for an Irish free state at all costs."

"My mother would say there is a very fine line between conviction and rebelliousness, and both border upon the unsavory."

"An' what would ye say?"

Where Pearse had revealed limited spirit in his features, Connolly showed the faintest glimmer of a smile—allowing the apples of his cheeks to rise above his mustache as he turned to whisper something to the rebel leader. Pearse nodded, his gaze set on the audience below, tapping an ivory-handled walking stick against his knee as if considering what the man had said.

"That I don't know all the facts—yet. But I aim to learn as much as I can."

"Rumor has it Pearse keeps a sword hidden in that walkin' stick. Want to bet on it bein' true? We can hunt newspaper articles until we find a photo confirmin' it. Sounds like yer kind o' fun."

"I don't bet," Issy snapped, though she had a difficult time keeping humor from her tone whenever he teased her. "It's unbecoming for a lady—as is discussing politics in an open forum."

"There's a first time for everythin'. I know ye have yer own convictions. Rebellious streaks too, if I might remark without drawin' yer ire."

"A vicar shouldn't speak of such things."

"Come now, Issy. I haven' changed all that much. I'm the same man."

Issy huffed in play—almost like they'd fallen into their usual rhythm—but found the blush lace of her opera gown so restricting, it punished her for daring to relax at all. "I've heard Rory mention Pearse before as though he were some mythical figure. But does he appear more of the schoolmaster than the rebel type? I daresay he gives the impression of calm, sitting over there so unassuming."

"Some say."

"Who?"

"The ones who haven't heard him speak. 'Tis said that man can cast a spell o'er a crowd faster than free pints in a pub, wit' a supportin' cast to match. Mallin is a ranked leader for the ICA an' the countess works alongside. She even designed their uniforms. An' notice—no tiara for her tonight. 'Tis said she sold all her jewelry to feed the poor after the Dublin workers' lockout, if ye can be believin' that. A woman leadin' with the men. Ireland's makin' strides."

"The ICA is building quite an organization. I found a newspaper article about it in Father's library just yesterday. You don't think it something to inspire men to ill-advised action, do you? With all the Irish uniforms parading through St. Stephen's Green, I don't know what to believe."

Sean stared down at the stage, though the quick deflection of a smile in his profile said his interest was piqued by something other than the ICA's activities.

"What is it ye were about in yer father's study then?"

Issy lifted her chin, ignoring his quip. "Perhaps I was fetching my Sunday hat."

"An' ye found it nosin' through the newspaper stack on the earl's desk, no doubt." Sean laughed, covering his chin with his palm like he was trying to master it and failed.

"Honestly," she shot back, wishing it were proper to whack him with her program. "As if all I'm fit to do is thumb through the latest copy of *Weldon's*. My father doesn't mind my interest in politics."

"Neither do I, truth be told. But ye know yer father's under the assumption yer on the unionist side o' the aisle—wit' him. What will he do when he finds out his daughter sympathizes wit' the nationalist cause an' Pearse's dreams of a free republic?"

"No need to wheedle about the details."

"An' I'm not tryin' to force ye to be the ladies' journal type. I'd be smart to avoid forcin' that mold on ye. But I'd say Rory would be the one to be askin' about affairs in Dublin. Ye won't get much from tiptoein' about in yer father's study. Ye need to ask a man on the ground."

"There you go again, feigning ignorance when you read more than I do, Sean O'Connell. I know you've been away from the city," Issy said without thinking, flitting her glance down to his clerical jacket before she could stop herself. She averted her gaze to the stage in haste. "But if you won't tell me, fine. Maybe I just will ask my brother."

If anyone can find him . . .

Rory Byrne had become a ghost. Interest in ICA doings in Dublin seemed to have absorbed him completely.

The lights flickered, signaling showtime.

"Issy, I wonder iffen I might . . ." Sean cleared his throat as the audience chatter faded out and the first notes of the orchestra drifted in. "May I speak wit' ye after the curtain call?"

Issy swallowed hard but presented a sweet smile over it. "Are we not speaking now?"

"I meant alone. If ye can spare me the time."

Issy peeked out of the corner of her eye.

Sean's gaze drifted about from balcony to stage . . . even to the program he rolled in his palms. She guessed he wasn't ready to talk of the past, and neither was she—especially not with the man who sat next to her now.

This wasn't the same friend from her youth. The brow that had been marked with a coltish spirit once had drawn serious lines. But then, war had a remarkable ability to remind one of weighted things. Life and death and the intertwining of both made men somber, and many a brow had been rendered humorless since the summer of 1914. Perhaps Sean was only taking on the same absence of frivolity as most others she knew in feeling grim events deserved their earnest.

The lights finally dimmed and a hush swept the crowd.

"We should—" Issy fanned her program in the direction of the stage. "It's starting."

"After the show then."

"I'll see Honor home after the play, so she'll be with me if that's alright? But . . . I haven't seen her since I sat down. Where could she be?"

Her friend had scooted off to the powder room some time ago, but as the curtain drew back and lights washed center stage, scene one fully engaged . . . still the aisle seat lay empty.

"There," Sean whispered, tipping his chin toward the balcony's center door and the young lady who'd squeezed through it.

Honor shimmied her way through the dark down to their row and eased into her seat without a word. Though Issy expected it, Honor didn't comment further, nor explain what had kept her. Just squared the shoulders of her evergreen gown to the stage as the actors continued their lines, ready to hold pretenses as long as she could.

"Honor McGinn, where in the world have you been?" Issy whispered, hoping neither Sean nor the theatergoers seated behind could hear.

"I told ye—the powder room."

"Liam passed our row and asked after you. I had a difficult time explaining where his fiancée was without telling an outright lie."

Honor's cheeks flushed. And instead of settling in for the show or rightly offering the barest of explanations, she fidgeted with the folds of fabric at her waist.

"Whatever's the matter?"

"Not a thing, Issy. Let's just enjoy the show."

Fidget. Squirm. Jostle and sigh. And then Honor repeated the sequence all over again. One thought hit Issy as she watched—a possibility that set her heart to sinking. She leaned in, heads close so she could whisper by Honor's ear. "Is it Rory? He didn't show up and catch you in the lobby, did he? I knew it was a terrible idea to come tonight."

"Honestly." Honor bit back a whispered scold in her fire-starting manner. It seemed her hair gleamed a brighter shade of strawberry blonde under the glow of the stage lights. "If I can't be trusted to stay away from yer brother for five minutes strung together, ye must be thinkin' I'm as weak as my father does."

"I do not think you weak. But I do think you in love with a man who is not your fiancé, and not terribly clever at hiding it—an awkward showing for the present circumstances. You're to marry Liam Devenish this spring, and he sits just two rows behind. How much more incentive could there be to cease in seeing my brother behind board?"

"Shhh!" Someone scolded her whispers from behind.

Issy and Honor hushed and set their spines straight, composing in unison.

Her friend's back grew more rigid as she watched the stage, but Issy could guess what was going on inside that head of hers. Honor McGinn was engaging in the precise activity she'd been reared *not* to do. It was one thing to be friends with an Anglo-Irish like Issy. That the McGinn family could tolerate because of a tidy fortune and a respectable family name. But it was quite a different beast altogether for an Irish-born lady of means to marry one of them—a Catholic marrying a Protestant, and an Englishman at that . . . It just wasn't done.

Any future for Honor and Issy's brother was a vapor at best.

Issy reached out, slipping her ivory satin-gloved hand over to squeeze her friend's and tugging until she looked in her eyes. Honor did look back, but sweet eyes of cornflower blue had glazed with tears.

A tiny flash of rebelliousness sparked within Issy and she leaned forward, decision made. "Come with me. I spotted an alcove in the lobby. We can steal away there until the show is over and sneak out in the crowd after. You won't have to see Liam tonight."

Honor's nod was so automatic, Issy leaned over to whisper to Sean. "I must go. I beg you that we may speak another time."

"I have a motor. I can be bringin' it 'round if ye want to leave—" Sean had half stood with her declaration, but now sat back down as she moved to follow Honor.

Issy mouthed, *"I'm so sorry."* She picked up her lace-and-bead train to hurry along.

Honor charged up the aisle, Issy hastening to keep up in tight-laced heels that punished with sharp pains in nearly every step from the auditorium, then gripping rails down the flight of stairs to the ground-floor vestibule. Once there, Honor buried her face into gloved palms and crumpled in Issy's arms, sending them into an off-balanced tilt against the wall.

"Dearest . . . what's this?"

Whatever *this* was, it was far more serious than a tear on the cheek. Honor was breaking apart.

Issy swept them into an alcove behind a green velvet curtain, just out of the lobby with ceiling lamps casting a glow onto the black-and-white tile floor, and the reflection against polished wood wainscoting on all walls. A stiff bench became their sanctuary and they melted down upon it, Issy holding her friend.

"Is this about Rory? You must know, if I had a choice it would be you as my sister. Always." She pulled a handkerchief from her beaded evening bag and dotted the underside of Honor's eyes. "I'm terribly sorry. I just wish there was something more I could do."

They were true but empty words—a clumsy way of drying tears, and Issy knew it.

"Ye don't understand . . ."

"Then help me understand, Honor. Tell me what's troubling you. Devenish is a kind man from a respected Irish-Catholic family. That suits the McGinns, doesn't it? Your father only wants something bright for your future. Do you see?"

"Could ye see without lovin', Issy? Tell me the truth."

Issy kept from speaking what would do no good to have said. She patted Honor's cheeks with the linen square, forcing a smile she hoped would help instead of harm.

"Issy—I'm with child."

The blood drained from Issy's head as the shocking words sank deep. She stilled her hand, the gauzy kerchief frozen in midair.

"You're with . . . ?" Issy exhaled as knots quick-tangled her insides and she finally dropped her hand to her lap. "And you're certain of this?"

Honor nodded: a pitiful, chin-quivering truth.

"'Tis what kept me in the powder room—the sick is terrible. I've had a time in tryin' to hide it. But I can' much longer, an' the season lasts through March. I don' think I can stand the dinner parties every night. An' when my father learns of it . . . I don' know what he'll do." Honor's cry was muted by a gloved hand she drew up to stifle it. She looked away, burying her face in the shadows.

"Have you spoken with Rory yet?"

"No . . ." Another muffled sob. Stronger. Wracking her as if it would split her in two.

Issy pressed the handkerchief into Honor's palm and slipped her arm around to hug her shoulders, drawing her close as she sorted the thoughts pinging wildly through her mind.

"Very well—first things first. I will send a message to the ICA this night. Someone should be able to reach my brother, and I'll demand he return home straightaway."

"Ye cannot, Issy. Rory can' know yet."

"Perhaps you can come back to Ashford with me tonight then? We will not tell my parents why, but we can travel south to the castle cove and you may stay away from the city to think things through. Once in Wicklow, we will summon Rory and discuss this calmly—"

"It's not what ye think." Honor looked up, doe eyes piercing even through the shadows. "Rory'd never dishonor me. Not in that way."

What a time for assumptions. "Then . . . who did, dishonor you in that way?"

In an instant the visage of Liam Devenish came to mind and fire blasted through Issy, burning from crown to toes. She shot to standing with fists balled at her sides, ready if she must to fight the world—beginning with the ill-mannered wolf in nobleman's clothing.

"If it's that rake of a fiancé in there, I'll march into the auditorium and box his ears. I don't care who is in attendance tonight—I will not let this stand if that brute has dared such a depravity!"

"No, Issy. Sit. Please."

Her dearest friend in such a condition as this? Issy wanted to make it all go away or else fling her fist into the man's jaw and at least feel better to land a blow he'd remember. But Honor's pleading was everything, and she obeyed. She swept her hand beneath her gown to settle back beside her friend—though she still perched on the edge of the bench on principle.

"I'll tell ye this once, an' then ye must promise me not a word of it will be spoken to anyone," Honor begged, her voice barely louder than a breath. "Promise me."

"I promise. Of course, but—"

"'Twas the night I walked home from the *Cumann na mBan* women's meetin' in October. Do ye remember? I was kept late, helping' wit' the ICA pamphlets."

Issy nodded. Of course she remembered. Her friend had suffered a fall that night . . . a bruise on her jaw . . . cut above the eye . . . and was quite shaken over the whole ordeal the next time they'd met. She remembered fussing over the state Honor had been in at tea days later.

"I had to walk through Portobello that night, near where the English soldiers are stationed." Honor's chin quivered and she closed her eyes for a breath, shaking her head.

Oh Lord . . . Please, no . . .

"Honor." Issy gripped her by the shoulders, staring dead in her eyes. "You can't mean that you were—?"

"Issy? Are ye there?"

She pressed a finger to her lips and squeezed Honor's shoulder with the other, shushing them from saying anything further.

"We're here, Sean." Issy slipped around the curtain to face him, hoping that would give Honor a few precious moments to compose herself.

He stood in the back of the vestibule, several feet away. But there was no lightness about him. No heart-confusing smiles or jests. Simply the friend she knew. Steadfast, hands buried in trouser pockets, waiting for whatever she might ask of him.

"Can I help?"

"Actually, yes. It seems Honor has taken ill. I'd much prefer it if she didn't have to wait for Father's motor to arrive at the end of the performance. So if we may, I accept the offer of your assistance home—with utmost gratitude. She's quite exhausted, and I fear the crowd may induce a swoon. If we could leave now, I think it best."

"I already passed an excuse to Devenish, though I'm thinkin' he's goin' to want an explanation at some point. Mine won' keep long."

"And he shall have one. But not tonight. If we could stop at her family's home along the Green, gather her things, and then drive back to Ashford Manor tonight? I know it's a lot to ask . . ."

Sean was astute enough to pick up that something was amiss but tactful enough not to comment. Whether he'd heard anything they'd said, Issy couldn't rightly know. He shifted his gaze—a quick peek to the broken young lady behind the curtain—and simply nodded, his usual discretion locked in place. "Of course. If it's what ye want."

"Good. Thank you. I'll just see to Honor and—" She turned, but the touch of his hand against hers drew her back around to face him.

He let go, almost in the same breath, and dropped his hands back at his sides. "Before we go, I've been needin' to tell ye somethin'. An' if Honor's ill I don' want to disturb her wit' it on the drive."

The cool blue of his eyes petitioned Issy to stay, and regardless of why, she was rendered defenseless. He hadn't reached for her hand in so long. Not in that way. Not since the last time they'd spoken, when he'd asked for a future she was unable to give.

If this was the moment to bring back the failed proposal, so be it.

"All right, Sean. I'm listening."

"I confess I crossed paths wit' Rory days back, an' he said ye'd be here tonight. Ye were goin' to find out sooner or later, so I may as well be the one to tell ye . . . Levi's bound for Ireland."

If it was possible to be hit with two tidal waves in one night, Issy was left swimming.

She dug her fingernails into the seams of her beaded evening bag, hoping he didn't see the one sign of how the news affected her.

Words, Issy. Find them. Say them.

"I see. And your brother will return soon?"

He nodded. "Seems a year in Brooklyn was enough for his likin'. He missed the old country more than he thought he would. Took some time for the letter to reach the island, but Levi could be on a boat an' back to Dublin anytime now. Workin' his way across."

"Well. How nice it will be for your mother to have him home. He'll stay with her, I assume."

"Levi's not one for the Dublin season, that's certain. Nor for bein' tied down under our mother's roof in County Wicklow. But he'll be about. Thought ye deserved a bit o' warnin' between Dublin an' those castle ruins o' yers."

"You mean in case we should pass each other in the street?"

Mustering courage to evade Sean's knowing glances, Issy determined to simply focus on helping her friend get home. Once there, they could both fall apart behind closed doors, instead of in the Abbey Theatre lobby with scores of patrons nibbling on their pitiful scene.

"Thank you, Sean, for thinking of it. Was there anything else?"

"If there is, it'll keep for tonight. I'll just bring the motor 'round." He started off, then turned, faltering a bit. "An' wait under the awnin' out front, yeah? Will keep ye ladies out o' the rain. I've an umbrella an' will come fetch ye."

The list of troubles Issy had considered at the start of the evening had been small—limited to what their social calendar might dictate for Honor's impending nuptials. But things were now to end quite differently. For Honor. For Rory, who didn't even know it yet. For her, as the combination of Sean's reemergence, Honor's news, and Levi's return fractured places she'd thought long since healed. And for a world at war, it seemed Dublin was its own powder keg with streets and lives rigged to the fuse.

Issy was loath to wonder, as they climbed in Sean's motor and she cradled Honor in her arms, whispering that everything was going to be alright as they chugged down Abbey Street, how their lives could have begun to unravel so quickly? And why, in the midst of such turmoil, did it feel so right to look up and find Sean O'Connell once again at her side?

THREE

DECEMBER 24, 1797
ASHFORD MANOR
COUNTY WICKLOW, IRELAND

It must have been him—*the thief*—lying in a motionless heap in the center of the snow-laden field.

"*AY-ra*. Whoa now, *AY-ra* . . ." Maeve Ashford tugged on Éire's reins, cooing to ease the mare to a halt. She twisted in her saddle and raised her lantern high, scanning the length of the road.

The lantern's glow proved paltry, lighting only a portion of rock wall that bordered the ridge up to the sea cliffs of Castle Chryn. There was no movement about, save for an army of snowflakes that painted the landscape into a blither of white. The outline of ancient ruins had become a silent specter on the horizon—Gothic arches rising in mist and mossy walls that weren't used to such heavy snow, the deep tawny stones standing as the lone witness over the glen.

Hoofprints led all the way from her family's stables through the rocky expanse of the ridge, indicating the posse of men had trampled away from the castle. The prints faded down the length of road in front of her, disappearing into the tangle-treed base of the Wicklow Mountains. In haste the men had overlooked the junction of a second, smaller trail that trekked over the rise in uneven plods . . . and ended with the dark mound crumpled on the ridge.

Even through the fall of shadows, there was little doubt—a man lay there. With no horse. No hat or wares strewn about around him. Just a twilight sky and sea and gently falling snow as his companions. Strips of something—wool from his coat?—flapped in the wind.

"I've found him—the brigand is here!" Maeve cried out to the group of grooms who'd gone on hunt, straining her voice into the wind.

The effort was drowned out by the backdrop of wind and waves, the sea's angry gale. Éire *clip-clopped* her hooves, dancing a nervous jig over stony ground, as if the animal, too, had surveyed the scene and understood what was at stake.

It seems I must apprehend him on my own . . .

Maeve slid from her horse, holding the lantern in a steadfast grip as her boots hit the ground. She looped Éire's reins around a jagged stone atop the rock wall and started up the ridge, step by easy step, the frozen field grasses crunching beneath her heels.

"Sir?" She grimaced at the automatic address and shook her head. Calling a thief "sir"? He deserved no such definition, not even from the propriety of her mother's hopelessly strict English upbringing.

Few men could boast they'd bested a stablemaster as solid as Leary Ó Flannagáin, but it appeared as though this one had, if reports of the violence at her family's Ashford Manor estate were to be believed. Maeve took it as a warning and would not give the vagrant a moment's worth of leeway.

She squinted into the wind, keeping her gaze fixed on what she could make out as an arm draped over his side. Had he a musket, or did he brandish a hidden blade? Maeve didn't doubt either was above him.

"It is futile to resist. You are taken into custody for the theft of my father's horse and injury to our stablemaster. When the local magistrate returns, you shall have a proper trial by representatives of the king's court." She paused to unsheathe the dagger tucked in her belt.

The aroma of a pub washed over her as Maeve stood over his feet.

Even the salt-sea air blowing across the moor couldn't mask it: heat, sweat, and alcohol—the latter being the robust, wheaty smell of Guinness. The man was a drunkard, no doubt. An overindulgence of black champagne at the local pub must have caused him to lose his sense of occasion, and here they were as a result.

Maeve kicked the sole of his riding boot, tensing in expectation he'd fight after. But there was nothing. Not fist or flailing arm. Not even the rise and fall of his chest to signal he was still breathing. Just wool dancing on an icy breeze.

"Why couldn't you have passed us by? They shall hang you for this." She sighed, shaking her head as she walked around him to search for weapons in the snow. "Such a waste that a man should lose his life for a momentary folly."

Without warning the man lurched, clamping down on her ankle in a vise grip.

Maeve slammed forward to her knees, the lantern tumbling in the snow.

Glass shattered to one side as the wind swept in, killing the flame. The hood of her cape fell with the gust, exposing her face and neck to biting wind—blasting, slapping, whipping her hair about her shoulders in an auburn curtain.

Breaths rocked in and out of her lungs as Maeve held the dagger in place, creating a shield of warning between them. The man eyed it, fixating on the length of blade in her hand, then focused on her face. Perhaps in seeing that the dagger was quite real, he released her. "I didn' mean to . . . hurt ye."

"So you are alive," she breathed out, more than half alarmed, and yanked the entirety of her skirts out of his reach.

"Am I?" He attempted to sit up on a drawn-out groan but gave up almost immediately and dropped back in the snow. "An' here I was thinkin' ye were St. Peter at the holy gates. I can' decide whether I'm relieved or disappointed that yer not."

Think quickly, Maeve . . .

"As I said, I am charged with bringing you in."

"Yer serious?"

"Yes. *I am*. And if you do not attempt trickery, then you haven't any worry about being sliced clean through the middle."

Maeve ignored his brass and rocked back on her heels. The dagger she held high, hoping enough twilight was left for the glint of the razor-sharp blade to help do her talking for her.

"I . . . don' . . ."

"You've had a pint or two down at the village pub. Yes?"

He struggled for each breath, stringing incoherent words so she could barely hear him.

Judas, he'll need help. No man in this condition could speak, let alone hope to stand on his own. And he'd have more than a thick head to contend with in the morning—a crude thing to awaken in a prison cell with no memory of the folly that brought him to it, but it appeared his future.

He coughed. And, on a moan, tried again. "I don' . . ."

"You don't what?" Maeve edged closer, straining to hear, then saw it . . . *crimson*.

A defiant half-moon patch darkened the snow beneath his coat in deep red-brown. The threat he could pose forgotten, she dropped the dagger in the snow and leaned over him. Riding gloves made the task difficult, so she ripped them off and fumbled with the buttons on his frock coat until she could pull back the side.

Dear Lord . . .

Blood.

So much, it had soaked from skin through linen shirt and waistcoat, spreading a trail down the side of his riding trousers. She pulled back his vest to find a hole: small but brutal in its meaning.

The culprit was a musket ball that had landed a target just under his ribs, bleeding badly enough it looked to steal his life unless someone saw to him—and soon.

"Try not to move." Maeve went to work, tearing strips of muslin out of her petticoat to press to the wound.

"Ye said don' . . . resist ye . . . So, I don'." He raised his wrists for mock shackles to encircle. "I surrender."

She sighed, the oddest sensation of a smile near taking over her mouth. Did he dare jest at a time like this? There was no real humor in it, just misplaced wit. An arrogance he shouldn't have possessed in his reduced state.

"How could you resist? Look at you. Have you no mind that you are quite possibly gravely injured along with being a foolish drunkard?"

"I've had no drink."

"The aroma would suggest otherwise. But hush. Don't try to speak." She looked into his face for the first time.

Curious, but the man didn't have the appearance of a thief.

Upon closer inspection Maeve could see he wasn't in tatters or unkempt rags. Besides the musket ball that had damaged him, his attire appeared clean, and though not stylish enough to be labeled foppish, neither coat nor vest showed wear at the seams.

Was he a gentleman or merely a thief in gentlemen's clothes?

Without lantern light there was little more to discern, save for hair that blew in dark waves about his forehead and eyes he'd clamped shut, squinting on what she read as fresh waves of pain.

"Nod, please, if you can hear me."

He obeyed, albeit with a notable clench to his jaw.

"Good. Just try to stay awake." She hated the sharp intake of breath she caused when pressing a wad of fabric against his side. "I shall see that you are properly cared for. You have my word on it. But I need you to be still and not try anything clever. May I trust you in that?"

He nodded again, eyes still clamped tight.

"You are in Wicklow, at the cove of Castle Chryn. And—"

"I know where I am," he snapped, his tone sharper than it should have been for his present circumstances.

"Fine. If you know that, then you may further know that we are without magistrate at present. No doubt the men will have to take you on to the authorities at Kilmainham Gaol prison."

He shook his head, furious in his refusal. "I won' go to Dublin."

"You haven't choice in the matter, sir. Not after you strike a stablemaster about the head and steal away with an earl's prized stallion. Theft is a punishable crime in Ireland the same as it is in England."

"A condition that means I must . . . stay here. I'll surrender after."

"After what, pray? Have you a more pressing engagement than your impending death?"

"Please . . ."

One word. Calm but strong was the petition that arrested her.

Maeve swallowed hard. The very last thing she should do was allow herself to be bought in by a man who was quite possibly schooled in deceit. But he opened his eyes, stormy gray and focused enough to stare through her. He said nothing, only looked back, hesitating, she was certain, out of something far different than the haze of pain.

"I will make allowance for the torment you must be in. And I suppose you would not survive a journey by road with this wound. On those grounds I will plead your case that you remain in Wicklow until we may hear your story on the matter. Will that suit you?"

"Turn me in after, an' I'll go without fight. But not until I've returned to the castle ruins," he forced out, drifting snowflakes collecting in his hair.

"I don't understand. Return to the ruins for what?"

"A lantern—in the tower facin' the sea." He lifted his gaze up to the ridge, the outline of the castle now shrouded in ghostly darkness. "If I don' be puttin' that light out, the ship will anchor an' boats will come to shore. The English will have soldiers alerted to a disturbance on yer land after all this, an' it'll sign the death warrant o' the souls aboard."

"There is a lantern in our castle ruins? How do you know this, sir?"

"Because 'twas my job to put it there."

It was Maeve's turn to clamp her eyes shut.

At once they teetered along the edge of a perilous cliff. His were criminal activities far more serious than a stolen horse.

"So you are using our cove for free trading, to port a smuggling vessel and avoid the Crown's tax on goods? And you thought you'd abscond with a horse to flee capture?"

"Ye think I'd leave men to their deaths?" His eyes flashed defiance.

She could see the horror on his face and felt a pang of guilt to have been rash in her judgment. "Somehow, I believe you wouldn't, if your confession about the lantern says anything of it. But I still don't know whether you are to be trusted, sir. So we'll leave it for now."

She swiped her dagger from the snow and stood, then resheathed the blade in the holder at her waist. "We must get you out of this storm. Might you be able to stand?"

"Ó Flannagáin—"

"Yes, the stablemaster. You needn't worry. He is not here right now. *I am.* And if you're going to live to see the dawn, you'll trust my judgment. I must see you over to that horse before the estate men return. We haven't time to quibble over details—not when you are injured and time is so dear."

"Ye don' understand . . . I can' go wit' ye." He shook his head and pushed her hands away. "I'm o' the clan O'Byrne."

The name leveled the blow he might have expected.

"You're an O'Byrne . . ." Maeve's breath froze in a cloud on air, the wind fairly knocked out of her with it.

The O'Byrnes were Irish. Catholic. And loud and proud about both. What's more, they were fiery in their dressing-downs of the English—landowners and soldiers alike—at every turn. The animosity simmering between the Irish and the Anglo families who lorded over them bled deep into the earth, enough that the man was ready to die before setting foot over the threshold of a Protestant's manor. Their prejudices against one another weren't likely to put out the flames of anger—only fan them, no matter how badly he was injured.

And they both knew it.

"I suppose an Anglo like me would let a man die because of his name?"

He didn't dispute it. Only closed his eyes again and lay still, as if willing her to defy his assessment of her virtues.

"Well, I shall have to beg your pardon later. I am an Ashford, sir, but I believe that a man's life—every man's life—is worth something, no matter his name or his religion. I'm sorry to disappoint you in your perceptions, but I have no intention of leaving you to die. Not before you've been delivered to the magistrate and justice has been rendered. Now, are you fit to stand or must I carry you?"

The man opened his eyes again . . . motionless . . . the darkness shielding any contempt that may have shot back at her. But no matter—if she'd been able to prick his pride enough that he'd stand, the provocation proved a win for them both.

He attempted to rise at the waist but crumpled back, falling in the snow almost as soon as he'd tried to move.

"I suppose that's a no." Maeve exhaled and held her arms out, hooking her elbows under his shoulders. "We'll do it together then. On the three count—"

Maeve counted and pulled on the third mark, hoisting his

deadweight like a massive sack of grain. He wobbled with her effort, still curled at the waist, but held fast once he was standing with his boots anchored to the ground.

"The ship . . ." He glanced over to the castle ruins, then turned to her as she tugged his arm over her shoulders. "I won' be leavin' it behind."

Maeve didn't return his regard—simply kept her gaze fixed on the path of snow and rock beneath their feet and started forward. Something could very well be stirring in her cove. And if it were true, she had a mind to keep the man alive long enough to find out what. If that meant giving the impression of passivity in the moment, she'd feed the lie.

"You'll leave no one behind. I'll put the light out and retrieve the lantern. You have my word."

"An' why would ye do that?"

She stared back at him, snowflakes drifting between them. "It's my castle, isn't it? My cove in which you're hiding? Well then. I ask you."

He tipped his head to the side, studying her. "Haven' ye a father an' brother who are masters here? Why 'tis not a commission o' theirs?"

"Please don't make me think on it a moment longer, or I may change my mind about this whole thing and leave you in your grave of snow. Our family and my role in it are of no consequence. As far as you're concerned, we are foes who have chosen to be friends for one night only. And that's your lot. Take it or leave it."

He didn't miss her spirit, simply leaned into her side, every ounce of his weight falling upon her mercy, as they edged toward the horse and leveled a most unexpected thank-you in his profile . . .

The hint of a smile.

"As I said, milady . . . I don' resist ye."

FOUR

PRESENT DAY
LES TROIS-MOUTIERS
LOIRE VALLEY, FRANCE

Laine paused in the shadows of the hall when she heard the telltale *clink* of crystal in the estate house kitchen.

For the late hour, everyone should have gone home. She peeked around the corner. Cormac stood at the central island with his back to her, collecting plates and champagne flutes and emptying them in the copper sink. He moved with ease—as a caterer might, always comfortable in a kitchen, even one not his own. Seemingly unconcerned with cleaning in wedding attire, he'd rolled the oxford shirt at his forearms.

Past him, an extended farmhouse table of rugged wood lay bare. Gone were Grandma Helene's pastries—Ellie's request for authentic French *pain au chocolat* instead of wedding cake—crocks of onion soup, mini towers of quiche Lorraine, and fig *tartelettes* that had seen the guests merry and full. The buffet had been swept up, and glass hurricanes were all that remained. A centerpiece of candles softened the room with its glow and spiced the air with cinnamon and cloves. A span of floor-to-ceiling windows showed off a million tiny shadows beyond, as winter continued its march through the vineyard rows.

Laine had snuggled Cassie in bed and rushed down the back stairs for a quick good-bye before Ellie and Quinn fled off on their honeymoon. Just a quick peck on her friend's cheek, a hug to the happy couple, and she could slip back upstairs before anyone saw her.

Instead, *he* was there.

Though she still wore her bridesmaid dress, she was undone with no makeup and mismatched argyle socks she'd pulled straight up to the knees. Laine tightened the charcoal linen wrap over her bare shoulders and turned on a dime, only to find her silent escape shattered in the next breath when aged floorboards groaned beneath her toes.

She clamped her eyes shut.

The clip of Cormac's shoes against hardwood drew closer, until he stopped in the arched doorway, turning over a dish towel and plate in his hands. "So, someone else is awake. Thought everyone had gone up."

"I was just going to say good night." At his tipped brow, she clarified. "To Ellie and Quinn. Before they leave, of course. Night train to Lucerne."

"I see. Then ye weren't hidin' around the corner? Because if yer still hungry, 'tis okay. I'd be takin' my life in my hands if I moved anythin' about in Gran's kitchen, but I think I can make somethin' o' what's left. Heat up soup. Or there are tarts in the pantry."

"Oh no. I couldn't eat another bite. The caterer's choices were wonderful. I can't remember ever tasting better."

"Thank ye. 'Tis high praise indeed."

She raised her eyebrows before she could stop herself and he smiled, aptly reading the *"You?"* in her reaction. It appeared he cooked. And showed up at the last minute to lend a hand at the wedding of a brother he hadn't seen in years—a combination Laine hadn't the first idea how to read.

"But I was mostly just doin' my grandmother's biddin', so credit's hers. Family recipes passed down an' all. Ye know how it goes."

"Oh yes. Family recipes."

Cormac paused, looking back a little too long, then quickly turned, as if trying not to notice an air of awkwardness that had befallen the room. He went back to drying and stacking plates on the open shelves. "Yer from Michigan? A little far west o' here, yeah?"

"We are. Cassie, the flower girl—she's my daughter, and we came together."

He turned, nodded with the hint of a polite smile. The kind that the mention of children could always bring to a conversation.

"She's a blessin'. Had the whole weddin' party charmed in under a minute, I believe. An' my grandfather seemed ready to give her anythin' short of a sugar bowl an' a castle had she asked for 'em."

Laine laughed. It was true—Cassie had a way about her. A quiet innocence with springy chocolate curls kissed by the sun at the tips, and a dimpled smile that melted the family patriarch's heart, even if he could no longer see it with his eyes.

Even so, in talking about her daughter, a tiny warning bell chimed within Laine. An unexpected laugh was fine. But a laugh attached to a man with an easy smile, who made witty remarks and would willingly dry dishes at midnight—the combination sparked a notion to linger in his presence, and that was a little too close for comfort.

Why not back out now?

"So, are Quinn and Ellie still here?"

"They are."

Cormac paused, and Laine thought she detected the slightest bit of wariness in him when he turned to face her. He almost looked . . . sorry. Was that right?

"Quinn said ye'd be down an' to send ye in. They're waitin' in the front room." Cormac tipped his head on the last word, toward the room with the rustic charm and the incredible fireplace seating area that overlooked the family's vineyards.

Laine peeked through the arched doorway, seeing the glow of firelight against ivory walls at the end of the hall. "Oh, okay. Thank you then." She smiled and turned—fast. The goal to be cordial but shuffle away as quickly as her feet could carry her.

"An' just so ye know, yer out for a *craic* wit' those socks."

Laine froze. While she had no idea what *craic* meant, she faced him, bound and determined to exude nothing but nonchalance. "It's cold. The hardwood and the marble entry, they . . ."

"Have a bite to 'em. Yeah. That much I remember. No doubt ye can find it warmer by the fire." He swung the dish towel onto his shoulder and nodded in a dismissive gesture, before he turned to hang a line of champagne flutes under one of the open shelves. "Nice to have met ye, Laine."

"Um . . . yes—you too. And good night."

Laine hurried out, having tripped over the newness of interest, attraction, or, heaven help her, whatever that mess was. With each step down the hall, she forced herself to forget how muddled her heart was at the moment and paste serenity back in her smile. Ellie and Quinn would be off to Switzerland soon, and the very last thing she wanted was to reveal anything that might shadow their happiness.

She eased in, stopping in the doorway. Ellie was nestled in a nailhead chair by the fire, a blanket in a spiced orange weave draped across her lap. Her elegant bridal updo was still twisted at her nape, but she'd changed into jeans and a cream off-shoulder tee. The fire danced, idling through cracks and pops as Quinn knelt beside the chair, already in his jeans and faded ringer tee, wedding ring reflecting from fingers he'd casually laced with his wife's.

They watched the fire, Ellie leaning into his side while he whispered something that made her smile, as if they alone had the monopoly on enviable, just-married moments.

"Sorry to interrupt. Cormac said you wanted to speak to me. But I can come back later if—"

"No. Come in, Laine. Please." Quinn smiled in welcome, then pressed a kiss to the underside of Ellie's wrist, pinning her with a soft amorous look, then released her. "I was just leavin'." He got to his feet.

Shouldn't they have left for the night train to Switzerland by now? The last few guests had trickled out the front doors of the estate house some time ago. Laine scanned the entry by the door. No suitcases or bags stacked and ready to go. Just an odd serenity as Quinn crossed the room and the fire continued its dance on the hearth.

"I'll just be upstairs if ye need me." Quinn smiled, nodded one of those tip-of-the-chin motions that harkened back to the days when Mr. Darcy characters bowed as they left a lady's presence. Save he was sporting hair tied at his nape and a chin in need of a shave, and probably wouldn't have buttoned up in an oxford if someone paid him.

The wedding was only the second time Laine had met Quinn in person, but his old-world manners told her the Foley brothers were far more alike than one might judge at first glance.

"I don't want to intrude." Laine hovered in the doorway after Quinn headed up the stairs. "I was just putting Cassie down when Quinn said you wanted to see me. But you could always call me when you two get home. We could talk then."

"Is Cass alright?"

"Tonight she is, yeah. Out like a light, thank heaven. I think we're still making up for the rough plane ride over. She's days in and hasn't been able to settle down." Laine drifted into the room, falling into their natural rhythm of normal, everyday sisterly talk. She pulled the wrap tighter around her shoulders. "And here I thought the—what were the pastries called, what you served instead of the wedding cake?"

"Pain au chocolat."

"Right. Those. I thought they'd have her up for several more hours. I didn't account for the fact that jet lag can triumph over French pastries any day—even in the bloodstream of a four-year-old."

"Then we'll have to get Cass used to the time change while she's here. And the sweets, for that matter. Grandma Helene has already made her a pet, and I warn you now that she communicates her love with food. I wish Auntie Claire had been here tonight." Ellie's face warmed in a smile of remembrance. "I only got to know Quinn's great-aunt for a short time before she passed. She was a rare one, and she'd have loved both of you."

Ellie scooted the chair opposite her out with her foot. "Come. Sit."

Laine obeyed, albeit on the edge of the cushion. Something told her the moment—serene as it was—had more to it than a relaxing chat by a fire. "Is something going on? I thought you and Quinn would have left for your honeymoon by now."

Ellie twirled one of the blanket's threads around her index finger.

"Oh no, Ellie . . . Don't worry about us. Cassie and I can get to the airport just fine. Don't change your plans on our account."

Ellie was beautiful—wedding makeup and hair intact and firelight twinkling against the diamond teardrops still dangling from her ears—but it was plain to see very real concern etched her features. Her eyes were damming back tears, and her forehead pressed in a deep crease.

"No—it's not that. It's . . ." A pause, a wobble of the head side to side. Ellie was stalling. "The honeymoon's kind of on hold for a minute."

"What? Why?"

"Because I wanted to talk to you first."

The wind was sucked out of Laine's lungs.

I don't know how . . . but she knows . . .

The absolute last thing Laine wanted to do was steal any of Ellie's happiness. Not on her wedding night. Not on the one day she was supposed to feel carefree and happy and remember always. Finding out that Evan had left them . . . that he'd moved out and moved on nearly a year before . . . had a new life in Seattle and signed divorce papers with no desire for reconciliation—it must have so upset Ellie that she wanted to talk about it. Right now, right here.

And I can't hide it anymore.

"Ellie, I know that I—"

"I have cancer."

They'd blurted partial confessions at the same time, but Ellie's arrow struck first, the force of which nearly shattered Laine in a million pieces. All of her concerns about the divorce, the secrets left unsaid, bowed to the numbness that rushed in.

"You have . . . ?"

"We might as well say the c-word as much as we need to. It won't make it go away if I treat it like Voldemort." Ellie paused on a nervous laugh and reached out to pull one of Laine's hands into hers. "Invasive ductal carcinoma. An awful long name for breast cancer."

"I can't believe this. I mean—how long have you known?"

"A few weeks. I was losing weight. Felt tired. I thought it was the stress of Grandma Vi's passing and trying to renovate an old castle—it's hard work to have timber put in ceiling vaults, you know? But then I found a lump and the doctor ran a few tests. Here we are . . . plot twist, as they say. So what better reason not to wait? Quinn and I thought we should get married and start this life together—even if we don't get on a train right after."

"So that's why."

"Yes. That's why, Lainey. And that's why I wore heels tonight . . .

why I walked through the snow and stopped at the chapel door . . . I wanted to feel it. To really *live* it. Because I might need to remember those very good things in the days ahead."

The firelight danced across Ellie's face, softening everything in the room. And suddenly, through her friend's resolve, her own cracked. Laine wrangled her newly chopped hair at the base of her neck, gripping a fist around it like it was the last bit of rope she had to cling to. It felt right to cry, so she allowed tears to come, free and open.

"So, what do we do? I mean, what did the doctors say? Is the treatment chemo or radiation? Or is it surgery? I feel stupid because I don't know."

"It's okay. I had a lumpectomy already and started chemo last week."

"What? How could you not tell me this?" Laine melted to the floor, kneeling in much the same way Quinn had before he left.

"I tried to—more than once. But I didn't want to burden you. I thought if I could call you after the wedding when you knew I had an amazing someone who'd stay by my side, then the news might come easier. I know you're busy with Cassie and everything at home. I can't believe it—*you're a mom*. It makes me cry to see you with her, after everything you and Evan went through to try for a baby." Ellie rolled her lips in on a wave of emotion. "Since the adoption, I just smile. Now you have one . . ." Her palm drifted to the apple of her cheek. Tears had tipped the length of her lashes. A soft swipe, and the moisture was gone.

"Ellie . . . I don't know what to say."

"I'm just so glad you're here. I couldn't keep talking on the phone, posting on social media anymore, and not say anything. It felt like lying to the world. And to you," she whispered, and squeezed Laine's hand. "And we don't do that with each other. We don't keep secrets, so I couldn't keep this one any longer."

And Laine's heart sank like a stone again . . .

"How long do you have to go through chemo?"

"I have more treatments that we know of, and then we'll have to see where we are. It's a common form of cancer, and our oncologist believes the prognosis is good." Ellie shrugged. Like it was no big deal that something was breathing fire on the inside of her. "At least I get a small break to go to Dublin, so there's a few things to work out and then we'll be back here for the next round of adjuvant therapy."

"Wait—Dublin? I thought you weren't going on a honeymoon."

"We're not. But Cormac showed up tonight for more than celebration. There's something to do with their father and a legal thing Quinn assures he'll give me full details on later. But the point is, it's serious enough that Cormac has asked Quinn to go home. At least for a little while, to get some things sorted out."

Laine let her gaze drift to the weathered wood door in the foyer. She pictured them leaving to board their train—turning over tickets and selecting a tucked-away pair of seats to speed off to their new life. Instead, she couldn't bear to think of them staying put to endure chemo—refused to consider that a diagnosis could wipe out that future.

"How could Cormac ask Quinn to leave you now?"

"He didn't know. Not any of this. In fact, we didn't expect him to show up at all. Quinn told him after the wedding—about all of this with me, why it's not the right time to go home. And they were going to leave it there. Cormac would go back to Ireland and Quinn stay with me. But I think it *is* the right time. If there's ever an opportunity to make peace with someone—especially family—then it should be taken. So I told Quinn he needs to go."

"I don't understand. Why would you want to go through something like this alone?"

"I won't be alone." Ellie smiled, a twinkle lighting her misty eyes. “We made a promise tonight, Quinn and I, in that chapel. That we’d travel life together. And I think now more than ever, I want that peace in our lives. We’re not giving anything up in this battle. In fact, when all is said and done, I’m afraid this cancer will be sorry it messed with Vi Carver’s granddaughter. But hearing the word? It changes you. As a person and as a couple. In a blink everything we thought we’d planned is different. The castle restoration is on hold—not forgotten, just paused for this bump in the road.”

Ellie was right. Words could change everything.

No matter if you watered them down just to make it through another day. For the last year and more, words had caused Laine to feel tiny clicks on the lens of how she’d looked at life. When *adoption* had been a blessing to a wife, but a *diversion* to her husband. When *divorce* had become a regular part of speech. When Realtors declared *sold* about their house—their whole world up to that point. And when Laine had packed boxes and marked *storage* on every one, more change was ushered in.

“But why did it have to be you? After everything. This was supposed to be your fairy tale.”

“It still is. Quinn’s not going anywhere. And just being able to talk about it with him helps, because it’s real and not going away if we ignore it. I want the freedom to fall apart in his arms if I need to. Or to fight it hard one day and wake up and stay in bed for most of the next, if that’s what will help in the moment.”

“And that’s what I want too. So how can I help? What can I do?”

Ellie leaned in to glance at the upstairs landing, then lowered her voice to a barely there whisper over the popping fire. “Quinn needs to make up with his brother—end whatever this feud is the family has going. And believe me, he’s taking me to task on it. My husband—”

She smiled, then caught her bottom lip with her teeth. “Okay. Gotta get used to saying that. Quinn is fine to talk about anything unless it's what happened between those two or why he hasn't gone home to see their father in years. And that's not like him. Quinn treats his grandparents with such care. He's gentle with Cassie. And he's always shown me love and respect, so I can't understand why there's this wall where the other side of his family is concerned. It's just not like him."

"Well, you know my family dynamic . . . So I agree with you—it's good to want to bring them together. But is it going to add more stress for you?"

"Somehow I don't feel stressed. I'm happy and scared and angry all at the same time. But not stressed. And while I didn't expect Quinn's predicament, this solution feels right in the right now. Cormac's asked for help, and I think we should give it if we can. But to do that, I have something to ask of you. I know it's a lot, so I'm just putting it here between us. You can say no and I won't say another thing about it. But . . . if you could stay, just a little longer, I wondered if you and Cassie might go with us."

"To Dublin?" Another something-new Laine didn't expect on top of everything else in her life. Her thoughts drifted over the uncertainty. "He spoke to me, in the kitchen. Cormac."

"Don't worry. I told him about Evan. Besides, we're family now. He wouldn't do anything to jeopardize that."

Laine had to avert her eyes from Ellie's perceptive gaze, since she didn't contradict any statement about her ex-husband. They were too close of friends for Ellie to miss the tiniest flinch of some deception in her face, and then the truth was bound to spill out.

"No, he didn't say anything out of line." Laine peeked down the hall. The glow from the candles had been snuffed, leaving only a passage of darkness. "But he was kind. And that was because he knew what you were going to tell me, didn't he?"

"Yes. He did."

"Ellie . . ."

Words refused to come. Laine didn't know what to say. All of a sudden, she was left unprepared to comfort the one who'd been her person through everything. The chasm of cancer and loss . . . It was too great a divide to cross with mere words. So she crossed it with her arms, enclosing her best friend's neck in an embrace that would speak for her.

"I'm so, so sorry," she whispered against Ellie's ear. "But I'm not going anywhere. Okay? I'm *in*."

Ellie bit her bottom lip, nodding, wiping moisture away with her palms, and they hugged like they'd never let go.

"Well." Laine straightened up and brushed tears from the underside of her lashes. "I'll let you go spend time with your husband. No more crying tonight because we've got a big trip to plan. Good thing Cassie and I already have passports. So I guess our next adventure is Ireland, hmm?"

"Ireland it is."

Laine rose and turned toward the stairs, slowing up when she gripped the cool iron rail in her palm. Thoughts swirled—too many for the moment. So she'd start with the easiest one for them both. "Um . . . Ellie?"

She looked up from the trance of the fire. "Yeah?"

"What's a *craic*?"

A smile later, Ellie whispered, "Oh, sweet friend, I'm afraid you're about to find out."

FIVE

January 23, 1916
Ashford Manor
County Wicklow, Ireland

Piano playing on the Lord's Day was generally frowned upon.

Issy supposed what her mother didn't know wouldn't hurt her. What was happening behind the library door may well hurt more if their parents returned from the vicar's parsonage to vivid tales from the service staff.

The cheery *Tabhair dom do Lámh*—"Give Me Your Hand" in traditional Gaelic—was a painful song choice given what was happening in the next room, but the only one Issy could think to play with halfhearted attention. If it might prevent the service staff from hearing the discourse as Honor told Rory of that which she could no longer hide, and if it masked the possibility of that news being taken badly, she'd play until her fingers bled. And she did play, though nothing—not a sound, not a breath at all over the piano melody—could be heard from the other side of that door.

Issy swallowed hard, fingers careful on the keys, the music that usually brought such comfort having become an ironic play of lyric and note sweeping in anxiety in cruel, gut-punching waves. The library door opened on a creak of hinge and wood, and she looked up, fading her fingers from the ivories.

Rory stepped out, tattered.

The usually carefree glint to hazel eyes had turned stormy, and that was frightfully new for the Byrne brother born the jovial one. He stood. Breathing softly. Motionless, with shirtsleeves rolled at the wrists and fists clenched at his sides. He stared off at the distant point of castle ruins on the ridge, far off past the windowpanes of leaded glass.

"Rory—" Issy whispered, hating the anguish in his profile.

He clamped his eyes shut and gritted out, "Stay out of this, Issy. *Please.*"

Of course. The last thing a man wanted after such ill news was consolation from a little sister. Issy connected glances with Honor, who stood by in the sunlight of the library's high-arched windows, a trembling hand cupped against her chin. They watched, helpless, as Rory marched through the music room, past the piano where Issy stood, and disappeared into the shadows of the hunting hall.

A slight *clink* of metal echoed off the ceiling as he tore a revolver from the wall, leaving a hollow space between prized red deer and elk antlers. He moved out of their line of sight, with the menacing creak of a cabinet door and the patter of metal scattering upon a tabletop.

Without a word he ventured past Issy, through the open door to the library, and focused his attention on Honor. "Stay on here at Ashford for a bit. My family will look after you."

"An' how long do ye expect that to be?" Honor took a step closer, as if hope had tied a string to her and had tugged in his direction.

Of course. The wedding to Devenish . . . It's just weeks away.

Devenish's family and hers were expecting a bride at a society wedding—what would Honor do if she hadn't any assurance from Rory of when, or even if, he'd return to her? He swept up his coat from a chair and stopped again before Honor, the answer to her question long in coming.

"I'll send word soon. Just stay, so I know you're safe. And do not go to Dublin. Too much happening now. But remember what I said—we do this together from here on out." He lifted his palm to brush the side of her face. "I love you. You know that?"

Honor nodded without another word spoken between them. He pressed a determined kiss to her forehead, and that was it. Rory Byrne exploded through the front door of Ashford Manor, leather case and coat in hand, with bullets weighing down trouser pockets and enough fire lit in him to slay a thousand dragons.

Issy hurried into the library and slipped an arm around Honor's waist. "What did you tell him?"

"Everythin'. I fear I love him too much to have held anythin' back," Honor said, as they watched the scene play out through the windows.

"You needn't worry. Rory is smart. And solid. He'll be all right." Issy hugged her shoulders, though the words, however kind and well intended, might well be a lie. "You'll see."

Honor hadn't even been able to speak to her about the events of the attack. Issy knew nothing but the consequences now. But for however painful it proved to tell Rory the details of such a terrible thing, she'd done it. And he'd taken it all in until his blood boiled over and pushed him out the door.

A motor turned around the circular drive and came to a stop before the front door, and Issy's parents stepped out—befuddled to arrive and find their son storming down the drive without a word of explanation. The younger Byrne brother had always been the passionate one, and it seemed he was to perform in character.

As the wind toyed with the feathers on their mother's black velvet toque and blew about the fur hem of her coat, she twittered about, following as their father attempted to run after their son, dodging icy gravel on the way.

Issy stood, arms now braced behind the shoulders of a quietly weeping Honor, watching as revenge twisted her brother from boy to man. She knew it carried Rory to Dublin—and to the enemy that had turned their world on end for the last time.

The camera lens painted a sight never to be seen again. A rocky beach below, with piles of round stones instead of just acres of sand and surf exploding against cliffs, and castle ruins that overlooked the mystery of the Irish Sea. It was a million exquisite angles competing for just ten spots on Issy's roll of film.

The ruins of Castle Chryn had been anchored at the ridge's peak since ancient times. Once the garrison of a seafaring clan lord, it had been built up in the twelfth century, was felled during Norman invasions in the thirteenth, and for centuries thereafter stood like a ghost haunting the rise. Its spires crumbled against Gothic-arched window frames and moss-covered walls. Bluestone and Celtic crosses stood as forgotten grave markers in an ancient cemetery. And there, with the castle's outer walls misted from moisture in the January air and the horizon bleeding in an endless palette of winter blues and grays, the ruins bearing the name of their family title called to Issy as the solitary space of peace left in her world.

Sea wind whipped strands of hair against her face, even under the cover of her hat. Issy pulled the collar of her coat tighter around the neck. Merlot wool and a thick border of fox trim kept her warm, despite persistent gusts. She positioned her camera into the height of the stone-and-sea view beyond the lens and squeezed the shutter.

Click.

"No one will ever see this view again . . . but that saved it."

Issy kept her gaze keen to the shifting sea, holding the camera steady in front of her torso as she stared down. Out of the corner of her eye, she caught movement on the path by the ruins—a clerical suit stopped at the top of the ridge, where the wind blew clean salt air and castle spires touched the sky.

She smiled inside. *Sean.*

"Good afternoon, Vicar. Out for a stroll on this winter day?"

"I looked in at Ashford after services. If yer not seated at yer Steinway an' starin' out at these castle ruins, then yer most likely takin' a photo of 'em."

Staring through the lens, Issy held her breath. Turning, focusing. Surrendering to the escape in capturing a shot of sky-against-castle-ruins and making it perfect.

"I stopped by Brook Camera Studio over Christmas. They've been low on stock for months, with the war. Mother gave me quite enough money to go to Clerys to buy a dress, so—"

"So ye bought the cheapest one ye could find an' spent the rest on that contraption. Were they cross when they found out?"

"They won't be once I show Mother the Eastman Kodak Company advertisements in *Harper's Bazaar* of society women with camera in hand. If the upper echelons in London and the States are fashionable enough in picture taking, I knew they'd allow it for me too."

"But that camera is more than a passin' distraction to ye, isn't it now?"

"It's a No. 3A Autographic Kodak, to be exact. Aluminum frame, nickeled parts. Seal-grain leather exterior. It's more compact, with sharper images, and loads in daylight with up to ten exposures. I must sound like an advertisement to you. But what was I to do? Let all of this inspiration go to waste?"

She shrugged off the question.

"Yer the only lady I know who would rather talk of seal leather an' aluminum than bonnets an' bows."

"I should hope. Even so, I've accepted it. As much as women like Harriet Chalmers Adams inspire others to put a lens to the world. Did you know she's the only female photographer allowed in the trenches in France? I read about it in a newspaper. She's actually a war correspondent. I'd find a way to go myself if it didn't sound impertinent to secretly hope for such a thing."

"I don' know that I'd prefer ye join her."

"My parents neither. But I confess, I do long for the day when I can take photos of something more than sea and sky and—though I dearly love them—castle ruins." She squeezed the shutter.

Click.

"Got that one too." Used to its gadgetry already, Issy was quick about folding the Kodak back into its case and pulling the leather strap over her shoulder. "But you bring a grand excuse with you—the lens is catching moisture. I ought to return."

"May I walk wit' ye then, see ye back to the manor?"

He held out his arm and she took it, lifting the hem of her skirt from the threat of mud and snow. Out of her mother's eyeshot, Issy had sawed the heels off her boots to make them easier for walking. But it also meant when she wore them, her hem was in danger of soil, which her mother wouldn't tolerate.

Best be on the safe side and tread with care.

"You must promise not a word to Mother. She thinks I went to Moira Dunne's afternoon tea. And I did plan to go, but the light diverted me. It's just the first time we've had sun like this nearly all winter." She sighed through the emotions of telling a clergyman a half-truth. "That didn't sound like a confessional, did it?"

He shook his head, a tiny glint of a smile in his profile. "No . . . ye would have to be remorseful about it first."

It was one thing to look for the good in dreary circumstances, but it was another to show him a half-truth. Sean knew her well, and Issy sensed he was waiting for something more as they walked, keeping silent, his attention focused on the gangly limbed tunnel of pear trees lining the path in front of them.

"In truth, I didn't know where else to go. A parlor party, what with Gard off to war and troubles at home? It didn't seem right to put on a hat and eat tea cakes in between smiles."

"I don' carry tales. Ye know that. But can I help somehow, wit' Honor?"

Issy didn't feign ignorance as to what he was referring to.

Perhaps he'd heard from outside the alcove the night of the play, or Honor had confided the worst to him back at the house. Either way, Sean wasn't a gossip. He knew, but he'd surely asked now because he cared.

"She won't speak of what happened—at least not to me. But I trust Honor to heal. Maybe not all of the brokenness and perhaps not right away, but she's stronger than even she knows. It's Rory who has me troubled."

"She had to tell him at some point."

"I know. And she hasn't yet told her parents. Or Devenish, the poor sod. To think I so wanted to dislike her fiancé because she did not love him. But he doesn't even know the wave of scandal that's fixed to wash up at his front door. Not for what Honor's done at all, but still for what's been done to her. She won't be accepted. Not in any society parlor in Ireland if this tale is carried—or England, for that matter."

"But she's still sittin' in yer parlor, an' that's somethin' at least."

"Maybe, but you know I've never truly cared for parlors, and that's where we differ. Honor does, and it will crush her if she's put out of them one by one. And when I think of Rory . . . I fear we've lost him for good."

Sean's profile showed he was attentive. He listened. Gave short answers after considerable thought. And was of a sort to look far down a path—he always said, to see the good that could come of something God was crafting behind the scenes, one had to keep an eye out for it. And Issy needed that view at present because she failed to see it.

His opinion on the matter carried weight that even she hadn't realized.

"Ye believe Rory's gone back to Dublin."

"Back to wherever he goes these days. But something, I don't know, shifted. I wasn't in the library when Honor told him what happened, but his expression when he emerged from the room . . . I've never seen him like that. It wasn't fits of anger. That at least I'd have known what to do with. But he didn't say a few words. And he refused the motor—just started down the road, a pack slung over his shoulder and something inside pushing him at a near run. I don't think he'll stop until he reaches the city."

"He's broken it off wit' Honor then?"

"Most men would quietly distance themselves from such scandal. But I've never seen my brother own such devotion. Apparently he told Honor he's ready to face down Devenish and her father both, if that's what it comes to just so he can marry her in the end. In any case, their private understanding is about to become a very public one. That he will stand by her in it is some consolation, I suppose."

Sean kicked a stone. It pinged ahead, rolling off the side of the path. "'Tis noble o' him. An' right. Yer brother's a good man, Issy. Wouldn' expect any less from him. But is that what ye fear, that his anger carried him off to enlist?"

"No. Remember when he was young and fell out of a tree, of all foolish things? He hides it well, but there's still a hitch in his step that will always remind him of a summer with a broken leg. The Crown wouldn't take him even if he wanted to go."

"But the ICA will take a volunteer pent up wit' rage any day."

"That's what terrifies me, that Rory's in over his head. I might agree with the heart of the Irish cause, but he's fully invested in it to the point of action. The Irish blood in him is raging against the English side of his ancestry—especially now. When my father learns of it . . . I will have to remain silent about my growing sympathies just to offset his."

"It is goin' to be possible for ye?"

"It must be. I won't argue with my father, but even I can see that Ireland cannot continue on this path forever. She's risen up before, many times. But the famine seems to have broken whatever spirit this country had to attempt peace with her English masters. The gap widens between rich and poor. Even on this estate it's said that tenants committed crimes to be sent to Kilmainham Gaol, because prison guaranteed they'd have food to eat. Families buried their babies, lost to starvation. And manors that once flourished now lay abandoned all around us. We're decades removed and yet we're digging graves again, what with the war. The newspapers say Kaiser Wilhelm is a madman, and the German Empire is being ruled by his generals bent on world domination. More death. When will the sorrow end?"

"I'm afraid I don' have an answer that'll satisfy, Issy. All I know is, God is not absent in our pain. Nor is He indifferent to our questions. He's only ever as far as we turn our back an' walk away from Him."

Issy slowed them to a stop at the junction of the path leading up to the manor and turned to him. "Is it wrong then to want to stay here instead of going back?"

Anguish clawed her insides, pulling tears from places she didn't know she'd stored them up. The emotions she'd held back for weeks on end finally overtook her. In the safety of an old friend's presence, they spilled out—vulnerability breaking her apart before him.

"He took Father's Enfield, Sean. Rory tore the revolver off the wall and emptied a box of bullets into his pockets. There's a vacant space now in the hunting hall, plain as day. My father will see it and then what? How do I tell him Rory's gone to find and kill the man who attacked his love? My parents are unaware of any of this.

I don't speak of it since they're already torn to strips with worry about Gard. They live in fear we'll receive a telegram any day. And how would I tell them they might lose their other son and daughter to their own convictions at the same time?"

"If I could help ye . . . Ask anythin' of me." In a soft, sudden gesture, Sean swept tears off the apple of her cheek.

It was a "you're not alone" kind of brush of his palm, and she couldn't fight his hand because of it. He trailed his thumb to stop a tear that had fallen from her lashes, and he slowed, curled knuckles along the line of her jaw in a butterfly's touch upon bare skin.

Familiarity startling her, Issy looked down. Away. Anything to ease the connection his eyes sought with hers. He dropped his hand but stayed close.

"Issy? Look at me. Please."

She obeyed, gaze rising to meet the one that held fast on her. Knowing and dreading what was coming, because she wasn't ready.

"I can' leave this unsaid between us. An' it's not the war or what happened to Honor—except heaven knows I'd do exactly as Rory. I've pledged never to raise arms against another man, but God forgive me, I'd march into Dublin wit' my finger curlin' 'round a trigger too, if I knew anyone dared hurt ye."

Seconds ticked by as Issy listened—silent, agonizing drumbeats of the heart in her chest, keeping her from thought or speech.

"Perhaps 'tis not how a gentleman would do it, to say such things openly, but I need ye to know when I asked ye to marry me last summer, it wasn' because I thought I'd lose ye. I didn' know yer affection for Levi, or I'd have stepped back an' let everythin' be. An' I didn't trip into a pew after." He paused, the warmth of his fingertips just brushing against the side of her palm. "I do have some pride."

Issy looked up, feeling she owed him at least that much. "I know that. And I'm terribly sorry. I wish . . . we could go back. I'd give anything to go back now and change it all."

"An' I. But we can' now, can we?"

"Is that what you've come to ask me? If Levi's returned, because he's paid no call at Ashford Manor." She shook her head, the crisp air punishing her eyes for daring to tear again. "I didn't expect him to come—not after what happened."

Once, a youthful romance would have forced Issy to run to an altar if she knew Levi O'Connell would be there waiting. She'd been blinded by sweet words and a dashing smile—she couldn't see straight until he'd boarded a boat for America, bound on testing his wings rather than being tied down to a wife. All she could think now was that if things had played out differently, she'd be standing before a brother by marriage, instead of a friend she was now terrified to lose.

"I can' speak for my brother—only myself." He swallowed hard. Stared back. "I would do anythin' fer ye. I swear it."

"I've never doubted it."

"Right, then. As long as ye know that," Sean whispered, leaning in, with the sun at his back and crisp air burning her cheeks with frozen tears . . . and grazed her lips with his.

Issy didn't move, just drifted her eyes closed and surprised herself to receive the sudden intimacy from him when he'd only ever been a friend before. And a brother. And now, in his own quiet way, was confirming that so much more simmered beneath the surface of the man. Sean owned pride that wasn't wounded or wrathful but laden with tenderness. That honesty awakened something deep inside her that had long been asleep.

Forgotten. Abandoned, even.

It was soft. And sweet. And over too soon.

"Sean, I . . ."

Stepping away, he cleared his throat as he looked down—a little tell that said he was showing just enough vulnerability to be real with her. "I came to say good-bye, Issy."

"Good-bye?"

The worst hit her—*the war.* Her feet carried her a step closer to him again. "You haven't enlisted?"

"No. But I must go where I'm needed. I pray God would sever this evil among men's hearts, an' the war will end. But if it does not an' I must go to France, I needed to wipe the slate between us." He paused over something that hitched his voice.

Was it regret? She was eaten with it too.

He recovered quickly, bestowing a smile. "Remember those times we pilfered guinea eggs from Seamus O'Malley's farm?"

"Yes, and we tried to flee his capture only to find you'd torn your trousers on the rock wall in the glen. And that gave us away."

"An' now the thief is tryin' to become a righteous man."

A laugh bubbled up in her with the remembrance of such innocent days from their youth. It seemed so long ago now—before love and war and the mixing of both had made them all grow up so fast. "I remember those summer days with fondness. But I fear I shall always be mistrusted if I happen by the O'Malley tenancy. And I remind you again." Issy bit her bottom lip over a smile. "A vicar shouldn't speak of such things."

"But I'll remember yer smile nonetheless, whenever I do."

Issy exhaled, the warmth of her breath freezing into fog. He looked up the path, to the manor house up ahead.

"Ye ought to go inside. 'Tis cold an' Honor will be wonderin' about ye. I can see myself out the front gates—I know where they are by now."

"But you will write to us . . . won't you?"

"If I'm able." He looked like he was about to step off down the lane but turned back, a twinkle in his eye. "Just promise me ye won' pack up that camera an' sneak off to join Miss Adams in the trenches, yeah? I came on official church business, so ye can' tiptoe out o' this one."

"I promise. No trenches." She paused to add her usual last word. "Unless of course they're on Irish soil, and then you cannot stop me."

"God be wit' ye, Issy-Girl." Sean smiled and tipped his head, not another word spoken between them when there was so much she ached to say.

"And also with you," she mouthed as he walked away.

Issy didn't need her camera to capture the view of two men she cared about, walking the same gravel road in a single day. She watched Sean O'Connell's back fading as he climbed inside his motor, its wheels cutting into the slush and snow of a melting winter landscape.

There was no Kodak in the world that could sear an image to memory like a heart when it was broken.

SIX

December 25, 1797
Ashford Manor
County Wicklow, Ireland

"How do you know he is a pirate?"

"Shifty eyes." The housekeeper stared at the man on the bed and crooked a finger, moving it back and forth over the bridge of her nose.

Maeve sighed, rolling her own eyes heavenward. "His eyes are closed."

"I may be old as cracked leather, milady, but I still know a freebooter when I see one. And he ought to go out of this house this very moment."

Dour to most and quite set in the ways of a strict English household, Mrs. Finnegan was immovable in such matters. But she was also loyal to the family Ashford—enough that she'd become the member of their slim staff Maeve could trust without reservation, no matter how shocking it was to find she'd managed to sneak a half-dead pirate into a tower room whilst her father slept down the hall.

Maeve stood at the foot of the bed, the front of her charcoal cape and palms still tinged with blood. She could only hope he wouldn't wake again . . . wouldn't cry out and stir the house, or mention the ship she'd conveniently omitted from her explanations to the steely eyed housekeeper.

"The bleeding has eased. But his skin is a ghostly hue. He still hasn't opened his eyes, and I cannot get him to take any drink. I suspect the only chance he may have is if we get the ball out of his side and stitch him up, but even then it's not certain he'll escape the fever after."

"We should summon a doctor. Or the undertaker." Mrs. Finnegan sniffed, no doubt the alcohol having come through his pores enough to hover in the air. "Preferably one with a tub of water and lye soap."

"We cannot. Whatever he needs by way of care, we must administer it ourselves." Maeve loosened the pearl buttons at her collar, releasing her cape. She laid it over a chair, stirring up a puff of dust to cloud the air.

Ashford Manor boasted multiple stories of tawny stone, lofty windows overlooking manicured gardens, and round spires on four corners, with rooms enough that a third-story tower was no longer in use and became the hidden-away haven they'd needed. Expending every ounce of energy to climb the flights of stairs, the man had crashed facedown upon the coverlet as soon as Maeve had closed the door, where he lay still upon the four-poster bed, his breathing even in sleep.

The need for a fire was the first thing Maeve thought to do and so hurried about the room. Matches she found in a mantel box. She had to pilfer logs from the woodbox by the stove in the servants' hall and carry the load up to the third floor, and though she hated to do it, she'd torn pages from an old book to use as kindling. She shuttered the windows. Even rolled the paisley rug and pressed it tight to the bottom of the door, so a room that was in a long-shut-up wing of the manor wouldn't give off any sign of occupation.

"Who is he, milady?" Mrs. Finnegan whispered.

"I don't know."

"But what's happened to him?"

Maeve shook her head. "I'm afraid I don't know that either. I found him in the east field—in the glen by the castle ruins. He's taken a shot in the side, rather badly. I couldn't just leave him there, no matter what he's done. He'd have died out on a night like this."

"Then this is the thief the estate men went to hunt?"

Maeve wasn't certain of course, but everything in her screamed yes. Who else could he be? He had no explanation as to his presence on their land, save for the mention of a ghost ship drifting somewhere in their cove, a lantern she'd snuffed out at the ruins of Castle Chryn, and the name of O'Byrne to haunt him. Everything else was a mystery that hovered too close to entering the grave with him.

"I believe he may be the same." Maeve moved to the basin on the bureau and rolled the sleeves of her mourning dress to wash the blood from her hands. "I've brought fresh water. A bottle of Father's whiskey to clean the wound. A stack of sheets from the linen room. I thought we could tear them—use them as bandages. We've no candles for the wall sconces. This room has been vacant so long they've all been removed. The candle from my chamber will have to do for now."

"Master Cian would not allow this, milady."

Mrs. Finnegan was correct on that score.

"No, I don't suppose my brother would. But he is on a boat to England at present and so forfeits any vote on the matter. As Father is quite unable to render a position in the midst of his grief, it is left up to me to do as I see fit. And I see fit to render him aid."

If Maeve could guess anything, it would be that Mrs. Finnegan was boring her glare into the man while her back was turned. But she also knew silence was a sign that the woman was considering. Teetering, even. It was a gamble to appeal to her sympathies, but seemingly more likely Mrs. Finnegan would rather help Mistress

Adelaide Ashford's daughter than abandon her—no matter how precarious the situation.

Loyalty was the one card Maeve possessed, and play it she must.

"The Irish would call him *suile shifty*," Mrs. Finnegan muttered, floorboards creaking as she crossed the room. Suppressing a hopeful intake of breath, Maeve turned, finding the woman bent over the edge of the mattress, peeling back the man's vest. She motioned to the bureau. "The light. Bring it here, please."

Maeve obeyed, retrieving the silver candlestick, then leaned over as she settled its glow on the bedside table. She unsheathed the dagger at her belt and held it out. "Will this work?"

The woman nodded and took the blade to cut through the wool vest and strips of linen at his side, until she'd shed soiled fabric in a small pile on the rug. She rolled him to his side, inspecting the wound, until his arm flopped upon the coverlet palm to ceiling, bearing a mark that stood out even in the dim light.

A tattoo covered the length of the man's forearm: a crest bearing a bracket and three open palms, topped by a sea wench with a long mermaid tail.

Hands frozen when she beheld it, Mrs. Finnegan rose up from the mattress like a shot and backed away, eyes narrowed to slits. "No, milady. Not whilst I have breath in my body."

On instinct Maeve covered the tattoo with her palm, as if she could hide the evidence. "Please. It's of no consequence in the matter of a man's life."

"Have you any idea what you've done?" the housekeeper whispered, shaking her head with each syllable. "If the countess were alive . . . God rest her saintly soul! Your mother would have died before allowing one of *them* under this roof. Have you forgotten what happened to Master George—your own brother? And tensions with these Catholics being what they are."

"Of course I haven't forgotten. It's all I can think of. But I feel

I'd be doing my family—myself—a disservice if I put a man out of our house in this condition." She left his side, chasing the housekeeper to the door.

"Then leave him to the soldiers."

"I cannot."

"Why? This man is a criminal. He ought to be brought before the authorities."

"I don't know what he is, but I have reason to believe there is more to this than a drunkard who simply saw fit to steal a horse from our stables. And handing him over to the men tonight would spell his death by morning. No matter what blood is running through his veins, it's still crimson he bleeds. If there's something I can do to save him, I must try. I'm sorry, but I pray George and Mother would agree."

"But he's a *creature* you speak of. An O'Byrne in Ashford Manor? He'll be the death of us all."

Maeve sighed, fully aware of the malice in Mrs. Finnegan's tone and why it was there. It hurt her, too, to know who he was. But Maeve could overlook it. Forget the sectarian divide even, for the moments it took to save his life. So long as she didn't have another man's death eating away at her conscience, she could deal with the repercussions later.

"He is not a creature, but a man. He's someone's son, isn't he? He may be someone's husband. Or father. And I don't care for the arguments of birth or religion . . . or the hatred that mark upon his skin means to the family under this roof. You don't have to say anything to Papa, or to Cian. All of this will be over by the time he returns anyway. But the man will find shelter here. So either help me, or I beg you to leave this room at once and forget you ever beheld him."

The fire crackled, a dance that should have brought comfort on a snowy night. But Maeve waited—as the wind swept against the window, as the man breathed, and as she stared down the woman standing opposite the bed, waiting to see what she'd do.

"I'll need a needle and thread, milady. You'll find them in her ladyship's sewing kit."

"I know where it is." Maeve could have cried. She bounded across the room and gripped the woman's hands. "What else?"

"Fresh water. A kettle to boil over the fire and a basin to hold water. But mind you go after the best porcelain to hold up against cracking. Fetch one of the soup tureens in the butler's pantry. And a pitcher. There'll be one with the mistress's special pomegranate print on the side. Chamomile tea—for the pain. And a cup for him to drink. Not a teacup, mind. He may thrash about and break it. We need a sturdy one from the silver closet."

"And the key?"

Mrs. Finnegan sighed.

To give up the key for a silver closet must have broken some code of ethics for a member of staff in a great manor. Mrs. Finnegan turned to the side, away from the man's earshot, on the slightest chance he could overhear and clean them out of their worldly goods. "On a hook in the larder. High up, behind the row of hanging pheasant."

Relief washed over Maeve. Mrs. Finnegan had a tender heart beating in her chest, Maeve knew it. One of forgiveness, and that gave her more hope than anything else. She squeezed again and kissed the woman's hand. "I'll go. I'll fetch it for you. All of it."

"Hurry. Before the pirate wakes. We can't keep his presence unknown if he's bellowing about in pain. And mind you go quietly on the stairs. Archibald will have an ear out."

Maeve nodded and headed for the door. Yes, their butler was too inquisitive for his own good. She'd avoid the grand staircase that let into the receiving hall; the lower half of the stairs groaned loud enough to wake the dead.

"I'll not make a squeak. I promise."

"A storm is brewing, milady, and I fear you've set your sails headlong in the thick of it. I pray we haven't brought a curse upon this house."

"I don't believe in curses, Mrs. Finnegan." Maeve held her head high as she gripped the doorknob, minding not to allow a creak of tired brass as she turned. "And it is after midnight. That means it is Christmas morning. And we will celebrate when we know one life has been returned to us at Ashford Manor, instead of lost this time."

"Water . . ."

The man's voice startled Maeve so, she blinked awake. She'd forgotten for a moment where she was, thinking she'd fallen asleep in the chair by her mother's bed again, instead of in the wingback by the tower room hearth.

The darkness that had been their ally through the night had given way to the peace of morning, with the room spliced by sunlight streaming in through cracks in the shutters. It drew a line from floor to plaster ceiling vaults, across the rug and onto a fire that had grown cold. The memory of it sizzled as a drop of water fell from the chimney to the pile of ash.

"Water . . . please?" Through a haze he stirred, cracking his eyelids to gaze from across the room.

Yes. Water. He'd need it.

Maeve discarded the cape she'd used as a blanket and jumped up, sweeping auburn locks back over her shoulder. It was rough and quick, but she unrolled the sleeves of her mourning gown, propriety reminding her to affix buttons at her wrists while she crossed the room to the bureau. She poured water from the pitcher—the last bit they had fresh—and paused a fair distance from the bed.

It was the first time she'd really seen him, eyes open, in the light of day. They were a strong, steely hue. Quiet. And unobtrusive as he waited for the water.

"I'll need to help you so you don't pull the stitches in your side. If you try anything at all, it would be more dangerous for you than for me. So have a care. Do you understand?"

He nodded. Just once, but with a veil of guardedness suggesting that in his discomposure, he might be as wary of her as she was of him.

"Here. Drink." She eased the sterling cup into his hand, and she slipped her palm to his nape to help him rise.

"Thank ye, milady." He swallowed with a sputter, then fell back on the pillow, the tiny action having worn him out.

It was then that he stared up at the ceiling and, perhaps finding a room with turret and timber an odd place to have awakened instead of the middle of a sea-cliff field, issued a questioning gaze back to her. "Where am I?"

"I'd have thought you already knew. You are upon the Ashford Manor estate, at Castle Chryn." Maeve stood, backed up a few steps until she was a fair enough distance to satisfy her comfort. "Have you any memory of last night, sir? You seem to have gone out on the lash at the village pub, yet you knew of illicit activities at our castle—and our cove—in rather striking detail for someone unacquainted with this estate."

"I don' touch drink," he contradicted, running a hand over his unshaven chin, but let out a noticeable catch in his breathing with the quick movement and dropped his hand down to hug the bandages tied around his middle. "But I seem to be rememberin' two things o' last night—an' a blasted shot in the side is the loudest one of 'em at the moment."

"Then I shouldn't need to explain the cause of your infirmity, though I don't rightly know how you came about such a trauma as a musket ball in your side."

"An' quite a wish I hadn'."

"You gave the impression you'd taken a bath in Guiness . . ."

"Nearly did," he started, then cleared his throat over a laugh about it. "A gentleman an' I had a disagreement over somethin'. He tossed a pint in my direction."

"I see." That wasn't nearly enough of an explanation. But she adjusted her stance, easing softness into her voice just a shade, thinking of how similar the man's recoiling the night before had been to George's when he, too, had been in the same agonizing plight of pain.

"You fitted most of the night, sir. Our housekeeper said if you woke at all you'd have garnered such luck. But perhaps Providence smiled upon you because it is Christmas morning and here you are."

"Ye stayed?" he whispered, looking to the flash of morning light from the cracks around the shuttered window. Then a swift change and he affixed his gaze on her.

Maeve swallowed, ignoring such an impertinent question, and placed her hands on her hips, her index finger just brushing the hilt of the blade in her belt: a silent warning to pay heed.

"I am Lady Maeve Ashford—mistress at this estate. And it was my duty. So yes, I stayed."

"An' the ship?"

"I put the lantern out, with no sign of a ship in the cove."

He sat up, or tried to, concern etched in his features as he flitted a glance from her to the face of the oak door across the room. Perhaps he'd decided to try a hand at making a run for it?

"You needn't worry. The door is locked and will remain so, for your safety as for ours. I remind you that you are confined to our custody, and propriety demands that you remember that fact until you are released into the hands of local authorities."

"An' propriety doesn' require a chaperone, as we're alone in this room?"

She backed up and bumped the bureau in sudden haste, jostling the mirror attached. Maeve stilled her hand on the top, composing herself—quickly. Even still, a glimmer of amusement registered in him, as if he chose not to smile but had still stopped to consider it.

"No. This room is one of many unused in this manor. But if propriety demands anything, it would be that a thief cease in asking questions. Our housekeeper has gone downstairs to instruct the staff to their morning duties. When she returns, she will bring you whatever you need and shall look after you. It's not yet known you're here, at least until I decide what to do with you. So, may we begin with your name—the first, as I'm already privy that you're an O'Byrne?"

"'Tis Eoin, milady."

"Well, Eoin O'Byrne. How is it you've come to my father's estate? The truth, if you please. Our stablemaster is just outside and no doubt can confirm whether you are indeed the man who caused this disturbance. I have but to fetch him if there is any inkling you may return to the violence of which you are accused."

"I don' claim violence, milady."

"Don't you? No drink and no violence, yet you stand accused of injuring our stablemaster and stealing my father's horse—all with clothing doused in Guinness. I daresay that does not strengthen your argument. What explanation might you possibly give?"

"I came by way of Dublin, to the crossroads at the edge o' yer father's estate. An' the truth bein', ye may think ye saved me last night when 'tis the other way 'round."

Was he goading her? Or truly, did he believe what he'd just said? She had to suppress a laugh at the absurdity.

"And I suppose you assisted yourself from a snow-covered ridge up two flights of stairs to this very room. How do you warrant such a claim?"

"The stablemaster, milady."

She withdrew, a tiny flinch registering uncertainty within her.

"His word is that a man struck him from behind an' stole off wit' the earl's stallion—as ye say, to flee capture for free tradin' in yer cove?"

It was a concise summary of the bloody affair, yes. "That is what our groom, Brennan O'Malley, recounted. Do you deny it?"

"Not in a way that looks to convince ye. But why then would a thief in need of a quick exit steal away wit' a horse he cannot possibly ride?"

"I beg your pardon?"

"Have the stablemaster questioned. If he can explain to his lordship why a horse sufferin' o' stringhalt in his left hind would be the one a thief would choose on which to speed his escape, then by all accounts, ye can be doubtin' me. But if he cannot satisfy the inquiry, I tell ye to be on yer steadfast guard."

Maeve swallowed hard.

To doubt him would have been easily done.

The circumstances of his condition were incriminating at best. But something stirred in her middle—instinct, maybe—that the manner of the man across the room was obstinate yet surprisingly open before her. That a grain of possibility existed he may be telling the truth meant the stablemaster her father had trusted for more than ten years had, in fact, presented a false account of a crime that could result in a man's hanging.

"As you say, you're of the clan O'Byrne. How then might I trust anything you say?"

"A liar an' a thief is afoot on this estate, milady." He stared back, his eyes challenging. "But ye'll find—'tis not me."

SEVEN

PRESENT DAY
10/11 O'CONNELL STREET LOWER
DUBLIN, IRELAND

Dublin breathed life.

It was music. History. The River Liffey drifting beneath storied streets. It was a street performer gigging "Danny Boy" on the violin as they walked by, Christmas markets on Henry Street, and Temple Bar pubs with doors open to the sidewalks, even in November . . .

It was James Joyce's pen come to life off the page.

Laine held Cassie's hand as they stood on the sidewalk in front of a corner pub.

"Here we are. 10/11 O'Connell Street." Quinn looked at the structure in a slow survey, all the way up four stories to the top. "Used to be Sackville Street once upon a time, but nothin' changes. Not in decades. Jack Foley's Pub is just the same as it always was."

It was classic Dublin—everything Laine had seen in Google searches for Irish pubs while on the plane ride over. She picked Cassie up, holding her as they looked over gleaming wood paneling on the rounded street-front corner, with wide windows painted over with the name in spirited Kelly green-and-gold trim. Menus and live music posters became artful ticker tape on the front window, a paper layer between the dining space and Dublin's bustling world outside.

"Why, you're right here in the middle of everything, Quinn! *Jack Foley's Irish House, established 1796.*" Ellie slipped her arm around Quinn's elbow and hugged tight as she read the sign. "I almost forgot—I'm a Foley too. I feel a little bit Irish now."

"Ye are. And it suits ye." He smiled, looking down, and dotted a fingertip to the dimple in her cheek. He turned back to Laine and Cassie. "What do ye ladies think? Do ye like our pub?"

"What's a pub?" Cassie whispered, her words light against Laine's neck.

"A pub is a place for friends to have dinner, remember?"

And a few pints, she thought, unable to stifle a laugh.

Laughs came packaged with four-year-olds. She must have told Cassie a hundred times on the trek over from France what Ireland might be like—green and hilly, with beaches, but airports and cities too. And little restaurants called pubs that served food and drink, and served as the place where strangers became friends over a meal and a good gab.

"Would you like to go in, hmm?" Laine squeezed her hand. "Let's see if they have fish and chips—fish sticks," she corrected, having learned the language that worked with the youngster crowd. "And fries."

"And red sauce. Ketchup packets to you Americans, mind." Quinn winked at them as he held the door, letting the ladies go on in front of him.

A bell chimed over the door, welcoming them to every Dublin pub Laine had imagined. Paneled wood covered the interior walls. Tiffany-style glass ceiling lamps kept it dim. And a long, weathered bar with leather nailhead stools ran down an entire side. It disappeared into a partitioned room of half wood and glass walls at the end—so cramped, it looked barely able to fit the table and chairs inside it, yet with the surprising addition of a rather remarkable piano peeking out from the back corner.

Was that a vintage Richard Lipp & Sohn? Laine strained her neck to see more of it as they walked by, making a mental note to come back and take a closer look.

A central seating area welcomed patrons under an arched, brass-stamped paneled ceiling. A short flight led to a second level in the back where TVs dominated an entire wall, boasting soccer on all screens and revelers eating up the action. And all around, the ambience was a hash of mismatched bottles, framed jerseys, knick-knacks on shelves, hung photos, and yellowed newspaper clippings from Jack Foley's great history of Dublin's local lore.

Their group paused in the front dining room while Quinn went in farther on his own, leaving Ellie a step behind as he approached the bar. He waited, burying his hands in his pockets as pub-goers passed them.

Ellie nudged Laine in the direction of a man behind the bar, with ice-gray hair and a goatee, focused as he filled a pint glass up to the rim, then set it on the bar in front of a patron. "I've seen photos—that's Jack. Not surprising on the name. Quinn told me their family has had a Jack Foley in every generation going back more than two hundred years."

"But he broke tradition with his sons?" Laine whispered.

"Not exactly. Cormac has always gone by his middle name, but he's the next generation Jack Foley. Quinn said his older brother may have received the family name, but that's where the similarities end between dad and sons."

The man's smile faded when he spotted the younger of his sons standing in his pub. "Look what rolled in wit' the tides." Jack froze as he looked at him, the bar remaining a buffer between father and son.

"Hello, Da. It's been a long time."

"I see yer still wearin' the long hair."

"A bit chopped, but yeah." Quinn stood still, a polite smile on his lips despite the cut about dark, chin-length locks he'd tied at his nape.

"Well, Cormac said ye were on yer way home. Could scarcely believe it till ye walked through our door." He eased back, lifting pint glasses from under the bar, then tipped them to the side, minimizing the foam as he filled them with dark stout. He finished and set the two pints on the bar with a loud *clip-clop*.

"Two pints o' plain!" Jack slapped his palm to the bar top, drawing a young lady's attention to load drinks on a tray and sweep them off. "Thought ye'd given up on Dublin for good. 'Tis a reason ye come 'round now?"

"Cormac. Showed up at Titus's vineyard. Asked us to come back with him."

Jack's notice fell upon their place by the door. Ellie stepped forward and slipped her fingers to lace with Quinn's.

"This is my wife, Ellie. Ye received the invitation to the wedding—last weekend."

"Couldn' get away. Got a pub to run."

"It's alright. Just thought ye ought to know. And this is a close friend, Laine, and her daughter, Cassie. They've come to visit with us while we're here."

Quinn paused and shifted his stance in a way Laine had never seen the confident Foley do. Uncertain. "They're my family, Da."

"Miss." Jack tipped his head to Ellie, then turned to them. "Ladies." He gave the greeting but offered no smile. No pleasantries, no affable Irish welcome. Just pints on the bar and indifference in the voice.

"It's nice to meet you, Mr. Foley," Ellie answered, her warm way always intact.

"Everyone calls me Jack here. Ye can do the same."

"Alright. Jack."

Laine's heart squeezed. A rocky greeting was the last thing

she'd hoped for her friend to receive. Ellie's parents had been killed in a small plane crash when she was eleven, so to have a would-be father figure in her husband's dad show such apathy to their presence made Laine feel sick to her stomach—or want to toss one of those pints in his face to wake him up to the daughter-in-law he'd been gifted.

Laine edged back against the wall a bit and pulled a menu from a stack in a hanging wood bin. "Are you hungry, honey? Let's see what they have," she whispered to Cassie and held the menu out, looking for the kids' section while the Foleys talked. The clock was ticking on her daughter's hungry meter, so best to know what she might like on a foreign menu.

"What ye here for, Quinn? Is this to do wit' the will o' that Dolly Byrne character? An' the legal mess o' the castle she left behind?"

A will? Laine's attention piqued. She looked up. *And a castle?*

"It is."

"A pile o' rocks an' a grand waste o' time." Jack laughed then, a hearty, humorless snort, and pulled a towel from beneath the bar to sweep it over the polished surface.

"If not for Cormac, we wouldn't be here."

"'Tis a mess I haven' time fer. Supper rush comes in an' the band at eight o'clock—we'll be too jammers to be fallin' behind. An' 'tis all Cormac's doin', so he'll have to take ye in hand." Jack tossed the towel across his shoulder and leaned over the bar, gesturing to the back. "Ye go all the way past the jacks to the kitchen. He keeps things goin' back there, so I expect he'll know what to do with ye."

Where Jack Foley's abrasiveness was on full display, Cormac was less easily read. He strode down the stairs at the back to the ground floor, looking far more at ease in worn jeans and a casual blue button-down than when he was at the vineyard estate. With a chef's apron around his waist and a pencil tucked over his ear, he didn't approach. Just offered a respectful nod their way before turning his attention to a waiter who'd stopped in his path.

The flicker of warmth gave Laine hope that Ellie would receive something from her in-laws that amounted to more than bristle and brash. And yanking in the welcome mat from the front stoop. Maybe Cormac would prove an ally in the midst of such strain between the Foley men.

"I see Cormac." Quinn edged forward with Ellie a few steps, to lead them farther in. "'Tis good to see ye too, Da."

And that was it. They moved toward Cormac, past tables of gatherings large and small. Families and friends and travelers—with far more cheer than the owners. Laine swept Cassie on behind, dodging patrons and waiters with full trays of pints and plates of food that distracted with their wonderful smells.

"Quinn. Ye made it. Flight alright?"

"Fine. Parked south, just to do a bit of walkin' across the river."

"Good night for it. We've had a bit of a warm snap. Won' last though." Cormac shot his gaze to Laine and Cassie, then back to his brother. "No bags?"

Quinn eased an arm around Ellie's shoulder. "We got rooms in a hotel across from Christ Church. Since Grafton Street and the Green are so close, thought the girls could be in the mix of everythin' when we have to see to this business ye have."

"'Tis less business an' more mess than ye think it's goin' to be. But ye really should just stay on here," Cormac said. "We did some renovatin' in the upstairs flat last year—new kitchen, loft area. An' we still have the rooms on the fourth floor, so there's plenty o' space."

"We'd love to," Ellie chimed in, face brightening. "Laine?"

"Cassie and I are fine anywhere." She smiled at her girl, who dipped her head into the crook of Laine's neck. "Thank you."

It was all set. They were staying on. Quinn, however, seemed less enthused. He turned back to Jack, who was busy tending the bar with the towel flipped over his shoulder, filling a row of glasses in front of him as if that was all there was in the world. "An' what does he say about it?"

"Not much—ye know that. Never has. This is my call." Cormac looked behind toward a bustling kitchen door. "I have to get back to the kitchen—but just bring yer things up an' set 'em in the loft. Door code's the same. Ye can come down, pick a table. Eat whatever ye'd like. I recommend the lamb stew—'tis the special tonight. An' I'll be back after close. We can talk then. Yeah?"

"Sounds fine." Quinn nodded. "Thanks."

There was no handshake between brothers. And no wasted words. Just an unspoken agreement that *detached* had been the order of things for quite some time and would continue to suit just fine.

Laine judged Ellie was right—the task of bringing these hardheads together would be an uphill battle. Whatever history existed between them, it didn't appear the Foleys had experience burying any hatchets.

It was late by the time the air settled—eleven o'clock at least.

Quinn had gone to retrieve their bags from the hotel, Ellie had taken Cassie to bed in the upstairs flat, and Laine had found the few moments she needed to slip downstairs alone.

She moved past a back wall of TVs, silenced after the soccer matches had ended. There was no music, just the hum of quiet conversation with tabletop candles flickering from shadowed corners. Pausing, she hovered in the doorway at the room of polished wood and glass, drawn by the vintage rosewood piano that gleamed with a deep polish.

Opening the top to glance at the pin block would be too

intrusive for a guest, but she longed to, knowing the original serial number would have been stamped inside. Laine brushed her fingertips along the fallboard, hooking her index finger under it to confirm it was indeed marked with the German "Richd Lipp & Sohn" insignia lettered in gold, just above the keys. It sent a rush of remembrance through her—happy years she'd spent in her family's antique shop.

Vintage photos dominated the space above the piano, in mismatched frames of gold and black and deep-oxblood wood. Laine inspected them, finding an old wagon in one, painted on the side with Roe Distillery and complete with horses, stacks of crates, and uniformed workers from what seemed the same era as the piano. An early twentieth-century barkeep stood in a vest, stiff-collar shirt, and tie under a merchant's apron pinned in a triangle point at his top vest button, his eyes piercing even through sepia.

Another photo drew her notice—a smaller, rectangular frame positioned high in the corner. Laine had to climb up, pressing knees to the piano bench to see it: a stunning sepia shot of a castle overlooking a span of cliffs and exploding surf below.

Edging in, she brushed a wave of platinum out of her eyes and ran her fingertips over the black gloss of the frame, studying it under the lamp's glow.

"Laine."

She jumped, waylaid by the sound of a voice behind her.

Yanking her fingers from the frame as if the touch had a bite to it, Laine stepped back, nearly cracking her head on the low-hanging lamp when she turned.

Cormac eased a hand to her elbow, saving her from crashing against the piano, and stilled the wobble of the glass bell overhead. "Alright there?"

"Yes. I was just . . ."

He released her elbow and Laine edged down to standing in

the tiny room, instantly regretting it. With walls closing in on all sides and the piano looming into the central space, there wasn't but a step between them.

"Can I help ye wit' somethin'?"

"I was just looking around." She fidgeted, tossing her hair like a schoolgirl before she could stop herself. "The piano . . . You've kept it in remarkable condition."

"Right. 'Tis that." He glanced out to the gentlemen who owned real estate at the bar—a stodgy row of sweater vests, canvas jackets, Guinness glasses, and eyes peering in their direction. "Uh . . . normally I wouldn' say anythin', but 'tis a Monday an' we have many o' the locals in here . . ."

"Oh yes." Laine followed his gaze, smiling back. "Hello."

Cormac ran a hand over his neck and leaned down, whispering, "Ye see, they're a mite concerned."

"Concerned. About what? The piano?"

He lifted his glance, almost a boyish gesture to the scrutinizing stares of the men. A gentleman with a houndstooth blazer and a rather determined brow tipped his chin in their direction, a "Keep goin', son" nudge if ever she'd seen one.

"No. Not the piano. That's just an old heirloom." He closed the cover back over the keys. "But this is the . . . *men's* snug."

Laine looked over the confined space—the humble wooden table and narrow, worn benches, the mismatched photos hanging like a jigsaw puzzle on the wall. "I don't understand. What's a snug?"

"Yer in it."

"You mean this little closet?" She laughed as she glanced over to the bar.

The row of roosters didn't see the humor, evidently. Their audience was serious—clearly in tune with the conversation at hand, though she hadn't a clue as to why. "Is it private or something?"

"Not private, exactly. But bein' an American, they know ye

didn' know any better." Cormac tapped the old brass doorknob. "This door closes on the men's side." Then he pointed to a curious window open at the end. "That's the hatch—where the barkeep delivers the new rounds. An' the ladies' snug is"—he tipped a finger to point to the nearly identical closet across the dining room—"that one over there."

Thoughts of women's lib reared up from somewhere inside as Laine cast her gaze across to the snug, its door ajar with a similar table and built-in bench. It boasted brighter light and a wide window, curtained against the street below. "You're joking."

"Not a whit, I'm afraid. I'm sorry, but they sent me to fetch ye out." Cormac blanched and shook his head, like he hated that some ancient expectations had reared their head in such a way.

"And what year is this?"

"I know. 'Tis not somethin' I can rightly explain, except tradition in long-standin' places like this."

Laine didn't know where her shock ended and annoyance began. "Tradition?"

"Hard-an'-fast rule. No ladies allowed. Up till the 1950s, except for rare exceptions of a few owners, women wouldn't have set foot through the front doors, let alone stepped up to the bar. Jack approved of the TVs for the football an' live music to cater to the tourists, but at last call an' durin' daytime hours, we hold to the old way o' things. A pub's a meetin' house. 'Tis for pints an' conversation an' brokerin' deals behind closed doors."

Laine placed her hand on the piano, as if defending the antique's honor. "No music, you say?"

"As I said, 'tis an old family heirloom. It's not to be played. An' as for the rest, snug mixin' isn't done."

"And you agree with all this?"

"I don' agree in principle, no, but I respect the history. An' to be honest, yer pretty enough that those old coots are goin' to keep givin' the boss-eyes until I get ye outta their line of sight. Best to solve those two problems at once."

Argument wasn't something Laine wanted in the moment—and certainly not to be goggle-eyed, or whatever that was, by a group of old men. The fact that Cormac had just called her pretty . . . She pushed that notion away as soon as it tried to register.

"Then I'll just . . . Excuse me." She felt him staring down as she squeezed by the piano, awkwardness following as she stepped out.

The soft *click* of the door sounded as Cormac followed behind, and the men offered a chorus of smiles as they turned back to their pints. It appeared they were sated as long as the snugs were looked after and all was right with their corner of the world.

"Did ye need somethin' upstairs?"

"No. It's great. Thank you." Laine shook her head and glanced over to the men—they hadn't turned away completely. Maybe it wasn't the snug? "I was waiting to speak with you, actually."

"Me?" He folded his arms over his chest, waiting as if curious.

"Yes. I didn't have a chance otherwise because everyone was around. But I . . ." Laine felt eyes on them and confirmed they were still putting on a show for the lookie-loos at the bar. It was one thing to have imagined such a difficult conversation, but something completely different to find Cormac's attention fully focused on her, and the locals peeking over their shoulders to drink in their every syllable. "Can we . . . step away for a moment?"

He nodded. "Fancy a walk?"

Thank heaven he understood. Laine tossed a glance up toward the stairs, not wanting to step too far away from Cassie. But she was in good hands with Ellie. "Sure."

"One second." He slipped behind the bar, untied his apron, and whispered something to a waitress washing pint glasses. He pulled a canvas trail jacket from a coatrack by the door, tugged it on, did a quick zip, and flipped the collar up around his neck. He held the door for her and she walked under his outstretched arm, the bell chiming them out. "After ye."

The rain had stopped but a slight breeze had kicked up, and Laine wrapped her cable sweater tighter around her waist as he followed her down the steps. "Which way?"

"Ye'll find all points in Dublin meet at the River Liffey." Cormac turned them to the left, facing a mass of lights twinkling against the deep-ink sky.

"So, anything else I should know about Dublin—women's side of the sidewalk I should keep to or something? Or where we all line up to protest in the morning?"

Laine won a genuine smile from him then—surprising, as she'd judged Cormac wasn't one to do that much.

"Tradition isn't as bad as it seems. 'Tis why none o' the buildings go over five stories high in this city. Why ye have monuments spaced out along the streets. Or how ye can have a row of thrivin' pubs all in a one-block radius, same as it's been for over two hundred years." He shrugged. "Ireland has a million pasts, an' even more stories. Ye stay long enough . . . ye learn them all."

"I wish I'd started with a different one, to be honest."

"Me too." He laughed, walking alongside her, hands buried in his jeans pockets. "It's a craicin' way to make a first impression."

"There's that word again: *craicing.*"

"Oh, right . . . A craic is a good time. You'll find we're always up for a craic in the pub, but we can be a sorry lot in makin' first impressions. Pigheaded an' unchangin', Dubliners are. But passionate when we believe in somethin', an' that makes it all even out in the end."

Walking in silence that came from unacquaintance, they passed storefronts and a crosswalk, while buses and taxis whizzed by. Streetlamps cast a circular glow on a colorful bakery window and bus stop signs as they crossed a wide intersection of rain-dampened streets, slowing up at the start of the bridge.

Cormac bit first. "Seems ye have a lot o' somethin' stewin' over there."

"Not a lot. But a few things on my mind, yeah."

"Ellie?" he asked, a sigh in his tone.

"Yes."

"Quinn said they were goin' to tell ye after the weddin'. I'm sorry—I know she's yer best friend. But from what I can see, Ellie's strong. She'll get through this."

They stopped when they reached the center of the bridge, and leaned over the stone rail. A breeze swept over them, stirring locks of hair against Laine's cheek as she watched the river toil in dark folds below them.

"Ellie's been more of a sister to me than my own, to tell the truth. And Quinn's your only brother. So that means you and I are on opposite ends of a marriage between two people we both really care about."

"And . . . ?"

"And whatever that was back there between your father and Quinn—you don't owe me any details. I'm not trying to overstep family guardrails or anything, but I'm only here for a short time and then Cassie and I go home. Knowing Ellie's half a world away and now this? Cancer? I just have to make sure—"

"That Quinn's going to be there for her."

Laine closed her eyes for a second—it sounded awful when he said it like that.

How could she question Quinn? She didn't even know him beyond a handshake, a few conversations, and an emotional "I do" with her best friend in a snowy French chapel. Outside of that, the entire family was a mystery. And she'd just laid judgment down thick. "Yes."

"I'm glad ye said it." Cormac sighed, his profile strong as he stared ahead, looking over the length of the river's stretched bend. "Someone should. Because I'd been wonderin' the same."

Laine turned to him, sparked by his honesty.

He turned too, his height and hers meeting at almost the same point to see the real person in the eyes. Cormac broke the connection a scant second later, like he cared and was concerned enough to have admitted it, but a sense of loyalty drew him back a shade from actually believing it could be true.

"Movin' about is my brother's way. We don' get to choose who another person becomes. We just accept them as they are. It's ancient family history, 'tis all I can say."

"It didn't look ancient from where I was standing. It looked alive and well."

"I realize that." He paused. Exhaled. Turned back to her. "But Quinn won't walk away. Not this time."

"So he's walked away from someone before?"

Laine stared back, Cormac's Foley greens unmasked as they studied her. His silence confirmed something of Quinn's character once upon a time, though she wished it hadn't. "How can you be sure he'll stay now?"

"Because Quinn asked me if ye could eat upstairs, so Ellie's weakened immune system wouldn't be exposed to illness in a crowded pub. An' he told me, three times mind, that it had to be plastic silverware. Said with the chemo metal leaves a bitter taste in Ellie's mouth. He even asked if they could take my room because it's got an en suite, in case she's sick in the night. Those are specific requests only to see to his wife's comfort. Details, mind, when he's never asked me for a single thing in his life."

Cormac buried his hands in his pockets while the River Liffey drifted on. "So yes, Laine. Quinn will stay because he loves her. An' I believe he's going to see Ellie through this, no matter how hard it gets."

EIGHT

March 17, 1916
10/11 Sackville Street Lower
Dublin, Ireland

Sun muscled its way through breaks in low-hanging clouds. Horse-drawn carriages lumbered along with autos chugging up Sackville Street, undeterred by the threat of rain. Pint-size newsies shouted from street corners, hawking newspapers and passing a cig between them as they received coin from customers. And the numbers of customers would grow.

They always did on St. Patrick's Day.

Already Issy had seen what had to be hundreds of uniformed Irish Volunteers, marching through drills down the length of Dame Street. The activity forced commuters into lines for packed trams and taxis that clogged the streets, requiring double time just to reach the city's north side. She'd watched from the back seat of her taxi, inspecting the faces of young men through the stop-and-go across the River Liffey, always looking for Rory . . . or, by chance, an O'Connell brother among them.

She exited in front of the shop-front sign that read: *Jack Foley's Irish House, est. 1796.* She allowed her gaze to follow ahead as traffic flowed up the street to the General Post Office—or GPO—secretly abhorring the sight.

Buried deep within brick and Corinthian columns and three stories of wide windows was the Irish communications hub for the British Commonwealth: the Central Telegraph Office. A newly renovated lobby with fresh varnish on teak counters and gleaming floor tiles should have offered a welcome to patrons and staff. But Issy imagined only darkness inside; the unmistakable shadows of a world at war. From there, families were notified when their Irish boys had been killed or wounded in action somewhere in the muddy trenches of France. Inside those walls was held the impending shatter of hearts by little rectangles of typed paper, and war couriers would make widows and childless mothers out of a knock to front doors.

Issy turned her back on the building, instead climbing the stairs to the pub.

Ignore what you see, Issy. Pretend it's not even there.

A gentleman stumbled as she stepped up to the door, nearly losing his bowler when she moved to slip past. "Madam." He tipped his hat right. "Are ye lost now?"

"Not at all, sir." She squared her shoulders, pulling the leather strap of her Kodak to keep it hidden under the coat flap at her side, and offered a smile meant to send his nose back into his own affairs. "Isn't it a glorious St. Patrick's Day?"

He looked on, an ill-humored bent to his features. "Glorious indeed."

Yes, yes. I know. You don't take to women in your pubs . . .

"Excuse me." She sidestepped him through the front door. Issy hadn't the time or the inclination to challenge a bearish Irishman on the front step. If he didn't take to the female persuasion in a traditional pub, then he'd best find a new barstool to occupy.

An old brass bell chimed over the door and floorboards creaked as she stepped in, causing heads to turn.

Inside was what Issy might have imagined a public house to

have been: The haze of cigar smoke in the air. Dark wood-paneled walls. A long bar and workmen sitting on all the stools, downing Guinness. She masked a cough from the smoke, refusing to show she couldn't pass muster in a men's establishment. The bartender behind the counter tipped his head—a ruddy crown with receding hairline—and kind eyes smiled at her though she must have looked lost.

"Ne'er fear, lads. This lady be a friend o' the Foleys." He stepped around the end of the bar, walking up to face her.

Though she still felt the scrutiny of the men in the room, they lost interest when the barkeep approached her, turning back to their local tales.

"Are you Mr. Foley?"

He nodded. "Might ye be the earl's daughter now? Lady Isolde Byrne?"

"I am, sir." Issy looked around. How many had heard the name—plus the title? If any saw the camera . . . potentially disastrous. "But you needn't address me so on my account. Issy will suit fine."

"We been expectin' ye. An' cheered to have another Byrne in house, when my niece said ye may come to call. 'Tis said the Byrnes an' Foleys go back generations in County Wicklow. Did ye know of it?"

The realization she'd been expected made Issy smile. "I did, as a matter of fact. We have some Foleys still in tenancy on our estate."

"Well then, this way, miss. To afford ye some discretion." The man's eyes reflected a deeper shade of goodwill, and he led her to a snug opposite the bar. "'Tis the ladies' snug, an' yer most welcome to it."

She followed, folding her ivory skirt and black woolen coat under her as she chose a corner tucked in by a frosted-glass window overlooking Sackville Street. It appeared the perfect spot to stay out of eyeshot inside but keep watch on the happenings out.

"Do ye wish for some refreshment?"

"Oh—no thank you."

The answer was automatic, so much Issy almost choked over the words. Her mother would have swooned to know she was inside a public house, let alone taking Guinness in one like the men. She already thought Issy too worldly—best leave something sacred.

"The call bell is just there." He pointed to a pull that was wired through a hole in the wall, next to a cast-iron match striker mounted beside. "If ye need anythin' at all, pull. I'll see to it through the hatch door."

"Thank you, sir."

"'Tis Aonghus, miss. Or Mr. Foley, if ye prefer. But any friend o' my niece 'tis a friend o' ours here." He tapped his knuckles against the doorframe in a jovial sound. "I'll send her to ye."

"Thank you then, Aonghus."

He clicked the door closed, leaving her alone.

More ICA uniforms marched by the windows. Many boys young as fourteen or fifteen she'd guess had joined men with graying temples and age lines at the eyes; those who were left after so many had gone off to war. They carried revolvers at their waists, rifles in their hands, and passersby backed up as they marched on.

Issy squeezed the camera case just to feel the leather against her skin. How she wished to capture the moment—anything to remind her that the world had so much more to offer than what transpired within the confines of ladies' parlors in County Wicklow.

Photography had become her window to see it all.

Who'd have guessed that a youthful jaunt to famed writer James Joyce's Volta Cinematograph would change her life? She'd once tagged along with Gard and Rory to catch the matinee picture show outlawed by their mother's staunch disapproval—the performing arts' underbelly, as she'd so eloquently put it. And yet it wasn't the thrill of seeing her first moving picture but the photography display in the lobby that had rendered Issy utterly captured.

The sample images of opera singers, stage actresses, and American starlets like Mary Pickford, and the mystery of far-off locales like India and the Orient, were engaging and vibrant, not the tintypes of old. The Stereoscopic Autochrome contraption she'd seen brought images to life in timeless renderings of color and light—enough that Issy had rushed home and begged her mother for every ladies' fashion journal subscription she could find, if only to see that same kind of life again bursting from the page.

Now the camera turned to electricity in her hands, with a pulse that cried out to be and do what it was made for, instead of remaining hidden and only snapping photos of castle ruins. All the bustle—the men marching and the build of emotion—triggered a longing in her to unlatch her camera case, squeeze the shutter, aim and fire for the life of it all.

The snug door creaked, snapping her back to attention.

And then—*Honor.*

That lovely crown of strawberry blonde shone in the sunlight as she poked her head in, a radiant contrast to the somber navy tunic dress she wore. She swept Issy into a hug as she closed the door behind them. "Ye came."

"Of course I did. Why wouldn't I as soon as I received your letter?" Issy drew in a deep breath, hanging on the question as if the answer should have been obvious. She leaned back, the edge of her hat just grazing the leather bench back as she locked eyes with her friend.

"Because I told ye not to."

"I thought you knew me better than that." Issy had to laugh then, and pointed to her camera as they sat, looking out over the bustle of Sackville Street. "What do you make of all this? There must have been hundreds . . . thousands of uniformed Irish Volunteers marching through the south side. And the English don't seem the least bit concerned. Not even a blink in notice."

"I'm sure I don' know what to think."

"They told me at the camera shop to keep the Kodak hidden and not take photos near any official government buildings, lest they think me a spy in league with the Germans. But there does seem to be some sort of plan at work. You think all these men are in the city to enlist?"

"I know at least one has—Liam is already on a boat. But not before he announced his engagement to one Vivien Carmichael from Lanarkshire." Honor heaved a weary sigh and rested a hand on the slight middle she was hiding under the drop hem of her dress and the lip of the snug table. "Their news made the society columns about the time this was makin' the rounds in the Dublin tea parlors."

Yes, the gossip had landed at Ashford Manor too, especially since Rory was linked to her situation. It was whispered among the hoity-toities that he was the father, making their name and the title of Lord and Lady Chryn the subject of taint just as Honor was. And without a shred of compassion for what a young lady had endured, their families were both, slowly, being edged out in one accord.

"Don't think on it. There are more important things to worry about now."

"My parents tried pawnin' me off on a cousin in the west. Out o' sight, out o' mind, ye know. But I couldn't be spendin' the rest of my days in a fishin' cottage on a Dingle hillside. So I came back an' the McGinn name is expunged in favor of a Scottish heiress. I don' blame the Devenish family though—'tis biscuits to a bear now wit' all o' this. I'll still light a candle for Liam each week, but a prayer to God's ear is as close as we'll ever be again."

"I'll pray for him too. And all of our boys who've gone."

"Any word on Gard?"

"A letter, just before New Year's. Last we heard he's captain in a battalion in France—near the Somme. He wrote of an abandoned old manor house they stayed in one night, curiously full of pianos. Can you believe that? Just like Ashford Manor. Even with the lightness of such a story, Mother grows more agitated with each day. I keep imagining he and Rory will walk back through the door for Easter, and it will be just like old times. Except we can't go back, can we? Now that so much has changed. I'd give anything for word from either of them."

"Ye mean if Rory found out I'm livin' on the third floor over a public house against his express wishes an' came to call anyway?" Honor looked up, a sheepish air melting over her face. "Then ye'd want to know it?"

"Rory's been here?"

Honor caught the edge of her bottom lip in a gesture that shouted an emphatic *yes* without the necessity of words.

"We set a date." She held up her hand. A tiny flash of emerald and gold winked back in the sunlight. "Will ye come?"

"Of course I will!" Issy held Honor's hand in hers, then swept her into another hug. "Honor . . . my sister. This is everything!"

A ring and a booked church didn't absolve all things.

It wasn't at all the way they'd have had their romance play out. But if Honor was to heal and that sweet smile was to return, a life with Rory would surely be the start of it. And for reasons even she couldn't explain, while listening as Honor exclaimed how he'd asked and slipped the ring on her finger, Issy's heart made a wild leap . . . drifting past memories of time spent under the spell of Levi O'Connell's dashing smile and, instead, stopping on the figure and familiarity of Sean.

Issy had never mentioned his proposal, nor that she'd fallen apart when he'd said he was leaving back in January. Weeks had passed, and still she'd had no news of him. No appearances in parlors or at garden parties. There was a ball at the Powerscourt estate, but he never showed. It was as if he'd kissed her, said goodbye, and fallen off the face of the earth.

"Issy . . . What's wrong?"

"Nothing. It's just—" She hadn't realized her eyes had glazed in tears and quickly masked it. "This is right. And I'm so happy for you. When is it?"

"We have to wait for the banns to be read, an' after Easter of course—for the church. But as soon as we can walk down an aisle after." Honor beamed with a sweet, girlish blush, making Issy's heart nearly burst.

"And . . . what about Rory? Did he tell you what he has planned after that day at Ashford?"

Honor shook her head. "Nothin'. Just that he had a fire lit an' intends to do what he can for Ireland. He believes in Pearse's leadership, an' the ICA. 'Tis not a popular opinion with most people. Even my parents believe we should support the Crown in the war an' pick up the fight for Home Rule after. 'Tis another reason we're waitin' until sometime after the holiday, as Rory says, when things settle down."

Horns blared and shouts erupted, drawing their attention out the window.

A tangle had flared down below, with motors forced to angle around a horse-drawn wagon that had slipped in curbside, blocking the street.

"Oh dear. Come with." Honor sighed and tugged her by the elbow to the snug door.

Issy swept up her camera, slipping the strap over her shoulder as she followed behind. "What is it?"

"The George Roe wagon. Uncle told me to watch for 'em because they're late. An' they'll stir a riot if they're not careful."

Issy followed behind, again absorbing the energy of Sackville Street the moment they stepped outside.

The sight of a horse-drawn delivery wagon she'd seen umpteen times, but the spark of such a day made the common occurrence of whiskey delivery a slice of Dublin she couldn't ignore. The sun had finally cut through the clouds, washing the sidewalks in spring light—perfect for a shot or two.

"No, gentlemen. Ye can' be parkin' here in the front." Honor waved down two workers already standing in the wagon bed, muscling crates out of the back.

"An' why not, missy?" One tipped his flat cap back on his brow with a bit of pluck in his tone to match.

Issy unsnapped her camera case—Honor wouldn't take to being called *missy*.

If they couldn't see the strawberry tint in her hair, they soon would when it blazed red. Making sure she was shielded from view by the whiskey wagon, Issy readied her lens, clicking the filter for gray conditions over to the highest setting for *brilliant*, as the sky was cooperating with an abundance of light.

"Yer new to the route," Honor shot back, hands on her hips.

"Nigh on two days now. I'm Killian Brent, an' wit' my associate over there, we'll be yer charge for the mornin' on delivery days."

"Well, gentlemen. Seein' as this is yer first day, I'll educate ye. See these tracks below yer boots? This is a tramline. Both o' ye an' yer poor horses will be flattened to a pancake in no mind. The sorry sight o' yer busted whiskey bottles will be all over the sidewalk, an' I'll have to sweep it up."

The distance Issy judged, sliding the lens for the wagon's place on the sidewalk. She focused in on the white block letters of *Geo. Roe & Co., Thomas Street* painted on the side, fixing and turning the viewfinder image until it was as sharp as she could make it.

"Then what do ye suggest now?"

"For Jack Foley's ye have to go 'round the back—down Lower Abbey, all the way to Marlborough Street. 'Tis an alley that connects to all the shop fronts on the block. Deliveries go through the back door. Never on Sackville if ye value yer life at all. An' back yer wagon down the alley, mind, or ye'll never get it out again at the end. We've had many a wagon jackknife because delivery boys couldn' follow simple instructions."

"An' why should we be believin' you? Isn't there a Foley here—by name o' Aonghus? 'Tis said he usually takes receipt o' goods. Or . . ." Killian hopped down to the sidewalk in front of Honor, swept a hand under his apron, and retrieved a slip of paper from his pocket. "Or a Breandán Foley, it says here?"

"Breandán is my cousin—he placed the order. But he's out just now so you'll have to do with me."

"How long will he be out?"

"As long as there's a war in France, I expect. An' yer late, so my uncle Aonghus is already in the back waitin' to unload ye."

Killian nodded acceptance to other deliveryman, who began stretching rope again to tighten the crates back for the short ride down Lower Abbey Street.

"Sorry we are about that then, missy. There's a certain parade pluggin' things up all over the city. Seems ye might have trouble in keepin' a schedule on St. Patrick's Day. But come tonight folks will be cheered, for their glasses will be full to the brim an' their tales all the merrier for the tellin'."

"Well, praise be for that," Honor added, her wit a tonic.

Click.

Issy smiled to herself, winding the film in back of the camera. That shot had been perfect. Honor's pretty profile taking the men to task, the snapshot of Dublin's daily life in horses and wagon, set against the backdrop of crowds, and the sun shining down on the GPO behind it all.

If she hurried, she could snap another just as brilliant.

The other man hopped from wagon bed to sidewalk. Issy stared down into the tiny lens image—the lighting, angle, street bustle . . . all pristine.

"Excuse me. Could you two just—hold for a second?"

Click.

"Marvelous." Issy turned the Kodak over, popped open the spring door at the back, and pulled the stylus from her coat pocket to jot a quick title to the margin between exposures.

"Hello, Issy."

Hearing her own name jarred her writing.

Issy looked up, and there he stood.

Sun on the shoulders of his work jacket. Turning a wool flat cap in hand. Waves of tousled brown hair tipping his crown, trying but failing to shield the O'Connell blue eyes that could always stare right through her. His features revealing he'd grown older somehow, though little more than a year had passed by.

The image she'd once longed for and so dreaded at the same time was no longer a mirage of forgotten things—it was real. *He* was real. Tall and dashing and standing right before her again.

"Levi," she breathed out, at once fumbling to tuck her camera out of sight. "You're . . . back."

He replaced his hat as Killian swept up to the wagon seat, goading him from behind that they had a schedule to keep and he should be about hurryin'.

"Aye. Sean said he'd told ye I would be."

She swallowed hard. "And Sean—is he well? We haven't crossed paths in some time."

"Wouldn' know. He's always about fightin' for some cause or another. Saw him for an hour at most last week before he headed off to the Duke of Connaught's Auxiliary in Bray."

Issy could finally breathe a sigh of relief; Bray wasn't France. At least Sean hadn't enlisted.

"He's working at the hospital then?"

"Been offerin' time to the spiritual needs of the soldiers in the limbless unit—beastly business, to be sure. Been burnin' many a candle there. Some days don' even come back to sleep. But there's nottin' else in Wicklow right now. Not for wages that amount to more than crumbs. So it's odd jobs in the city—deliveries by day, mason work at night. I'm gettin' by well enough. An' seein' as neither of us would join up to fight for the Crown, it's do what we can here."

Killian whistled, raising the reins in his hands with a "what's the holdup?" in his direction.

"You have to go." Issy plastered on a smile, though it took everything to muster it.

"But can I . . . ?" He edged back, then paused. "Can I come call on ye? Have a mite to catch up on wit' Rory too. Yer at Ashford still, yeah?"

No letters. No word for a year. You leave . . . return . . . and it's pick up again, just like that?

"Um . . . we're at Ashford Manor, yes. But Gard has gone off to France. And Rory is . . ."

Issy looked to Honor for help, finding none but a perplexed look upon her face, questioning why Issy was inviting a deliveryman to her parents' estate. But of course—the McGinns hailed from Enniscorthy, County Wexford, and didn't know the Wicklow locals as she did. Honor had been introduced to Sean in the months after Levi had gone and only knew the younger from Issy's recounts of an unrequited love from her youth.

It wouldn't take but a moment to explain the blue eyes after they'd gone. But in this instant? She was stuck without answer or assistance.

"Rory is busy these days."

Levi swung up to the wagon seat, pulling back on the fervency of Killian's near slap of the reins to get the horses going. They jolted, then stopped.

"Hold, Killian." Levi strained to hear over the sound of car horns and chugging motors passing on the street. "So, can I come call?"

"You are welcome, of course. It would cheer my parents to see our old friends again. Seems everyone's scattered with the war."

Killian kicked the horses into a walk around the corner, and Levi flashed a characteristic smile as the wagon lumbered away.

"Will be just like old times, yeah?"

"Levi—" It was so unladylike considering everything her mother brought her up to be, but Issy couldn't hold it back. She'd simply shouted his name the next heartbeat that thundered through her. "Please do invite Sean to come with you. We should like to see you both."

Issy watched him ride down Abbey Street Lower, with a bit of devil-may-care still alive in his smile.

Yes, that's what she feared most: that it would be just like old times.

NINE

December 25, 1797
Ashford Manor
County Wicklow, Ireland

Crisp winter air outside the stables sealed in the scent of fresh straw inside them. Maeve tapped her riding boots against the doorframe, freeing them of snow, then stepped in.

Horses stirred in their stalls, energetic and awake, looking for their breakfast. The clank of metal—the jostle of bridles or currycombs—echoed from the back row. Maeve knew who it was and what she must do. With shoulders held high, she walked toward the sound, then stopped to pat Éire's nose as the mare poked it over the stall wall when she happened by.

A mixture of thoughts disquieted Maeve's spirit on such a morning.

Only six months prior, she'd expected to celebrate Christmas as they always had. The earthy scent of Scots pine should have perfumed decorated halls. Spiced cider would have simmered in the kitchen, while Mrs. Finnegan saw to a breakfast feast of her mother's annual request: the last of the season's Williams pears in deep French red, imported from the groves near their Berkshire estate, smoked salmon with dill, and scones with sweet *fraochán* berries and cream. The stable rafters echoed the jovial spirit of

Christmas in her mind with each step: laughter . . . celebration . . . memories where all of them—George, Cian, and their parents—gathered around the hearth as Maeve played "The Wexford Carol" on the pianoforte.

But now, even the familiarity of their stables presented a bittersweet welcome.

Both George and her mother were in unsettled graves beyond the gardens, in the shadow of the castle ruins. Cian was at sea, having swept off to manage their holdings in England. Her father was inconsolable in his grief. And the pianoforte had gone quiet; Maeve's heart could no longer hear the memory of its melody in her mind.

Her entire world had been upended, and if she were to believe the intrepid traveler in Ashford Manor's tower room, then it would be again. It was on Maeve's shoulders now to battle back—to defy an increasingly volatile climate in Wicklow and, instead, forge peace and happiness for every tenant upon their estate.

That began with a visit to the stables, be it Christmas morning or not.

Maeve paused at the open door of the last stall, finding Leary Ó Flannagáin combing tangles from King's mane.

Despite his injuries of the previous night, the man had continued working on a holiday, with a bandage taut 'round his crown. He was older than her twenty-one years by nearly two decades. Tall and broad, and feral in his way with the grooms employed under him. And though she'd never seen a direct flash of anger in him, Maeve positioned her frame paces away from the strength of muscle he owned in favor against her, just in case. And as added security should things go badly, Maeve had tucked a flintlock dueling pistol at her side, hidden in the folds of her mourning dress.

"Shouldn't one of the grooms be doing this, sir, with your injury?"

"Oh, milady—I did not see ye." He bowed. Offered a smile in greeting, pausing with currycomb in hand. "Happy Christmas morn to ye. But I'm quite well an' wanted to see all put right after the blackness o' events last eve."

"How is King?"

"He be quite fine an' cheered. No damage, thank heaven. An' safe back where he belongs."

"I was worried that we might not recover him at all, given all that occurred." Maeve stepped forward, keeping her words flat and her glare pointed. "Did you apprehend the thief then?"

"'Tis sorry news to bring, milady, but no. Iffen Master Cian were here, he'd have bid we search all night—which would have been right by him to do. But the men had their families, an' wit' the storm it seemed fittin' to draw back an' leave it to the soldiers to ferret the thief out o' his hidin' hole. 'Tis believed he's fled up into the mountains." He kept working, words stout and sure, but . . . eyes cast down and away from her.

"I see. King got free from the thief then?"

"Nigh an' farther than the east fields. We had to search well into the hours—down the Dublin road an' up into the trees shieldin' the mountains. Quite a scare the thief put into him, to run as he did."

"But the horse has suffered no injury."

"Not a whit, milady. Fine an' a matter o' no concern. I'll have 'im cleaned up rightly."

Eoin's words of caution raced through her mind: "*Watch for King to lift his hoof . . . a jerk or hop about the hind leg—especially when he's turned or backed out o' the stall. Ye can see it plain as day. That horse couldn' run. Not as he is. An' as it doesn' come on suddenly, yer stablemaster would have to know.*"

"I'd like you to take him out—to see him trot."

"Milady?"

"King. I'd like for you to back him out of the stall." Maeve eased back several steps, giving space for her request. "Bring him out so I might see he has suffered no injury. He is, after all, his lordship's prized stallion. We should see that he's of no lesser state after that long run through the fields. Would you not agree it's better to err on the side of diligence in such matters?"

Leary stood tall, comb lowered to his side, the smile fading from his lips. "I don' understand. I just told ye he—"

"I am mistress here, and I gave you an order." Maeve squeezed her grip on the pistol in her palm. "Let him out to walk. *Now.*"

Leary shrugged, ever on the slight side, as if her wishes were nonsensical but he'd entertain them for her benefit. He untied the reins from the hook at the hay manger and tugged to turn King through the door.

"Back him out, please."

He eyed her with more mettle this time but turned the horse to do as she bid. And without warning, a sharp hitch caused King to falter and kick—twice—nearly sending his hoof into his abdomen.

"*Shhh* . . . hush now." Leary raised his hand over King's brow, taking hold of the noseband to ease the horse to a halt. "'Tis shaken up, milady. An' not wise to agitate him further. He'd best be put back fer now."

Maeve tipped her chin higher. "Again."

"What is this, milady? Ye'd damage yer father's horse on a whim? I take orders from his lordship or Master Cian—"

"I said *again*, Mr. Ó Flannagáin."

"Ye be givin' orders now, eh?" He did laugh then, revealing his nature with a glare so direct it could have lit fire to the walls. "Ye haven' called me but Leary in all yer born days, child. I'll saddle yer mare, iffen ye fancy a ride. But if not, off wit' ye. I have work to occupy my day."

"I am not a child, and you would do well to remember that."

Maeve stepped forward and swiped the reins from his hand, blistering him with an iron scowl she knew he'd not soon forget. "You are dismissed, sir."

"Dismissed?"

"You heard me." She flitted her gaze over to the stable door, then back again, challenging him with cool confidence. "Gather your belongings. I expect you out of the cottage by nightfall. I will be by to ensure you have done so. Now go."

"Ye cannot dismiss me. Not without cause." He stepped out of the stall, rage seething between gritted teeth as he turned to the tack room shelving on the opposing wall. "I be employed by the earl fer more than ten years!"

It was exactly as Eoin had warned her: the stablemaster kept a musket hidden in the bracket of a low shelf. Though Maeve hadn't any clue how a stranger on their estate would know such details of their stable operation, she was cautioned to listen.

Without flinch or tremble Maeve raised her pistol shoulder high, training it on the center of his back. Slow and steady as she could, she clicked the hammer back with her thumb. Leary was bid to stop, his progression arrested by the echo of the noise against the high ceiling. He turned to the sight of cool metal staring him down.

"Your employment arrangement ends now. Forward an address so we may send what is owed to you, sir. Good day."

Maeve watched him, pistol firm, as Leary challenged her with scorn burning in his eyes.

"And if you dare one step in the direction of the musket on the shelf, I will be forced to discharge this pistol between your eyes."

"This will not stand."

"It already does," she insisted, finger curling around the trigger, ready to snap with the slightest provocation. "I am agent on this estate until further notice, and my decision is firm. You may leave with your dignity intact, or I shall have you removed from the premises forthwith. What say you then?"

He turned then, little to do but thrash about like a fish on a hook, beating leather straps against stall doors and tossing a pitchfork the length of the stable row, until it crashed in a pile of tools and hay in the corner.

Maeve held back a flinch when he slammed fist to door, swinging it until the edge caught in the snow and hung open, spilling morning light inside. The pistol she kept high, trained on the door until her muscles screamed with the weight and she finally had to drop it to her side. She could scarcely hear anything after, save for the heart slamming in her chest, breaths rocking in and out of her lungs, and the stirring melody of neighs from horses rustling in their stalls.

The stable door crashed open at the opposite end and Maeve did jump then, drawing the pistol back up in a split second.

Eoin stood there, boots in the snow, his breath a rapid in-out cadence like he'd sprinted the entire way down two flights of stairs. He cradled an arm around his waist and in the other, shirt untucked over his trousers, brandished Cian's second dueling pistol in a confident grip.

"*Judas*—it's you." Maeve exhaled, closing her eyes to catch her breath. "You are late, sir. He's already quit the stable . . . and shortly, this estate." She lowered the pistol and leaned against the haven of the stall door, submitting to the wave of adrenaline that washed over her.

"Have ye no sense at all? I said his lordship should question him—or a man from the estate. Even the butler could have done. Why would ye come out here in their stead?"

"Someone had to do it."

"But it didn' have to be ye, did it?" Eoin scanned the stable, seeing she'd indeed been left alone with only horseflesh, a mess upon the aisle, and bits of hay still drifting on air. "Do ye realize what a man like that could have done to ye?"

"Not with this cocked between the eyes. Though I might think to actually load it next time just in case." She held out the pistol's mate, still locked in her grip, though she eased the hammer back down to rest against the barrel. "Where did you find the other one?"

"That housekeeper o' yers doesn' hide the fact she despises the air I breathe, but she did tell me where to find the pistol box when I guessed what ye were about an' told her it could mean yer harm."

He exhaled and his shoulders relaxed, the tension replaced by an unexpected smile that eased onto his lips. "Ye dismissed him?"

"Must you sound so surprised?" Maeve stooped to the shelf, feeling around under the wooden bracket.

"I'm impressed."

"Well, you needn't be. I've been looking after myself for some time."

When she felt the cool of metal against her fingertips, Maeve pulled it out—a musket, just as he'd said.

"An' why is that, milady?"

Maeve turned back, standing tall before the stranger wearing her brother's clothes, with a hint of the tattoo peeking out at his wrist. He was an enemy to the family Ashford, and she'd allowed him sanctuary under their roof. It did not sit well within her, even as her instincts had proved correct in one point of his character—but that was not enough to absolve everything.

She couldn't disentangle the rest to him, so she avoided past doings altogether.

"Because I don't need anyone to take care of me. And I wasn't quite sure you were telling the truth. It appears as if you were."

"Try to on occasion, even if I am o' the clan O'Byrne."

"I don't judge plainly for that. But King is indeed lame on his left side. However did you know it?"

"He won't put weight on it at a walk. Could see it soon as I looked at him."

She stared back at the horse. Her father's prized pet. The one her mother had gifted him not two years prior. "What's to be done?"

"A few things to ease the symptoms, to get him back to a better form. But stringhalt is believed somethin' a horse is born to an' won' ever leave him. Any stablemaster worth his salt would have known it. 'Tis somethin' that should've been reported to his lordship long before now."

"Yet our stablemaster chose to hide it instead. The questions is, why?" Maeve studied him. If he knew why—and she suspected he did—the man wasn't saying.

While the stablemaster they'd trusted for years had covered deceit, Maeve would have guessed it of a similar man, the one standing before her. Eoin knew of horses—more than simply as one who rode them. That was evident enough. But Maeve couldn't stop herself from thinking about the extent of the man's knowledge in things far more severe. Like dueling pistols. The smuggling of goods. Musket balls cutting into flesh and skirmishes with soldiers. Everything about him spelled *reckless*, and any measure of the cavalier in him could have repercussions Maeve was not willing to entertain.

Eoin leaned against the stall without masking his need to brace against a firm foundation. Sunlight filtering down the aisle illuminated slim streaks of red that had seeped into the white linen of the shirt beneath his palm. He was in pain, no doubt, but didn't remark.

"You'll catch your death out here."

He looked up, crossing the impediment of space between them with a fixed gaze. "As ye almost did, ye mean?"

"Not remotely. It's reason why I keep a dagger in my boot. And now I've two firearms instead of one. I'd have been fine, I assure you. The grooms can look after the horses at present, and I'll think about what to do for a stablemaster later. Right now, we ought to go in. The soldiers are likely still hunting you."

After easing King back into the stall, Maeve tied the horse's reins to the rail over the hay manger. When she was satisfied the animal would keep for the moment, she turned back to Eoin—trying not to think about how he'd been concerned enough to follow her all the way to the stables. Why he'd thought to bring some defense of her. And why he'd insert himself into affairs on her father's estate.

She eyed the pistol in his hand, not thinking of it before, and was struck with curiosity. "Was yours loaded?"

"Aye. Pirates prepare for the worst—especially we shifty-eyed ones."

Maeve repressed a smile. Mrs. Finnegan would have appreciated the fact he was awake just enough the night before to pick up on the quip she'd made. What else had he heard?

"Our housekeeper does apply sea-roving descriptives quite liberally, I'm afraid."

"'Tis hard not to notice." Eoin turned the pistol, offering her the butt of the weapon though she stood paces away. "But I've done what she asked o' me, so now I return this to you."

Maeve eyed him. Instead of accepting the pistol, she kept her stance firm—and far—from where he stood. "Will Ó Flannagáin give us any further trouble?"

"He may."

"Well, Mr. O'Byrne, I shall be ready in the event that occurs. For now, I'll ask that you place that pistol in the box where you found it and, if you wish to stave off death a while longer, that you return to the tower posthaste before anyone sees you."

"If ye wish it."

"That'll do for present. But shortly, I'm afraid I must demand an explanation. And I assure you, I won't be shy about asking for it."

He accepted with a nod. "An' I assure ye, milady—I'll hold nothin' back."

TEN

Present Day
10/11 O'Connell Street Lower
Dublin, Ireland

Cassie's tears had almost stopped.

In a tank and yoga pants, Laine paced along the stretch of loft windows overlooking O'Connell Street holding Cassie bundled in her favorite pink pj's and fleece blanket. She walked a back-and-forth trek, with streetlights bright enough to avoid bumping into the couch or end tables, and rain that *pitter-pattered* down the windows.

It should have been quiet and peaceful, but it was late. They were exhausted. And Laine's heart was breaking apart again.

"It's okay, sweetie," she mouthed against Cassie's temple, over the sound of her bare feet padding across the hardwood. "It's okay."

This time had been bad.

The nightmare and Cassie waking to uncontrollable crying . . . Laine had thought they were past the worst of it after year one of adoption. But like clockwork, two a.m. had ticked over and Cassie had awoken with screams and tears, with only Laine there to comfort her. She just prayed it wasn't because she'd packed them off to a strange city, with too many new things, loud noises, and unfamiliar faces.

Too much, too soon.

She hugged Cassie tighter, guilt pricking at her insides.

Laine hushed and hummed through the shadows, from couches and exposed brick in the open living space, to the kitchen, along a wall of open wood shelves, and a table and chairs set against the windows. She paused, her gaze drifting over the print image of cliffs and sea and sky hanging on the back wall, when she heard steps on the stairs.

Cormac came down in jeans and a plain white tee and black-rimmed glasses he hadn't worn before. He flicked on a light at the base of the stairs, washing a soft glow across the hardwood.

"I heard, uh—" He stopped paces away and looked toward Cassie's mop of chocolate curls. "She okay?"

"We're okay. Thanks. Her internal clock is off, and sometimes a new place can be a little on the scary side. But we know how to get through it." Laine hugged Cassie closer, knowing she wasn't asleep but wasn't ready to let go of the tight hold on Laine's neck either. "We didn't wake you, did we?"

He took off his glasses, folded and set them on a bookcase that spanned a wall with color-arranged spines on its shelves. "No. I wish." He laughed it off and ran a hand through his hair. "Was in the office when I heard ye come down. Kickin' the books, actually. Seems the only time to do it these days 'tis the dead of night."

"Oh. Right." She nodded, glanced upstairs. "Anyone else awake?"

"Doesn' look like it. An' Jack sleeps like a stone. Don' mention I said so, but I wouldn' count on him wakin' before the night wears off. He talks a mean game but takes Guinness like my grandmother."

Laine had to laugh at that—funny to think of the gritty Jack Foley she'd met downstairs sleeping off a pint like a lightweight.

Cormac stood there, arms folded across his chest, watching over the sprite bundled in her arms but clearly able to see her undone appearance too. Laine swept her tousled hair back behind her ear and lowered her gaze to the folds of fleece in her arms, hoping he couldn't see that Laine had been crying too.

"Well . . . I guess we'll go on up then."

He took a half step toward them. "Are ye hungry?"

"No, we're—"

But Cassie straightened, nodding. "I am."

"Right. Let's fix that." All business, he crossed to the kitchen. Laine followed, Cassie looking on with interest as he flicked on a trail of lights and opened the refrigerator behind the long, concrete-topped island.

"This is goin' to shock ye, but for a public house we're slim. A couple o' bachelors live here an' just about every meal's eatin' while standin' in between shifts. We've got Guinness in here aplenty. But besides that"—he popped up, a thick loaf of bread in hand—"grilled cheese. An' we've got apples an' pears. Good enough?"

Cassie gave a wary nod, slightly interested in being won over.

He pulled a stool out from the counter and patted the seat. "Here." He smiled at Laine with a whispered, "An' coffee for Mom—like the Yanks do it?"

"Please," she mouthed, having spotted a Keurig a while back and so wishing she knew where the pods were stored to get it brewing.

Cormac went to work—cutting thick slices of soda bread and halving fruit on the wooden cutting board in perfect portions, like he could do it in his sleep. He talked slow and quiet so Cassie wouldn't have to say much. She'd nod if she liked; that was her way. And somehow, he knew to ask whether she wanted the "square yellow" or "white circle" cheese instead of giving a choice between cheddar and provolone. Laine even had to hide a smile behind her hand when he let Cassie make a game out of him flipping the grilled cheese on the griddle.

Watching, Laine felt the gentle fade-in of a longing she'd once given away.

She'd once dreamed nights like this would exist, where she and Evan could raid the kitchen at two a.m., talking and laughing over a cup of coffee. And where for a few precious moments, no cares existed as rain cried on the great big world outside the windows. A little girl would be seated between them, smiling, maybe even healing a bit, and she would have become the center of their world together.

But Laine's ring finger was bare now, and Dublin was not home.

Sharing middle-of-the-night heartbeats with a man they hardly knew . . . Laine feared what Cassie had seen—and liked—for the first time, what it might be like to have a father. And that she wouldn't know. At least not now that everything with Evan was severed, and he'd settled in a new life in Seattle while they waded through heartbreak in theirs.

Cormac looked over, flashing a grin at something Cassie had said. Laine had missed it, muddled by questions instead of sharing in their smiles.

"Laine?" A tiny flicker of confusion crossed his face. "Did ye hear us?"

"I'm sorry—what?" Laine shook out of her thoughts and raised her coffee cup up in joined hands.

"Miss Cassie here wants to see the princess castle wit' her uncle Quinn an' aunt Ellie tomorrow."

"That's right. They were going over to see the estate that a woman left in your care?" Laine swallowed a sip of coffee, watching as Cassie munched on apples and perfectly cut squares of grilled cheese.

"Yes. Dolly Byrne. She was a patron down at the pub—one of the regulars."

"Did you know her well?"

"That's what keeps me wonderin' . . . hardly at all. She'd come in at noon meal most days, sit at the end o' the bar on the same stool.

Never tried to sneak into the men's snug, mind." He gave Laine a light tip of the brow and a half wink. "She listened more than she ever talked to anyone. Did have an eye for the piano though. She'd step into the snug and run her hand along the side as she walked by."

"Yes—the Richard Lipp? I've never seen an early 1900s in quite that condition. You have a real treasure there."

Cormac paused and studied—really studied—her. "How in the world did ye know that? Ye turn it over while I wasn't lookin'?"

Laine toyed with her mug handle. She knew much more than she'd offer up. She'd have guessed it was a 1912 custom build, and it was worth far more than to keep shoved up against a pub wall where patrons might scratch or nick the wood. She'd have had it removed and brought up to the loft. The alcove overlooking O'Connell Street was crying for such a piece to add character to the space.

"No . . . I didn't. It's just that all things vintage was a hobby of my grandfather's. And my father's. Just die-hard memories from childhood, I guess."

"Happy memories?"

She smiled. "Most of them, yes."

"I can't imagine what Dolly's were. Not wit' us at least. They say she had no kin. She passed, nigh on three months now, an' nobody knew she owned a thing, let alone some grand estate house an' castle ruins in County Wicklow. An' to think—she left it all to a pub owner who scarcely had time for her, but to set a pint at her chair an' slide a bill across the counter."

"I assumed she left it to you. You mean she left everything to your father?"

"To see to dispersin' it, yeah." Cormac nodded, cleaning the counter, keeping his hands busy while they talked. Maybe it was easier than looking at the other person. Keep busy. Keep things light. It was always safer that way.

"He'd like to bring in an auction house, sell what we can, an' wash our hands o' the whole messy business."

"But you don't."

"No. I don't. I'd like to learn more. To find out who Miss Dolly was an' what she wanted us to do wit' it all. I don' know why exactly, but it seems important or she wouldn' have involved us." Cormac shrugged, like the answer was the simplest thing in the world. He dropped the pan in the sink, the cast iron sizzling in the water and soap. "So? How about it, ladies? Want to go?"

"Well, I'm sure you have to work. We didn't come to cause any problems. If Ellie still wants to see it, maybe Cassie and I could go exploring or something."

"Cleanin' up the books or cookin' up a feast at two in the mornin' is easy. But when a guest asks to see a castle—a princess castle at that, I can' be sayin' no. Don' make me the bad chap in this story." He winked at Cassie, who shared the hint of an apple-filled smile. "This pub has survived more than two hundred years—even took a direct hit durin' the Rising. After all that, I don' think these walls will fall apart if I step away for a few hours."

He brushed his hands on a towel, flipped it over his shoulder in a carbon-copy of the elder Foley from the downstairs pub.

Castle ruins and a manor house that contained who knew what treasures? The prospect did prick her heart a little, Laine had to admit. But Cassie smiling after a bout of nightmarish cries that could've lasted all night? Remarkable. If taking a few hours to drive some Irish back roads and walk around the ruins of a castle was all it took to see her little girl smile, then Laine didn't see what harm it could do.

"Well, Cass—you want to go?"

Cassie nodded, her matter-of-fact, quiet way having returned.

Cormac smiled in victory, the thing Laine guessed he didn't do often but seemed to ease into a little more regularly since they'd crossed paths—in two kitchens and a snug and a little chapel that hosted a fairy-tale wedding in the snow.

"Okay. You win. I guess it's grilled cheese for breakfast and castles for lunch." Laine set her mug on the counter and eyed Cassie with the motherly stare she'd become quite good at. "And that means . . . time for little princesses to go back to bed." She gathered Cassie in her arms.

"Uh, Laine . . . ?" Cormac tipped his head toward the window, and the rain still streaming down the glass from ceiling to floor. "There's boots in the closet in yer room—Keira, our sister's. They should fit. By the look o' it, ye'll be needin' 'em tomorrow."

"Boots. Thanks." Laine hugged Cassie close, standing on the edge of the shadows from the kitchen light. "Can I come back, Mr. Foley? Help you clean up?"

"It's Cormac to you." He shook his head. "And no. 'Tis my pleasure."

Was there anything like a pair of cherry-red wellies on a dreary Dublin day?

Laine found the Hunters in the closet and silently thanked Keira for the loan as she pulled the boots over skinny jeans and slipped on a rain jacket. The boots brightened her view, even in the back seat of Quinn's rental, as he drove them all south out of the city, to the back roads of Ireland waiting beyond.

The drive was only about forty or so minutes from the pub, but the view was an extraordinary mingling of greens and blues popping up in hills and sky and sea.

Cassie glued her nose to the window with Laine close behind her as they passed port towns and level stone-laden beaches one moment and, seemingly in the next, cruised along a cliff-side road, barren save for a rocky rise and an endless view of the Irish Sea.

The terrain bordering it was wide with green- and yellow-blanketed ridges, then the Wicklow Mountains appeared behind. Trees tangled and twisted up over the road . . . like God couldn't make up His mind in the Emerald Isle's design and included all master creations at once.

Their car followed Cormac's lead as he turned his Renault past a thin wall of perfectly pieced rock fences arranged with no mortar, Quinn said, which was Irish custom. The remarkable limestone structures meandered as far as the eye could see and still stood after hundreds of years. Sheep wandered beyond, their coats splashed with a stripe of royal blue against white wool, showing off expert climbing skills as they scaled high-up crevices notched in treeless ridges. And then . . . a drive. Long. Winding. Lined with rows of mature, gangly limbed trees painted over in autumn colors, and beyond it the heart-stopping image of crumbling stones—the ruins of Castle Chryn sitting high up on the rise.

"Looks like this is it." Quinn checked the GPS on his phone. "Castle Chryn. In Bray, County Wicklow."

"See, Cass?" Laine rubbed her palm on the fogged window and pointed. "Back there . . . It's the castle."

"Oh, Quinn," Ellie breathed out as Quinn eased the car to a stop at the drive's end. "Look at it. It reminds me of home. Just a different kind of Sleeping Beauty, right? And look—the manor house is still standing! Think of all the books, Laine. And paintings and vintage whatnots that make your heart sing . . ." She turned to eye Laine in the back seat. "Tell me this isn't your Christmas morning right now."

"It would have been once." Laine laughed. "A long time ago."

Ellie wasn't accepting that. She turned back to the manor, sighed, and whispered, "It should be again."

The manor sat off to the side, quite alone, in four stories of burnished stone and glass, sleeping in the hollow between castle, cliff, and tumbling waves.

Its grounds were tired—electric green and autumn toned in places but choked by bramble and thorns in too many others and overgrown with brush trees that sprouted along the rock wall base. Autumn hadn't been kind. From the mix of rain and neglect, the stone needed a good washing. Double front doors stood weathered and worn by the salty air, with corner towers so high they whispered to the Irish Sea on the horizon.

Cormac was already out of his car, walking up the path to the front steps.

"Well, at least there's no moat. Must say I'm a bit jealous of that feature." Quinn no doubt referred to the headache of the bog that surrounded their castle. "And don't get any ideas, sweetheart. We've got more than enough to keep us busy wit' our own renovations for a good while yet."

Quinn kissed Ellie's cheek, hopped out, then trotted to catch up to his brother.

The girls hung back, opting to explore the path between ruins and manor. They strolled down a tree-lined lane—not paved with stones but blanketed with dew and fallen leaves. A rock wall edged bowers of trees clothed in the last of autumn's crimson and deep purples.

"What do you think these trees are?"

Laine kept her gaze on Cassie skipping along the path, but she couldn't help but find herself drawn to the palette of painted leaves. It was something they might see in an orchard row at home—not cultivated along a path leading to a sea cliff and castle ruins. "I don't know, but they're beautiful. Cormac might want to find out."

Laine reached out and plucked one of the leaves from an outstretched limb. She ran the silky color under her thumb.

Leaning over the rock wall, Ellie scanned the grove's floor. "There's an orchard not far from Grandma Vi's cottage back home, remember? I think these are pear trees. I don't see any fruit though. Maybe it was already harvested. But pears seem out of place here, don't they? An orchard bordering a sea coast? I wonder who in the world would plant pears here."

"Manor houses had gardens, right?" Laine said. "Maybe this is what's left over from that. Looks like it needs some work though." Weeds sprouted up along the rock wall. Field grass and a thick carpet of thorny yellow flowers drifted over the rise, where the colors bled into a landscape that fed all the way to the mountains. "Are those the Wicklow Mountains?"

"So Quinn said. He was right—this road has quite the view."

Laine snapped a couple of print-worthy photos on her phone, then stood back, watching Cassie's sweet innocence dancing against the toil of wind and sea past the castle walls. "Has he said anything else, like there's progress between him and Cormac?"

Ellie shrugged. "I don't know. Those two . . . They're good at business. See?" She tipped her chin in the direction of the manor steps. "They can talk restorations all day, but they won't even look at each other while they do. What I want to know is, how did they get this way? And why is Jack able to connect with Cormac, but he can barely say two words to Quinn? Even then there's snark behind nearly everything."

"So we've learned." Laine paused, her thoughts interrupted as Cassie teetered on a flat stone, then jumped—imaginary fairy wings flapping as she landed on the edge of a puddle. "Wish we could all be as free as she is. Though I have a feeling those jeans are going in the trash when we get home."

"Jeans come and go, but this view is worth it. Right? And look at her." Ellie laughed. "She's in heaven."

"You're right. How often will we have a view like this?" Laine slipped her arm around Ellie's, supporting her as they walked elbow to elbow, watching Cassie trot up the path toward the manor.

Birdsong joined in as they walked on. The sound of wellies crunching stones and leaves . . . the crash of distant waves . . . even the whistle of sea winds carrying over the rise, loosing leaves to drift on it like sparks of color in the sky—Ireland lulled the traveler with quite a melody, and it was fast winning Laine over.

"So, I've been meaning to ask you something, Laine."

"What?"

"Why did you—?"

"Cass. No, honey. Go around," Laine tossed out, shaking her head. Her little sprite looked at the evidence of last night's rain, then went around the giant mud puddle and began hopscotching up the manor's front steps. "I'm sorry. Why did I what?"

Ellie stopped short with a gentle tug at her elbow, and turned to her with one of those *I-want-a-real-answer-here* looks. "Lainey, why did you cut your hair and go platinum?"

She couldn't help but laugh—quite a nonchalant question for the pointed glare her friend was issuing. Laine patted a palm to the platinum waves at her nape, shaking them out against her collar. "What, you don't like it?"

"No—I love it. It looks beautiful." Ellie shifted her stance, thinking with her feet. "It's just not *you*. It just seems like a big change out of the blue."

"I can fly across an ocean, surprise you at your French vineyard wedding, and that's not big. But an appointment for a cut and color . . . is?"

"For some, no. But I think it is for you, and personal at that. You've always loved your long hair. It's how I've pictured you in my mind for as long as I can remember, with that brunette curtain framing your smile. I just wondered, because something about that girl is . . . I don't know. Different. And I wondered why such a change now?"

Laine looked down at the cherry tips of her boots, feeling the warmth of a blush take over her cheeks. *Please don't ask me for any more . . . I'm not ready to tell you.* "That girl grew up. A while ago."

"How long is a while?"

Laine ground her heels in the earth, gave her boots a distracted tap like Dorothy spouting, *"There's no place like home."* "A while is long enough that I don't imagine what my life was supposed to be like. Now, I accept it. I just want to live each day as it comes."

"You mean Cassie."

"I mean everything. Cassie was my niece, but she's part of me now. She's my daughter. Maybe not from my body, but of my heart. And I wouldn't change that for anything. I don't think about how things should have been—packaged and perfect, with a big house and white picket fence. But who said we should always be chasing perfect anyway? I think I'm learning I'd rather have something real. Something to fight for, you know?"

"Right." Ellie stared up at the manor, seemingly lost in Laine's comments. "Who'd have thought I'd end up building a French fairy-tale castle in between chemo treatments?"

"Oh, Ellie. I didn't mean it like that—"

"I know you didn't. But it's true." She waved off Laine's show of emotion with a soft smile. "I'm fine. Don't worry about me. I've got a fighter spirit too, you know."

Laine wrapped her in a hug, her heart breaking. "Too late. I'll always worry. That's the best part of being friends—they're the family we get to choose, right? And maybe God asks us to cut out the old every now and then, just so we can be sure there's enough room for something better on the horizon. He's got a plan at work, even when we can't see it . . . I mean, a couple of weeks ago Cass and I were at home. And now we're here, walking this stunning road with you. I can't believe any of that's coincidence. I'm not sure God works like that."

"I've never heard you talk that way."

"Maybe I should have. Things change. We start to look at life through a new lens. And hope can take us to simple places—like a tree-lined path, or a salon chair—for a chance at something new. Maybe a few trees or a pair of scissors at the right time are exactly the kinds of things we need to keep us moving forward."

Laine gazed up to the manor, watching her pink-jacketed daughter as she hopped to the top step, drawing up on the Foley brothers from behind. A chill that had nothing to do with the weather crept up her spine as Cassie slowed . . .

Step, longer step.

Stop.

Laine watched as if in slow motion as the little girl who'd been damaged and forgotten and forced to fight back so early in life took a heart-stopping chance. Without word or warning she reached up for the warmth of Cormac's hand. If it startled him, he didn't show it—just turned and looked down to the path, searching for where Laine stood.

A breeze drifted over the ridge between them as Cormac found her. He stared back, making a silent request for permission to enter the sacred space of a little girl's affections.

And though Laine's heart begged to give him a response, she couldn't move. Not to give a nod or a word, or even a smile. Because it felt right to stand back and, instead, let him choose.

Cormac held fast for a moment, then turned away from Laine, breaking their connection. He took keys from his pocket and, holding Cassie's hand, turned one in the knob and pushed the double doors wide at the center.

They opened without ceremony, a breeze toying with the edge of gauze curtains at the side windows. And Cormac stepped in, his back to them, allowing Cassie to stay as long as she wished right by his side.

Quinn called out to Ellie, waving them over.

"Well, looks like we're being summoned." Ellie slipped her arm around Laine's elbow to lead them toward the stairs. "Let's go and find out what secrets are waiting inside."

ELEVEN

APRIL 23, 1916
ASHFORD MANOR
COUNTY WICKLOW, IRELAND

The colors of war were muted versions of their brighter cousins.

Where the *Maison Paul Poiret* was once the darling house of Paris fashion, the designer's lavish fabrics and bold designs had become frivolities as bombs blew trenches to bits half a country away. The colors in Issy's fashion journals turned to steel gray, deep blues, and the earthy military-styled greens that had become staples in the Irish woman's wardrobe. Because of it, Issy wouldn't have minded wearing her gray gabardine suit for Easter morning services. Or the long, serviceable royal-blue skirt and ivory blouse she favored from the last season. Even black would have felt more appropriate, given the state of things.

When a luxuriant pink box was delivered from a dressmaker on Temple Street, Issy was crestfallen to find it had been purchased for and delivered to her. The style was all wrong—not her at all and certainly not functional. Nothing but drippy layers of dusty rose, with tiers of silk gauze lining the bodice and hem. The imported Lanvin hat she left in its bed of pink tissue paper.

The reflection in her chamber's floor-length gilt mirror rendered her unable to see past the pomp and the practical worry that the fabric would surely snag on the mechanism of her camera. Yet still not wishing to injure her mother's already-frayed sensibilities, Issy had dressed without complaint. But in her heart, she was increasingly bound by the desire to involve herself in a different, purposed role in the war effort.

Rose silk and Lanvin bonnets had no place in that world.

Women were stepping outside the home to work now in offices. As nurses in war hospitals. They muscled it out as fine as the men in munitions factories—some even wearing trousers and flat caps by choice. Unionists and nationalists alike were rolling up their sleeves and aiding the war effort—something she secretly but ardently wished to do.

With rose gauze floating in waves around her, Issy hurried down the staircase and stepped into the drawing room, carrying the morning's copy of the *Sunday Independent* she'd found on the library desk. "Father—have you seen this? It's remarkable."

"Ah! Here she is," her mother chimed as the butler closed the door behind her. "Dearest Issy. We have a surprise."

Issy lowered the paper, enough to catch the suited figure of Rory advancing to encase her in an affectionate hug. He drew back and shook his head slightly, silencing her from any questions of the ICA, or Honor . . . or where he'd been for the last few weeks.

"I thought to come home for the holiday, Sister. And I've brought an old friend with." Rory added a deliberate layer of cheer to his voice.

He stepped to the side, revealing Levi, his blue eyes smiling back from across the room.

"Mr. O'Connell." Issy swallowed, then recovered quickly. "What a surprise to see you."

"Hello, Lady Isolde." Levi bowed after giving the title—for her parents' benefit, of course. "*Cásca sásta.*"

Happy Easter indeed.

With the honorifics, Levi's charm was on full display. But with his natural mannerisms so similar to Sean's, Issy felt a pang of longing to search the drawing room over in hopes he'd be there. Her mother looked on with perfect posture from her seat on a blue brocade settee, and her father stood near the mantel, beaming an ignorant smile to it all.

But . . . no Sean.

"Mr. O'Connell says you crossed paths in Dublin?" Her mother—the titled Lady Mildred Chryn on display at the moment—could always be counted on to be the skillful combination of aloof yet direct about matters concerning her children.

"Uh . . . yes, Mama. We did. A few weeks ago now, while I was on a shopping excursion. Just in passing, in the city center."

Issy didn't lie—she had stopped by the camera shop for film on St. Patrick's Day, just stopped at Jack Foley's to see about Honor first.

She darted a glance Levi's way, checking for discomfort. Had he any, he hid it like a master fabler.

He was ever composed in a crisp suit of charcoal pinstripe, charismatic, and seemingly without a care in the world that he'd asked to call on Issy weeks before but hadn't made a peep since. But to show up on Easter Sunday, out of the blue, raked Issy's insides with hot coals. She was fast becoming a woman who might lose all civility if he dared swindle her thrice, especially if he did so before she was finally able to confront him for boyish capriciousness.

"You should have said you'd met, Daughter." Her father's scold was amenable, as usual. "We posted a letter to Gard not two days ago and could have included mention of his old acquaintance. It might have cheered him to know that some of his childhood chaps are still on the island. But what is this in the paper now—not something of concern on this fine holiday? I'd thought to read it after your mother's fine meal and Fairyhouse for the horse races tomorrow."

Suddenly under a microscope of eyes, Issy recovered, slipping the paper down at her side. "It's nothing. Truly." She backtracked, as if it were inconsequential enough to feed the fire.

Her father stepped forward, some of his jolly having faded. His mouth tightened, concern showing around a white mustache as he took the paper from her. "Come now. What is it?"

"It's not ill news, is it, Hugh?" Her mother gripped the armrest of the settee, no doubt the welfare of their older son flashing through her mind. "Please say it is not news of the war."

"No, Mama. Not exactly."

Her father sighed at the article—as expected. It was assured that the one thing able to sour his mood would be maneuvers of the Irish Volunteers and the ICA, when all good Irishmen were supposed to be supporting England's war effort.

He slapped the paper over to Rory, and Issy held her breath—thinking of her brother's illicit involvement with the nationalist cause, her own gaining sympathies, and yet the fact that their father was ignorant of it all. Were Rory to see the report, she'd know in an instant whether or not MacNeill's order was a critical matter. But it could also prove disastrous if the rage feeding his sympathies crossed with their father's staunch support of the Crown.

Father and son's opposing views were a powder keg, with the potential to blow.

"It is nothing." She passed a glance between the parties in the room.

Rory scanned the article, quick and silent for a moment only. But when his eyes flashed, she guessed he'd reached the critical junction of the announcement. An order from the Irish Volunteers' officer Eóin MacNeill himself had been communicated to the press the evening prior. It gave strict orders that whatever had been planned for Easter was canceled—full stop.

"It can't be." Rory muttered a curse and kept reading.

"Rory, dear. Please do remember yourself. This is a holy day." Their mother shushed on a twittering laugh.

His palms curled the paper edges in a visceral reaction as he read aloud: "'All orders given to the Irish Volunteers for tomorrow, Easter Sunday, are hereby rescinded . . . Each individual Volunteer will obey the order strictly in every particular.' MacNeill cannot do this—if the Volunteers don't show, we're finished!"

Levi placed a cautionary hand to Rory's elbow, whispering low, "'Tis not the time. Let's see to yer mother's fine dinner now, yeah? We can do this later, when we've had a chance to calm to the news."

"Time for what?" Mother asked, just as singsong and oblivious as could be.

"Yes, Rory." Issy stepped in, anxiety feigning the sweetest of innocence to pacify rising tempers in the room. "Let's enjoy Mother's dinner—leek soup and roast lamb with cabbage, as always. Your favorite. We can speak of this little annoyance after our Easter celebratory."

"I'm sorry, Sister—but no." Rory folded the paper, dropped his hands to his sides. Like a soldier standing at attention, he addressed Father. "You'll say this is the Catholics' war, Father. And to many, it is. I know you won't like me for saying it, but this is our time for Ireland to be free."

"What can you mean, Son?"

Issy closed her eyes tight, dreading what was coming.

"I've joined the ICA."

Mother's gasp echoed off the ceiling.

Issy opened her eyes to the aftermath. Mother had nearly fallen away with the shock, her face washed of all color as she sagged back against the settee. In striking contrast their father stood frozen, breathing heavy, staring his younger son down with the coldest glare she'd ever seen etched upon his face. "You have not, sir."

"It's true." Rory tipped his head to Levi. "Both of us. Sworn allegiance months ago. Levi in Brooklyn, and I in Dublin. It's why he came back now—to take up arms with us against our English oppressors."

Father's features tightened, tension building so the buttons looked ready to pop off his white linen shirt. He avoided Levi thereafter, not even acknowledging his presence with a look.

"You dare take arms against your own blood?"

"The English blood in me is dead."

"Our title is English, man!"

"My *brother's* title is English. I am Irish now, and if you could truly see what this is about, you'd blame me not for a second. You'd take every weapon down off the walls in the hunting hall and go with me today."

"I *do* blame you. I knew you took the revolver weeks ago—the coward's way out. You think I didn't notice, when your brother fights for his king? Or that I haven't heard whispers you've been seen about in a green uniform, skirting after the McGinn tart?"

Rory stepped forward, passion causing his fists to form boxing mitts at his sides. "*Do not* call her that. You don't know the truth about it."

"I know enough to have rumors reach our door and degrade our good name in any house of polite society. Have you not considered what your mother has been forced to endure in all this? It's been the tittle-tattle of Dublin for months."

"If these houses were so polite in society, I wonder whether they'd carry such tales at all. You act as though you don't know her. Was Honor not a guest in this house until only a few weeks ago?"

"Yes, but I could not have such a one in attendance with your *sister* here." Their mother spoke up, her voice emboldened by the notion that Honor would be welcomed back. "Issy still has a chance to marry well—a name that might be accepted in Dublin. Or even

London. Would you seek to tarnish whatever hope she has left with such an ill association?"

"Mama, I really don't—"

"Hush, Issy. We are speaking to your brother."

Issy flitted a glance to Rory and then to Levi. What in the world must have passed through the minds of both men at the mention of matrimony? The O'Connell brothers were born with just enough status to render them acceptable acquaintances for the Byrne brothers to associate with in youth, but certainly not for Issy to have found a possible suitor.

It was evident now, more than ever, that her parents knew her not at all. Their concern of war was just, but the rest they treated as if her only cares should be in selecting a new dress or filling her dance card at the next party. The youthful summer romance with Levi, her burgeoning affection for Sean, and, of course, her own sympathies to see Ireland free—through the lens of her camera, wherever it might take her . . . They were as ignorant of her heart as they were of Rory's.

And they knew their children not at all.

Though not in total fault, as they'd kept secrets well hidden.

Issy watched as the earl stood his ground, her heart beating nearly out of her chest as tension burned like fire consuming the room. Caution. Rage. And bitter contempt . . . They'd begun their hemorrhage on both sides.

"You insult a woman who has committed no sin," Rory whispered, too calm for the moment. "And you mar your own character by believing such idle tales."

"You dare speak of character when Gard has gone to defend our heritage, our land, his title—because you could not? What have you done but sully everything he stands for? So the Ashford heir is risking his life in a trench in France while you're dogging for the scraps of a bunch of hell-bound *Fenians*."

Issy exhaled, balancing a grip on the back of a parlor chair as the severity of their father's rebuke clung to the air.

Levi straightened his spine but remained silent. And Rory—passionate always, but clear and direct under pressure—stood his ground before their father, conviction maturing him by the second. "So that's the way it's to be?"

"This is the way it has always been. And how it will always be. Rebellion isn't brave—it is against God. And you blaspheme your Creator with this taint on such a day. So go if you must. Out of this house if it is your wish. But you'll never return. Not for a half crown of living. Not while I'm alive."

Rory nodded, staring their father down with strength emerging through a steel skeleton.

"Good-bye, Mother. If you have need of me, Issy will know how to send word."

Their mother gasped, crying out as Rory turned to the door. He thrashed it open, sending the wood to clang against the iron door stopper, then stormed through without another word.

"I'll go after him, Mama." Issy rushed behind, running down the hall to the grand foyer.

She gave chase into the hunting hall this time, remembering the last time Rory had plucked a weapon off the wall in the name of vengeance. He was plotting cold-blooded murder in his heart and she knew, given the chance, he'd surely pull the trigger.

Issy caught up to him, pulling at his elbow. "Rory—"

"I told you before, Issy. Stay out of this. You can't change my mind."

"I'm not trying to." She swallowed hard. "But if you're going into Dublin, then I am too."

Rory didn't try to hide his shock.

"Not on your life, Issy. Do you think I'd allow you to walk out on our parents when they need you here?"

"Allow *me* to walk out?"

"I know you're freethinking. I don't ever try to change that about you. But this won't be tea in a parlor. This is rebellion. And if it's anything like what Gard is fighting through, it'll be machine guns and artillery fire and agony on both sides. Men who seek freedom must be prepared to die for it. I've signed up for that. But you mean to tell me you wouldn't faint at the first drop of blood or cower as bullets fly past your head?"

"Dare me to prove you wrong and I will."

It must have been the oddest of combinations to see his pink-frock-wearing sister grandstanding about how she was ready to run off to war. All Issy knew was that a set of convictions had grabbed hold deep inside, just like Rory's had, and wouldn't let go until she was walking Dublin's streets with a shutter under her thumb and a camera lens at the ready.

She'd think about the ramifications later. For the moment, all that mattered was seeing it through.

"You're my brother, and I know what's ticking in that head of yours. You love Honor more than anything—" He looked away. "And that kind of love can inspire us to challenge ourselves in ways we mightn't have before. So if there will be a fight on Irish soil and you're called to it, then so am I. I'm of age and you cannot stop me."

"Why do you have to be so blasted headstrong?"

"Let her go, Rory." Levi's words cut the tension, silencing them from behind.

"You don't get a vote in this, Levi. It's a family matter."

"No, by all means—keep the votes to yourself," she shot back.

Levi stepped through the archway into the glow from the gaslights overhead. They cut sharp lines through elk and red deer antlers, drawing ominous bramble and vine shadows against the marble at their feet.

If Rory wouldn't answer her, Issy knew Levi would.

"Where are you going, Levi?"

He tossed his gaze to Rory, then answered firmly: "We meet at Liberty Hall this day. Eden Quay, North City. 1430 hours."

"I'll kill you, Levi. If anything happens to her . . ."

"You've enough killin' on tap already, Rory, an' God save us from even one. But ye cannot keep Issy caged. Ye know it as well as I do. I'd say that camera o' hers is burnin' a hole through the ceilin' as we speak. She has her own reasons for goin', an' who are we to hold a man—or woman—from their convictions? It would be no different if she was in *Cumann na mBan*. If ye go to join up for yer own reasons, then ye have to take Issy for hers, or whatever we're all tryin' to do here is a lie."

Rory looked to her then, his brow crimping in question.

In that moment, Issy knew her heart rested not in chasing him or in angling for political positions, but in something else entirely. She hadn't known how to admit it even to herself. But Rory was correct—it wouldn't be a garden party. War was real. And raw. And ravaging their world.

Was she ready to see it?

"Is this true? You'd go anyway?"

Issy abandoned safety and nodded.

Just once.

"I'll be fifteen minutes behind after you two leave, I swear it."

There were no words to explain why, not with Levi standing mere feet away. She had to sort out her loves—the former feelings that had burned so bright for Levi O'Connell during the years of her youth, the growing affection for the brother who'd bared his heart once and asked for her hand, and the stories in film and lens that for the first time in her life made her feel fully alive when in her hands.

If God was to grant freedom to Ireland, then from somewhere deep inside, Issy knew she had to be a part of it.

"Mother and Father will think I convinced you."

"Never. I'll leave a note explaining why. And I won't be gone forever. Just in the event that something's going to happen, I want to be there, Rory. I'll go to Honor at her uncle's pub if you want. Stay with her on Sackville Street."

"My sister in a pub . . ."

"I'll refrain from telling you I've already been there once. At least we'll be out of any danger. It may not be the best-laid plan, but this is something I must do."

Raking a hand though his own cinnamon hair—a gesture so common to all three Byrne siblings it sometimes felt like looking in a mirror—Rory tossed his glance over to Levi. The O'Connell brother contributed nothing, just stood with hands in his pockets as he waited for the decision to play out.

Rory sighed as he looked back at the drawing room, the door still ajar.

"Say your good-byes. And go get your things. We'll wait ten minutes, but not a second more."

Issy grasped his wrist, squeezed, and mouthed, *"Thank you,"* before she fled up the stairs to her chamber.

She slipped into a blouse and movable skirt and her trusted boots with the sawed heels. Wares she tossed in a bag: journal, Bible from the shelf, pencils for marking exposure paper and a pencil knife for sharpening, an extra blouse, stockings and underthings, and if there was to be a rebellion, the leather case and Kodak that would be her eyes to capture it.

Issy tore open her top bureau drawer, the one that held jewelry she'd never cared to wear, with piles of scarves and evening gloves she'd used only as insulation for the treasure hidden behind them. She reached to the back, feeling around, panicked until her fingertips felt a single cardboard box.

Only one box of film left.

She tore into it, hating that she'd lose landscape shots when she yanked undeveloped film from the back of the Kodak. She loaded the new film, snapped it secure in its case, and pulled the leather strap over her shoulder as she stared back at her reflection in the mirror.

There was no choice now; one roll of film meant she'd be granted only ten images—ten shutter presses and *clicks* to capture scenes of what could be a miraculous birth or an agonizing death.

Ireland was at war again—this time, she'd make herself bleed.

TWELVE

JANUARY 1, 1798
ASHFORD MANOR
COUNTY WICKLOW, IRELAND

Wilfrith Ashford, the seventh Earl of Chryn, sat alone by the fire.

Companioned by grief, he'd wearied through weeks in the same lone chair in the shadow of his wife's portrait, with heavy brocade curtains drawn about the library windows both day and night. It was dim, but the firelight illuminated enough of his silhouette that Maeve could see the grayed crown and deeply creased brow lines that aged him, it seemed overnight, taking him beyond his fifty-four years.

Balancing the dinner tray in the crook of her elbow, Maeve rapped her knuckles on the doorframe—a light *tap-tap-tap* that should have stirred him, were he not under the spell of the firelight's dance. Booted legs he'd stretched out before him and he still wore his frock coat, though he hadn't left the manor in days to have need of the outer garment. It was unbuttoned at the waist and his collar drawn, linen wrinkled at the neck.

"Papa?" She stepped in, the door hinges creaking a weary song as she eased it wide.

"Maeve." He turned a quarter-profile at the sound of her voice but looked away as she entered. A decanter of Jameson reflected the flicker of firelight—sitting near empty on his side table.

"I've brought you something to eat, Papa. You must be feeling quite peckish by now." She edged in toward his desk, the firelight casting the library in a golden glow.

"I said I didn't care for any."

"Well, you said you did not care for our usual holiday affair, so I've brought a humble feast with me . . . for us to share. A sort of picnic for our New Year's. And we may discuss business if you like—from one concerned estate master to another. We could discuss placing a new stablemaster. And perhaps a new steward, as Cian may be in England for some time."

The desk of her father, her grandfather, and generations before him owned a remarkable presence in front of a curtained oriel window, but it went unused now. For weeks correspondence had piled up in the letter tray. Book stacks had sprouted out of the floor all around, leaving bare spots on shelves where they'd been plucked and never returned. Papa sat adjacent to it, the contrast of a sharp-edged crystal tumbler in one hand and the softest white gauze in the other—one of her mother's kerchiefs, embroidered in her favorite rosebud spray along the edge.

"I told Mrs. Finnegan the staff needn't fuss over a seated meal in the dining hall. We should save that for Cian's return. Maybe invite some of the tenant farmers for a planting celebration in the spring? Like we used to do in the old days."

Maeve made room on the desktop, scooting unopened missives and stacks of dust-catching books out of the way, and slid the tray in their place. "Tonight we shall have to suffer through the delicacy of Mrs. Finnegan's quail pie and plum pudding—both your favorites. Tea. And . . ." Maeve picked up a burgundy pear. She crossed the room to his chair, knelt beside it to gently ease the tumbler from his grip, and replaced it with the fruit. "Look. This will cheer us."

Remembrance seemed to be in the physical contact of pear flesh with skin, instead of in seeing the deep French red in his palm. He looked down, turning the deep burgundy over in his hand. "The Williams' *bon Chrétien*."

"Yes—the shipment of 'good Christian' pears arrived yesterday. A mite late this year, but still in time when all is said and done. We can take them 'round to the tenants tomorrow."

"Your mother ordered them before . . ."

Maeve's sorrow rose, unexpected and fierce, when he couldn't find the words to hold tears at bay, triggering almost physical pain in her chest. But she did, swallowing the emotion. Her mother had placed the order months before she'd fallen ill . . . before George had been killed . . . and now they couldn't even speak of it. Maeve hid all behind the confines of an empathetic smile.

"Because she knew it would not be New Year's without them."

"No, it would not," he whispered, holding the pear limp in his hand. But seconds later, he gripped tighter. Knuckles squeezed fierce, the tips of his fingers bruising the pear skin in a growing vise.

Maeve leaned in, turning her face to his. Instead of inviting her to share their grief, he clamped his eyes shut. "Remove them."

"But you've always loved them. I thought it would help us to remember. And she wanted the tenants to have them, just as they always have. To ring in another new year at Ashford. Perhaps it would help us . . . to heal some."

He shook his head, a white-knuckled grip piercing the beautiful French red as he shoved the pear back at her.

Maeve took it, her fingertips gentle, feeling the ridges where his nail marks gouged the flesh.

"I said take them away. *All* of them."

"But we have crates filling the storehouse—the last of the season. We cannot just throw them out. Papa, the tenants expect us to engage them as we always have. The master of the estate must do it."

Even as she said it, Maeve questioned who that was. In truth, Ashford had been without a master for some time.

"Did you not hear me, girl?" He slammed his palm on the leather armrest, making her jump. "These will feed the fire or rot the rubbish pile, but they go out. Now."

Maeve backed up, edging away as he returned an ardent grip to the kerchief. He rubbed his thumb over the rose petals, staining the delicate gauze with pear juice from his fingers.

"At least have something to eat . . . Please."

"Go," he countered, far too easily and with graveled tone. "And take the tray with you."

The portrait looked on. Watching. Pitying.

Maeve petitioned it, silently wishing her mother were here to help but seeing only an angel in paint strokes of sky-blue silk, with a basket of vibrant yellow gorse—Ireland's *aiteanns*—in her hand. Maeve feared most that one day she'd walk into the library and it, too, would be gone—another memory surgically removed from her life.

Lord Chryn would carve and cut Ashford Manor until there was nothing left.

"Of course. If you wish it, I'll go." Maeve hated the abrupt sound of her own voice, but she'd not beg.

It may work to try again tomorrow. And the day after that. And again, each day until Cian returned. But begging achieved no purpose save to make one weak. Weakness wasn't going to step into men's boots. And if Ashford required it—even in the interim—Maeve would rise to slip them on.

Decisions could wait no longer.

She hoisted the tray, leaving the mountain of letters and book stacks to gather another layer of dust. "Good night, Papa."

Whisking down the hall in an automatic gait, Maeve balanced the tray so the pears wouldn't roll off the edge. But instead of descending to the kitchen as he'd ordered, she stopped at the junction of the floors.

An idea sparked—a tiny glimmer of hope.

Sending a letter to Cian in England was the obvious next step, as he'd need to be aware of their father's despondency. But a letter sailing all the way to their estate in England would take time, if it arrived at all.

Needs at Ashford were here. Now.

Polished wood stairs twisted around and up, carrying through shadows to the third-floor corridor and a wing of the manor that now went unused. Maeve looked from the upper floor back to the pears on her tray—a traditional symbol of peace.

If Ashford Manor was to survive, what had she but to place trust in the only ally she had left?

Where the earl had tumbled into decomposure, burning away his pain with drink, Eoin was the opposite.

Not unlike the man two floors below him, he was sitting in the wingback by the fireplace. But the decanter they'd used to clean his wound hadn't been touched from its place on the bureau. He'd tied his dark hair back at the nape and was clean shaven, wearing one of Cian's shirts and navy waistcoat and boots as if ready to depart somewhere, though he hadn't anyplace to go.

He read by a single candle lit on the side table.

"Milady." Eoin dropped his boots down from the footstool and stood, book closed at his side. "I didn' expect ye."

Maeve was slow and steady to close the door behind her, remembering to make tired hinges soundless down the stairs. "You're well?"

"I am. Better at least. Thank ye."

She looked to the hearth. "You have no fire?"

"I didn' want to chance the smoke drawin' from the chimney durin' the day. Too easy to be seen from the glen."

"But you cannot stay up here in a freezing room. It's inhumane."

He walked to the mantel. "I haven' much choice, have I?"

It was then Maeve noticed a row of books, stacked the length of the timber above the hearth. As if he could read and, further, valued Latin and Greek. Books on economics and agriculture. Stacks of novels. Shakespeare. There was even a volume or two of German poetry. Not inquiring but so wanting to—if he wasn't a gentleman, he gave quite the impression of it. Only a man of affluence could have such an education, couldn't he?

Eoin slid the book to the end of the stack, then turned to face her. It was too dark to see; which one did he read?

"It seems you do have a choice, if you wish it. I believe with Ó Flannagáin gone, the danger has passed." Maeve set the tray on the bureau, keeping her place by the door. "And so, I have a proposition for you."

"A proposition?"

"I plan to promote Mr. O'Malley to the position of stablemaster. As lead groom, I should expect him to be sufficiently qualified to the duties. But with my brother gone, a greater need is to fill the vacancy of steward—to work alongside me in the management of daily operations on the estate. If you can satisfy my questions on the events of Christmas Eve, then I should like to offer the latter . . . to you."

He made a slight flinch, the upturn at the corners of his mouth fighting a ghost of a smile as he stood by the hearth. Perhaps the notion fed his arrogance a little? Maeve didn't mind. They were both in the stable that day and knew what had occurred.

"Seein' as ye tried to start a duel wit' the last stablemaster, am I to expect a loaded pistol if I step out o' line? I don' know how I feel about the ferocity in such workin' conditions."

She cleared her throat.

No cheek. And certainly no familiarity.

"Rest assured, there is no threat of violence. I'll pay a fair wage, and you may have the stablemaster's cottage on the estate, as O'Malley already has a tenancy at the closest farm. You can move into the cottage tonight if you'd like. There's firewood and it's been cleaned. There will be various duties of the estate grounds, some manual labor, and you'll oversee the stablemaster and grooms. All of this is, of course, if you are able to accept orders from a woman."

"An' that woman bein' you?"

"Well, not Mrs. Finnegan, you'll no doubt be relieved to hear." She tried not to smile when she added, "At least you may stop worrying your meals have been laced with arsenic."

"A relief, to be sure. But what ye mean to say is . . . yer askin' for my help."

"I'm simply offering you a position, Mr. O'Byrne. I haven't time to search the county over for someone qualified to step into my brother's boots—not when there is much to be done. Unless, of course, you have family or . . . someone waiting for you outside of County Wicklow and wish to speed your way from here."

He shrugged off the notion of a sweetheart, or anyone, waiting. "I've cousins in Belfast."

"Is that where you're from—Belfast?"

"An' a few other places. But I've none waitin' for me. Not now."

The confirmation he was without family lit a spark of sympathy within her, for it leveled them in an instant. Maeve knew the weight of loss, and the absence of family was a heavier burden than she'd once understood. She stood before him, feeling the twinges of compassion, but only able to offer what a master could on their estate: no frills or friendship. Just hard work and coin.

"Mrs. Finnegan tells me you're well enough to travel. You may accept this offer, or if you choose to quit this estate, it is fully within your right. But I caution you: I will personally monitor the castle ruins, and any attempt at free trading in my cove will be met with the swiftest of response. I may show mercy, sir, but only once. It will not be extended a second time, as I have now become an expert at loading a dueling pistol."

"I should be wise to remember that fact. Ye brought dinner to sway me?" He looked to the bureau, walked to her side, and lifted the silver plate cover. "Quite a bribe—Williams pears."

"That's right." Maeve's spirits brightened without time to stop them. "From my mother's Berkshire estate. She has them shipped in every year."

"But they're not grown here?"

"I don't believe we'd ever considered it, no." Maeve straightened her shoulders, crossed her arms over the plain smock of her mourning dress. "But that is of little consequence. Unless you satisfy my inquiry for the position as steward, you needn't worry about anything on this estate. We can part ways for good."

He paused, replacing the cover on the tray. "I pledged to answer yer questions, milady. Without reservation."

"Why did you come to this estate on Christmas Eve?" A pointed glare was the best Maeve could render, yet she was both anxious and hopeful at the same time. She needed to place her trust in someone. Could it be him?

"Very well. There was a meetin' of United Irishmen in Dublin that night, in the corner snug at a pub called Foley's. There was a plan to smuggle French arms into the cove nearest the point between the city an' County Wicklow. That happens to be yer castle ruins. I was to rendezvous wit' the local leader—yer former stablemaster—an' take receipt o' the arms from him, then transport to a group waitin' in the mountains."

"The purpose of which was to . . . ?"

He stared back, his gaze direct, and too close for her comfort.

"Mount a risin' against English aggression, milady."

"I see." Maeve eased back a shade as waves of angst hit her midsection. "And are you . . . one of these United Irishmen?"

"I am."

"But how can you be? Is this organization not outlawed by the king of England himself?"

"On account o' our fight to shed the brutal oppression left from the Penal Laws o' this country an' establish an independent Irish republic for every man an' woman upon this soil? Or to prevent any more innocent Catholic blood from bein' shed at the hands o' English soldiers an' Protestant enablers who look away as they torch churches wit' parishioners inside, burn farms to the ground, an' level villages on a whim? Then aye. We are such—until our dyin' breath, God help us."

It was Maeve's turn to flinch from words spoken.

Her father and brother had painted the United Irishmen as bloodthirsty rebels who'd attacked the estates of innocent Anglo landowners in their rage against the Crown's rule—not passionate revolutionaries fighting for the lives of innocents the likes of tenants on their estate and the families she'd come to care for in the village.

Her defenses began to fall with the weight of truth that tumbled out, and his position started to sound far less ill placed than her father's and brother's.

"What happened then, that you should end up here with a musket ball in your side?"

He attempted to close the space between them—a tentative movement that whispered of empathy.

"I was made privy to a plot to divert the English soldiers from French ships comin' ashore. The plan was the torchin' of Ashford Manor an' the murder o' all Anglo-Irish on these estate grounds, o' which yer stablemaster was set to employ wit' his own hands."

Eoin didn't deny Maeve the brutal truth as she thought he might. He simply stood before her, breathing with a slight rise and fall of the chest as he stared back, so open, she swore she could detect truth in his eyes.

"Leary . . . He couldn't have. He wouldn't."

"He could, milady. I assure ye. An' would have done without a second thought. I'd agreed only to see arms to shore—not to kill estate owners. As a result o' that meetin', I came to the stables straightaway an' met wit' yer groom, O'Malley. I sent him on to warn the house wit' the story o' a disturbance on the grounds, an' stayed behind to deal with Ó Flannagáin. It was he who set King free, knowin' he was by far the most valuable horse, an' when caught, I'd go to the gallows. He didn' expect I'd see King's ailment though an' catch him out because of it." Eoin brushed a hand against his ribs. "Wasn't quick enough to catch out the musket hidden on the tack room shelf though, even if I did get a blow in on him myself."

"And . . . what of the lantern at the castle ruins? I removed it."

"Aye. An' its absence sent a message to the ship to stay at sea an' instead port at the next cove down the coast—at Arklow."

"And did it?"

The shadow of a smile tendered the corners of his mouth. "I'm afraid I don' know that, milady. I've been shut up in this tower since then."

"You jest, but you risked your life to save ours?"

"I wouldn' say that. 'Twas bad luck. An' I didn' know ye." Then he whispered, "But I do now. A musket ball is a small price to pay in gratitude for what ye've done for me in return."

Never had someone treated Maeve as an equal in such a manner as to have been so blunt and honest in explanation. She'd lived a life detached of the reality that faced the common man, save for the tenant families she'd befriended on the estate in the last year. But now, as her moment of greatest decision collided with her greatest need, Maeve couldn't shed the gut instinct that she could trust Eoin O'Byrne.

True, his was a reckless conviction. But it was not a murderous one. And that, in contrast to everything else she knew, carried weight far above the rest.

Maeve nodded. Once. "If you wish to stay on, you will not question my orders?"

"Not a whit." Though his acceptance appeared less assured and more laden with surprise.

"And you would swear to no violence or drink while on this land?"

When Eoin looked poised to issue a vehement protest to the implication of drink—which he'd already denied—she quieted him with a raised hand. "I know you do not take it, but I still need it stated forthwith. No violence. No drink. And no rebellion attempts under my nose, or I shall turn you over to the soldiers myself."

He cleared his throat—louder than was necessary, she was certain, to make a point of contention known. "Agreed. No violence, no drink. An' I'll always be honest wit' ye."

"Right. Then we understand ourselves." Decision made, Maeve took a plate, muslin napkin, and sterling fork from the tray and turned, offering them to him. "Can you drive, Mr. O'Byrne?"

"Drive, milady?" He stepped in front of her, taking the wares in hand.

"Yes, a loaded baling wagon over rutty village roads. Do you think it should pain your injury? I've no wish to cause you further grievance from it."

"I believe I can drive, milady."

"Good."

She moved to leave and Eoin took a half step forward, searching her, a lightness in his eyes that told her he'd misunderstood, thinking she'd intended to stay and share the New Year's dinner with him. It seemed out of character for him to misjudge an action—or intent—yet he had in this instance.

The extension of a pear in peace offering was all Maeve could extend at present.

She reached for the unmarked one and held out the ripe burgundy. Eoin stepped forward and accepted it with his free hand, fingertips barely grazing hers.

"Tomorrow. Sunup. Be ready to go." Maeve nodded to take her leave but paused to retrieve the remaining pear from the tray. She held it close as she opened the door. "It's time you meet the village—or, rather, time that they meet you."

THIRTEEN

Present Day
Ashford Manor
County Wicklow, Ireland

Ashford Manor was a time capsule hidden in the Irish countryside.

Laine followed Ellie through the front doors into a world she'd only seen in a handful of Jane Austen films. A vast foyer with a lofty arched ceiling, windows that stretched up so high they brought views of the Irish Sea indoors, and furnishings with brocade fabrics and intricately carved wood—they drew her in at first meeting.

Cassie was already peeking around doors and in corners, high and low. She'd detached herself from Cormac and ran over to Laine's side when she walked in, grabbing her hand, holding tight. A woman in her fifties with a petite build, blonde pixie cut, and wary smile looked up when their shadows cut the sunlight streaming in through the front doors.

"So this is Ashford Manor," Cormac said, welcoming Laine and Ellie into the foyer. "An' Deborah Rooney—resident historian at the estate."

"Glorified housekeeper is more like it." Deborah waved him off. "But I can be tellin' a bit o' the history from what Miss Dolly relayed to me."

"Startin' wit' ye have no clue as to why she'd choose us, unfortunately," Cormac said. "Other than frequent visits to Foley's pub."

"Well, she was an odd duck, Miss Dolly. Didn' have much by way of acquaintances, but she took the role of estate caretaker as seriously as any who'd gone before. So the story from her, datin' back to the first major rebellion in 1798, there was a leader dubbed "The O'Byrne" who challenged the peerage an' took over this estate, as a fierce rebellion swept through the glen. An' again in the 1916 Rising, there were ties to a family member joinin' up wit' the ICA, but by then they'd dropped the 'O' an' were just the Byrnes—though the title followed. After that, the castle grounds lay quiet."

"What's the ICA?" Laine asked.

"Irish Citizen Army—an organization that once sought to see Ireland as the free republic it is today." Deborah walked their party from the foyer into a large hall with coffered ceilings and an impressive array of hunting rifles and game heads arranged on the walls. "Do watch yer step—this wing doesn' have electricity."

"Tell them why," Cormac piped in, a smile on his face that said he was intrigued by the answer.

"Well, Miss Dolly was somethin' of a purist—that's plain to see around here. She'd only upgraded the flat in back, wit' rooms for her to live in without affectin' the original state o' the manor. This is the huntin' hall—ye'll see gaslights still hangin' from the ceilin'. 'Tis said the Byrnes were avid outdoorsmen. I don't know all o' the tales, save for the red deer that once ran wild in the hills were abundant at the base o' the mountains." She pointed to a pair of game heads: immense deer antlers centered over the hearth. "These are the only native species we have to Ireland. Extinct here in County Wicklow, but they are still under protection out west, in Killarney National Park."

Ellie squeezed Laine's elbow from behind, her smile bright as she whispered, "Don't you think we need a game hall at our castle? It reminds you of the huntsman in *Snow White*, right?"

"Uh, no. If you don't inherit them, then where are you going to buy animal heads to decorate your walls? It's a little creepy, don't you think?" Laine bit her bottom lip to keep from laughing out loud.

If only Quinn had a real understanding of the trouble he was in. His wife was fully enthralled with the idea of building a fairy-tale castle, and he hadn't an ever-loving clue as to how deep he was in it. If Ellie thought their castle needed a hunting hall to be authentic, he'd be bidding on game heads at online auctions before he knew what hit him.

Their informal tour moved into the library—massive oriel windows gave sunlight free rein to pour in, showcasing rows of floor-to-ceiling bookshelves with weathered and worn spines facing out, and a vintage wrought-iron rolling ladder tucked in a corner . . . Laine's view shifted and it suddenly became her own version of a fairy tale.

And time to rebuke that former judgment of Ellie . . . I'll fall in love with this place if I'm not careful.

"'Tis the formal library, wit' the turret windows spannin' the front o' the manor. What's left of the stables are just there, down at the edge of the rise leadin' over the glen." Deborah opened a set of double doors wide. "An' the library connects through these doors at the end wit' windows overlookin' the ruins of Castle Chryn."

Walking Cassie through the library, Laine drew in a deep, steadying breath. Tucked away, silent and forgotten, was a stunning room—polished floors, a high coffered ceiling with a crystal chandelier refracting sunlight around the room, and the showcase of an immaculate rosewood Steinway that peered out a wall of floor-to-ceiling windows.

"This is the music room . . ."

Laine breathed out, her heart beating double-time.

"One o' them at least."

Cormac stepped up next to Deborah, a curious smile in place. "An' tell them about the pianos."

"'Tis an oddity here at Ashford. There are six pianos in the manor, that we know of. But no one's done a complete inventory, as Miss Dolly wouldn't allow anyone in—not even when historians came a-callin' from the National Museum of Ireland. Wit' a reclusive heiress lockin' doors on rooms teemin' o' history, who knows what's to be found?"

Ellie sent Laine an enticing glance and held up six fingers, as if to say, *"We need six pianos too, right?"*

After seeing concern melt down over Quinn's features, Laine took pity on him and shook her head to the idea.

"Cormac here hasn't seen all yet, but Miss Dolly left two pianos up on the first floor—one in a sittin' room, the other in a private chamber. An upright in what used to be a servants' hall on the lower level. One in the drawin' room, but 'tis in disrepair. Another in a smaller sittin' room here on the ground floor, an' of course the grand in this formal music room. She did tell a story of a seventh, but 'twas lost somewhere along the way an' there's no further record of it. Nevertheless, it appears these walls were once filled wit' music on all sides."

"Why so many of them?" Laine stepped in, drifting her fingertips over the Steinway's fallboard. "Was this the home of a composer or musician?"

Cormac met her by the piano, as if tour duties had shifted onto his shoulders. "We can find nothin' on it. I did some diggin' an' 'tis similar to a French château along the Somme—Château de Pont-Rémy. It was found wit' a number o' pianos inside the abandoned ruins, but no one quite knows why. An' it's gone now but there's a myth that persists about it, same as here."

"But any myth is kept quiet here. Miss Dolly wouldn' allow tours, mind, so 'tis a bit o' a mystery hangin' over us. Which is why the new owners—these Foley boys"—Deborah tipped her brow at Cormac—"have their work cut out for 'em."

"You said there's a drawing room. Can we see it?" Ellie asked, inching Deborah back toward the library. "We're restoring a château ourselves and I'd love to get some ideas . . ."

"Oh no—" Quinn mumbled, looking green in the face. "Not on yer life."

Ellie's face had flickered with excitement for the first time in a while. And for however laid back Quinn always appeared, he seemed to read that flicker in terms of multiplying euros and tracked after the ladies as they ventured back through the library.

Laine ran her fingertips over the Steinway's music rack—the fluid, rosewood carvings of pears and leaves intertwining along the top was a delicate pattern she'd never seen before. Cormac stood paces away, hands in his jeans pockets, looking as lost in the space as she was. Cassie hopped up on the piano bench, oblivious, happily making herself at home in someone else's elegant manor.

Watching the shadows disappear through the hunting hall, Laine looked to Cormac and whispered, "Do you think it's okay?"

"If she sits?" He leaned in, whispering back, "Aye, since we own it."

It felt good to laugh then.

"I guess I forgot. You do—or Jack does. And what does he think of all this? I mean, if he's set his mind on an auction, I'd say this piano is a pretty good place to start."

"He's never seen it."

"The piano?"

Cormac shrugged. "The estate." Matter-of-fact. As if Jack viewed a vintage manor and the things inside as nothing but old ghosts that didn't matter in a modern world.

"I can't believe someone can own a place like this and never even want to see it." Turning wide circles, Laine moved around where peacock-blue walls met with crisp white wainscoting and looked at trim that drifted to the ceiling coffers. The regal chandelier twinkled overhead, getting caught up in the rays of sunlight streaming through the windows. Chairs were pressed up against the walls. Paintings hung between leaded glass. The tiled hearth had a wide marble mantel. And not one speck of dust on anything.

"I can guess what yer thinkin'. 'Tis worth a lot. What's to see to know it can all be sold?"

"No, actually." Laine knelt before Cassie, showing she'd not forgotten the child was there, and dotted her finger to Cassie's nose. "I was thinking that I agree with you. You've got something special here, and it just might be important that you're trying to learn why Miss Dolly wanted you to have it. The owner of a manor kept up like this had to have been a remarkable lady."

"I don' know if I ever said two words to her, an' she came into the pub near every day."

"You can't feel bad about that now. She left this place to your family. That must mean she thought enough of you, even in what you did say."

With Cormac's back to the windows, the sun had cast a glow around him. Laine had felt his gaze settle on her, and she responded by looking away—fast. Before those Foley greens could persuade her into wondering things she shouldn't. Castle ruins were safer. Solid and certainly not handsome enough to tempt her out of a shell, so Laine shifted her focus to them.

She stepped forward and pressed her knee to the window seat, gazing out over the ridge. "And what about the castle? You plan to sell instead of trying to open it to the public? If it's money Jack wants, he could probably make a heap of it by giving a few tours to eager Americans. Who wouldn't pay to see this view?"

"It'd have to be more than that. Right now, Jack's view is that it's just a very big, very expensive pile o' stone an' weeds."

"Only on the outside," she shot back, smiling because . . . *the music room*.

"We'd have to prove somethin' significant that ties this manor to a worth of sellin' tickets or trampin' tourists through the halls. The cost o' upkeep alone sets my mind reelin'. It would take some doin', an' that's what Jack doesn't have interest in. The history o' the pub is all he cares 'bout or wants to know."

Laine sat, tucking a leg under her as Cassie climbed up to the window seat beside her. Wood creaked beneath the cushion as she crawled over and pressed her finger to the glass, tapping at a butterfly that had dropped onto a sprig of yellow blooms outside.

"Then maybe that's your 'in'—find a connection to the pub, and your father won't be able to say no."

"It was somethin' like that, yeah."

"And you thought if you brought Quinn home, Jack might listen to him when he won't listen to you?"

Cormac nodded, staring into the vast length of rooms and foyer stretching before them. "We get used to the ones always at our side. Jack hears my voice so often, he no longer knows what it sounds like when I have an opinion that differs. He might reconsider if the son who's stayed away came back an' made him see sense. I'm not cryin' over it, mind. I just want this. Somethin' tells me it's worth it. I suppose we choose our battles, an' sometimes ye just move on. Ye know what I mean?"

Of course she did. More than he knew.

His was a quiet way that drew her into comfort and ease when she hadn't expected to find it. It turned out those mannerisms were what now spoke loudest—especially how he was with her daughter. And it would have been fine if Cassie hadn't hopped up and ran off to look at something out the library window . . . But she did. And he locked gazes with Laine over the span of inches that the little girl had left void.

Taking it as an invitation, it seemed, he sat—though left space between them.

"Did Ellie tell ye they're going back to France?"

That came as a surprise. They had just walked down the lane together, having a best friend heart-to-heart, and Ellie hadn't said a thing about it. "No. I mean, we haven't been here that long. I thought they'd stay for a while."

"Quinn told me just before ye came in, that Ellie has a doctor's appointment they don' want to postpone."

"Well, I guess we all go back on Friday. They to France. Cass and I . . . back home."

"Actually, 'tis why I wanted ye to see the manor." He tipped his head to the Steinway, gleaming gold in the sun. "An' the piano. Because I need more help than Quinn can offer right now. I can't ask him, not wit' everythin' Ellie's goin' through."

"That makes sense. I think it's weighing on Quinn more than he's willing to say."

"I agree. An' while Mrs. Rooney knows a bit about the estate, 'tis still a fraction o' what's here. So we're left wit' a library full o' books that haven't been sorted in ages, endless rooms of furnishings I have no notion what to keep or lose, an' I haven't the foggiest idea what to do wit' six, maybe seven pianos . . ." He rested his elbows on his knees, easing into a sigh. "An' Ellie suggested ye might be interested."

"I don't understand—suggested me for what?"

"To help me go through everythin'. To stay on in Ireland, just a week or two. She said yer family owned an antique shop for years, an' that yer father still has an auction house in New York, for estates like these. Is that true?"

The room that was oversize before shrank down to minute size just then, and the space between them grew smaller. "Yes, but I wouldn't count on my father's help. He's . . . well, we're estranged. It's a mess really—too much to say now."

"Well, good thing yer talkin' to someone who understands a bit about it."

It was one thing to tool around Ireland with her best friend. But with her best friend's brother-in-law? A good-looking brother-in-law who hadn't the slightest notion how an Irish brogue flowed from his lips in melodic cadence.

No, sir. Not on a leprechaun's life was she staying in that kind of scenario.

"Cormac, it's not that it doesn't sound wonderful . . ."

"I'll pay ye, of course."

"No, it's not that. But you need an expert."

"An' what year would ye say that piano is again?" He crossed his arms over his chest like he was considering the argument, but only for the split second it took to beat it down. Laine swallowed hard under his scrutiny, pushing the answer away.

"I'm tryin' to catch ye out, Laine. I saw yer face when ye walked in here. Couple that wit' yer interest in the piano down at the pub, an' I'd say yer hidin' a talent or twenty."

"Well, there's Cassie. I don't think she'd want to stay in a strange place too long."

"Ye mean that little girl who's sittin' on the floor, thumbin' through a stack o' books?"

"What?" Laine looked up to find it true. Cassie had pulled a stack of weathered books from a library shelf and was already turning pages. Flipping and looking and fluttering Laine's heart by giggling at something that had tickled her.

Cormac laughed in return. "Must have found a Beatrix Potter volume to her likin'."

"I'm so sorry. She shouldn't be—"

Cormac held up a hand, his fingertips just grazing Laine's shoulder. Easing her away from the instinct to rush over and restack what could have been priceless heirlooms and, for the moment, to let her little girl be.

"'Tis alright. She's happy, isn't she? An' she's not hurtin' a thing."

He was right. Cass wasn't crying. She wasn't contorting her tiny features in fear after a nightmarish sleep. Not this time. Sunlight shone in through the library windows, creating a glow around the little girl. Her springy hair, lovely and full, framed the most beautiful thing Laine had only seen from Cassie on rare occasions since the adoption: a contented smile.

Laine sank to the bench and sat on the edge. "You're right. She does look happy. It's been . . ." A wave of heart-swell threatened to trip her up. "It's been a long time since she's looked like that."

Courtrooms. Broken relationships. Zero stability in the past and now a shaky future . . . They were the opposite of what Laine had wanted for her. Every little girl deserved a home. A family who loved her and safety that was assured.

She dotted a tear that tried to escape her bottom lashes. "I'm sorry."

"For what—lovin'?" Cormac stared at Laine, as if something in him understood. "Don't be ashamed of that. Looks like whatever yer doin', it's workin'."

It did strike a chord inside, that the estate could make them feel free somehow. It wasn't just Cassie's smile or an Irish manor, or even Cormac speaking truth she needed to hear. Maybe it was everything mashed up together. Maybe it was a persistent whisper inside telling Laine it was okay to walk a path she'd never intended. That there was something to be said for boldness in the face of the unknown.

Maybe she didn't need to have everything figured out to say yes to something new—bravery could be as simple as a yes when she was at her most afraid.

"If Ellie's coming back after the doctor's appointment, then okay. I guess we can stay a bit longer. But I warn you—I don't know a red deer from an elk, and I certainly can't play any of your six pianos. Finding out what all of this stuff is will be as much *craic* as I can help with."

"Noted," he said, a steady smile in his profile as he stood. "Miss Cass? Want to go see our castle now?"

She looked up, grinning, and almost stumbled over the stack of books in her speed to dart out the library doors. Laine rose too, biting her bottom lip over a laugh at the sounds of the little girl *clip-clopping* down the hall, heading toward the elegant foyer.

"Cormac?"

"Yeah?" He turned back to Laine.

"The piano? It's early 1870s. A Steinway centennial grand with custom woodwork. I knew it the second we walked in."

Cormac hesitated, then stuck out his hand. "Yer hired." He accepted her hand and shook on it. "I think you an' Cassie are just the girls for this job."

FOURTEEN

April 24, 1916
Sackville Street Lower
North City
Dublin, Ireland
1235 Hours

Uniformed ICA men carried mammoth reams of paper out the front doors of the *Irish Times* reserve printing offices. Issy squeezed the shutter on her first photo, capturing the bizarre events unfolding.

Click.

Taking the stylus from her inside jacket pocket, Issy opened the spring door in the back of her camera and jotted a date to the exposure as the men marched up Abbey Street. And just as Honor had said they would, they crossed Sackville Street and stormed through the front doors of the GPO.

Issy wound the film in the back of the Kodak, slid the mechanism back in place, then tucked it safely under her coat so she could follow in pursuit.

Honor had loaned her clothes her cousin had left behind when he'd gone off to war: sturdy wool trousers, a linen shirt, black suspenders, and a herringbone hat in coffee brown to cover her long hair. It was defying her parents. The promise, too, she'd made to

Rory to stay out of it—everything that said a titled lady shouldn't be running about in the middle of such mounting aggression. But the ICA and Irish Volunteers were taking strategic garrisons all across the city: Boland's Mill and the bakery at the Grand Canal Dock, points all along Sackville and Abbey Streets—including the *Irish Times*—Clerys department store and the Imperial Hotel across from Foley's pub.

Even the GPO.

It was rebellion, and that realization both stirred and terrified her to the core.

Dublin's streets were quiet, businesses closed due to the holiday. Few citizens still walked about, curious but not alarmed at unfolding events. Some even stopped to window-shop the displays in Clery & Co. They remarked on the unseasonably warm temperature, but the oddity of men carrying newsprint across the tram tracks and a young lady whisking by in gentlemen's clothes was simply passed by.

Issy crossed over to the front doors of the GPO—not surprisingly, she was met with hands raised and rifles gripped, meant to intimidate her into turning back.

"Away wit' ye," a uniformed Volunteer issued, matter-of-fact. "Watched ye come clear across from the pub. Go on. No citizens allowed."

Issy had kept her hair tucked up in the cap, her freckled nose and delicate features turned down under the brim, so he may well have thought her just a curious young chap who'd trotted over to investigate. Regardless, she wasn't about to be put off.

"I must speak with Pádraig Pearse."

"Ye must now? Yer English, too, with that talk, an' ye think we'll let ye in?" He guffawed, hugging his rifle as he leaned back against a column. "Might be a spy an' no account."

"A spy wouldn't bear a message from Michael Mallin." She

looked up, steely-glared enough she hoped to gain admittance. "Carried directly from St. Stephen's Green."

His face turned pallid. "How do ye know Mallin's at the Green?"

So Honor's information had some truth to it . . . Good.

"As I said, I've a message for Pearse. So you'd better let me deliver it."

He tipped his brow, looked to another—a more mature rebel with a gaze that lingered far out down Sackville Street, like he could envision soldiers marching toward them already.

"Iffen he's of a mind to get in, just let him go. Does no good to crowd out here."

The lobby was intact when Issy was led in, surprisingly so. One didn't know what to expect of a rebel coup, save that there may have been broken glass or hostages shivering in corners. But the tile floor was clear, the lobby wide and empty. Down a wood-and-glass-lined wall, offices appeared abandoned. Smoke curled from an ashtray on a desktop behind the counter as uniforms rushed by—more reams of paper coming in and men going back out. Everything appeared in a state of semiorder, even for rebels who were fast barricading windows and doors in preparation for what was to come.

The soldier led her in, stopping her at the front counter as he went behind to whisper to another uniform sitting at a desk.

Stand tall . . . head up . . . Look like you belong.

A woman with a twisted brunette chignon at her nape looked up from a typewriter behind the window marked *Postal Service*, eyeing the men with conjecture. She owned a pert nose and deeply expressive eyes, pinning a fierce glare on the uniforms whispering at the lobby counter.

The woman pulled a pencil from her hair and stood, crossing her arms over the chest of her prim ink blouse. "What's the trouble here?"

Such cheek—the uniform didn't flinch. "An' you are?"

"James Connolly's adjutant. 'Tis safe to say I'm ranked miles above ye, my boy," she countered with hands at the hips of her military-style skirt, with what looked like a Webley tucked in the leather belt at her waist. "An' ye'll leave this lady be."

"Lady?" He stared back, clearly inspecting Issy for the truth in it.

"'Tis right. A *lady*."

"Well, she's not to be in here, though she claims to have a message for Pearse."

The woman tipped her brow a tad. "An' how do ye know she doesn'? Ye know women wit' the *Cumann na mBan* will be runnin' messages for us. I've less than twenty-four hours to issue an edition o' the *Irish War News*—under Pearse's orders. Now who do ye suppose is goin' to help me do that, if ye pounce on all the couriers who bring me news?"

"She's a . . ." He did a double take, trying to work out how a female could possibly serve as a journalist—especially one in worn workmen's clothing.

"That's right, genius. Can't ye see the camera peekin' out o' her jacket? Only a journalist would risk arrest by carryin' that for any o' the English to see."

The woman addressed Issy directly, raising her voice across the lobby with a shout. "Show him yer camera."

Issy slipped her arm out of her jacket, then pulled the strap over her head and held it out so the Kodak was in full view.

"Now, I'd ask that ye see to yer own affairs. An' if ye need somethin' to do, there's always the rest o' the furniture to carry out to the street. The English won' bomb our property, but we need barricades against all windows—as thick as ye can, please—out in front. Use chairs, desks . . . whatever ye can find that'll stack. Save yer fightin' for the men behind the English guns."

There was no ill taken up, apparently. The rebel nodded. And the others went about their work, wedging paper reams in rows against the windows.

And Issy could finally exhale.

"I assume ye don' really have a message for Pearse." The woman stood as the rebels scattered, a glint of respect flashing in her eyes.

Issy shook her head as she walked around the phone box and came back behind the counter, unable to refuse an automatic smile.

"Yer name, soldier?"

"Issy Byrne."

"Well, Issy Byrne. Ye do realize if the English see ye wit' that camera, 'tis arrest on sight."

"I do." She raised her chin.

"Then any lady who steps out wearin' trousers an' keeps a Kodak protected like a prize at her side, that's hatchet for me." She smiled, thrusting her hand out to accept Issy's. "Winnie Carney. What brings ye here today? Other than this business we've got goin' on—which is why Pearse is presently engaged an' unable to receive yer fake message."

"I suppose the Kodak's my message. I'm a little short on film, but I'm here to work."

Winnie threaded the pencil into her chignon, back to business. She checked her watch. "Didn' expect to find a photographer willin'."

Issy inhaled deep. "I'm willing. I'll work under you, if you'd like."

"An' how do I know yer not sent in by the English to infiltrate our ranks?"

"Because I'm taking my life in my hands even by standing in this lobby."

"Well, Issy. If yer prepared to do that, then I'd say ye meet the minimum job requirements. But no need to work under. We can just go alongside." She tapped the face of her watch. "I'll send a chap up to Campbell's Camera Shop to get film. Will that do?"

"It will. I also have reason to believe my brother is here

somewhere in the ICA ranks within the city—Rory Byrne? I'd like to find him, just so he knows this is my post."

"An' I have reason to believe ye'll find yer brother in no means an' can tell him yerself. 'Tis time to go outside."

"Outside for what?"

Winnie tipped her head as a chorus of footsteps echoed through the lobby.

And there he was. Pearse. As if on cue.

The pioneer poet himself, the rebel leader and passionate orator . . . the man Sean had pointed out at the Abbey Theatre but months before was marching through the lobby, with Connolly and an assemblage of men gathered in force behind. He gripped a poster-size roll of paper in his fist, headed for the front doors.

"Let's go, Byrne," Winnie chimed, whisking off to the door. "Camera at the ready."

With members of the Irish Republican Brotherhood, military organizations of the Irish Volunteers and Irish Citizen Army, and a sparse crowd of curious onlookers present, Pádraig Pearse began to read a stirring proclamation—that Ireland was now *free*.

"Irishmen an' Irishwomen: In the name o' God an' o' the dead generations from which she receives her old tradition o' nationhood, Ireland, through us, summons her children to her flag, an' strikes for her freedom . . ."

Pearse's oration declared the rights of the people of Ireland to the ownership of her land. That religious and civil liberty would reign. And sectarianism would have no foothold in a provisional government. Instead, Irishmen and Irishwomen would henceforth be free. And equal. And Ireland would rely on God's strength first, and her own second, to govern that equality—for all souls working and living and dying on Ireland's shores.

"We declare the right o' the people o' Ireland to the ownership o' Ireland, an' to the unfettered control o' Irish destinies . . ."

Issy watched, moved to silence by Pearse's voice echoing strong over Sackville Street, and the sight of him nailing the Proclamation to a column as rebel flags were raised.

The wind flapped a tricolor and another in vibrant green with the words *Irish Republic* waving against a cloudy sky. And through the mist and gentle rain and Pearse's voice flowing free, Issy found and connected gazes with a familiar face—Rory. Standing tall with a group of rebels atop a flat-top wagon barricade in Sackville Street.

". . . The Irish Republic is entitled to, an' hereby claims, the allegiance o' every Irishman an' Irishwoman . . ."

Rory nodded to her and she understood. Maybe what she hadn't before.

This was their chance. One moment. One time . . . for freedom.

Issy looked up to find a shadow in the third-floor window over Jack Foley's pub. Could Honor see it all, and was she crying too? Just as the men standing shoulder to shoulder with Rory. Just as Winnie and the rest.

Just as she was.

In that moment, Issy couldn't make out the differences between Protestant and Catholic, nationalist and unionist, man and woman. Their numbers mattered not; they were Irish. They were free, and they were beautiful.

". . . In this supreme hour the Irish nation must, by its valour an' discipline an' by the readiness o' its children to sacrifice for the common good, prove itself worthy o' the august destiny to which it is called . . ."

Who could know what was to befall them in the days ahead? In that one furious, passion-filled moment that Ireland drew its first gasping breath, Issy squeezed the shutter.

Click.

Photo number two.

FIFTEEN

JANUARY 2, 1798
ASHFORD MANOR
COUNTY WICKLOW, IRELAND

A long ride into the village meant she'd need to warm up before they departed.

Maeve had woken and dressed in the dark. Downed a few sips of breakfast tea. And over her black riding habit she pulled a cloak of deep aubergine. The garment was the warmest she owned, so she'd have little choice in wearing it—appropriate color for mourning or not.

The sun had not fully cracked the horizon and the world was just beginning to wake, yet she'd found Éire saddled in her stall—meaning Eoin was already about. She hurried her horse out the stable doors and found him leaning against a stocked baling wagon, one leg crossed over the other, waiting for her to arrive.

"You're on time," she said. "I trust the cottage is comfortable?"

Eoin stood up straight when she came into sight, offering a light bow. "It is, milady. Thank ye."

"You received my instruction on what to stock in the wagon?"

She didn't wait but held her hat brim against the wind and looked over its bed, finding pears stacked high and crates tied down against the sides.

"I did. 'Tis the way stewards should mean to get on wit' their masters—by bein' early to task an' on the nose about their duties."

"One last order of business. My father would ne'er allow an O'Byrne to work as our steward. And as I cannot reveal the entire affair at present nor my reasons for your presence here, I believe we ought to alter your name. At least while you are working on this estate. What is your full given name?"

"'Tis Eoin Brádach, milady."

"There are many Byrnes in County Wicklow, and no one should question another, especially not if I present you as my brother's supplant for steward before he left for England. Would Brádach Byrne suit you?"

"I've no objection—especially not to a mistress who carries a dagger in her boot an' pistol in her pocket."

And don't forget it.

"Quite right," she said, finally agreeing to smile openly. "Mr. Byrne it is. Shall we go?"

Eoin climbed up in the wagon seat, awaiting her instruction. She goaded Éire into a trot, and he slapped the reins to stir the horses, beginning their trek down the lane.

Maeve gazed over the horizon as they passed the glen. Snow had drifted into piles, windswept in waves around the base of tree trunks and dusted over the outstretched arms of limbs. Castle Chryn stood out on the rise, a skeleton of walls jutting up from the ground—watching, as if waiting for ships to come in cove. Rock fencing created tension in the peaceful landscape, cutting sharp lines of stacked stones that hemmed them in on both sides, transforming the road into a tunnel of white.

"I'm assumin' the crates an' wheaten straw are holdin' pears ye mean to sell in town."

"Actually, we're giving them away, Mr. Byrne."

"Are we now?" Eoin's voice raised against the creak and crawl of the wagon wheels. "'Tis a prized lot to be givin' away to tenants. Most common folk don' see luxuries like imported pears often, if ever in their lives."

"Perhaps, but here they receive them every year."

The talk of luxuries went far deeper than a gift of fruit. Maeve knew that. Theirs were the long-standing divides between rich and poor, Protestant and Catholic, Anglo and Irish, even oppressed and free—for hundreds of years. They'd bled into the very earth beneath their boots, and it was tasked to her to either uphold or endeavor to change attitudes around them.

Humor showed up in his profile, prickling her insides. "You mock me?"

"On the contrary, milady. I meant no impertinence. 'Tis to say I understand the task ye have ahead o' ye to convince them to respect the third child—an' daughter—of a lord, as she seeks to take over the reins o' leadership on a grand estate. If that's what ye intend."

Maeve eased Éire to a stop and inhaled deep, unsure whether to reveal the protected parts of who and what she intended to become. But Eoin followed suit, slowing the wagon alongside. Remaining quiet. Waiting for her to speak, as seemed his way.

"My brother prefers our estate in England. He's never hidden that fact from me. With my father unable to step back into his role as master, it is left to me."

Eoin stared ahead, slapped the reins lightly, again urging the horses on. "Then . . . I mean to help ye. As I said I would."

"Alright." She directed her gaze toward the horizon. "Our story may be full of mirth and myth now, but traditions date all the way back to the thirteenth century. My father's title goes back to that time. And it is the traditions we carry that bind us to each other—despite our differences—and to the land. The first farm over the rise belongs to Mr. Brennan O'Malley, whom you know. He and his wife, Brigid, have two daughters: Eilís and little Madailéin. They raise sheep on the land that runs from the ridge along the sea cliffs to the glen below the castle. Just there." She pointed out over the span of fields passing to their right. "And all the way to the rock wall here in the east field."

He locked eyes with her. "Where ye found me that night."

"Yes. Where I found you."

Eoin was introspective but rash, a lowborn, as Cian would have so grossly labeled him. Yet he also gave the impression of a quite learned man. One who made her want to trust him in earnest, which was both astonishing . . . and dangerous.

Maeve broke connection with those eyes that so often betrayed what he was really thinking and kept Éire at a slow walk.

"At the start of every new year, the master and mistress of Castle Chryn travel the estate lands with their children. Cian, George, and I ride behind the wagon. We stop at each tenancy. Listen to their grievances and wish good cheer in the year ahead. And then in the village center, we greet the people and offer the symbol of peace and prosperity to each, until all of the pears are gone." It pained Maeve to think of it, but she added, "And the mistress always greets the village children, giving each a gift. So these are not common folk. Not to me. And I intend to learn every one of their names."

"'Tis a mite more than tradition."

"Some would say, yes. But it is the genuine and right thing to do. And I will be honored to celebrate with them through the feast of Epiphany."

"Aye. To celebrate *Nollaig na mBan*."

Eoin didn't seem the celebratory type. Maeve flitted a glance his way, meeting a smile that just tipped the edge of his profile.

"Don' look so surprised. O'Byrnes are known for our . . . spirit. Some things are constant about this fair country, even as far north as Belfast."

She returned a smile, hers unhidden. "Every 'Little Christmas'

Father would acquiesce to the tradition that women should rest while the men cook and tend house. And I can guess what you're thinking—the only women tending chores at Ashford Manor are servants, and they work day by day anyway. But perhaps I'd like to change that. Would that shock you?"

"Nay." He turned to scan the fields and tiny homes that dotted the horizon with smoke curling from chimneys. "I was thinkin' more that yer tenants would be wonderin' why a stranger is drivin' a wagon o' pears about the village, instead of his lordship on his lordship's land."

"They won't question a thing if I introduce you as our new steward."

"I'm sorry, but I canno' be agreein' to that, milady."

"But why?" She turned, challenging him with a pointed stare. "It's how it's done."

Eoin shook his head, looking at her as he eased the wagon to a stop in front of a stone-and-thatch cottage set behind the rock wall bordering the road.

"Because *I* am not master here. Either ye ride out front an' greet yer tenants as their mistress, or we ride side by side an' do it together. But I'll not ride in front or speak for ye. As that's how things are done where I come from—the leader leads an' doesn' find shame in doin' so."

They were abrasive but wise words, Maeve hastened to admit. And his suggestion was one that would accomplish what she'd set out to do. But if the O'Byrne endeavored to be brackish about his dictations, she'd show him the measure of the worker he'd pitted himself up against.

Maeve slipped down from the saddle, and her boots hit snow.

After the wind loosened and tossed waves of her hair from under her cape collar, she brushed them out of the way as best she could, turned toward the back, and lowered the wagon's gate. She tugged her skirt and climbed up, uncaring that a cultured lady wouldn't lift crates and deliver goods on her own—especially not in a wool cape with satin trim that seemed to attract every splinter of straw the wagon possessed.

Eoin hopped down and rushed to the gate behind her. "What are ye doin'?"

"Well, we're doing this together, are we not? Your words, sir." She lifted a crate—heavier than expected—and offered it down to his waiting arms. "Here."

"But ye have no gloves."

"It seems I've misplaced them after an episode in a field on Christmas Eve." She hopped down again. "But I hardly think that matters. If I mean to repair fences and herd sheep, who's to care if I have hands to match?"

"But yer flesh will be torn in no mind. Let me see to it, milady."

The cottage door opened and tenants emerged. Mr. O'Malley approached down a snow-laden path, his wife tucking loose wisps of hair into her pale-blue kerchief as she walked behind. The little girls haunted the doorway with curious eyes and hopeful smiles.

Maeve waved to them as she walked, Eoin a half step behind, crate steady in his arms.

"Milady." Brennan smiled, bowing to her. "We didn' expect ye this year. But we're honored by yer presence, to be sure."

"Well, how could we miss out on this opportunity, Mr. O'Malley?"

His wife approached, offering a curtsey so polite and perfect, it was as if she'd been schooled for presentation at the king's court.

"Milady, we are but cheered to see ye this morn."

"As we are to be here," Maeve answered.

Brigid bowed, smiling. Her heart so evident and open that it struck Maeve with a pang of remembrance of times they'd seen each other across the glen—almost as if they'd been friends, and would be, had they all lived in a very different world.

It was then that Mr. O'Malley noticed Eoin O'Byrne stalking behind Maeve, and without his wife's notice, his face fell white as the foam in the nearby cove.

"Uh . . . We'd have expected his lordship an' all, but most pleased to greet ye, milady," Brennan noted, then called over his shoulder to their daughters, "Come now, girls. Greet yer mistress." He received Eoin's crate of pears. "An' a new stablemaster, I assume?"

"As Mr. Ó Flannagáin has lately left our employ, this is Mr. Brádach Byrne—our new steward. And he should like to discuss the position of stablemaster with you. But I do believe you've already met? No doubt you two will have much to discuss in the near future."

"To be sure . . ." Brennan paused, nonplussed, it seemed, to find Eoin had confided their association to her. "Of course, milady."

"Good. I leave it to you gentlemen to discuss the best way to assure this estate remains secure from threat on all sides." Maeve checked Eoin out of the corner of her eye, judging his reaction.

As if reading her thoughts, he stepped forward, missing not a beat. He held out his hand to shake Brennan's at the bottom of the crate, then nodded to Brigid standing alongside.

Engaging in conversation of sheep and farming, Maeve inquired after their enterprise, telling Brennan the Ashfords were aware the rock wall below the castle was clearly in a state of disrepair, and they had plans to reinforce it at the earliest possible occasion when the weather broke. She stooped, eye level with the girls, exchanging pleasantries and bestowing a small gift before they left them to move on to the next tenancy.

The same occurred with regularity after that. Each house. Each tenant.

The names she worked to learn, and it seemed Eoin was interested to do the same. He greeted them with tact, handing crates into grateful arms. Engaging in talk of the estate, they worked together, using repetitive language that established Maeve as their leader. And it seemed each time they rode away, the tenants had forgotten she was a daughter of the estate owner and had spoken as if she was their ally all along.

When they reached the village, Eoin opened crates and Maeve filled market baskets with pears until the baling wagon was near empty. She listened to the villagers' cares with new ears after Eoin's stories of oppression against Catholics. And in that tiny breath of time as Maeve kneeled, handing a pear and a gift to each of the children who'd gathered, smoothing braids and patting cheeks, instinct told her to look up—that Eoin's gaze had settled upon her.

She rose to meet him at the back of the wagon.

They stood together . . . silently watching . . . smiling . . . as if something had triggered mutual pride in what they were doing.

"I should tell you that your convictions border on the revolutionary, Mr. Byrne."

"I should hope so, milady. As do yers, by the way."

He didn't look back, just continued watching the children play jacks with pebbles in the courtyard. Several little ones laughed and ran about, with a closed fist around the gift Maeve had given—a trinket that cost nothing, but something that meant near everything to her.

"What did ye give them?"

Maeve smiled, thinking of the polished and perfect stones she'd gathered from the cove of Castle Chryn.

"Not much—just a round stone from the beach."

"That's a kind of hope, isn't it? An' looks as though they'll treasure it." He tidied the straw and locked the wagon gate. "There's but one crate left. Where does it go then?"

"I'll show you." Maeve pushed back the doubts as they rode on to the crossroads.

It had been a rare and beautiful morning. One that in the

course of recent days had ushered in joy instead of sorrow. And she wanted more of that prosperity and peace. As they neared the rocky landscape at the edge of the estate and passed by the crossroads that bore his cottage, Maeve slowed Éire to a stop.

She looked down the road to Dublin, wind toying with a lock of hair against her cheek. "There."

Eoin didn't mask his furrowed brow—surprise taking hold, for the steward's cottage stood before them. "For me, milady?"

"Yes. For you." Maeve sat tall in the saddle, decision made. "I will no longer live in sorrow's shadow. Nor in suspicion either. Whoever you are, Mr. O'Byrne, you've shown bravery to defend us, and generosity to stay on doing so. I cannot forget that. I believe my mother would agree with me that we must move forward from past events. That peace can be forged for Ireland—and if God wills it, we begin here. On this estate. With its mistress."

"'Tis why ye gave the children a stone from yer land."

She nodded. "The children will grow with a reminder not to hate. Not Catholic or Protestant. Not Anglo or Irish. Not anyone. Whether Ireland fights for freedom or not, we can be free if we choose to be. It starts with one."

"Is that . . . ?" He paused, something weighing down his features. "Why you are in mourning, milady?"

"In a manner of speaking, yes. My mother has lately passed from illness. But I choose not to hate an O'Byrne for another reason—even when six months past, a man who owned a mark identical to yours filled my brother with musket shot and left him to die on the Dublin road."

SIXTEEN

PRESENT DAY
16 HIGH STREET
MERCHANTS QUAY
DUBLIN, IRELAND

The sign read SHORN in clean block script.

"This is where they said to meet." Cormac slipped his phone in his jacket pocket. "16 High Street."

A chic white shop front with black-and-white ticker-stripe awnings stood out from a merchants' strip just past the bustle of heart-of-Dublin street traffic. Laine held tight to Cassie as the three of them stood on the sidewalk, looking in the salon windows as passersby whisked past in the rain.

Quinn spotted them from a seat in the foyer and stopped drumming fingertips on his knee to wave them in.

"Come on, Cass. See? Ellie's in there."

They entered one of Dublin's trendiest corners, with reclaimed wood walls and a door leading to an adjoining espresso bar, pure white salon chairs, black-framed floor-length mirrors anchoring hairdressing stations, and mustard-yellow mini-chandeliers hanging from the ceiling at even points all the way to the back wall.

Ellie wrapped Laine and Cassie both in a hug. "Glad you made it." She smiled, then looked at Cormac. "And thanks for bringing them. I know you have a lot of work ahead of you at the estate."

“’Tis no trouble. Happy to do it.” Cormac nodded, offering a respectful smile. He slid his hands in his jeans pockets and eased back a step to stand just inside the front door.

“So, we have a plane to catch tomorrow, and you three have a castle to return to. But first.” Ellie tugged on one of Laine’s platinum waves that drifted over the collar of her rain jacket. “Scissors, remember? At the right time, they’re exactly what we need to keep moving forward.”

“I had a feeling,” Laine said, her heart sinking to hear the truth spoken. “Are you sure you want to do this right now?”

“Come on—it all has to go anyway. This way, I get to choose. And I’m not alone. That’s as good a reason as any to just get it done.” Ellie nodded to a stylist behind the counter.

Everything happened so fast, there would have been but seconds to back out if her friend had wanted to. The stylist led Ellie to a corner chair, swept an ivory cape over her shoulders, fixed it tight at the neck, and tousled Ellie’s silky ebony locks at her shoulders.

And then . . . switched clippers on.

Ellie breathed out a deep, shaky exhale as the humming trimmers were placed in her hand. “Ready.”

Even before they’d arrived, Laine had an idea of what was about to happen. But she guessed Ellie knowing it mentally and actually making the first cuts were completely different beasts to battle. The rough sound of metal tines churning—the damage they’d do and the change they’d bring—flipped a switch inside Laine she wasn’t prepared for.

Her friend held on, breaking apart in silence, hands gripping tight but nothing happening.

“Ye don’t have to, Ellie.” Quinn squeezed her shoulders from behind. “We can go. Right now if it’s what ye want.”

Watching someone she dearly loved seared with pain and loss and slogging through grief . . . Laine couldn’t stand it. And for reasons even she couldn't explain, the memory of her own brokenness drifted away and was replaced by something—or someone—else.

She searched the length of the trendy salon until her gaze found and rested on *him*. Cormac locked eyes with her, in far too open a manner for her to brush off. Triggered to decision, she reached down, taking Cassie by the hand, and walked her across the foyer. "Could you?" she whispered to Cormac. "Um . . . just for a minute?"

"Of course."

Laine transferred Cassie's hand to his with a quick kiss to her cheek and turned away. She drifted back the length of the salon, until she eased up behind her friend's chair. "Ellie?"

Ellie looked up in the mirror, piercing Laine's heart with reflected pain.

Emotion flooded. Laine started to say something to Ellie and stopped. Sniffed over tears, remembering their conversation on the road to the castle. "Do you want me to . . . ?" She cried softly, with hard, hitching breaths. "I'll do it if you want."

"Please." Ellie bit her bottom lip and, with closed eyes, shook her head. "I can't . . ."

Laine reached down, loosened Ellie's grip, and eased the clippers from her palm. She swept a hand over her friend's brow. Brushing back her bangs she cut, feeling the silk against her skin as locks of hair slid down the sides of the cape, drifting into piles on the floor. Ellie alternated between tears and chin-quivering smiles of solidarity through it.

Quinn eased in to kneel at her side, whispering, "I've got you . . ." He held her hand as Laine repeated clean sweeps from front to back, smoothing brow to nape.

It was beauty and agony together. Rising up. Fighting together in a stunning portrait no one ever wanted to see.

Love and loss and marriage—Laine watched as they melded together, maturing a couple who'd only just walked down an aisle.

Evan and Laine had walked in marriage ten years. *Ten years.* And never had the connection Ellie and Quinn did in the first few weeks of their life together.

A moment sped by and Laine flipped the switch so the clippers fell silent. Ellie stared back at her reflection. All of a sudden looking new. And exposed.

Shorn—like the sign.

Piles of who she'd been before cancer surrounded them on the floor. And the dam broke. Ellie crumpled in Quinn's arms. He cupped a palm to her bare neck, holding on, crying in unison as hair slid down his tee and over the front of his jeans.

Laine watched, not understanding their same kind of pain, but having tasted the bitterness of a different kind. She trusted Quinn to love her friend, needing no further proof of his devotion after the gut-wrenching moments she'd just witnessed. But before the walls closed in around her and panic won, she had to get out.

After backing up, step by step, Laine fled and burst through the front door, stopping on the sidewalk.

Deep breath . . . Inhale. Exhale.

As rain sprinkled down, Laine drank in a series of deep breaths, welcoming the cool, calming oxygen. She heard the door open and close. Cormac walked up to her side and stood there, Cassie in his arms.

"I'm sorry about that in there . . ." She paused, trying to catch her breath. "I . . ."

"'Tis alright. I said good-bye. An' yer both fine now that we're outside." He smiled at Cassie. "We'll see Auntie Ellie an' Uncle Quinn tomorrow, an' then they'll be back in a few days, yeah? An' all will be right as rain. Speakin' of it—I can get us a taxi. Dublin weather can be a messy affair now an' again."

"No. We're brave girls, right, Cass?" Laine reached out to take her daughter back. "We can walk in the rain."

"*Wight,*" Cassie said, and high-fived Cormac with a tiny hand.

They drifted a block down as silence hung heavy, Cassie flirting with sleep under a rain jacket hood, still snuggled in her arms. Cormac walked in step but seemed lost in his own thoughts. And Laine tried to process what had just happened—why she'd been so marked by witnessing another couple's pain.

"Did they tell you ahead of time?"

"I guessed it was a salon when I saw the address. I don' think it was intentional to keep it from us. Maybe they thought we wouldn' come if we knew what they were about. 'Tis a tough decision Ellie made back there." Cormac paused, looked at the bower of trees covering the sidewalk overhead. "An' you."

"If I didn't have the warning before we walked through the door, I'm not sure I could have kept it together to stay at all. I tried to stay back, but I thought if it were me . . . I couldn't have done it. And maybe another woman would understand that somehow? Not more than a husband, just in a different way."

He guided them around a line forming at a bus stop. "I think she did. 'Twas a similar reason I stayed back."

"Why is that?"

"Quinn. He'd have told ye he once stayed in the back of a room, so to speak, when our mother passed. I don' blame him for it. But when ye don' step up, ye can have regrets later. Ellie is his wife, his family now. An' if I had a family o' my own, I'd want the courtesy to be the one steppin' forward to be strong for 'em. I owed Quinn that much to let him work things out on his own this time."

Regret seemed something Cormac knew better than she'd thought.

Laine slowed up in front of a massive church with columns and a medieval façade that looked as though it belonged in a Greek tragedy. "What's this one?"

He stopped alongside her, gazing up to where the top of the

structure cut against low-hanging clouds. "St. Audoen's. Been here forever it seems. Built over twelfth-century ruins an' still has mass every day."

"Is there one in the afternoon?"

"I don' attend here but sign says 1:15 on Tuesdays."

"It's Thursday." Her heart sank a little. "Can we still go in?"

"Yeah. Dublin is always open to travelers. Not hard to find a welcome here—both in the pubs an' wit' the Almighty."

"I'd like to say a prayer for them." Laine swallowed hard. She didn't even know how, just that her heart was pinging in her chest, telling her to respond. "Would that be alright, if we stopped for a few minutes?"

"Let's go."

In the few moments Laine had watched Ellie and Quinn in the salon, she realized she hadn't understood love or sacrifice in the ten years she'd been married. All Laine knew was it felt right to step into an ancient place like St. Audoen's. To slip into a pew and lower herself against a kneeler, then look up to something so much bigger and mightier than they.

Worshippers dotted long rows of wooden pews—they, too, carrying burdens, praying out their own stories under the vault of a cathedral sky. Cassie wasn't used to church, but she stirred from sleepiness while under arches and sky-high coffered ceilings, leaning back in the pew between them and staring up in wonder at a white-and-soft-green rosette design over the altar.

Cormac closed his eyes at one point. Praying, maybe. Or just being reverential for where they were.

Laine waited until he opened his eyes again, whispering, "You've been here before?"

"Yeah. Beautiful each time though."

"And what brings you back?"

He turned to her with an openness that blighted any resolve she had against finding comfort in his presence.

"What brings me to a pew or back to God? Because there's a difference."

"I guess I'm asking whether God was in that salon—in everything Ellie and Quinn are going through. Or is He only here now with people looking up at an altar? I need to know if God sees us in the middle of our worst moments. Because for the life of me, I can't believe pain like I saw in that salon can exist, and God would not be a part of it."

"That's the answer people been tryin' to pin down long as this church has been here. If yer askin' for a theologian's view of it, I don' have an answer that'll satisfy. But if yer askin' a man who's flawed an' faithless at times, who doesn' know why a pew offers the peace it does but comes back anyway . . . then I'd have to say yes—we find God there."

"In which place?"

"All of 'em."

If that was true, was He in the nights Laine had cried herself to sleep in the last year? Or when Cassie was hurting, and frightened, and didn't understand why her own mother had given her up? When Evan packed a moving van? When the For Sale sign went out in the yard? When she had to clean out her desk at the Maple Ridge Care Center? Laine closed her eyes against the questions.

"It's my wedding anniversary," she blurted out.

When Cormac didn't respond, Laine opened her eyes to find him no longer looking at the effigy of Christ at the front but watching her. Waiting for whatever she wanted to tell him.

"I couldn't expect Ellie to remember, with everything else going on. Especially since she doesn't know about the divorce. But my husband left and I couldn't do a thing to stop him. I don't know why after I've had a year to accept this, but standing in that salon . . . watching them going through something so terrible . . . It made today hurt more than I thought it would."

Cormac leaned forward, elbows on his knees, as he shifted his gaze to Cassie, peaceful in sleep in an ages-old pew. He sighed. "I'm sorry, Laine."

"You don't have to say that."

"But maybe I do, so ye don't think ye were alone in that salon either," he whispered, turning his attention back to her. "Funny thing about Dublin—the rain *always* stops, just not in the moment we may want it to. So like God. His plan, His timin'."

They didn't say much after—maybe both lost in their own thoughts of regret and pain and anchoring through storms. They lit a candle and stepped back out onto High Street, walking in the direction of the River Liffey and Jack Foley's boisterous pub world.

The one thing Laine knew was that Cormac's honesty had struck a chord. Faith wasn't prepackaged. It was messy at times. And raw. And present, even as the rain continued to fall. As they walked and talked, Cassie skipped along between them, opening her mouth to catch raindrops on her tongue—how was it that her little girl was only four and had already grown far braver than she?

Laine wished she, too, could reach out and hold Cormac's hand.

SEVENTEEN

April 25, 1916
Sackville Street Lower
Dublin, Ireland
0700 Hours

Dublin had fallen deeper into darkness, even as morning dawned.

By the time the clock ticked over to seven, rebels owned all corners of the O'Connell Bridge and up Sackville Street to the barricaded doors of the GPO, shoring up strategic points as heavy rain fell over the north side.

Word trickled in overnight that English troops had arrived east on trains from County Kildare—an endless stream of soldiers from the Curragh Camp at steady twenty-minute intervals—pouring into the south side areas of Kingsbridge and Dame Street, soon engaging rebels in intense battles around City Hall. And then . . . looting. It had begun on both sides of the River Liffey and scourged in furious waves, with fires popping up to light the night sky.

Issy and the other women had gathered in a spacious office on the first floor, their lone window barricaded against the corner of Prince's Street. There they sorted intel and Winnie wrote dispatches for Connolly, alongside nurse Elizabeth O'Farrell and dispatch rider Julia Grenan—both members of *Cumann na mBan.*

Having convinced Issy that her camera was of no use at night, Winnie solicited her to work through until morning, helping them pore over accounts that flooded in.

Like clockwork, the deep shatter of glass, the sounds of shouting, and the pronounced echo of bullets ricocheting off buildings would jar them. It did then, jumping Issy out of a sleepy oblivion, causing her to blink until the GPO office came into focus and she remembered where she was.

"More looting—or is it troops advancing?" Issy looked to the window, though they couldn't see much past the reams of paper packed against the wall.

Winnie read over a sheet of paper sticking from the top of her typewriter, not looking up from the ink on the page.

"Ye'd think the first thing Dubliners would do is support the cause instead of pickin' up a brick to smash a store window. Doubtless we'll be the ones blamed—though most o' the bloody business has been citizens takin' advantage. But we can' worry about that now. There's an English boat trollin' the Liffey, bombin' points this way. 'Tis said the Dublin Bread Co. took a nasty hit. Had to send some o' our boys out there to keep the fires at bay in buildings leadin' up Sackville."

Honor.

Issy edged forward in her chair, ready to spring if necessary. "Any fires close?"

"No. We're safe thus far around the GPO an' Clerys, all the way down to Abbey Street." Winnie pulled the sheet of paper from the typewriter roll. "Look at this."

She slid the paper across the desk to Issy, then stepped to a back sideboard they were using as a makeshift kitchen counter and poured hot water through a strainer to a teacup.

Issy read, *"If the Germans Conquered England,"* and looked up. "What is it?"

"Front-page article to run in the *Irish War News* this morn. Pearse has given us a bit of leeway with editin', an' I've been wantin' that one front an' center since a clever bit of satire ran in a London paper weeks back. We're sendin' it across the street in minutes—the *Irish Times* building ought to be used for somethin' good, so we're printin' news from the inside."

"'*The writer draws a picture of England under German rule, almost every detail of which exactly fits the case of Ireland at the present day . . .*' You think people will read it?"

"They'd better. We don' have overwhelmin' public support an' we'll need it if this is to end well."

She lowered the paper back to the desk as Winnie slid a cup of tea over. Issy took a sip, hot and bitter, but so completely lovely was the warmth that she couldn't care what honey would have added.

It woke her in seconds. "Any word on City Hall?"

Winnie shook her head. "Fallen. Early this morn the men were cordoned off on the roof an' all captured. Seán Connolly was leadin' an' he's been shot dead—a great loss. We also know men stormed the gasworks at South Lotts Road. Tore apart the machinery an' sent the poor souls on the south side into utter darkness through the night."

"That means the streets along St. Stephen's Green would be dark then too."

"Perhaps, but the Green has its own misfortunes."

"Which are?"

"Heavy losses. Trams down. Streets barricaded an' machine guns hummin' through the alleys. The English can't even tell who's rebel an' who's not, so they're shootin' anyone who steps into their line of sight. An' not much better here, bein' dressed down with gunfire for the last hours. But Julia made it out on a dispatch ride to Boland's Mill. Elizabeth tried to get to the wounded down Sackville, but 'tis too risky. They've had to bring men in to her, inside through the back doors. Pearse even wrote to the church on Marlborough Street, askin' for a priest to come take confessions. A Father Flanagan arrived this morn an' is takin' letters out for the Volunteers' families."

"Because they think they're not coming back . . . ?"

Had Rory left one of those letters?

Should she?

Issy was drawn to the window by the call of fight and fury outside, staring through a line of glass still visible through reams of paper.

"I was there at St. Enda's School last month when Pearse said blood would need to be shed for Ireland to be free." The depth in Winnie's eyes darkened. "He's known from the beginnin'. They all have. Connolly, Clarke, MacDiarmada, an' Plunkett too. All leaders inside these walls knowin' the same thing yet still goin' through with it all."

Issy turned to the window, watching rain paint the glass in too many tears. "Knowing what?"

"'Tis a battle we can't win."

Though dawn had awakened them to morning, the skies were cloudy, and rain fought to wash the streets of lingering black smoke. All appeared quiet on Prince's Street, though Issy did see shadowy figures running back and forth in front of Clerys' windows. The displays were ravaged: broken glass, strips of fabric torn and hanging from the ceiling, and colorful department store whatnots strewn about the sidewalks.

The corner of Jack Foley's cut a distant silhouette through the haze of mist and fog—wooden pallets still secured shuttered windows, and no flames ate buildings at its sides or upper floors. Shut up and burrowed in was a good sign, if anything could be. She had to believe Honor and her aunt and uncle were holding steady.

"Bullets can still cut through paper, so I'd back up from the window, Byrne." Winnie set her cup and saucer by the typewriter, then rolled her chair back up to the desk. "Unless yer thinkin' of goin' out there, of course."

Issy was, and she wasn't.

It was why she'd worn trousers—for the ease of mobility. Yet she'd been hunched in a chair, sorting missives all night. She had a camera and lens ready, but it meant nothing if she let fear hold her to scouring accounts on the off chance the names O'Connell or Byrne would come in. Didn't she want to step out, to see and capture what was happening, instead of reading about it afterward? But how could she step out of the GPO . . . and leave Honor behind?

"Campbell's Camera Shop's been burned out, so no extra film there. But ye may wish to know that several units of our boys had to fill in ranks over the Liffey, to hold the bridge an' support down to the Green."

Rory would have gone with them. As his belief was coupled with rage . . . anything to take him closer to killing the English and he'd have been the first to volunteer. Somehow, Winnie had known to strike that chord.

"And my brother went with them."

She nodded.

"Connolly released his unit before dawn. An' if that's the case, yer askin' why yer still standin' here when ye'd like to be out there too."

Issy stared out the window, trying to convince herself the rapid cadence of gunfire and the errant booms of artillery fire were only bouts of spring thunder. Deciding. Wondering if she was so brave or would cower, like Rory had predicted.

"Writers are the caretakers o' history, Byrne. We document the livin' an' dyin' of the human cause. But our pen, however noble, however well-intended, will always bleed the color of our convictions. That's where ye come in." She eyed Issy's camera case on the desk and tapped it with the end of her pencil. "This lens never lies. It tells truth as it is. An' in a hundred years from now, as it will be. I'm the writer, but yer the real truth teller. *Go*. Tell our story."

It felt right, every word Winnie had said draining in a fury, from Issy's ears down to her heart.

"Here." Winnie took a piece of paper from a stack, folded it, and held it up. "I'll even make it official this time. We're usin' *Cumann na mBan* women as runners between the GPO an' garrisons to the south. I was told this should wait for Julia to return, but I think ye have enough grit to get this dispatch through. Ye know the streets below the river?"

"I could walk them blindfolded."

"Ye have to go at a run. But if ye can do it, we need this to get to Major Mallin at the Green quick as ye can. An' that'll take ye past the camera shops, mind, if they're still standin'. So ye can get yer film—just don' get a bullet too."

Decision made, Issy swept her jacket from the back of the chair, buttoned the missive in the chest pocket, and pulled it on. Rain and long hair made for a bad combination unless she could keep it tucked out of the way. She grabbed her hat stacked with her things on a cabinet in the corner.

"Keep talking." She tucked her hair as Winnie talked. "Anything else I need to know?"

"There's a Captain John Bowen-Colthurst sending English soldiers north from Richmond Barracks, stirrin' heavy fire in that whole area. Wit' a hospital in Portobello scheduled for openin' next month, doctors an' nurses were already transported there. Some may have joined the fight, as many came into Dublin from the Duke of Connaught's Auxiliary on Sunday. Even the clergy from the limbless unit came over to support. Word is there's losses en masse, but Mallin an' Countess Markievicz need reinforcements at the Green, an' this dispatch could bring help for the scores of wounded."

Issy froze. She turned, hair half tucked, hands falling at her sides, as her heart jammed in her chest.

"You said clergy—from the Duke of Connaught's Auxiliary hospital in Bray? They've gone to the area of the south side that's under assault?"

"That's right. To Portobello Church, across the canal from Richmond Barracks. One of the worst areas to be in as it's overrun by English troops. But 'tis the doctors an' nurses we need over at the Green—if they can even get there."

Issy's heart whispered one agonizing word: *Sean.*

All this time, she'd thought he was well out of it. Ministering in the safety of a military hospital in County Wicklow—as far from English guns as could be. But it seemed fate wished to tempt her, and she was forced to consider Sean might have fallen trap into a more savage war zone than they had even at the GPO.

"You're certain the clergy went too—to Portobello Church?"

"Yes, I'm certain." Winnie planted her hands on her hips. "So what's what about that?"

"Nothing," Issy said, though the missive in her pocket was burning like hellfire to get her legs moving. She swept up her camera, tugged it over her shoulder, and headed for the door. "I need to go. *Now.*"

Winnie pulled her back, issuing a squeeze to Issy's elbow.

She whirled around, breathless, scared out of her sawed-heel boots that Winnie would see her fear. That she'd demand an explanation as to why Issy had fallen rattled, and so quickly. She needed every ounce of courage to step from the front doors or lose her nerve completely.

"Love, is it?" Winnie asked.

Issy couldn't linger over why; time was bleeding. "Which way is best?"

"That dispatch is signed by Connolly himself—show it if ye

need to so the rebels will let ye through. Ye may have cover over O'Connell Bridge, but 'tis not assured. Don't dare go in the direction of Dublin Castle once yer over. It may have been thin with English during the Irish Grand National yesterday, but 'tis a different story today. We didn't even try to take Trinity College either—it's a stronghold. So yer best bet is side streets between the two, comin' around the Green at Fusilier's Arch, if ye can make it. But not as far as the south side by The Shelbourne. We had a dispatch that the English are rainin' machine gun fire down from the hotel's upper floors."

Machine gun fire . . .

Issy's heart nearly bottomed out of her chest.

"Now, Byrne—repeat it back to me."

"I'll have cover to O'Connell Bridge. Take the side streets between Dublin Castle and Trinity. Through the Arch. Find Mallin." She took a steadying breath. "And don't take a bullet."

Winnie pulled the revolver from her belt—the Webley that was always fused to her side, and offered it. "Need this?"

Issy shook her head. "No. If I'm running to save my life, I'll be lucky to shoot a photo along the way."

Winnie nodded, tucking it back in its home before whistling with pinkies in her teeth. She drew attention from a gaggle of Volunteers guarding the lobby doors at the end of the hall. "*Chaps!* Let this one pass. She's *Cumann na mBan* an' has a dispatch bound for Major Mallin. Give her cover to the bridge."

Issy eyed her before stepping out. "Since when am I *Cumann na mBan*?"

"Since now."

The last thought that swept through Issy's mind as she hurried from lobby through front doors was what a real member of *Cumann na mBan* would do: run straight to the Green as she was told, or follow her heart to Portobello.

April 25, 1916
20 Sackville Street Lower
Dublin, Ireland
0720 Hours

Taking a dispatch via horse may have been faster, but it would be heard for miles and that would make it far easier to get picked off by a sniper's bullet—especially in daylight.

If Issy could weave in between buildings, blazing sprints and then tucking back in alleys, she could make connection with rebel outposts from garrison to garrison until she reached the Green. Ideally, at least, that was how it was supposed to work. But in reality? The sight of black smoke curling into the sky and the terrifying *zing* and *clink* as bullets claimed the sides of buildings forced her feet to keep moving.

The first sprint was over the corner of Prince's Street and a daring dart across the wide-open space of Sackville Street.

"Better to cross here under cover than down near the bridge—may well be impassable now. Run over to Clerys. Inside, down the block, an' then run like the devil himself's at yer heels," one of the Volunteers had advised, and raised his rifle, waiting for her to flee over road and tram tracks.

Issy nodded to him.

Inhale . . . Exhale . . .

Go!

With the camera flopping under her coat, boots clipping the rain-dampened street, and eyes fixed on the corner of Clery & Co. department store, Issy raced the wide expanse from sidewalk to sidewalk. Jumping bricks strewn in the road. Hearing the shattering sound of rapid-cadenced gunfire echoing somewhere not far off.

Don't look . . . Issy darted past a man crumpled facedown in the street, at the base of the immense granite Nelson Pillar monument that split Sackville in two.

Just run . . .

On the corner she fled past shops of demolished walls and scattered brick, stopping only to kick out a shard of plate glass that cut up like a human-size knife in a Clerys' window display and jump inside.

Careful not to fall in the pile of Easter chapeaus that greeted her, knowing it could be teeming with razor-sharp splinters of glass, she righted herself. It would take an entire block of running through shattered glass and past demolished counters, soiled dresses, and splintered wood creating a minefield across the flooring, spanning the street front of the iconic store.

A countertop display of gentlemen's shaving goods had been upended, littering razors and brushes, manicure scissors and combs across the floor. She stooped and grabbed an ivory-embossed straight blade—any weapon now might be an advantage later. Issy slipped it in her trouser pocket and kept going.

She ran through the elegant wares strewn in her path, careful to go with the least sound, not knowing if rebels or looters—or worse, soldiers—owned the inside.

Though the storefront ended with barred, arched windows, Issy would have cover from the Volunteers at least another block or two down. She'd have to sprint out across the rest of the shopfronts to the corner of Abbey Street and blow a kiss to Jack Foley's as she sped by in the direction of the river.

Rousing her nerve, Issy reached for her camera.

She unsnapped the case, pulled the lens out, and adjusted with mere seconds on the clock.

Breathe . . .

Issy turned the lens, focusing on a scene of soiled curtains and gas chandeliers hanging off-kilter, out to the mountains of barrels and mismatched furniture barricading the center of Sackville Street. Men were hiding out behind, rifles raised on the top of a wood-carved sofa back, trained in the direction of the city's south side.

And easing her thumb over the shutter . . .

Click.

Photo three.

It was then that movement caught her eye—just a shade through the shadows.

Issy ducked, keeping low under the open window. She slid the mechanism of her Kodak back to its flattened posture without the slightest sound, then eased it back in the case under her jacket.

Nothing to do but tuck and run.

She drew in a deep breath and flew—her boots hitting the sidewalk. It was but a split second before she halted and backed up, slamming her back against Clerys' outer wall. A half block away on the corner, where she'd once watched a whiskey wagon fade in between the buildings, lay upturned barrels and a stack of crates with broken whiskey bottles crying a pool in the center of Abbey Street.

Behind them sat a girl, with cornflower-blue eyes and strawberry-blonde hair, cradling a dead man in her arms.

EIGHTEEN

March 4, 1798
Ashford Manor
County Wicklow, Ireland

Maeve had just put down her quill to close the estate ledger when the alarm bell clanged outside. She turned at once, the wooden desk chair creaking as she rose to the library windows.

Twilight had taken hold of the glen, the sky painted in sweeps of purple and gray. She pressed fingertips to leaded glass, scanning the fields, looking in the direction of their stables but finding nothing definitive. A chill tended the length of her spine as the bell clanged again—this time drawing her to gaze out on the horizon, where the ominous sight of black smoke infected the peace of an early spring sky.

Blasting from behind the desk, Maeve tore open the library door, lifting her skirt hem as she ran through the great hall.

"Fire!" she called, and rang the service bell through the foyer to summon the staff from down below. "Fire—everyone out!"

She threw open the front doors, leaving them wide as she ran down the manor steps. While the bell had indeed been rung from the Ashford Manor stables, the closer she came, Maeve could discern it was not a threat upon their estate buildings that had drawn alarm. To her horror, thick plumes billowed up in the sky past the distant wall of rock . . . fire and smoke and ash . . . roaring flames eating an entire side of the O'Malley cottage.

It may have been better to rush down the lane on horseback, but Maeve's heart carried her through the meadow on foot instead, her boots crunching rock and grasses with each running step. She fled to a gate—weathered wood with hinges rusted stuck and choked with hedge mustard growing through its tines. She kicked it with her heel, uncaring if the sheep would get out and pour into the road. They'd fetch them later. Nothing mattered in the moment but getting the O'Malley family to safety.

For weeks Maeve had taken to wearing a pieced-leather pierrot—it was far more serviceable than a muslin gown or full riding habit of brocade. All she could think of while running through the glen was that her arms would be covered at least in some measure, protected by the thicker garment if she needed to go in after the girls.

Perhaps there was hope—if she hurried.

Maeve reached the farm, finding only one she could see fighting the fire—a soot-smudged young lad, no more than fifteen, muscling bucketfuls of water to toss upon the flames. The sea wind fed the inferno, agitating so it licked up the front door threshold and ate the lintel overhead, making his efforts near moot.

"I'll take it," she cried out, running to his side, taking the bucket from the young man. "Get another!"

After she tossed it, the bucketful of water sizzled and died, evaporating against the flames.

"The children? Dear God—don't let them be inside!" she cried out as the roof became fully engulfed on one side.

A window blew out, shattering glass with a sputter of flame and smoke. Maeve ducked, yelping as the heat blistered them back by steps. She kept her forearms raised in front of her face, furiously looking inside the front windows, praying that none of the precious souls had been caught up inside.

"They be out, milady! Safe—all o' 'em," he shouted from behind. "Save fer Mr. O'Malley, I seen 'em!"

"Out? Where?" In a flurry Maeve scanned the glen . . . the rock wall and the ridge beyond. Even the path that led down to the beach. No O'Malley family. Just a rain-drizzled glen dotted with sheep and the toil of the sea beyond.

"They be there, milady!" He pointed her to the rise and the castle ruins standing guard atop it.

Beyond the arched Gothic window of the glen-facing wall, hidden up against the stone, stood Brigid O'Malley. The fall of night was dropping shadows too quickly to see if she'd escaped uninjured, but they appeared sound—she holding one daughter in her arms, and the other squeezed up against her side with face buried in her skirt.

They're alive . . .

"Right. They've gone up to the castle."

Breathe, Maeve told herself. Breathing would be good.

"And Mr. O'Malley?"

The lad shook his head.

"Don' know. Haven' seen hide nor hair of 'im. But workin' far off past the rise he was, wit' yer Mr. Byrne. He told me just this morn they'd be about repairin' the stone fence linin' the estate road."

"More water," Maeve called, snapping him to action again.

The cottage looked to be a total loss. If Mr. O'Malley had indeed been inside . . . She prayed not. It was all they could do to keep battling until the flames were put down.

The barn hadn't caught fire, but it could with the action of a single spark of ash carried on the wind. Ferrying buckets of water from the trough may not have been enough to save the cottage, but they could stave off further loss by wetting down the barn roof. It may stop a spread to the field, if it could even light afire, and God willing, a spark wouldn't reach far enough to claim Ashford Manor.

"Go see to the livestock—if there's any inside, drive them out!"

The smoke-tinged air burned with each breath, causing mad fits of coughing. Maeve tore the gauze kerchief at her bodice and hastily tied it over her mouth. Hoisting a full bucket at her side with a sure grip, she began climbing a ladder to the low, pitched roof over the corral.

Clouds of smoke took over the sky, lighting the air with embers as the cottage died.

Maeve dumped the bucket, one hand holding her grip sure upon the roof and the other fighting—and failing—to spread the flow of water in better than a single round spot. She attempted to climb down several steps, hurrying, watching her step to avoid tripping on her skirts, as the air became tinged in a deathly black.

The cottage roof fell in with a resounding crash.

It sputtered smoke and flames, devouring what remained as embers flew up into the air. Flames grew. Sparking through the twilight sky, floating from the cottage to the barn. A patch of straw lit on the ground . . . close . . . too close to the corral. She filled a bucket and splashed it down, tamping the fledgling flame under her boot, causing the fabric to fall from covering her chin and dangle around her neck like a flimsy necklace.

"Lady Maeve!"

Exhaustion fell at once with the call of her name.

She turned at the sound of the voice . . . gulping for air . . . wind from the sea tossing locks of auburn to splay across her face. The bucket suddenly felt weighted to more than she could lift, even without water, and Maeve fell, hands and knees flat in the field of mud.

Eoin bounded up over the rock wall at the road, then eased his arms around her waist, drawing her away from the burst of heat that blazed inside the cottage bones. "God in heaven! What do ye think yer doin'?"

She stumbled back, feet tangling in her skirt.

"The alarm bell sounded at the stables. And the children—I had to make sure . . ."

Wind carried smoke, blasting Maeve in the face and burning her lungs until she couldn't continue.

Brennan fled over the wall close behind, eyes wild—the sight of his home engulfed sending him into a frenzy that nearly had him run into the heart of the fire. Eoin halted him as he tried to sweep by them into the flames, grabbing hold of his shirt with a firm fist.

"No, Mr. O'Malley—look to the rise." Maeve coughed, drinking in breaths as Eoin returned, holding her up. She tipped her chin up toward the ridge. "Your family is there. See? They are . . . safe. Well and safe at the castle ruins."

Brennan ran past, sailing through the glen in a furor in the direction of his family.

With twilight taking over the sky, the fire cast a glow over Eoin's face, and the fear that had overtaken it. Raw and wholly unmasked, as if every emotion he laid claim to was shaken loose before her.

"Milady? Are ye hurt?" Eoin stared into her eyes, palms gripping her cheeks. "Look at me. Right here." He patted her cheek and brushed stringy, mud- and soot-mixed waves back from her face. "Are ye hurt at all?"

Maeve couldn't focus, no matter how she wanted to.

The haze . . . the smoke . . . the fear—they rendered her unable to carry on. Maybe even unable to stand, for she felt her limbs tingling and her sight riddled with a haze of blackness.

She fell victim to its trance and tumbled down.

Or was she lifted? Her forehead bumped against the underside of Eoin's chin as he pushed her up in a saddle and swung up behind her. He rode them through the gate and down the lane in the direction of the manor, leaving the last blazes of fire reducing the cottage to a sputtering pile of ash behind them.

Finally she was safe. And known in his arms.

"Ye need a doctor."

"You're late again," she whispered back, ignoring his worry. "Remember? In the stables on Christmas morning?"

"Aye, seems I'm always late wit' ye when yer fixed on killin' yerself under my watch. Could we set a schedule for these jaunts so I might arrive afore ye?"

"I don't need anyone to take care of me."

"Ye did say that. But seein' as yer too willful for yer own good, I'd suggest ye keep friends 'round ye at all times. I know I'd feel a sight better knowin' ye weren't temptin' fate by skirtin' around the grave on a daily basis."

Maeve swallowed, her throat raw, what felt like a trail of fire burning the length of her insides. She leaned her head back, fear fading out and falling away as she was locked in his arms.

"Is that what we are to be now . . . friends?"

Eoin wasn't one to give an easy smile, or even to reveal when he wanted to. Maeve had learned that in the weeks he'd been tending the estate. They'd worked alongside each other—he as tirelessly as she, without good humor most days. While he wasn't boorish, he had opted for quiet solitude in the crossroads cottage and disassociation with her, save for when they met for an estate duty. But in that rare moment it mattered not at all.

Without mask he relinquished the hold, smiling down on her with every bit of tenderness she hadn't known she so ardently desired.

"Aye. We're friends." He paused—his brow shifting from tender to furrowed, an intense gaze straying to the view in front of them.

"What is it?"

"Look," he whispered, lowering his chin until it brushed the side of her cheek. She rose up, her heart squeezing in her chest when she saw that flames had erupted at the end of the manor facing the castle.

"I didn't even know . . . It must have been on the other side when I ran down to the cottage."

"And that's why so few were there to fight the fire at O'Malley's farm. There was more than one blazin' at the same time."

Before them was a sight Maeve had never expected to see—her father had been broken of his despondency and had become master again.

Lord Chryn toiled alongside the others who'd gathered from the estate. His waistcoat hung open and linen shirtsleeves were soot smudged and blowing against the wind, but he battered flames with the rest. And at his side was Mrs. Finnegan, animated in slapping at sprigs of flames with what appeared a wetted bedsheet. Archibald had shed his butler's coat, and he, too, tamped out the fire with buckets of water brought up by the footman.

There had gathered not just the paid staff, but tenants—Brennan O'Malley, too, no matter that he'd just lost his own home—all fighting the throngs of a blaze together.

"We must help them." Maeve attempted to right herself out of his arms, then raised her hand to steady her brow, for it had sent her swimming.

"I'll see to that after I'm sure no harm has come to ye." Eoin took her instead up to the castle, easing her down from the saddle to the base of stones far enough from the blaze. Carefully, he checked her face and arms, then called Brigid over.

"No burns that I can see. But I'll send for the surgeon from the village straightaway. Keep her here until I return?"

"Of course, Mr. Byrne. We'll tend milady."

He knelt and whispered, "I have to go. But we must speak later." He brushed a wisp of hair from Maeve's brow. She barely felt it before his fingertips drifted away, and he was gone again.

Exhaustion claimed her, and Maeve slumped against the castle stones at her back. "What happened, Brigid?"

"I don't rightly know, milady." She stooped down, the girls huddled in close, all watching the flurry of activity at the stables. "One moment, we were takin' bread from the stove. The girls were about the washin'. An' without warnin', a rock sailed through the window an' a blaze of fire followed it through. We got out, but just."

Thinking not to scare the girls, Maeve lowered her voice, feeling the tinges of pain in her throat as she whispered. "But it doesn't make sense. I can venture a guess as to who might desire the manor burned to the ground. But why would anyone wish to harm you?"

Unless they seek to silence witnesses about arms arriving in the castle cove . . .

"I'm sure I don' know, milady."

"Well, you needn't worry. I shall speak to Mr. Byrne. You can stay at the manor until he is able to find another cottage on the estate. You'll be looked after—all of you."

In the midst of buckets being carried, and Eoin directing the men to wet down all sides of the manor, and a fidgety old housekeeper making the most of her defiant spirit against the fire, was the same lad running buckets to and fro from a line of villagers pulling water from the shores of the cove.

"Who is that young man?"

"'Tis a new groom. Mr. Byrne hired 'im from Dublin just today, an' glad he did. He might be a spot o' luck here on the estate," Brigid said, taking Madailéin up in her arms to rock her, as they watched the activity begin to slow and the last of the flames being stamped out into sizzling smoke. "He showed up nigh an' but seconds aft' the fire started up. Helped us out, he did. Had me believin' Providence sent him to save us from such a perishin'."

"He showed up as the fire started . . ." Maeve watched the young man. He owned a sure gait, strong arms, and wiry frame that moved as Eoin bid. He looked sturdy, but could he be trusted?

"What is his name?"

"His father owns a pub in the city. I believe he's called Foley, milady. Jack Foley."

March 12, 1798
Ashford Manor
County Wicklow, Ireland

While they still hadn't a witness for who'd set the fires, Eoin recounted the actions had been intentional. The knowledge put all on their guard—shifting Maeve's unofficial estate duties over to him until she could heal from the smoke in her lungs.

Finally up and about, Maeve held a missive in her hand, addressed to the master of Ashford Manor as a matter of urgency.

Fearing it may have contained ill news of Cian in England, Maeve had opened and read it first. While it was not ill tidings of her sibling, the relief was short-lived; the news proved jarring enough that her father might be the only person with whom she could discuss its contents.

It was shocking then to find that the one thing that had remained absent from the manor in the past year—laughter—now hailed unfettered from inside her father's library.

Peeking in, she found her father playing chess with a gentleman seated opposite, a deep indigo coat and shirt cuff the only thing she could rightly see. Tumblers of brandy were in supply, and a robust fire consumed logs in the hearth. Her father's glass lay with a trickle of spirits left in the bottom. The stranger's was as yet full.

"Maeve, dear. Do come in." Lightness was evident in her father's voice. "You do not need to hover at the door."

She'd thought to leave and return when it was assured he'd be alone but was caught out instead. Maeve parted the doors at the center, hiding the second page of the missive in the marigold folds of her gown.

"Come, Daughter. We've a dinner guest on this dreary eve."

The two men stood as she entered. Maeve recognized the crown of dark hair tied at the nape, the broad shoulders and build, as she'd worked alongside him too many hours not to recognize the association.

Eoin turned, bestowing a bow. Her father turned back to the chessboard, his focus drawn to the strategy of the game.

"Lady Maeve."

She swallowed hard, giving a customary but cool curtsey.

"Good evening, sir." What manner of business could have Eoin in attendance as a guest, playing chess with her father, instead of as a man in their employ?

"Mr. Byrne here has come each day since the fire to discuss business of the estate. And to see when you might be ready to resume your duties."

"Has he?"

"And, of course, he inquires after your health from the ghastly business. I've told him you're just up and about this day. A kindness, is it not, that he should act as steward for us? Perhaps we could entice him to remain in his post after Cian's return?"

"If Cian would agree to that, Father, we still do not know."

That Eoin overlooked the praise of her father was not lost. But neither was the tiny flinch of his brow, reading that he'd caught the air of doubt in her tone. "Are ye well, milady?"

"Quite. Thank you." She cleared her throat, expertly slipping a second folded bit of paper into the pocket hidden in the folds of her evening gown.

"Is it not fortunate, Daughter, that Mr. Byrne was in a position to look after our estate, just as Cian set sail and Ó Flannagáin left our employ?"

"Fortunate. Yes. I'd say so."

Maeve could see the story he'd told of Christmas Eve unravel as Eoin studied her. She raised the first missive, palm outstretched.

"I do not wish to disturb you, Father, but we've received a letter. I feared it was news of Cian, so I'm afraid I read it first. I would beg pardon for doing so."

"It is quite alright." He took the letter and read in haste, then handed it over to Eoin. "What make you of this?"

Eoin stepped forward, took the letter in hand, and scanned the penned words upon it. He looked up immediately after, locking gazes with Maeve. She lifted her chin in response but kept all else about her stance resolute, fully for the benefit of challenging him.

"We are hereby notified by Dublin Castle to be on our guard. As you've read, Mr. Byrne, a magistrate has arrested a man by the name of Oliver Bond—and some fourteen associates who, it appears, were planning violence against the Anglo-Irish in Dublin and surrounding counties. Suggestions are that we fortify our holdings and keep close watch for treasonous activities in our cove. As steward in proxy, what would you advise we do?"

"I would advise, milady, that we all have a care over such events—especially after the fires." Eoin returned the letter to her father. "My apologies, Lord Chryn. 'Tis not grave news, but I must see to duties on the estate without delay." He tipped his head in a bow and headed toward the door.

Maeve followed a step, the second page of the missive near burning a hole in her pocket as she watched him go. "And if we should suspect the fires on this estate are a result of violence aimed at Anglo-Irish—say, from the United Irishmen? Surely we cannot rule out that the responsible party could be upon this estate as we speak?"

Her father chortled. "United Irishmen? In County Wicklow? Honestly, Maeve."

Yet the veiled accusation halted Eoin's retreat, and he faced her with a far-less-humored countenance.

It had been days since Maeve had looked on Eoin—healing as she was from the inhalation of smoke that terrible night of the fire. Until the missive had arrived, she'd hastened to admit to herself . . . she'd missed the estate management.

Missed working alongside Eoin.

Missed . . . *him*.

The eyes that stared back at her were steely and determined, almost as if she'd wounded him.

"If ye have any suspicion at all, milady, then I would bid ye not to worry, for any man on this estate would surely give his life to see ye safe." He bowed again, quick and quiet, and with a respectful, "Good night, Lord Chryn," took his leave.

"An oddity to be sure," her father said from across the room. "I asked Mr. Byrne to begin accepting post from the mail coach as it happens by the crossroads cottage."

"And why would you do that?"

"He's the steward." He paused. "Why would he not? It is customary for an agent to accept correspondence of an official nature. And you gave him the cottage, did you not?"

"I did. Yes." Maeve swallowed hard, willing tears to stay inside where she could hide their secrets. "But he was here this eve, and therefore unable to receive the urgent summons that had to come to the manor instead."

Father was oblivious, of course.

He downed a gulp of his chess partner's untouched tumbler of brandy and settled into his chair by the fire, his laughter silenced and dinner in the hall evidently abandoned.

"Just as well," he mumbled, loosening his cravat as he surveyed the chessboard. "He'd have won anyway. That one is a shrewd player—sharper than he gives appearance to be, even for a Catholic."

"Oh, Papa. What manner of talk is that?"

He sat back, eyes registering surprise that she'd dared speak out in a misstep of her station. "I meant no disrespect. Why would you lecture me, Daughter? When I see fit to put the past behind and allow one to manage this estate? If it was Cian's arrangement, then we should not question it, should we? We might try to get along with their breed—if the missive received tonight is any indication."

"I lecture no one. But don't you see? The people on this estate . . . the families . . . your tenants—they are real people. Not a *breed*. Not creatures from a lost world. They are right here, in your midst. And just because one man took George from us—"

"Don't say his name!"

"But I must. Someone must, or he really is lost forever." Maeve wiped a tear that escaped, rolling unchecked over her cheek.

The day in the village came flooding back to her heart. In hues of the winter sky and the color of the tenant wives' dresses. In the sounds of the children's laughter in the square. In the way she'd so wanted to believe in something—in someone—again. And in the way Eoin had looked at her, over everyone else.

Had she not seen it, or only imagined tenderness upon his face the night of the fire?

To doubt him now broke her heart. And to see that the divide hadn't really been crossed and minds not really changed . . . that shattered the splintered pieces that remained.

"I remember the beloved master on this estate driving a wagon with his wife and children every New Year's Day. Listening to the tenants on his land. Working alongside them. Taking their concerns to heart. He saw them as human. As beautiful souls, and not as enemies because of a handful of opposing beliefs. Do you remember that man, Papa? Before George died and before Mama fell ill. Were you truly that man, or had you simply buried your prejudices under a veil of false concern? Who was battling a fire with men and women on this very estate just days ago, putting out the flames that might have consumed all we have? I do not recall you inquiring as to whether a Catholic or a Protestant handed you the next bucket!"

To stay in his presence would have heightened her insubordination, so Maeve mumbled, "Excuse me," and quit the library, slipping out to the adjoining music room that faced the cove.

What had cut Maeve's heart, and somehow she couldn't bring herself to say, was that a second missive had arrived with the first. Addressed only to her.

This one she'd hidden in her pocket when she looked into Eoin's eyes again.

It bore an article from the *The Freeman's Journal* dated 1796, reporting of a fleet of French ships that had failed in an invasion, with many to sink in stormy seas off the Irish coast. It was rumored that insurrectionist and United Irishmen leader Theobald Wolfe Tone had lost a cousin in the Hoche disaster—a high-ranking clan leader in his own right known simply as The O'Byrne—who had perished with the rest of his men when their ship went down at Bantry Bay, County Cork.

"I agree with you, Father," Maeve whispered to herself, watching out the window as Eoin jogged down to the stables. "Our steward is much sharper than he looks."

If it was true that one Eoin Brádach O'Byrne had been dead for nearly two years, who was the gentleman who'd stood in their library using the very same name . . . and who wished her to know it?

NINETEEN

PRESENT DAY
ASHFORD MANOR
COUNTY WICKLOW, IRELAND

"Laine?"

By the sound of it, Laine guessed Cormac was shedding rain gear in the foyer again. The road to the castle ruins had become a mud trap to both tires and shoes in the past few days.

"We're in here," she called, adding another book to one of the stacks she'd made on the ground-floor library desk.

They'd opened the shutters on the library windows, but with the late-afternoon hour and the gully washer of a storm outside, light was fading fast. They'd found several glass hurricanes and lit candles upon the desk, but that would only offer enough light for another hour at least. Cormac had offered to get them LED lanterns to help, but something felt wrong about dropping modern touches into Dolly's stunning old place. So they'd have to either move back to work in the flat where electricity would help out, or just call it a night.

"Sorry I'm late. 'Tis the music festival this week. Wall-to-wall tourists an' buskers giggin' all the way down O'Connell Street."

"Buskers?"

"Yeah. Street musicians. Addin' to the traffic nightmare, we were jammers in the pub all through midday. Took me forever to get out o' the city."

"It's okay. We've been making good use of our time."

He stooped. "Ye alright there, Cass?"

"I'm building a castle . . . like yours. See?" Cassie crawled through an imaginary arched entry into a play area, with a doll and a smart tablet and a pillow propped in the corner of the inlay hardwood.

"Right ye are, miss." He nodded along with her enthusiasm.

Laine smiled at Cormac, as though Cassie's building towers of blue-and-green spines was as official as Laine's marking nineteenth- from twentieth-century volumes. He stood and eased in next to her, took a book from the top of a stack of German poetry she'd been sorting.

"So, Ms. Expert. What've we got?"

"Well, to start . . . more than you'll be able to go through in a few days. This library is mostly economics, philosophy, poetry—that kind of thing. And a lot of it's in German and French. I remember some from college, but not enough to be dangerous. I looked up a few titles though, and there are a few really early volumes. We're talking late-eighteenth century. I put those in the crate by the door because I think you need an appraisal. I was half afraid to touch them for fear they'd fall apart in my hands."

"Any first edition James Joyce hidden in these shelves by chance? That'd convince Jack to go along wit' this scheme from the word go."

"You're joking, but you may not be too far off. There's an upstairs study too, connected to one of the larger bedrooms. Deborah and I didn't even have a chance to touch it today. But it's got twice the amount of books you've got in here."

"Right. Books. But no seventh piano?"

Laine shook her head.

Deborah had taken them through all the rooms, just to get a

layout of the ground floor, upper levels, and attic space. What they found was a massive question mark with rooms shuttered up and only sheet-covered blocks of unknown furniture or antique wares to greet them.

It was a picker's dream . . . but an estate owner's worst nightmare.

"To be honest, I think that's going to take some time. Every room is a mystery. And while I won't pretend it's not making my heart beat a little faster every time Deborah turns the lock on another door, I don't think this will be an easy task. You need appraisers for just about everything—the pianos to start, but all the books, furniture, paintings, and the property overall. If there is another piano in this house, it'll take some effort to dig it out."

"Well, fer the property, I've already seen to that. I've got an estate appraisal scheduled early in the new year. Just wanted to go through things on our end first—see what we've got, ye know? Do our homework before we open the doors to experts with calculators. Somethin' tells me it's what Miss Dolly would have wanted."

"Makes sense." Laine pulled another couple of treasures from their safe spot in the desk drawer. "And speaking of which, we found these today. In a shoe box tucked in the back of her closet."

Cormac took the photos in hand and turned over images of a young woman in wasp-waist dresses and Sunday hats—some with others in the photos, some just of her—and flipped them to see the dates on the back.

"I like this one. It's different from the rest." Looking over his shoulder, Laine pointed to her favorite. "October 1968."

A remarkably young Dolly in farm duds and a kerchief over her hair posed in front of a sixties-era truck loaded with crates of pears.

He held it up to the light. "Wow. She was a dish."

"Right?" Laine smiled. "But I didn't know people still used that term."

"Ah, it fits. Vintage photo. Reluctant heiress an' castle ruins. *Pretty* just doesn't go far enough as a word sometimes."

"I agree with you there."

Cormac dropped the photos back on the desk. "So the estate . . . She may look pretty as a picture, but Miss Dolly's books are an ugly mess. An' I don't mean the ones yer lookin' through here. As far as I can see, Jack's right about one thing—she left a few problems behind."

"But you take the good with the bad, right?"

Cormac nodded, eyes on her again. And staying there. "Right."

Laine smiled. And bit her bottom lip, though a flutter in her midsection forced her to look away from him.

There'd been a shift after the day of the salon and what she'd shared with Cormac at St. Audoen's Church. It broke down walls between them, and they were easing into a space they couldn't easily back out of. They were rolling up their sleeves, working side by side. Sharing take-out dinners from the pub. Carpet picnics by candlelight, their little group of three sitting on the floor in the music room, laughing and talking about childhoods and memories and princess castles by the Irish Sea.

It was nonsense, but then, it was everything too.

He'd been a perfect gentleman, of course—maybe too perfect because everything was business. But to have Cormac standing so close, easing into conversation again as if they'd known each other for years . . . with Cassie making a book tower on the floor . . . with candles burning and rain interrupting the silence by flowing down leaded-glass windows—it cast a spell of comfort she didn't want to end.

"What else?" Laine looked around, hoping to latch onto anything else but how it felt to stand under his gaze. "You've got some impressive pieces in the kitchen. There's a valet's pantry that was mostly empty, but some things could bring a price at auction. Thomas Furnival & Sons serveware. A Doulton Burslem pitcher and cups set—really beautiful, with a pomegranate design I've only seen once before. And then there's this." She left him, moving to the door.

Laine knelt by the crate holding the potentially valuable books, pointing to the faded stamp on the side. "If you liked the photo, this is even better. Deborah said there are stacks of empty crates in the old servants' hall on the lower level. See what it says?"

Cormac knelt beside her. "Ashford Pears?"

Feeling a tiny surge of victory, she nodded. "It seems Miss Dolly harvested the pears from the orchard along the road to the castle every year. Deborah did confirm that. And while we know that goes back at least as far as 1968, you're right—the books are a complete mess. I tried to make sense of the finances in the spreadsheets too. But one thing just doesn't make sense to me. If Dolly was as secretive about this manor as we've been led to believe, she still took meticulous care with its upkeep on the inside. That tells me the story of this place can't be lost—not if she was trying so hard to preserve it as it once was. I think the answer's hidden in these walls somewhere."

"'Tis an expert's opinion?"

"No. Just a granddaughter's opinion. My grandfather would have said every book has a story—you just have to open to the right page. In our case it could be the right door. Now, Dolly didn't allow many people into her life, so I think we should start with the ones she did."

"An' that would be . . . ?"

"I found a name for a buyer in Cork. She sold pears to a Mr. Thom Cullen. I already called. His Irish is a little thick, but I could make out that he'll be at the English Market in Cork City tomorrow if we want to go. Quinn and Ellie will be back in the morning, but I think they'd understand if we stepped out for a while to go talk to him."

Cormac tipped his head. "What yer sayin' is, we've got to go to Cork."

"If you want to. Yeah." She shrugged, though Laine's heart was grinning ear to ear.

Pushing back the terror of what it might be like to her little family of two to form a bond with this man and have it ripped away, Laine tried not to think about it. She wanted to live in the music room picnics a little longer.

And finding out who Miss Dolly was would keep them there.

"Then let's go to Cork."

Present Day
Princes Street Centre
Cork City, Ireland

"So this is it? The English Market."

Laine looked up at a three-story building, unassuming from the sidewalk but whimsical enough for an eighteenth-century covered market. It stood out with red brick, black-and-white-striped awnings on the front windows, and a grand entrance with the proud name *English Market* splashed on the front. She peeked in, seeing a large fountain, lofty ceilings, and vendor stalls that snaked their way behind the streets.

"This is what a day trip from Dublin will get ye." Cormac stood on the sidewalk, hands in jeans pockets, looking up with her. "One of Ireland's gems."

"You've been here before?"

"A time or two when I was young. Like I said—don' get much time away from Foley's."

"Looks like you've already changed that practice," she said with a smile. "A few days into estate research, and we're heading south on the back roads of Ireland?"

"Southish," he teased back. "An' I don' linger, Laine. If there's somethin' that needs done, I do it now. Catalogin' the estate is one thing. But yer the one who's agreed to help me learn about Dolly. This is really all yer fault we're here."

"And to think I thought we'd have better luck with the music shops in Dublin. Yet here we are—our first real lead."

"They might not have pianos, but at the English Market, ye can find just about anythin' else ye fancy. Come on." Cormac led her inside and they entered a world within a world.

Princes Street was not dissimilar from the high-end shopping district on Dublin's Grafton Street or St. Stephen's, but the old English Market still thrived in the heart of Cork City. Vendor stalls mixed both delicacies and everyday sundries alongside one another, and tourists mingled with the locals, filling baskets to the brim during their weekly shop.

They passed a bakery stall—a sweet shop, as Cormac called it—and Laine couldn't help but think Cassie would have been curious to explore every inch of it by filling her cheeks with colored macarons or apple tarts that looked like they were iced in liquid sugar. "Cass would have loved this."

"Ye sure we shouldn' have brought her?"

"No, it's okay. Ellie said she'd take over from Deborah because she wants to spend time with her when their plane gets in. And honestly, I don't think butcher cases and produce stalls can compete with an afternoon trip to the Dublin Zoo in a four-year-old's eyes. The macarons, maybe. But I can bring her some of those."

"An' we are here on official estate business. Even if they don' sell pianos, we might just get an answer or two. Deborah said to go to the back produce section an' find Cullen's stall. Been here for ages, so maybe there's a sign posted or we could ask someone if we get turned around."

"Cullen on a sign. Got it." Laine peeked in stalls as they moved together, scanning signs for the name.

An Italian grocer popped out on the corner, looking provincial and smelling heavenly, its olivewood bowls filled to the brim with kalamata olives, sun-dried tomatoes, fresh mozzarella, or honeyed figs. They passed glass cases with farm cheeses. Stalls with shelves of honeycomb in jars and loose-leaf tea. Boxes of shortbread biscuits. Baskets overflowing with fresh-baked bread. Wine. Cases with Cornish hens and bacon rashers . . .

It was loud and crowded and colorful, and Laine could barely hear herself think with the chatter, but nothing felt more alive. All she needed was a basket hooked in her elbow and they could have been locals too.

"Cormac!" She patted his sleeve and pointed down an aisle. "Cullen's. Over there."

He saw what she did—a sign spanning a wide stall, with mini Republic of Ireland flags strung across the front, turquoise shelves stocked with jams and jellies in the back, and a spread of Ireland's best produce mounded like a rainbow out front.

"Good eye." He smiled and brushed her hand to tug her with him.

A man of seventy at least—tall, in canvas overalls and a fisherman's sweater—was at work, bustling about to move crates of produce from the back, refilling empty spots out front.

Cormac rapped his knuckles on the wooden frame entry. "Excuse me?"

The man looked up with a smile lighting behind a thick gray mustache. "Aye. Can I help?"

"Yeah, actually. We're lookin' for a Mr. Thom Cullen. Are ye him?"

"Standin' here to offer ye the best produce in Ireland."

"Good. I'm Cormac Foley. This is Laine Forrester. We called yesterday?"

"Right. The folks from Ashford Manor. Yer a sight for sore eyes." Thom set a basket of cabbage down to lean into a high stack of crates. "We've been out o' yer Williams pears fer weeks."

"Yeah. I understand ye used to purchase produce from the estate at one time?"

"That's gas! At one time?" He laughed, like it should have been common knowledge how he sourced his stall. "Try every season for this family since 1967, lad. An' am I cheered to finally see ye. I don' know what to tell our regulars. They think I'm a chancer holdin' back the best o' Miss Dolly's pears for meself. An' the jars o' pear butter all sold out back in September. I know she's been ill, but until ye two came in, I hadn't hope we'd see any more stock from Ashford this season. Best Williams on the island, mind. Everyone wants 'em for Christmas. An' New Year's Day."

Laine connected glances with Cormac.

"I'm sorry to be the one to tell ye, Mr. Cullen, but Miss Dolly's passed on. In her sleep some months back."

His shoulders slumped and his mustached mouth hung open. "Ye don' say . . . I'm but sorry to hear. She was a craicin' lady."

Laine smiled. What a short and sweet testimony—with a bit of Irish slang threaded in.

"Well, my family's been left wit' the estate, an' we were hopin' as someone who knew her, ye might be able to share some information wit' us."

"What information now?"

"We don' know much about her family, an' we're tryin' to locate any she might have had, to share the news o' her passin'. Or if ye had anythin' else ye could tell us about yer dealings wit' her, we'd be grateful. She didn' leave much back for us to follow."

Thom bristled a shade, tossing his glance from Cormac to Laine and back again. "So . . . no Williams then. Is that it?"

"Right—I'm sorry, but no."

"I thought that's why ye were comin' down from Wicklow today, wit' a shipment."

"Well, there are pear trees on the estate, but we're lookin' at maybe havin' to sell the land. The orchard's all cleared out this season, an' I don' expect to keep up the harvest, so . . ."

Seconds ticked by on the clock. They waited. Thom nodded, staring down at them over the bridge of his nose, tossing his glare between Laine and Cormac like he was thinking something through. "Ye got a new buyer?"

"I'm sorry?"

He tipped an eyebrow at Cormac. "Or a better price? Is that what ye two be after?"

"What? No!"

Cormac's shock made Laine have to cough over a laugh. The innocence of finding anything out about a reclusive but craicing lady seemed to have morphed into distrust and a threat to the livelihood of a decades-old enterprise that Thom Cullen appeared all too ready to defend with his life.

"Because I pay a fair price—like me father an' his father before. Our suppliers an' growers are among the best in this fair country!"

"Look, Cullen—"

"Um, Thom, is it?" Laine stepped in to place a hand on Cormac's sleeve and squeezed, trying to ice his irritation. "What Mr. Foley is trying to say is, what if we agreed to Miss Dolly's usual price for the pears next year—plus five percent of the yield?"

"Five percent?" Thom nodded, his smile returning. "How's that now?"

"Yeah, Laine. How is that?" Cormac stood still, watching her with a gaze that begged to know how he could get an extra five percent out of the next year's yield, when he'd intended none at all.

"We just need some time for Mr. Foley to get his feet under him with the estate operations. And if he eventually has a new owner, we'll ensure they give you first pick at next year's crop. You send us details of the usual order and we'll ensure it's filled—pear butter and all—down to the last jar. All we need is a little information, and we'll be all too glad to continue working as your supplier. Any agreement you had with Miss Dolly is good enough for us."

Thom eyed Cormac. No craic between those two. They were men sizing each other up over produce, by rows of jams and jellies and frilly lid covers to boot.

"What do you say we talk this over while Mr. Foley goes to find me some honey?" Laine shot Cormac a *Please?* look as she stood by, tilting her head toward rows of golden jars.

"We have a nice Wexford Ivy in the raw o'er there, lad. Late autumn blend."

"Wonderful." Laine smiled. "Wexford Ivy it is. Cormac?"

It took a few minutes to iron out what she needed. The inflated price tag of eight euros and a miniature jar of honey later, and Cormac's reluctance to hand the grump any money at all, meant they were more than ready to go.

"Well, miss. Ye have a deal." Thom shook Laine's hand while giving a half-squint look to Cormac for good measure. "I don' know a lot about Miss Dolly. She kept to herself. But what I do know is she had the best pears this island has ever seen, an' she was hatchet at negotiatin'. Just like ye."

"I take that as a high compliment, Mr. Cullen." Laine smiled, half wondering what he'd said as she began tugging Cormac away from the stall. "We hope to see you then next season."

Halfway around the corner, Cormac stopped in his tracks, pulling Laine to the side of a long dairy case stacked with artisan goods. "I am not sellin' my pears to that man," Cormac blasted out.

"Are you kidding me?" She laughed—full and unabashed, standing right in front of him. "Cormac, you do realize you're not really selling pears unless you want to. Right?"

"Right." He backed down, shaving a little stiffness off his shoulders.

"And you probably never have to see him again, especially if you end up selling the estate to a new owner. Adding five percent was just a little insurance policy to see if he'd talk to us."

"He takes produce a bit too seriously fer my likin'."

"And Dublin pub owners who remove Americans from their snugs are any less serious about tradition?" Laine held up a business card, then handed it to him. "What I needed was this. Miss Dolly was in her nineties when she died. There's no way she could have carried all those crates to Cork alone. She had to have had help. I've already called all the music shops in Dublin and Wicklow. No one's ever heard of any pianos at an Ashford Manor estate. But the Steinway is in too good of condition to have gone without some kind of attention over the years, right? Wouldn't it stand to reason that if she'd sell to one produce vendor all of her life, Dolly would have the same kind of relationship with anyone actually visiting the manor—including to tune the pianos at least once a year?"

Cormac smiled. "An' if she came all this way to sell the pears . . ."

"Why wouldn't she stop in a trusted music shop while in the city? There are pears carved in the music rack of the Steinway, Cormac. It's a custom add. And I believe it's worth a shot to visit the longest-standing music shop in Cork City, which just happens to be a few blocks from here. A little reassurance with Mr. Cullen bought us the name."

His smile widened. "Well, I admit Cullen's right about one thing—ye are hatchet."

Irish slang. She needed a dictionary just to decode it. "And what does that mean?"

"Brilliant."

TWENTY

April 25, 1916
10/11 Sackville Street Lower
Dublin, Ireland
0800 Hours

Issy stared down the barrel of a rifle.

The one Honor had raised over a dead man's body—his head and shoulders buried in her lap—and pointed straight at her. Step by step, with hands raised, slow and steady Issy walked, praying a bullet wouldn't find her as she crossed Abbey Street.

"Honor . . ."

Her friend lowered the rifle a hair.

The brim of Issy's hat cast a shadow, but if she could present a familiar face coming forward, she only needed to be feet away and Honor would surely recognize her.

"It's me, Honor. It's Issy." She slowly removed her hat, hair tumbling down over her shoulders. She pushed it back from her face as rain fell around them.

"Issy?" Honor lowered the rifle and broke, sobbing over her uncle's body. Issy ran the rest of the way, then ducked down on her knees behind the stacks of crates with them.

So much blood. And whiskey. And rain pouring down to add more torment.

"Are you hurt?"

"No . . ." A cry and a barely recognizable voice collided as they tumbled from Honor's lips. "But . . . 'Tis Uncle Aonghus." Honor pressed her hand to a wound in his chest, though it looked as if it were no longer bleeding. Who knew how long she'd sat there, beloved uncle in her lap, with gunshot to the chest and she pinned down on a street corner as bullets whizzed by.

"Oh, Honor . . ."

"I was tryin' to get Uncle to come back in. But wit' the fires comin' closer to Abbey an' knowin' looters would hit Clerys on the next block, he thought he could defend our corner."

Forgetting that she'd never seen a dead body until that day, and in the span of about a minute had jumped over one and was agonizingly close to the bloody remains of a second, Issy reached over to ease Honor's palms from twisting in the front of his shirt. "He's gone. Do you understand me?"

Honor stared back, crying but numb at the same time, with black soot and tears making tracks down her face. Her skirt and belly were a tragic sight, all streaked crimson and wetted down with the pungent aroma of whiskey and rain.

"We have to get you out of here."

"No! He only came out to fend off the fires. An' hold back the looters. We hadn't used these crates yet . . . How could he know the bullets would come straight through?"

Issy picked up the rifle, slung it over her shoulder. And with hands gentle as could be, she swept trembling fingertips over Honor's. "Let go? Please . . . Honor." She drew bloodied palms away. "I will make sure he's brought inside. But first I need to get you and the baby to safety, alright?"

"I can' leave the pub—we have fires at Foley's. Ragin' in the back at Marlborough Street. If they hit the alcohol stores, we're through."

"For right now, I will get you over to the GPO. We can cross safely."

Honor tensed, hands tangling back at the collar of her uncle's shirt, signaling Issy to backtrack. Choose words that calmed—anything to get them out of the street.

"Listen to me. Where is your aunt?"

"In the back. She's beatin' the fires . . . wit' tablecloths."

"You both can shelter at the GPO. Right across the street, remember? I have friends over there. They'll see you safely inside and look after you until I return. And we will send Volunteers over to fight the fire. You will not lose Jack Foley's."

Honor came alive then, hands squeezing Issy's shoulders as if they both were about to fall off a cliff. "Where are ye goin'? Ye cannot leave!"

"I've something to do, but I'm going to fetch Rory for you," Issy vowed, will as ironclad as ever.

It had better be more than a sniper shot trying to take her down, for Issy felt nothing but grit rise in her middle as she stared into the depths of her friend's eyes. "Do you hear me? I will send Rory back to you. I promise."

The reply was a nod—a pitiful tip of the head that signaled exhaustion and shock were fast taking over Honor's limbs.

She couldn't run. Not as she was.

Issy looked around, seeing the edges of the barricade, knowing rifles were held up by men behind it. Surely the Volunteers were still watching. It had felt like a lifetime, but only seconds . . . mere moments could have ticked by. The Irish Volunteers around the GPO would have watched for her in order to provide cover fire down to the bridge. Or at the very least, they'd have watched for Issy to take a hit and her body to fall. Nevertheless, they'd have a keen eye when she popped back up.

She stood, calling out to the men in the street, waving them over.

Two of them ran, one in street clothes of shirt, coat, and hole-in-the-knee trousers, and the other in an ICA uniform like Rory had worn. Their feet swift, help was upon the corner of Abbey Street within seconds.

"Go, miss." The uniformed one's eyes bore a stalwart urge for her to hurry. "Ye have a dispatch, an' that's more important than the rest o' us. We'll see her safe."

Issy backed up a step as the men took charge. The street clothes chap shed his own coat, put it over Honor's shoulders. Had he seen her condition, Issy didn't know, but he helped her stand.

"What are ye doin?" the uniform spat at Issy, patience wearing thin as he supported Honor's elbow. "We have her. Now go!"

"Right." Issy nodded, breathless as she searched for the quickest words of explanation. "Of course. This man was the owner of Jack Foley's. His wife is battling the fires in back of the pub, on Marlborough Street. You'll have to bring her over too—notify Winnie. And here." Issy swung the rifle over her shoulder and offered it to the uniformed man, then began the hasty business of tucking her hair back up in her cap. "I can't take it where I'm going. It'll only mark me."

He took the rifle and whisked Honor away, supporting her at the elbows as they ran through the rain, and Issy was alone again.

Alone, with guns and foxes hiding in urban holes all along the street, Issy ran the block down to the Dublin Bread Co. on Eden Quay—the open-air street along the River Liffey. Barricades were set up there too: stretching in front of the O'Connell statue, a mismatched defense of wagons and barrels and toppled furniture, across Sackville to the five-story brick M. Kelly & Son fishing tackle manufacturers on the opposite side.

Though the rebels owned a stronghold on Sackville all the way to the GPO office, it was start-and-stop, heart in her throat as she listened to bullets *ping* and *whiz* all the way across O'Connell

Bridge. Issy hunched, sprinting until her lungs burned. Until the sound of gunfire became as common as the buzzing of a bee in summer.

Shocking though it was, few citizens were still about.

Broken shop windows were evidence of looting down Westmoreland through to Grafton Street, as if it were a free shopping day and the city was not under siege. Shut-up shop doors didn't matter; looters had gone through the windows. Knowles & Sons Florists in the heart of busy Grafton had suffered shattered windows, bricks lying about and flowers strewn with trampled petals, as if roses and violets had been laid to carpet the sidewalk.

Ignoring the height of unrest, Issy urged her feet to keep moving. To take one step after the other. To not look memorable or important in any way and pass by unscathed. It wasn't until she neared the end of Grafton Street and beheld the once-beautiful Victorian-era St. Stephen's Green park that her heart sank to her shoes.

Earth was mounded around the entrance at Fusilier's Arch. Trenches had been dug along the iron fencing, and torn-up grass and mud mixed with rain on the sidewalks. The unmistakable hammer of machine gun fire rocketed through the streets—Winnie's claim that the English had taken over The Shelborne on the park's south side had to be true. By the sound of it, they were firing bullets down on the rebels like raindrops from the clouds.

As she slowed up on the street corner, Issy's worst fears were confirmed: The rebels were in an active state of retreat.

Men and fighting women, with guns drawn—some muscling pallets of the wounded and dying, others carrying buckets and arms over the littered street—were, in heartbreaking fashion, fleeing the Green. Issy hovered in the doorway of a shopfront, watching, not even realizing where she was until she saw the last half of the lettering for the Brook Camera Studio on a busted plateglass window, the sorry remains of a shop she'd frequented.

Smoke continued to rise as rebels ran supplies across the street.

What did it matter if Issy was spotted with her camera out now? Arrest would have been a kindness over taking a sniper's bullet, and either could befall her.

The Kodak lay safe in its case, resting against the small of her back. She reached for it and unsnapped the latch, hands expert and fingertips ready to capture what the world might never see again. She attached the shutter and adjusted the lens—pulling, turning, finding the perfect angle of trench and park and rebels in the street . . .

Click.

A quick wind of the film meant photo four was captured.

"Issy Byrne!"

She'd just turned 'round to check for dry film boxes in the window display when a voice careened over the cadence of gunfire.

A body tackled her, shielding her from the noise and the bullet hits in brick and glass over their heads as they tumbled to the ground. Tiny splinters of glass cut into her knees through her trousers and the skin of her wrists as Issy went down, cradling the camera against damage.

Arms came around her, shoulders covering as more glass and chunks of brick rained down. Her breathing caught up in her throat as she looked up—his profile so familiar.

"I swear to the Almighty." Levi scanned over the top of her head to the road. "Either ye or that camera are goin' to be the death o' someone. An' I sure hope 'tis not goin' to be either one o' us. Are ye hurt?"

Issy checked herself over. She bled at the wrist from a cut that made her arm burn like fire but was otherwise rendered whole. Levi appeared so too, covered in mud and rain dirtying his shoulders down to the puttees of his ICA uniform, but no worse for wear. And alive, when bullets could have taken their heads off.

"I'm not hurt," she breathed out, dusting glass and brick from her front. She blew on the camera lens, clearing it of dust. "And blessed be, the camera isn't either."

"I don' care about that contraption right now. I'd almost wish it would meet its end iffen it would stop ye from this madness. What are ye doin' out here—besides tryin' to tempt St. Peter to escort ye through the holy gates?"

"I have an official dispatch," she blurted, breathless and relieved to see him at once. "For Major Mallin and the countess . . . From Connolly at the GPO."

Something twinkled in his eye. "Yer runnin' dispatch for the rebs?"

"It seems I am. I don't really do things in a halfway manner. That includes joining ranks in uprisings. But I have urgent news. Sackville's under siege. The English haven't broken the line yet, but fires are already tearing through around the GPO." She paused, drinking in precious breaths before continuing. "Honor's uncle . . . He's dead. And I need to find Rory to tell him. Is he here?"

"Aye. He's here." Levi nodded, lifting her to standing. "Can ye run?"

"Faster than you."

"Right then. Down to the Royal College of Surgeons building. I'll be on yer heels so keep runnin' no matter what."

Leading out into the fray, Issy held the Kodak still against her chest as they hurried the block down to the haven of the white, multistory, massive-columned building. She looked back—just once—to boxes of film strewn on the sidewalk. Like too many souls in Dublin, they'd been scattered . . . ruined . . . trampled over by bullets and rain.

Inside was no less chaotic.

Rebels muscled furniture up to block the windows, as more ran in through the front doors—muddied, carrying wounded comrades by an arm slung over their shoulder. It was blood and dirt and agony at first glance. Issy breathed in deep, willing her hands to refrain from shaking and giving away the effect such wanton violence had upon her.

Through the bustle of loading rifles and moving supplies and wounded in through the front doors, she spotted Michael Mallin—the leader Sean had dubbed as owning an impressive mustache that night at the Abbey Theatre. He was bent over a desk, unrolling what looked to be city maps, and pointing out orders to men gathered around. Countess Markievicz was there too. She'd donned an ICA jacket and trousers with military-issue puttees wrapped up both calves and a revolver tucked in her belt. The faint traces of bloodstains were smudged on her hands and face as she gave opinion on the map.

Issy reached for the button on the front of her jacket and was met with burning that radiated down her right arm when she tried to retrieve the dispatch.

A chair that had been lost and lonely, overturned in the hall, became her sanctuary. She righted it and fell upon the seat, with hands shaking and a haze of exhaustion compelling her to lay her head back against the wall as if it were the most inviting pillow.

"She's here," someone remarked.

Voices surrounded her. She felt a hand patting her face and cracked her eyelids, wishing they'd leave her alone.

"Issy?"

Rory was there, kneeling over her, tugging her jacket off.

"I have a dispatch . . ." She tried to remove the paper again, feeling a weight holding her arm down. "It's in the pocket."

"Oh no you don't." Rory ripped her shirtsleeve up to the shoulder. "We'll worry about all that later. You sit tight. I've got to get this bleeding stopped."

"Bleeding?"

"Levi? The dispatch for the major is in the front pocket," he yelled, tossing her jacket out of sight. "I need bandages—now! And get a nurse over here! This is my sister."

"Rory . . . There's fire at Foley's pub. Honor's there . . ." She swallowed hard, her mouth feeling chalky. Why was she so tired? "I told her I'd bring you back. To the GPO. She . . . needs you."

Someone tried to steal the camera from her hands and Issy fought against it, snapping the Kodak tight against her chest.

"It's all right, Issy," he whispered, a strange combination of pride and concern in his voice. "You did well today. We got the dispatch to the major. So let me take it from here? I need to see to this first."

"See to what? We have to go."

"Yer not goin' anywhere, Issy." Levi reappeared, kneeling at her side. "Ye've been shot."

TWENTY-ONE

April 28, 1798
Ashford Manor
County Wicklow, Ireland

Maeve watched the cove each day, always looking for the sign of French sails on the horizon.

The ruins of Castle Chryn had become her hidden watchtower over the estate, and she frequented the arched window that marked the place where she'd once found a lantern and put it out.

Gripping the outline of the arch, as if it still had roof and glass attached instead of wind that blew through unobstructed, she stood. Alone. With sea and sky that once painted a portrait of beauty, but somehow felt like they'd become a foe conspiring against the estate.

The crunch of a boot alerted Maeve to someone behind.

She spun, unsheathing the dagger at her belt. With breaths rocking in and out, she stared down at Eoin—the steward who her father had no knowledge was a traitor in their midst.

"'Tis only me." Eoin held his hands up. "Can ye put that down?"

"And if there are liars and thieves afoot?" She raised it higher just to spite him.

"Ye shouldn' be here, milady. 'Tis not safe."

"*I* shouldn't be here? And if I were not, who would prevent a ship from anchoring in our cove? Or are you here to alert insurrectionists of the opportune time to come ashore?"

"Insurrectionists, ye say?" He scanned the span of sea before them, seeing the same nothing she had each day for weeks. The salty sea air blew in, brushing his hair back, toying with the edges of his collar. "I don' see any at the moment."

"Perhaps I do—one, at the very least."

Slowly, Eoin took a step away from her until he'd leaned his back against a rock wall. He crossed his arms over his chest as if they had a business interaction to complete and he was quite content to wait it out.

It wasn't a stance of weakness; he'd never acquiesce to that. But it was enough of a retreat that she loosed her fingers from their white-knuckled grip—just a bit, in her palm where he couldn't see.

"Might I venture a guess as to the reason for yer hostility these last weeks? I'd wager I haven' received two words from ye."

When she refused an answer, he continued. "Someone wishes ye to mistrust me, milady."

"Shouldn't I?"

"An' yer reason?"

That unmatched nature of reckless and steady at the same time—he had fooled her with it once before. And further still, she was forced to admit to herself that same nature and a well-told story had managed to draw affection from her—a childish folly she did not wish to fall ensnared to again.

Maeve edged back toward an opening in the wall, should she need to flee. "Very well. Have you not sought to infiltrate our estate?"

The tiniest flinch crinkled his brow, indicating the arrow struck its target.

Good.

"I endeavored to save your life. You fool me with a well-crafted story, when all along you've lied about your intentions. And now that you've put out fires and played a few rounds of chess with my father, he's taken a liking to you—enough that you have a place of authority on this land. At least until ships arrive. And by then, it shall be too late. Ashford Manor will be caught in the crossfire of rebellion."

He offered no words for a moment, just a keenly placed gaze. "I never lied to ye. Remember? No violence, no drink, an' I'd always tell ye the truth."

"You never lied? Who is Eoin Brádach O'Byrne then, and why have you commandeered the use of his name?"

Eoin straightened, uncrossing his arms, countering her accusation with a stance more rigid before her.

"The night I encountered you in my father's library, two letters arrived by courier. You were unable to intercept these summons from your cottage along the Dublin road, as I believe you've been lately doing. I showed you one letter. In it, we received word that the arrest of United Irishmen leaders in Dublin may have thwarted a larger rebellion attempt that is still ongoing. And you promised to be forthwith about any plans, especially if it could impact the lives on this estate or in the village."

A flash of anger lit in him, the line of his jaw flexing as if it was only just restrained. "An' as a result, any men in Leinster Province thought to be associated—linked, in truth or not—were set upon wit' floggings, half hangings, an' the evils of a pitch-cap set aflame upon their heads. Ye think more houses cannot be burnt, more floggings an' executions won' be enacted at the hands of English soldiers? Because I assure ye they can, wit' or without my involvement in a rebellion."

"Perhaps it is why a second missive was addressed only to me. Someone wished to warn me about a cousin of a known insurrectionist leader in the United Irishmen—'The O'Byrne,' he was called—who died at sea, bearing a striking resemblance to your name and precise situation." She raised the dagger again. "Did you kill him?"

"Aye. I did," he whispered. "Because I am he."

"You . . ."

He heaved a sigh. "Wolfe Tone is a cousin, from Belfast."

"You said you had no family!"

"I said none were waitin'—there's a difference. Most all my kin thinks me dead."

"Splitting hairs," she shot back, shaking her head.

"I didn' lie. I answered everythin' ye asked of me. But if the English think me gone down at sea, then that was better for all to be believin'."

At his admission, Maeve's hands trembled enough that she fumbled the dagger.

It slipped and clanged against the rocks, falling out of sight.

She tried to follow it—even stooped, but it was flung down the ridge into a tangle of seagrass at the cliff's edge. Eoin took the opportunity to draw closer, still not touching her but edging up to where he could in a matter of inches had he wished to.

She attempted to retreat until the small of her back pressed up against the ruins. He knelt, picking through the grass, and flipped the dagger so the handle was offered to her.

Maeve lifted her chin, defying him with the courage of her convictions on the outside, even if her middle was fast turning to mush. She took it and could have held it up, but he appeared no threat, so she sheathed it in her belt. "Why have ships not come to shore with arms in the months since you arrived? They could have at any time."

"Because I sent word against it." His eyes confirmed it.

Of course. That was why he'd kept himself reclused at the steward's cottage—it proved the perfect scenario. He could watch for and send word to would-be rebels from the crossroads, and neither she nor her father ever would have known.

"Why should I believe you?"

"I told ye—I was against violence on any of the Anglo estates, an' I still am. But hatred runs deep an' can lie in wait for longer than that. A parish chapel was burnt an' a friar was killed wit' his congregation in Melancholy Lane more than a hundred years back. 'Tis not forgotten. Nor the chapels burnt to the ground in Monkton Row these recent years. Nor the Penal Laws that have kept Catholics chained since the Jacobite wars. 'Tis not about bein' barred from parliament or servin' in the king's army. 'Tis about people—like the children in the village—who've been bloodied an' bruised for generations. These people are patient in death, an' they do not forget."

Maeve began sliding back against the length of the castle wall, careful steps over fallen stones to get away . . . wishing it was not on her shoulders to have to think in that instant. What to do with George and her mother already dead, Cian gone, and now the realization that the lives left on the estate were all in jeopardy . . .

And she was again forced to trust a man despite serious doubts.

"But you talk of rebellion on this very land! Of outright war against England. In a province that is peaceful—even prosperous. And you say you wish no one else to die, but wouldn't war bring more death than you've already seen?"

Eoin darted to her then, hands easing over hers not in aggression but in entreaty. "I don' claim violence. I told ye. But I will bow if 'tis our best chance against English guns murderin' innocent Catholics an' keepin' all o' God's rights in birth to the hands o' the landed gentry . . .'Tis our chance against the people of Ireland bein' oppressed for one second longer than they must. Please understand I'd never let anyone hurt ye. Or any soul on this estate or in the village. 'Tis why I intervened at the stables that first night."

"But you still would have allowed our estate to be destroyed."

"Not one stone, I swear it. 'Tis why I stayed here with ye. Reports o' my death had already circulated, so the English wouldn' come lookin'. An' any kin I have believe their leader is already gone." His eyes searched hers, pleading, looking deep enough to see the hidden parts of her heart. "There are enough Byrnes in South Wicklow that no one would make the connection. Not to a common name as Brádach. Not unless someone already knew who I am an' wanted to get at me . . . through *you*."

Maeve willed herself to disbelieve him, to disassociate from the recklessness that followed his every step, though her heart was lurching. "You must leave this estate at once. If you promise never to return, I shall not relay this blackness you've planned."

"I couldn' leave after that first night. Not now either."

"But you must. If the English find The O'Byrne here, they will not be so accommodating as I in letting you go."

"I said I remembered two things about that night." He reached for her, swept an arm around the small of her back, and lowered his forehead until it grazed hers—so close, his whispers could warm the skin of her neck. "An' the other one was ye, in that field. A fire-haired vision blindin' me in the middle o' a godforsaken storm. When I should've died, instead ye were there fightin' for me. I can' forget that no matter how I try."

"Eoin, I . . ." She shook her head.

"Tell me I'm wrong, that ye wish me to stay. That night o' the fire, when I thought ye were hurt—" Eoin clamped his eyes shut for seconds as if battling thoughts, for the first time showing a fierce anger that darkened his brow on her behalf. "Why, Maeve? If ye believed all this about me . . . why didn' ye turn me in when the letter arrived?"

"I couldn't."

They were but whispered words—the only defining measure of bravery she had left.

"Why?"

Desperate, she averted her gaze. "Because if I'd turned you in, they'd have taken you. And I wished you never to leave."

A kiss at castle ruins that should have had her fleeing, instead had Maeve crashing headlong into the moment with him. Eoin pressed his lips to hers, and she met him. Threading her fingertips at his nape. As far as the cliffs were to the rocks below, she fell into his embrace as if it were the last moment they might have.

Ardent in surrender. Complete. Happy. *Lost.*

The sound of a flintlock pistol cock echoed loud, startling Maeve out of Eoin's arms. Her lips still a whisper from his, she focused her gaze behind Eoin to the hollow between the crumbling stone walls.

Cian stood on the path between castle and manor, a dueling pistol raised high. "Unhand my sister, you thieving, murderous rogue."

"Cian!" Maeve blasted around, pressing her body as a shield against Eoin's chest. "No—I let him!"

Cian stared down his hawk nose as he took an angry step forward, the rise and fall of his chest beneath a gray frock coat showcasing his rage.

"I let him," she repeated, breathless.

Eoin responded, though with actions far more measured than Cian's twitchy confrontation. He raised a hand waist-high and stepped out so Maeve was positioned behind the whole of his shoulder and his body would take the brunt of any shot aimed in their direction. "Yer quarrel is not with her, sir."

"Then the vile rumors I've been fed have no foundation? Present circumstances would suggest otherwise."

Maeve looked over Eoin's shoulder as Cian held fast to the flintlock. He hadn't even removed his traveling coat or hat. He must have been alerted to the unrest on the estate from the second he'd arrived in England—or worse, had sped his way there in learning that arms and ships were expected in their cove any day. Perhaps he sought to kill The O'Byrne and end a rebellion before it could begin.

"An' what rumors might these be?"

Cian looked over Eoin's shoulder, addressing her directly. "Is it true, Sister, the depravity that has managed to pervade this house since I took my leave? You stayed in this man's chamber—in our manor—the whole of a night?"

The complete turn of events rendered her speechless.

"Oh . . ." Maeve hadn't any preparation for such a thought. A night of complete innocence that someone had twisted to filth? Who would do such a thing? "Cian, I don't know who . . . but it's not what you think."

He turned to Eoin. "What say you, Mr. Byrne? Is it true?"

"Aye. 'Tis true." He stated the fact without shame, it seemed, or hesitation.

Her brother nodded, resolute. "And for that, there's a pistol waiting for you in the glen."

"Cian—I will not allow you to stage a duel with our steward without proper explanation. There was a disturbance on the estate the night you left. He was shot and we took him in. We saved his life. Ask Mrs. Finnegan if you do not believe me!"

"It is by Mrs. Finnegan's confirmation that I came to seek out this vagrant and defend your honor. It is the twitter of all the servants under our roof. And in the village, I'm sure. Which marks it astounding that you are not yet privy to it."

Maeve swallowed hard. "I have heard nothing of this. And Mrs. Finnegan would not pass such vicious tales. She was witness that night, there almost the entire time."

"But not . . . all night, I gather."

"He was unconscious—waking enough to hear what we said, but only just. There wasn't time for a doctor . . . We stitched him up and staved off the fever sickness after," Maeve pleaded, words tumbling from her mouth without restraint. "There is an explanation for all . . . if you would just listen before turning rash. I will not allow another of my brothers to die such a cruel and untimely death! Our father would surely not survive it. Nor will I allow two men that I love to kill each other while I stand by and watch. If you do not believe me, then by all accounts you must listen to him."

She turned to issue a scathing glare to Eoin, who for some reason had lost all measure of composure just then, his eyes widening. No doubt he was as embarrassed as she by the accusations of what had transpired that first night.

"Eoin—tell him!"

"Eoin, is it?" Cian countered, pistol holding fast.

"I meant Mr. Byrne." She drew her fingertips up to her brow before turning to address Eoin directly, praying it was not too late to avert a crisis. "I swear by all that is holy, if you do not set this matter straight immediately, I shall take that pistol and shoot you myself. Now tell him. It was innocent, and you mean to do right by this false accusation by declaring it so."

Tipping a brow, Cian turned to Eoin. "Well?"

"Aye. She speaks the truth. I'll do right by it."

Maeve exhaled—a breath she hadn't realized was stifled in her lungs. She pressed a hand to the flutter in her midsection, finally able to breathe again.

"And how is that, sir?"

Eoin nodded, decision apparently made. "I mean to marry her."

TWENTY-TWO

PRESENT DAY
WANDESFORD QUAY
CORK CITY, IRELAND

Freeny's Violin Shop was nestled in a corner spot beside The Time Traveller's Bookshop and a walking bridge that spanned the River Lee.

They stepped in through a door of weathered wood and pebbled glass. Cormac spotted the counter and went to the young man behind it, while Laine drifted over to rows of shelves.

So much of Ireland was steeped in history—castles and manors, and cities built upon centuries-old foundations. This was a tiny shop of books and musty shelves that told so many of those stories, of antiques and nostalgia more than modern music. It reminded Laine of happy times so long ago, when she'd stood behind a nineteenth-century shop counter to greet curious antique hunters who'd wandered in from the street off the old town square.

Now she and Cormac were the wanderers.

Drifting past rows, Laine thumbed through boxes of vintage vinyl—album covers of Irish rocker bands with names like Horslips and Thin Lizzy. She found books, shelf after shelf of music, secondhand novels, and biographies with jackets curled and cracked at the spine. Acoustic guitars lined the brick of a back wall. The polished cognac wood of violins gleamed from inside a glass case. Racks held sheet music, and an entire case was dedicated to wires and gadgets for modern acoustics, though she hadn't the faintest idea how to tell what was what.

"Laine?"

She turned at the sound of Cormac's voice. He peeked down a row of books and headed her way when he spotted her.

"Young lad's gettin' the owner. Seems he lives in the flat just upstairs." He wrinkled his brow. "Ye okay?"

Nodding was easy. Easier than explaining why he must have seen tears trying to build in her eyes. Memories were beautiful, but hard sometimes—too much to say right then. "Yeah. Fine."

"We're goin' to meet a Martin O'Brien. He's owned the shop only since the late nineties, but it's been here for ages, an' he's supposed to know about the clientele goin' all the way back. If Dolly did come in here, I'm bettin' a Steinway like hers wouldn' be easily forgotten. Not a manor an' castle ruins either."

"Mr. Foley?"

They turned in unison.

A man walked their way down the aisle, wearing a Mr. Rogers sweater with leather elbow patches, a crown thinned and gray, and a smile. "'Tis a pleasure to see ye. How is the Richard Lipp?"

"Do you know him?" Laine whispered to Cormac.

He shook his head. "No."

"Well, he thinks he knows you—and your piano at the pub."

Short-statured and kind around the eyes, Mr. O'Brien stopped in front of them with every contrast to the fiery Cullen they'd just met, greeting them with a hearty handshake.

"When young Conor came up an' said a Mr. Foley was downstairs askin' about tunin' a piano, I just assumed Jack come down from Dublin. But ye must be Cormac then, yeah? His older son. The one who still lives in Ireland."

Cormac shook hands with the gentleman, all the while something strange melting over his face. Was it shock? Or anger? Laine hated that she couldn't tell which at the moment, except that it certainly looked like Jack Foley had some explaining to do when they returned to Dublin.

"Aye. I'm Cormac an' this is a friend. Laine. I'm sorry, uh . . . Mr. O'Brien. Ye know my father, Jack Foley? Owns a pub on O'Connell Street."

"The very one. Wit' a nice 1912 Richard Lipp tucked in the snug? I tried to convince him to sell it on more than one occasion, but he'd never take a price. Said it was stayin' put long as the pub has walls."

There was no denying it: O'Brien was talking about the same Jack Foley who held dominion over his pub in the heart of Dublin. Whatever the association there though, Cormac looked knocked over by it. Laine didn't know why exactly, but to show solidarity, she brushed closer to his side in a light shoulder-to-shoulder touch.

"I'm sorry. My father's never mentioned ye to me. Or comin' all the way to Cork to stop in a music shop."

"No? Ah. 'Tis years ago, but I remember the Richard Lipp. A real beauty. Jack there paid us to ship the piano to the pub, all the way from London. Quite a task, mind. But he said he'd pay whatever it cost. An' we've only seen him here a few times since, when he'd stop in to schedule a tune for a friend's piano."

Cormac swallowed hard—something Laine knew she'd have to wait and ask him about on the drive home. Since they'd walked in the door, nothing was adding up. Had Jack really known Dolly . . . and kept it from everyone?

"We're here about a piano, Mr. O'Brien. An' now I'm wonderin' if the friend might have been the same. Was it a Dolly Byrne?"

"That I can' say, son. Jack would come in, pay in euros on the spot, an' send me to an address. That's it. I didn' mind, because it's not often ye get to tune a piece like the Steinway they had. An' wit' such a view o' the sea in County Wicklow. One o' my better commissions to get to make that drive once or twice a year."

"You said 'they,' Mr. O'Brien. Did you ever meet the owner?" Laine asked, watching Cormac's jaw tense out of the corner of her eye.

"No. Can't say as I ever did. But I can give ye the address just the same."

"Yes. Thank you. That would help us a lot."

Mr. O'Brien stepped back to the front of the store, then moved behind the counter and opened an old-school leather-bound appointment book. He searched through pages until he spotted what he was looking for, then penciled something on a piece of paper by the register.

"Cormac—I don't understand what's happening. You mean Jack really did know Dolly?"

"We don' need whatever address that man is writin'. He's just goin' to lead us home."

"Are you sure?" she whispered, watching as Mr. O'Brien finished his task and headed back their way.

Cormac thanked him and shoved the paper in his jacket pocket. He led Laine out of the shop after that, weaving through the downtown streets of Cork, calm and quiet until they reached the car.

Clouds followed them home in silence, and it rained all the way back to Wicklow. The former nostalgia Laine felt for vintage stories was lost a little after that. The things she'd hoped to ask Cormac on the drive home faded into the background. What was ticking around in that head of his?

The rain had stopped, but the Irish Sea was still stormy.

Cormac stood at the castle ruins, his back pressed against the stones. Laine walked up behind, her footsteps drowned out by the sound of waves crashing against the rocks. He looked over when she stood at his side, wrapping her sweater tight around her middle though the wind tried to toy with it.

"Ye ready to go back to Dublin then?"

"In a minute." She leaned into the cutout of a Gothic arched window frame, watching the sea's turmoil with him. "I called Ellie. She said they went to the zoo. And Phoenix Park. And ate cookies at a little bakery on Henry Street. Now Cass is watching cartoons in the flat and eating fish and chips from your pub kitchen—completely happy at the moment."

"That's good. I'm glad ye didn' have to worry about her while we were gone."

Worry about her . . . He didn't know how close he was.

Laine watched the last battle of sunlight trying to cut through the clouds. It cast a glow on Cormac's face, his hair, and the shoulders of his jacket as he stared out past the cliffs.

She noticed everything she hadn't allowed herself before. Cormac was steadfast and strong, in ways she hadn't seen in someone before. Always courteous, asking questions, letting others be the fools who'd rush to judgment while he kept a cool head. It was evident Jack had some major issues with his sons—about some very big questions they still didn't have answers to—but Cormac didn't respond with anger. Instead he was there. Waiting for her to talk. And wanting only that a mother shouldn't have to worry about her daughter for the whole of an afternoon.

Cormac Foley might be the only person in her small corner of the world who could understand what her little girl had gone through.

"Cassie's not mine, if you were wondering."

His attention shifted from the span of ocean over to her. "I wasn'. But she's yers now. That's all that matters, isn't it?"

"No, I didn't mean it like that. My niece wasn't born of me, but I adopted her after my sister, Bethany, went to prison. We don't know who her father is, and we'll probably never know. But we're a family now—Cassie and me—and I wouldn't trade that for anything."

He looked to her, hands buried in his pockets, but he didn't move. Just stood there in the waning sunlight. Too solid and silent to put her off from telling him more. "What happened?"

"Dominoes fell a while back—our grandfather died and we closed up the family antique shop we'd had on the town square, I don't know, for like forever. My parents divorced a few years later. Mom remarried and moved to Florida, and our dad left for New York. That was it. Our little white-picket-fence youth was over. But we were grown up, so it shouldn't have been as hard, right?"

"I remember hard. But Quinn an' I had all the memories o' when our parents were together. It still bothers me that Keira doesn' have that."

"Sometimes memories can bring more hurt than healing. I felt for a while like I'd abandoned Bethany because I got married. And when Evan left, I blamed myself even more because I'd given up my sister for him.

"She still made some really bad decisions she had to own. It was trying drugs once at a party and she was hooked. Lost her job. Gave up on school. She got in trouble with the police and then I lost her, Cormac. The Bethany I used to know—the little sis I remember watching cartoons with on Saturday mornings or curling her hair for the junior prom—was gone. She *is* gone. In a federal prison for the next few years for drug charges she couldn't deny, because they were true. And there's nothing I can do to help her."

"An' Cassie? What happened to her, wit' the nightmares?"

"She wasn't three yet. Bethany left her in the apartment while she went out to a party, thinking she'd sleep through the night. The complex caught fire—some freak accident with a tenant cooking on the stove. By the time police arrived, they found Cassie alone in a smoke-filled apartment, and I got a call at work in the middle of the day—come quick, your niece is dying."

"But she didn' die."

"No. And I still don't know everything she went through before Child Protective Services brought her to me. But I wondered that night you and I were sitting in St. Audoen's, with her between us on the pew, if it wasn't just the biggest blessing of my life to get that call. Because the hardest day turned out to be what would heal both of us, years down the road, before we even knew we'd need it. So no. I'm not worried about Cassie. She's right where she needs to be right now. And I'm okay with that. We'll handle tomorrow, tomorrow."

It would have been too easy for Cormac to cross the mere inches of space between them, to slip his arms around her and dare her heart to try again. He seemed to feel it too but didn't move as the wind whipped blonde waves against her neck.

He cleared his throat and pushed away from the ruins. "Well, I'll go ahead an' take ye back. They must be wonderin' where we are."

"Yes. I imagine Jack will need you at the pub tonight."

"I imagine he will."

They started down the rise, Laine stepping over patches of stubborn yellow flowers that refused to yield to a late-November chill. Cormac walked alongside her. Head down a tad. He opened the passenger door and waited for her to climb in—a gentleman's act that put a painful, businesslike punctuation on the end of the day. He closed it behind her and slipped into the driver's seat.

Before kicking the car in gear, he looked over at her and said, "Cassie's story is what it is. But the future—ye can change it for her. Ye are changin' it. Don't forget how valuable that is, even if it's not how or when ye planned."

"Reminds me of your words at the church. 'The rain always

stops . . . just not in the moment we may want it to.' Life never happens in our own timing, does it?"

Laine watched as the castle ruins disappeared behind them, gazing at the sea rolling in and the sky bleeding desperate hues to meet it, wishing for the first time that their time at Ashford Manor didn't have an expiration date attached. But they were leaving. Cormac's life was in Ireland, a world away. And carpet picnics by candlelight could only go on so long before someone got hurt.

How she wished one sunset over the water could change it all.

TWENTY-THREE

April 25, 1916
123 St. Stephen's Green
Dublin, Ireland
1900 Hours

Issy cracked her eyes open, vision slow to focus.

Prostrate and foggy, she looked around in the darkness, finding she was lying on a cot against the wall of an infirmary-type office.

Rain pattered the glass of a rounded window high up, preventing her from seeing out, save to discern that night had fallen while she'd slept. A blast shook the walls, and specks of something—dust or plaster—floated down from the ceiling. Issy needed little else to revive her senses as to where she was and what was happening when rapid gunfire echoed outside. She wore the same shirt as before, but the sleeve was gone and the placket bloodstained. Her arm was wrapped tight with a bandage from shoulder to elbow. A slight move rewarded her with a white-hot flash of pain that fled down to her fingertips.

Slower . . . Don't do that again, Issy.

She surveyed the tiny room. Whether Rory had seen to it or not, whoever had laid her there had patched her up—and must have known she'd want her camera close. The Kodak sat atop a desk nearby.

A knock echoed against the door and Rory stepped in, leaving the door cracked to noise in the hall. He set a lamp on a desk beside the cot, the slight flicker of a flame casting a glow between them.

"You're awake. That's good." He stooped in front of her. He had rings under his eyes and the shadow of a beard trying to grow upon his face, exhaustion, it seemed, plaguing them both.

"Where are we?"

"Royal College of Surgeons still." He held out a steaming metal cup. "Tea. Thought it might revive you a bit. Foodstuffs are running low by now, but there's beans. And soda bread. I'll see you're brought some before it's gone."

"I'm not sure I could eat right now."

"Slowly . . ." He anchored her good arm at her elbow so she could sit up and swing her legs to the ground. Arm a painful deadweight, Issy could do little else but cradle it in her lap. "Thank you."

"Luck favored you—just a flesh wound. But you won't be able to use it in full for a while."

Issy shook her head and braced her hand to her temple, her vision murky. "Does that account for the haze I feel? I'm afraid I don't remember much."

"Some from blood loss. Shock, maybe. But I'd say it's a healthy dose of lack of sleep or food, and running for your life down the length of Grafton Street after deprivation of both. You may not know it, but you've earned a heap of respect around here to have made it through at all."

Another blast shook them—reverberating the walls this time.

"The English are getting closer?"

"They are, but you needn't concern yourself too much. The building is sturdy and this room's on the alley. There's no danger of gunfire. We're digging our heels in."

Good. If a fight continued, then so must she.

Issy took one last sip, polishing off the tea, and set the cup on the desk, switching it out for the camera. She pulled it into her lap, finding the case had a fine scratch down the side. But in checking the inside, pulling the mechanism and turning the lens as best she could with one arm, she was relieved it had been spared more serious damage.

Her hair hung down in her face, and she swept it back over her shoulder. "Where's my hat?"

"Rubbish bin. With your jacket. And those trousers and shirt should feed the fire too. There are women here, but Lily Kempson and Mary Hyland are leaders, so I've appealed to the nurses to track down a dress for you. May end up being a uniform, but it'll be better than nothing."

She stared back, incredulous. Had he learned nothing? Were bombs not blasting trenches in the Green? How could she possibly run with a skirt tripping her every step?

"Rory, you were the one who said rebellion is no afternoon tea. Or have you forgotten? What on earth would I need with a dress at the moment?"

"Well . . . it's unseemly to go about in men's clothes, Issy. For you, it is."

"But Countess Markievicz is a titled lady and she wears her ICA uniform better than most men. And I bid you to take notice of Connolly's adjutant when you do return to the GPO. Winnie Carney wears what she likes and carries a Webley as she gives men orders. If they can do it, so can I."

"You've done your part. You promised Honor to carry a message that I return to the GPO—and I will. In fact, I'd only just stopped by to tell you I was leaving out that way. The south side's still without gasworks, so it's better to try in darkness. You carried a dispatch through, which is more than anyone could have expected. But you needn't think to do any more than remain here. Stay low and stay safe. Levi's said he'll watch over you."

Defiance rose, and as gingerly as she could, Issy swept the camera crosswise over her shoulder. “Please do thank him for the offer, but I’m sorry, Rory. I cannot stay.”

“That’s a fine lot—where do you plan to go in the middle of a rebellion?”

“Portobello Quay.”

Rory did laugh then, derision in his tone even as she stared back. It took some balancing of fingertips to the desktop, but she stood. “I am quite serious. The dispatch and getting a message through to you were only part of why I’m here. That being done, I cannot stay. I made it thus far without Levi O’Connell’s watchful eye. I wonder if I might muster enough courage to go on another day without it?”

That was unkind, but there was truth in it, and revelation behind it. A youthful romance was one thing; letting go for something and someone real? The chance to see Sean again was what drove her on now.

“What in heaven’s name is in Portobello, save for an army of soldiers that would seek to put a bullet clean through you this time instead of just nicking your arm?”

Issy walked the room slowly, finding that each step without falter gave her confidence.

“In Mallin’s dispatch there was word that a team of medical and clergy had been placed in advance of a military hospital opening in Portobello next month—near Portobello Barracks. If they could be summoned, then they might aid the heavy losses you are sustaining here at the Green. Someone needs to go and, if the team is still there, send them back here.”

“But you’ve been asleep for hours. Surely a dispatch rider has already gone and seen to it. You’re not even a signed-on member of the ICA! Why are you doing this?”

Issy walked up to him, blasting him with defiance, eye to eye. “Consider my name inked in blood then, Rory, because I’m going.

I realize I'll be pegged as a rebel the moment I walk outside with bloodstained clothes, so if you wish to help, find me something other than an evening gown. Trousers—I don't even care if they're clean. Suspenders will do if they're too big. A shirt. And I need a hat to cover my hair. A jacket, too, so I can hide my camera. I just need enough help to get me through to Portobello. If you can't do that, then I'll go up and down this hall until I find someone who can."

"Issy—this is madness!"

"What would you do for Honor?" she shouted back, tearing out the only truth she knew would sway him. "Tell me, Rory! What made you take Father's revolver down from the wall and weigh your pockets with bullets, save for thinking you'd do absolutely anything for the woman you love? Now tell me I can do anything less."

Love.

The word Issy hadn't realized and certainly hadn't intended to say aloud had come tumbling out her mouth.

"Who is in Portobello?"

She clamped her eyes shut for the second it took to say his name, willing herself to show no emotion that would betray whether she was brave enough to continue.

"Sean."

Rory sighed, the desk creaking as he leaned against it.

"I can't tell you how I'm beginning to regret befriending the O'Connell brothers."

"Well, I'm not." Issy reached over and took his wrist in her palm, turning it over so she could read the timepiece there. "It's after seven o'clock. That's far later than I expected."

"And if the ICA won't let you out the front doors?"

"I'll make myself available to run another dispatch. They don't have enough ill-minded rebels willing to dodge the delights of sniper fire."

"Or enough mad sisters, to be sure."

Issy slid her hand down to his, squeezing tight. "Please? Go to the GPO. Keep our promise to Honor. I'll get to Portobello, and I swear I'll stay put as soon as I find Sean. They said that the English have a Captain Bowen-Colthurst holding soldiers back at Portobello Barracks, so the streets just might be passable without troops marching north."

A shade of something she couldn't place bled over Rory's features. He eased his hand from hers and with a barely there whisper gritted out, "What did you say?"

"The streets should be passable."

"No. What name?"

"There's a Captain . . . Bowen-Colthurst? He's residing officer over the English troops at Portobello Barracks. Why? Do you know him?"

A helpless feeling washed over Issy as Rory stormed out the office door and, without explanation, continued down the hall.

Something about the darkness inside a vast palace of a building, with artillery fire just outside—and the fact that she was left alone—did not sit well at all. She grasped the lamp from the desk and followed him to the hall. Shouts, frenzied and broken, rose from the lobby. Men cried out in agony in chairs and pallets everywhere. The sounds mixed with the undercurrent of random *booms* and voices shouting orders.

Issy pressed her back to the wainscoting rail against the wall, feeling her breaths hollow out, as though they were in the belly of a sinking ship. She felt the tug of fingertips against her trouser leg, looked down to find a young man, eyes clamped in pain, grasping out on air.

She set the lamp on the floor and knelt there, it seemed like ages, holding his hand until his skin had grown cold—not knowing what to do but be a stranger who'd wait with him until death arrived.

Rory quick-footed it down the hall in her direction. He'd changed into street clothes and had a rifle strapped crosswise over his chest, a stack of wares in his hands, and Levi following at his heels. "You still bent on going to Portobello?"

She raised her chin. Said a quick prayer and released the man's limp hand back to the pallet.

No fear.

"Yes."

Rory took the lamp from her hand, exchanging it for a stack of clothes. Levi eased by her, setting a pair of lace-up boots on the floor inside the infirmary office, then retreated as if to stand guard in the shadows of the hall. He braced the butt of a rifle on the floor, leaning on it like a cane as he watched the stairs.

"Get changed," Rory said. "And we're gone."

April 25, 1916
Portobello Bridge
Dublin, Ireland
2000 Hours

Most of the south side was still cloaked in darkness from the gas-works disaster. There was just enough light left from the glow of lanterns on the bridge that Issy was confident a photo would still turn out. She angled the camera with her good arm and squeezed the shutter . . .

Click.

Photo number five.

Stalking in the shadows of an alley overlooking the canal and Rathmines Road, their party of three watched as English troops paraded through Portobello. Rory and Levi would tense on either side of her, keeping eyes trained down to both ends of the alley in case a threat should sneak up from behind.

They hadn't expected to be pinned down so close to the church. But three gentlemen traversing the bridge on foot had drawn the soldiers' notice and stalled their advance to cross the last few streets until Portobello Quay.

Issy squinted in the shadows, trying to roll film in the back of the Kodak. Knowing the fabric-knotted sling holding her arm could already be an impediment to their flight, she'd need to be ready when they had to run.

"That's a lieutenant's uniform? The English in front?" Rory asked.

Issy hadn't the faintest idea, but Levi nodded, ever so slightly.

"Don't say . . ." Rory breathed out, shaking his head when one of the men turned, his face washed in light. "That's Skeffy they've stopped. The one with the beard. I'm certain of it."

Slender, in a smart suit and with the faint outline of wire-rimmed glasses on his nose. The other two gentlemen wore suits too. They'd halted, hands in the air, soldiers standing with rifles raised and bayonets glinting in the light.

"Who is Skeffy?" Issy asked.

"Francis Sheehy-Skeffington. Editor of the *Irish Citizen*. He was a member of the Peace Committee during the Dublin lockout just three years back. Could have been influential in the ICA, had he not advocated against all use of arms against the English. He couldn't come to terms about the force Pearse believed was necessary for rebellion, so he's stayed out of it."

"Why have they stopped him?" Issy peered through the shadows, watching as the soldiers continued their interrogation. "For carrying a dispatch perhaps?"

"No. Skeffy owns a strong conviction for peace. He'd never have gotten involved willingly—not to raise arms or to deliver messages for those who do. This is another matter."

One of the men with Skeffington was accosted with the butt of a rifle slammed to his temple, forcing him to swing down to his knees. Issy tore her gaze away, the ferocity of the violence making her stomach turn. Had she eaten anything, she'd have surely retched on the cobblestones.

"Can we not do something?" she cried, biting her bottom lip.

"Those men are unarmed, Rory." Levi raised a rifle with his shoulder braced against a brick building corner.

"We can't give away our position. One shot and the soldiers would be upon us too. Look—they're shackling them now." He tilted his head toward the bridge and the sight of iron vises being affixed to the men's wrists. "If anything, they'll take them up to Portobello Barracks. They'll be imprisoned, but at least they'll be alive. If we attack, it could mean everyone's end—including ours."

Issy tucked the Kodak under her jacket flap as quickly as she could, around the stiffness of her arm still in a sling.

"They're leavin'," Levi whispered, following the gaggle of uniforms with his rifle end until they were over the canal, moving out of sight.

"And once we're certain they're gone, we'll make a run of it—all the way to Portobello Quay. That's three blocks down. We'll decide what to do about the soldiers after."

Eyes sharp, Rory looked from Levi over to Issy, then continued. "Ready when I say go?"

She nodded. "Ready."

It was unnerving that dodging sniper fire had become the order of the day. Issy had already run, and hid, and felt her heart lurch in her chest once that day—not to mention endured the nick of a bullet to her arm. To do it again felt near impossible, not to mention fraying upon already-stripped nerves. But Rory called it, Levi bolted first, and Issy followed at his heels.

They flew past busted shop windows. The haunting sight of

a pub, ransacked and ghostly quiet, bathed in darkness when it should have been lit with gaslight lamps and pub-goers who reveled in tales and talk over a pint.

Weaving in and out of sidewalks, ducking into alleys, they traversed streets Issy didn't know. It was fortunate Levi appeared to have a map in his head, because they followed his lead from a shop corner with buildings lining the sidewalk to the open-air block corner of an iron-fenced cemetery courtyard. Budded trees reached up like bones in the dark, and a church with a high steeple rose up to tip the clouds.

Levi tried a metal gate, finding it locked. Instead of showing her a way around, he leaned his rifle against the iron fence and wasted no time in lacing fingers to a cup, ready to help boost her over. "Go easy. Yer arm. There's a door to the church down below, at the back along the curve of the path. Ye get over an' ye don' stop in runnin' for it. No matter what happens to us. Yeah?"

"I can do it." She slipped her boot into the bridge of his laced fingers.

Levi hoisted her over, grabbing hard to her shoulder when she faltered with her one-handed grip and almost slammed into the iron spindles face-first. Levi's push of momentum carried her over the top and she slid down the metal tines until her feet touched down where a cobblestone path wound its way through a shrub garden, just as he'd said.

Not waiting for Levi and Rory to catch up, Issy flew like the whole of the Crown's army was on her heels.

The back door was rounded atop and half-buried with steps jutting into the ground, like a cellar dug out of the church's side. Stained glass lined windows with intricate arched tops on either side of the door, their meld of hues still brilliant and not fractured yet. It was as if Dublin had fallen into the shadows of rebellion and this little corner of the world had been spared from any knowledge of it.

Wrangling the iron door handle was a desperate dead end—locked. She pressed up against the door, not crying out but wanting to, pounding her fist upon wood, praying Sean was inside and could hear them before soldiers did.

"Issy—no!" Rory's shout was a whisper raked over gravel, but it was too late.

Someone inside had heard.

A bolt unlatched.

The door cracked, hinges crying into the night. Levi stepped in front of Issy, pushing her back by steps until there was ample room to raise his rifle between them and the door. Rory pressed in behind her.

Light beyond the door cast a glow on the path at their feet—soft, flickering rows of beeswax candle jars in an alcove. A man stepped out with hands raised. He'd shed his clerical jacket, wearing a neck band with sleeves rolled at the wrists and black waistcoat undone across his middle. "I can' let ye in, Brother, unless ye put that down."

Levi lowered the rifle. "Sean. Praise be."

Issy finally exhaled when she saw him.

Weary and worn in the candlelight, he looked as though they'd been struggling inside the church same as the rebels were fighting outside of it. But he was standing feet from her. Whole. Unmatched in her affections. After weeks of an aching absence, it almost didn't seem real that she could reach out and touch him.

"Almost didn' recognize ye without the uniform. But ye best come in an' take sanctuary wit' the rest, before a sniper puts a bullet in ye. They're all over the Quay."

"Aye. But I'm not certain ye need a uniform for that." Levi edged to the side so she was in full view. "Seems our girl here managed it even without the ICA duds."

"Issy . . ." On a concerned half step forward, Sean begged, "What's happened to ye?"

Every dirt-smudged, trouser-clad, wounded bit of her was laid bare before Sean, and she couldn't have cared less. He looked her over in a quick survey, his pools of blue questioning and then concern marring his brow when they reached the sling.

All thoughts gone, Issy flew past Levi and fell into his brother's arms.

She wrapped her one good arm around Sean's waist. Holding on. Burying her face in his shoulder until her flat cap slipped off and her hair tumbled down. She eased deeper into the embrace when he cupped the back of her head with his palm and held tighter, as if clinging to that one moment would make all right in their crumbling world.

"Come inside," he whispered against her ear. "Yer safe now."

TWENTY-FOUR

May 24, 1798
Ashford Manor
County Wicklow, Ireland

The fire had died long ago.

Maeve tied a robe over her chemise, went to the tower room's great window, and brushed back the drapes to look out at the thick morning mist that had settled over the glen. Green hills were already dotted with sheep, and the rocky coast was still blanketed with the ghostly morning fog around the castle ruins. Gorse covered the high hills in reams of gold.

Summer was nearly upon them, yet she felt a chill and wrapped her arms around her waist.

"Ye woke early," Eoin said, half startling her through the darkness.

"I could not sleep."

He pulled a shirt over his head and joined her at the window, offering his warmth with arms that encased her from behind. The featherlight brush of his chin rested on the top of her head. "Why, milady? Have ye a worry?"

"A few, perhaps." She traced a finger along his forearm, lost in thought. "And you must stop calling me 'milady.' It's ill humored now that I am your wife."

"No one could call a man married to ye ill humored. But this is . . . still new, aye?"

She hugged his arms tighter around her. It was a relief that he could read her enough to state the obvious, without her having to actually say what was on her mind. Waiting three weeks for the banns to be read and then, in a breath, finding herself standing in the front of Wicklow Chapel in blue muslin with yellow aiteann flowers laced in her hair—that had been anxiety-inducing enough. But the newness of married life, the outright scorn of her brother, even the days she'd looked to the Irish Sea, both expecting and dreading the sight of ship sails to fly upon it . . . There was a cavalcade of emotions, and Maeve was still processing. Who knew how to be a wife in the midst of it?

"Yes. This is new."

"But yer not sorry."

"No. I am not sorry. I wonder, though, what would become of us if your clan learned you're still alive, hidden away in a tower on a Protestant estate."

"I prefer the tower. It assists in duckin' yer brother's constant glares in my direction. He cannot dismiss me from estate duties now that I've wed his sister, but I'm bettin' that means we won' be celebratin' in the same parlor. He still has hate for a Catholic name that's been added to the front page o' the family Bible."

"But he acquiesced to this, along with my father. Acceptance should be granted with it. Would it be shocking for your kin to accept an English wife?"

"I haven't a care for a social calendar, iffen that's yer fear. I doubt a Catholic would be received in any Protestant parlor in County Wicklow. I hadn't thought ye'd consider it disparagin' if we don' receive an invitation to our first ball at Powerscourt, nor my family to accept ye in return."

"You know I wouldn't care for invitations. But there are reasons why I choose to work alongside our tenant families and stay within the bounds of the village. After losing George, I wanted to repair what's been broken in any way I could. I hadn't given a thought to a social calendar, or even marrying in order to secure a place in society."

"Well, it appears ye managed to destroy that plan, seein' as we stood up in a church in our Sunday best. Ye should've seen yer brother's face when I had to borrow his mornin' coat. I'm afraid that gamecock looked taken ill. My apologies that it cheered me considerably."

"I'm quite serious."

"As am I." Though the last thing he appeared was serious. Not with the cheek in his voice and no concern evident whatsoever as to their present circumstances. "Cian's accepted the fate he cannot change in choosin' a brother-in-law. But don't be worryin'—I signed wit' my real name, so this is bindin'."

"I know it is." She leaned back against him. "Wherever life takes us, we go together now."

"Is that yer clever way o' sayin' ye'd like to move to Belfast? Or South Wicklow, if ye please, where there's an O'Byrne on every corner?"

Castle Chryn stood tall as Maeve looked out. Its walls carved up through the fog, like it owned the very rise it sat upon. The sea was calm beyond it, blue and gray and so vast she could see it even when she closed her eyes. The land had a song that called her—drifting and melodic enough that she wondered if she could be content on another of Ireland's shores.

"I've never contemplated leaving. Not even to go back to England after George and Mama died. But Cian's made it known he abhors this estate, and Ireland's troubles with it. I believe he'd prefer to return to England with Father and leave us here to be forgotten."

"If he does not prefer Ireland, why did he return?"

"I do not know, save for a sense of obligation at my letter informing him of Father's faltering in his grief. Perhaps he will not stay." Maeve closed her eyes as she turned her forehead to the crook of his neck. "What will we do if the fight comes to our shores and your cousin calls for his crusader? Will you defend us or join your family in taking up arms against mine?"

"The answer's not an easy one, not when an O'Byrne killed yer brother."

"Yes. A robbery gone bad. Only that man was Catholic, fueling the hatred. He was caught and hanged by the king's soldiers, if that's supposed to be justice. But it was too late to make things right. George is dead. And I wonder whether Mother fell ill more of a broken heart than anything. I believe . . ." She paused, emotion choking her words. "I believe my father cannot even say George's name without abject grief overwhelming him. Have you noticed how he turns away if I mention anything of what and who we've lost?"

Eoin sighed and stared down at the castle ruins with her. "The books in this room, they belonged to George?"

"They did."

"An' that's why ye couldn' part with them."

"My brother was a rare soul. Kindly and generous. Where Cian's nature is severe, George's heart was to show concern for the tenants and the village. He'd always had his books and I had music—the pianoforte my father removed from the manor after his death. No more melodies. No laughter. It seems rather foolish to think on now, but I loved them so. And until you, I didn't believe George's books would ever have an owner, or that I would ever enjoy music again. But now, somehow . . . I do."

Maeve held her breath as he released her, the admission of hope spoken between them. She knotted her hands in front of her as he stepped around to face her, hands at his sides. With palms open to the timber vaults above them.

"So a pirate an' a lady, from either side of a chasm, have wed. The question is, can they be meetin' somewhere in the middle? Seems to me we both have some trustin' to do, one to the other. I'm but willin'."

"My trust is not easily surrendered, Eoin. Not anymore."

"Ye said ye loved me that night at the castle ruins. Was that true?"

"I did," she whispered, slow and near silent. "And I do, yes."

"Then after today, I would ask that ye never again think yerself below another person. Not yer father, nor yer brother. Ye've taken the reins o' leadership here an' cared for the land an' the people on it as any master would. That's repairin' more than 'tis required. An' if any man dare speak a word against ye—either on this estate or in the village—he will have every misfortune of a hotheaded O'Byrne husband to come huntin' him down."

With gentle fingertips Eoin unthreaded her hands so he could take her palm in his. He pressed his lips to her knuckles.

"Must I really share you?"

"I think, milady, were we to go from this estate, that I'd be bringin' an O'Byrne back who is far more capable a leader than the man my kin might remember. I'm not certain they'd be ready for a woman o' yer strength. Might be enjoyable to watch the young lads trippin' themselves over the sight o' ye, though."

"Your faith in me is appreciated." She looked around their tower room. Remembering. Daring to hope for peace even with what might come. "But perhaps we can stay here for a while longer? At the castle ruins. In this tower, even. Not make any decisions right away. I'd like to stay just as we are for now."

"But there is one decision we need to be makin' . . ."

His reply struck a chord, and she sent him a mock glare. "And what, pray, might that be?"

"I ordered a weddin' gift for ye, but 'tis a bit o' waitin' ye'll have to do before it arrives across the Irish Sea out there. So I've a surprise to tide ye over."

"I don't need a gift. What surprise could I want, save for land with families who are safe and peaceable upon it?"

He leaned down and pecked a kiss to her lips—natural, as if they'd always done that, though it, too, was new. And wonderful, because it felt like home.

Eoin took her hand, drawing her away from the window. "'Tis across the estate. Come. Let's go watch the world wake up."

The Wicklow Mountains sang with the last notes of spring—alive and striking—every shade of green, slate, and cranberry proving vibrant on the peaks. They saddled horses and rode to them, over the glen, Éire stretching a bit of pent-up energy out of her legs as they tore down the lane.

Wildflowers bloomed gold and violet along the road and mingled in patches of color across the rise. Their horses' hooves *clip-clopped* on a bridge spanning rocky waters below. And Eoin laughed as Maeve passed him up, winning the informal race declared between them.

Winded, she pulled back. He winked as he rode by, leading her to the familiar sight of the stablemaster's cottage. The road to Dublin that had once proved so painful greeted her this time with hope anew.

Eoin slowed at the gate in the rock wall and slid down from his horse.

"What surprise? This is a sight I believe I've seen before."

He shook his head. "Not this one. 'Tis inside. I've an idea, see, to show ye I mean what I said at our weddin'. I won' allow ye to be hurt again. An' ye extended peace to me once. I've a mind to be the harbinger of it fer ye in return."

He walked her through the gate to a hidden world of green just behind the rock.

Seedlings.

Young leaves reaching for the sun. Pots and pots of them lined up in a row on the other side of the fence. It was a pretty promise of future *Williams' bon Chrétiens*, young and beautiful and longing for a permanent home to stretch their roots deep into Irish soil.

Maeve knelt, knees and rust-red riding habit pressing into the earth, surveying the sprouts. She brushed glossy leaves in her palms. Pressed down the rich, dark earth of several pots, feeling the life beneath her fingertips. The seedlings were remarkably well grown, and now hungry for sun and soil in a permanent home.

"Where did these come from?"

"From the crate ye gave."

She looked up at him, the gesture more than she'd imagined. "You did this?"

"Fer you." Eoin nodded. "Took months to grow 'em from seed. An' now we must decide where they will grow. So peace will no longer have to be shipped over an ocean each year—we can forge it here. Startin' on this land, with the Ashfords an' the O'Byrnes at Castle Chryn. That is, if ye wish to stay on, then I'll abide wit' ye."

Maeve jumped up with muddied skirt and soiled hands, forgetting that a lady would never behave in such a manner. She leapt into Eoin's arms, accepting the gift with a full heart and knowing it meant more than any she'd ever received in her life. Because he'd known how much it meant to her to stay. And it meant not that they forgot who they once were, or the differences that could divide them. They'd come together despite the chasm and would forge something new out of that bond.

It was respect and love despite every bit of a sectarian world battling against them.

"I will never let anythin' happen to 'em. Or us," he whispered against her ear. "Do ye hear me, love?"

"I hear you." She wiped at tears on her cheeks.

With a final squeeze she drew back. "Along the road—that is where they belong. Beyond the rock wall. Let's line it as far as these first trees will go, and each year we add more. Pear trees all the way to the Wicklow Mountains. We will make peace grow here for every generation that comes after. What do you think?"

"I think ye have dirt on yer face." He laughed, so easily, and wiped at her cheek with his thumb. "An' 'tis a fine idea."

"It is." She kissed him, boldness in such an action new and thrilling—that she could do such a thing on a fancy.

The clamor of a speeding horse approached, breaking the magic of stolen moments at a humble cottage. They turned to find a rider yet far enough away that he couldn't quite be made out.

Maeve squinted, staring through the mist. She dusted her hands on her skirt and came closer to his side. "What's wrong, Eoin?"

"A rider makin' tracks is never good is all." He reached for a pistol from his saddle as he edged in front of her.

She didn't question, just stayed still so she was sheltered by the haven of his shoulders. Watching as the horseman drew near—soiled linen coming into focus on his shirt and jacket flapping in the wind.

"It's young Foley?" she said, not understanding why their groom could be in such a state. Unless . . . trouble.

Jack Foley rode down the road from Dublin in a flurry, his horse's hooves cutting deep into the softened earthen road, kicking up clods in his wake. He pulled up, stopping at the crossroads when he saw them. "Sir."

"What's this, Foley?"

"'Tis an urgent message fer The O'Byrne." Uncertainty on his face, Jack looked down at Maeve.

"Ye can speak freely. I don' keep anythin' from my wife. An' yer still groom here, so she's yer mistress."

"Beggin' yer pardon, milady. 'Tis only orders. I had to ask,"

Jack said on a bow, and walked his horse a few steps closer. He lowered his voice. "They sent me on from me father's pub to relay the English caught wind o' the plan fer Dublin mail coaches to be stopped on this day. An' . . . Fitzgerald has been gravely wounded, sir. Happened when the soldiers came to arrest him."

"Who is Fitzgerald?" Maeve hadn't heard the name before.

"'Tis Edward Fitzgerald, milady. United Irishmen leader—one o' the last we had at the top."

Maeve drew in a steadying breath. Talk of mortal wounds and officers arresting known rebellion leaders did not bode well for who and what Eoin was—if anyone learned of it.

It felt right, so she reached down and gripped his hand from behind.

"We're found out. Dublin may be spoilt, but I'm to alert the province that we're goin' ahead in Wicklow an' Wexford. All as planned. I'm to ride all the way through an' relay a call to arms. We form a garrison at the base o' the mountains. Wit' few leaders left, they could use ye, sir."

Eoin turned his head, three-quarter profile enough to look at Maeve.

It was a risk—greater than she'd considered.

"I'm afraid I'm required here." He never broke connection with her. "An' what o' the castle cove?"

"This night, sir."

Eoin finally looked away, staring at the ground beneath his boots. He anchored his free hand to his hip. Though it seemed some reluctance gave him a few seconds' pause, he finally nodded. "Report that we'll be ready to accept ships should they come in."

"Very good, sir." Jack tipped his caubeen to her. "Milady."

Easing in at Eoin's side, Maeve laced her fingers with his as they watched Jack speed down the road. It couldn't be that days into their marriage, they'd be forced into an impossible situation.

Would they fight together? Would Maeve have to choose—her husband or her home?

Eoin's eyes betrayed him. For the first time, they looked on her not with openness or even the simple tenderness she'd seen in him. These were the steel-boned eyes of a leader. Of a rebel who was ready to fight, and defy, and even die if need be. And a tepid response to ships arriving in their cove would not be possible. Not when Cian and her father would surely take up arms on the opposite side to prevent it.

Praying she was wrong, Maeve dared ask, "What does it all mean?"

"Rebellion." Eoin gazed back, strength fading to sorrow before her eyes. "We have until dawn."

TWENTY-FIVE

PRESENT DAY
ASHFORD MANOR
COUNTY WICKLOW, IRELAND

Music floated up the stairs.

While working at the estate, Laine had heard the creaking of the manor's aged walls and roof under the persistent sea wind. Rain hitting the windows. Deborah's laughter and Cassie's skipping about. Or the few times one of their cell phones rang and sent echoes of tunes off the high ceilings.

But never a piano.

The melody was so faint, she might have missed it had she not paused in her note-typing. Laine closed Cormac's laptop at the desk in an upstairs office and followed the sound down the hall to the landing at the top of the grand staircase.

Twilight cast a glow into the foyer and the hunting hall as she approached, a stair at a time, descending age-old steps oddly without a creak. Shafts of sunlight fractured the front windows in bright-gold rays, the day's light quick-fading into the fall of shadows.

Laine eased in toward the music room and hovered in the doorway. Anchoring her shoulder against the doorjamb, she listened as Cormac played, fingertips flying over the Steinway's black-and-white keys.

Favoring his brother's casual side just then in jeans and a *Jack Foley's* tee, Cormac perched on the bench, his black hair slightly mussed and his glasses having been discarded somewhere along the way. He looked up then, meeting her gaze in the window's reflection. Notes faded as he turned.

"All this time, I was droning on about pianos and music shops, and you could have put me in my place. You never said you could play." Everything in Laine said not to find the moment as breathless as it was.

"Ye never asked."

"I guess I'm asking now. What was the tune?"

He smiled and tumbled his fingertips over the keys one last time. "'*Tabhair dom do Lámh.*' Traditional Irish song."

"And you were playing from memory?"

"Yeah." He pulled the fallboard down, covering the keys as if he was almost embarrassed by it. "Lessons since I was eight, I'm afraid. Bein' the youngest, Quinn got to indulge the rocker guitar vibe. I was forced into the more traditional path."

Cormac stood, leaving the piano bench behind, but not before sending a last look over his shoulder, as if the Steinway was at once an old friend. "The Steinway's got the best sound though." He crooked his head in the direction of the castle ruins beyond the glass panes. "An' the best view."

They stood in silence for a moment. Cormac's hands went back into his jeans pockets. And Laine tried to examine the room, as if surveying it for their task, though she'd seen each corner a hundred times.

They were just two people who had something to say and wouldn't.

"Ye headed back to Dublin then?"

"Almost. Just waiting on Ellie and Quinn to pick us up. Cass is watching TV with Deborah in Miss Dolly's flat, and Jack's going to need you behind the bar tonight, so I was trying to hurry through a few things."

"I think I'm actually goin' to stay out here. A day or two at least."

Sunlight streaked the floor, painting gold behind his feet.

"Cormac, you don't want to try to talk to Jack about all this?"

"After years o' workin' elbow to elbow behind the bar, an' he couldn' even tell me he knew Dolly? There's a bit o' history at play here, Laine. I don' expect ye to understand that. But I'll have to let it be. For a while yet, anyway."

Laine tried to ignore that he was hurting. That she cared. That she was trying so hard to ignore the fluttering in her stomach that was fast becoming unbearable the more time she spent with him. From the quiet kindness he showed, to genuine care of Cassie, to now . . . piano playing? All that after the disastrous night of the trip to Cork.

Layers were being peeled back faster than Laine could manage them.

She tucked back errant blonde locks that had wrangled free from behind her ear and, list in hand, stepped into the center of the room. "Well, before I go, Deborah gave me an inventory of the upstairs rooms. Most of them have furniture and paintings—like we expected. And a few pianos, as you know. I phoned Mr. O'Brien and he's willing to take a look at them whenever you want. I told him it would probably be in the new year, after you have the estate appraisal. But that was before I knew you played. So you'd know when the Steinway needs tuning better than I would."

"A custom piece can always do wit' an extra look, yeah?"

"Yeah." Laine smiled, soft and quick—he probably didn't even notice through the quick cast of shadows. "I've also been making calls about the books. A few shops in Dublin have appraisers willing to come out. There's a list of them here. And I emailed my father's company about one of the paintings in the upstairs hall. I'm waiting on a response to that."

"That's fine. It'll work for now, until we can decide if it's worth it to bring in all the appraisers or just put it all to auction outright."

"Well, I did find something I'm not sure what to do with." She stepped over to him and handed him Deborah's pencil-scrawled legal pad list.

"Three flights up—it's a tower room, I think? There's a door tucked behind a stack of boxes, so I almost missed it. I was going to check it off the list, but it's locked. And the wood is too sturdy to try to push in. So if you have a key or . . . ?"

"I've never been up there." He scanned the list. "Didn' even know."

"Okay. No problem. I'll just go ask Deborah and see if she knows where there's a key for it. Or we could call a locksmith if there's one in town. The room is probably empty like most of the space up there, but I'd still like to check it off."

Taking the list back from him was a capital mistake.

When her fingertips brushed his, something clicked. As if they both read what was building between them and neither could deny it.

"So, tomorrow maybe we can move down to the lower level? Though I think it's just the old kitchen and closets . . . ," Laine added, losing focus—fast.

A tendril of her hair fell over her brow as she tried to look away. She brushed it from her forehead to tuck it behind her ear. "Probably only empty space and old furniture stacked in the cellar. And the pear crates. But it's worth a look if you haven't been down there. Deborah said it's mostly just storage now, so it should go fast."

Trying to flee, she pivoted as if to sidestep but half turned and smacked into his shoulder. She backed up, mumbled an apology, but for the life of her couldn't look any higher than the pub logo emblazoned on the middle of his chest.

Don't. Look. Up.

"Laine?"

She swallowed hard, unable to gaze into eyes she knew were staring at her in a far more intimate way than "Let's explore a manor house together."

Cormac didn't move but a few inches.

It left her breathless when the edge of his chin just brushed her temple. He hadn't shaved. And beyond the butterfly-light feel of his breath warming the side of her cheek, he didn't touch her. Just the softness of breathing and standing and sunlight streaming in, and trying to avoid what they both knew was there . . . She forced her eyes to close.

She felt the stroke of his palm, electricity grazing her from wrist to elbow.

"Laine," he said again, so whisper-soft it jarred her.

It wouldn't happen. Laine respected Cormac too much to allow him to cross a line he must have known he shouldn't. She was free. She'd told him so. Signed divorce papers spelled it out. But to everyone else, and maybe even to herself, she wasn't.

Not yet.

Not to take a chance as big as they might be facing.

Ellie and Quinn could be right outside. That should be enough to stop this.

"What I told you about the divorce . . ." She paused, pain clawing her insides. "Ellie could walk in here at any second. I'm just not ready to explain all of this and they'll think I'm . . . That we're . . ."

He tensed against her. It was faint but still there. "If I read anythin' wrong, Laine, I'm sorry."

She stared down at the tips of her shoes, furious with herself for caving to fear.

"This has been a lot in a short time, Cormac. And we don't even know if Ellie's going to—" She covered her mouth with her palm, unable to say more. "We're going home soon."

This time, the fight or flight instinct wasn't dismissed. Laine swept around him, list in hand and heart aching as her ballet flats carried her away from him. "I'll just go get Cass so we can head back. And we can start on the lower level tomorrow."

The sun had begun to set. Shadows drifted across the music room floor as she chased them out, leaving Cormac and every possibility of something new behind.

And she still couldn't look him in the eye.

TWENTY-SIX

April 26, 1916
Portobello Church
Dublin, Ireland
1015 Hours

"Issy? Ye must wake." Sean knelt over her, patting a hand to her cheek.

He took the clerical coat laid as a cover over her and set it off to the side. Cradling her arm, he helped her to sitting. She was stiff from curling up on a wooden pew but, thankfully, could withstand the pain in her arm that seemed to be easing by the hour.

With everything shut up, doors having barricaded them in the sanctuary, it might have been the middle of the night still. But daylight brightened brilliant hues behind stained glass, telling her she'd slept through to morning. "What time is it?"

He pressed a finger to his lips, admonishing her to whisper. "Ten o'clock. Can ye stand?" He took her hand to help her up. "Was goin' to let ye sleep longer, but . . . somethin's happened."

"Did Rory and Levi make it out alright?" Issy scanned the sanctuary, finding the candles still aglow, pews empty, and stained-glass walls eerily still.

"Make it out, they did."

"Then whatever's the matter?"

Sean led her behind a stone column in the shadows of the nave, curling his hand toward a door at the back of the church. Dropping his voice to a deadly whisper, he mouthed, "There are English soldiers outside."

"Soldiers?"

With her instinct to flee growing stronger, Sean must have known it because he settled her with a hand blocking against the column on one side and a hand raised in caution between them.

"*Shhh*, Issy. There's a captain sent word he's seekin' bricklayers. I don' know why save there was an incident on the bridge last eve. The captain remembered there have been laborers offered board at this parsonage in the past, an' he beckoned them to come straightaway. Soldiers are waitin' to escort them, under guard, to urgent work at Portobello Barracks—right now."

What they'd seen on the bridge flashed in her mind. "The incident on the bridge . . . It wouldn't have to do with three Irish journalists taken into custody, would it?"

"I don' rightly know. But somethin's amiss. An' I came to beckon ye to hide this instant."

"Why? Do they know I'm here?"

He looked down at the stone beneath their feet. That sent terror to bleed through her. Sean never did that. He was always resolute. And he'd never drag his feet in delivering news unless . . .

"No, but they have Rory an' Levi."

"What? How?"

"Rory determined to go out to Portobello, instead of straight back to the GPO. I couldn' hold 'em, so we devised a story ahead of time as a precaution. The soldiers caught up to them in the streets overnight, an' they told a story of masonry work in Portobello that was enough truth it matched mine. Please believe me in that I tried. But Rory bid me to leave ye be until mornin' an' tell ye then. So I need ye to hide here in the church until we return."

"*We* . . . Wait—you're going with them? And return from what?"

"The group of bricklayers are bein' taken to the barracks. I'm to accompany as clergy."

Issy ducked under his arm, frantic in searching out her hat and camera. She found them tucked in the corner of the pew. With effort, she slid the leather strap over her shoulder, thinking that she could hide, just until the soldiers were gone, and then get a message back to the rebels at the Green that some of their men had been taken prisoner.

It was a shot in the dark, but a chance at least.

"Issy . . ."

"I made a promise to Honor—to myself, that we wouldn't lose anyone else in this fight. And now you're telling me that soldiers are outside ready to take you all away?"

"Ye can't go out in those streets alone."

"But I could have convinced Rory to come back . . ."

"Ye couldn't have convinced him to stay any more than I could," he whispered, taking her hand. "Rory knows that if Captain John Bowen-Colthurst is the English officer at Portobello Barracks, then that means the lieutenant under his command will be there also."

"I don't understand. Why does that matter?"

"Because Lieutenant Malcom Corley is the man who attacked Honor, an' Rory's ready to give his life to avenge hers."

The weight of Issy's ignorance washed over her.

How had she not known who the captain was . . . What Rory's intentions were . . . All the time she thought her brother was helping her get to Sean, he was plotting his own revenge. One that he surely wouldn't survive.

"It's all my fault. I'm the one who told him the captain was there."

"Don' blame yerself."

"So Levi must have known?"

"He did."

All along, they'd both known yet given her no warning of their plans. It stirred determination anew.

"But then . . . why bring me along too? If they endeavored to enact revenge on a company of soldiers, why risk a wounded photographer holding them up?"

"Because they wanted ye to be taken care of, Issy. An' they knew ye would be here . . ." He paused for a second, enough that she felt tenderness light his eyes. "With me."

"Because they think they're not coming home."

Sean nodded, appearing quite sorry for the truth.

"Then I'm going too. I'm a bricklayer," she vowed, wiping a tear from under her eye. "I can't just stand here and let all of the people I love walk out that door—" She shook her head, stopping short of a declaration that might carry no weight.

It was too much to risk in a moment that meant everything.

"I'm going with you."

"No," he whispered back. "Yer not."

"You said yourself there's a group of workers going. I won't be noticed among them. I can be one bricklayer in a nameless crowd."

A weight in her trouser pocket reminded Issy of one thing that would allow her to blend into a line of young men workers. She slid her wounded arm from its sling. Then, retrieving the straight blade she'd held on to from the first run through Clerys department store, she placed the ivory-embossed tool in his palm.

"Sean. We haven't time. If I'm a bricklayer, I must look like one. Please? I can't stay in this church without you. Do not ask it of me," she whispered, eyes entreating as she curled his fingers around the sheathed blade. "I need your help."

Issy swept her braid over her shoulder and carefully, with her wounded arm, unwound the long rope and threaded her fingers through the waves until they were fully combed out. Turning her back to him, she swept her hair so it tumbled down, long and unbound, asking for his touch.

By the flickering of prayer candles and the hidden shadows of a sanctuary alcove, she closed her eyes and waited, asking him to enter an intimacy she'd never allowed another man before him. It took seconds—no doubt from the decision Sean was wrestling. But she held her breath, and then he was there.

In a touch that first grazed her neck, he swept her hair back, smoothing locks in his palms. And with the softest care, she felt him draw and cut, giving the first lock its freedom. The cinnamon wave danced to the ground, painting a line on the tile at her feet. And then another. And another . . . trusting, cutting, letting go, until she was shorn, and her neck was cold.

Sean came around to face her, brushed back the hair at her brow and, ever so gently, cut it so the final wave fell and what remained curled at her chin.

"I find you've changed, in the months you were away." Issy met his gaze reflected through the candlelight.

"I told ye before that I'm the same man. Same convictions. Same flaws. But I was already on a path to this moment. Do ye think maybe 'tis not I who did the changin'?" He swept the errant wisp of hair so it barely tucked behind her ear. "I know I can't hold ye back, Issy. An' I'd never try."

April 26, 1916
Portobello Barracks
Dublin, Ireland
1215 Hours

The three journalists were dead.

Whether bitten by arrogance, fear to cover up the executions of innocent men, or sheer idiocy, Captain Bowen-Colthurst hadn't the inclination to look his bricklayers in the face. Neither were they searched on their person, praise be—just surveyed for weapons under their coats. The soldiers had not inspected closely enough to discern a woman had infiltrated their workmen's ranks. Instead, a tall, dour-faced lieutenant marched them into a barracks courtyard and supervised the work while soldiers kept watch a rifle's distance away.

Issy kept her head down as Lieutenant Corley nursed a cig, trying as she might not to think of the towheaded evil standing paces behind her, nor how he laughed over some amusement in the background as they cleaned the blood-soaked cobblestones beneath their feet. She'd never touched a brick hammer in her life. Levi was a swift teacher, instructing her in the manner to remove areas that had been stained crimson or with bullets that had passed through the bodies of the three men and become lodged in the brick.

She'd go between wheelbarrow and tools, from wall to bricks and back again, more pretending to work than anything as they prepared lime mortar replacements. And though nerves twisted in her stomach that Corley remained close, Rory worked diligently, keeping a steady head as they splashed buckets of water to drain the blood-evidence from the stones.

They worked in silence, no more than an hour or two, as if the rifles weren't there.

And when the soiled bricks had been piled up, tools stowed, and their lives properly threatened umpteen times, soldiers marched the stoic line of bricklayers away from the courtyard with bayonets drawn. The others employed in the cover-up had scattered once they reached the barracks gate, leaving Rory and Levi to assist Issy out.

Sean stood in his clerical collar and long coat at the barracks gate, and Issy chastened herself not to fall into his arms the instant they were free, for Corley and his men watched with a keen eye as they fled out to Military Road.

Sean swept his arm around her back as he ushered her down the sidewalk, Rory and Levi following behind. "Issy, yer shakin,'" he whispered, sending his gaze back to Rory and Levi. "What happened?"

"They killed Skeffy . . ." Issy gripped her jacket tight around her, fighting for breaths that wouldn't hollow her out. "All three of them. We saw the bodies carried out!"

"Killed?" He snapped a look over his shoulder again.

"Too much to speak of now," Rory said. "We'll tell you all once we get to the church."

"At least ye weren't found out." Sean squeezed his arm tighter around Issy. "At least they let ye go."

Sean ushered their group in haste, Issy feeling herself pulled along in a fog, barely recognizing their trek down the length of Rathmines Road, up toward Portobello Bridge.

"An' Lieutenant Corley? What say ye about him, Rory?" Sean asked, leading their party to a thin strip of road off Grove Park, along shop alleys up to the bridge.

"I know what he looks like now."

The ominous tone wasn't unexpected—Rory was patient in rage.

Issy prayed that once back in the haven of Portobello Church, she might speak with him. Convince him that vengeance was the Lord's, and he could not return from crossing a line of cold-blooded murder to satisfy it on his own. She could think of little else as they cut across to the canal and hurried along the street up to the bridge.

Yes, they'd get back to the church. They'd hide in safety. And one day, it would all be over . . . and perhaps then Rory could see his future with Honor more clearly.

An armored truck blasted over the rise without warning, decimating her plan.

A plated monster with a long cylinder bed chugged up to a stop before them. They slowed along the bridge, looking across the canal to the sanctuary of the church steeple but with no way to reach it. It appeared the worst was now upon them as a pair of soldiers jumped from the back and blocked the bridge end at Rathmines Road.

Levi's words from the night before rang through Issy's mind; like the journalists, they, too, were on the bridge, soon to be accosted, and unarmed. But did the soldiers know they were not as innocent as the men who'd just been executed at the barracks?

They were rebels with bullets owed to them.

Sean edged in front of Issy with careful steps until they were both pressed up against a gaslight lantern and the stone rail overlooking the water. Rory and Levi stood before the soldiers, exchanging eyes-only glances, feet planted in place.

The armored truck waited like a beast before them, until a door opened and the lanky arrogance of Lieutenant Corley stepped down. The flash of a pistol caught the light, illuminating a barrel gripped in his hand.

Oh no . . .

This was no official visit; there was no unit of troops to indicate it, just a pair of soldiers flanking the devil. Whatever Corley had planned, it appeared as though someone had changed his mind, and they'd decided to silence the witnesses.

Rory was eerily calm. Levi too. They stood without word or movement, just staring down the officers blocking their path. Issy gripped Sean's hand from behind. He squeezed her fingers in solidarity, squared his shoulders, then let go.

"Good day to ye, Officer. As clergy, may I be of help?"

"The captain bid me to check in with your workers to see that they arrive safely to their destination, Vicar. No doubt rebels are afoot, even on the bridge to Portobello Church. I cannot ensure their safety without escort."

"A kindness, sir." Sean clasped his hands in front of his waist as he bestowed a priestly bow. "But we are quite safe. Thank ye."

Corley raised the pistol, training Sean squarely in his sight. Issy nearly gasped aloud, for how swift the action had turned the temperature of the encounter.

"Then I'd like to humbly request, Vicar, that you and your party accompany us back to Portobello Barracks. Immediately."

"An' why is that, sir? The masons have been discharged o' their duties to the Crown. They'd like to be returnin' to their families posthaste. An' I to a place o' the Lord's service."

"Says the captain, someone recognized the young boy there." Corley tipped his chin in Issy's direction.

Her breath caught in her throat. Surely they couldn't recognize her. Not when she'd changed clothes and cut her hair . . .

"One of the soldiers here seemed to remember a similar face making tracks over in the area of the Green. If you don't mind, we'd like to have a physician examine him, just to see that he didn't take an unfortunate injury to the arm . . . or that his camera wasn't damaged as he ran into a rebel garrison."

A pale wind blew over the bridge, stirring lost papers in a swirl at their feet.

They waited, all frozen as each contemplated their options.

Issy flitted her glance from the soldiers back to Levi and Rory, who remained statues before the armored beast. All she could think was that she'd promised Honor no one would be hurt—not because of her. And if Rory didn't come home or if Sean or Levi lost their lives in her defense, she wouldn't be able to live with herself.

Decision made, Issy gripped her camera in front of her, willing to step out and go with them—if only it meant no one else would die. Sean seemed able to read her intention and drifted an arm back, slowly curling it in a shield to stop her.

"May God forgive me, but I'm afraid I cannot allow that, sir."

The soldiers kept their rifles raised, though they didn't seem to take the masons with any note of seriousness. Issy could see they knew them all to be unarmed. Why else would Corley keep his weapon raised on a vicar—a man no one would have suspected to have loyalties on either side of the conflict? His was a vow of nonviolence, and Corley's intimidation hinged on it.

Without warning Sean pulled a pistol from under his clerical coat and raised it high. He shoved Issy down, her knees crashing to the pavement as shots rang out.

When the smoke cleared, two men lay on the ground.

TWENTY-SEVEN

May 24, 1798
Ashford Manor
County Wicklow, Ireland

A storm raged from the depths of the Irish Sea.

Lightning streaked within the cloud formations in the distance. Maeve looked out from the tower window, chewing her thumbnail as the flashes of light carved the shape of castle ruins into a turbulent sky.

Eoin was out there somewhere, shoring up positions across the estate for what may yet occur by morning. It may be men attacking Protestant estates, piking loyalists. Or English soldiers hunting down Irish rebels. Weapons and warfare, she prayed not, even as she watched for any movement upon the face of the water. No spark or flickering flame appeared at the castle ruins either. All was still save for the storm clouds deciding where and when to punish.

The fire crackled on the hearth, drawing Maeve's attention.

Her gaze swept over the books lining the mantel. They'd once been a row of the intellectual that in so many attitudes defined George and the way things used to be. Yet they also defined a man so his opposite in matters of politics and religion, but who shared aspects mirrored in a steadfast character.

Eoin's convictions would never be hidden away like books on

a shelf or the forgotten music from a pianoforte. He'd pretend he liked being confined to a tower on a Protestant estate, for her. But it was not who he was.

And it would not pass for her to ask him to be less.

Though leaving the manor would defy him, Maeve could see no other way but to be true to herself and seek him out. She retrieved her leather pierrot from the wardrobe and pulled it over the deep evergreen of her round gown, hastily fixing the buttons down the front, then slipped into riding boots. She'd not taken time to bind her hair—just fixed it with a ribbon in a loose braid.

She blew out the candles on the bureau and, with a final glance to the ruins below, cracked open the door.

Cian and her father wouldn't have yet woken, for the early hour. Even still, she admonished every stair, every click of the heels of her boots, to remain as silent as to allow her to slip out of the manor undetected.

"Have you need of something, milady?" Mrs. Finnegan emerged from the shadows at the bottom of the stairs.

"Oh." She started, hand calming the fast-moving drumbeat in her chest. "Nothing, thank you."

"Are you set for riding at this early hour?"

"Not just now," she whispered in return, though she battled not to find impertinence in the woman's inquisitive manner—riding jacket or not. "I bid you a good morning, Mrs. Finnegan."

Maeve proceeded down the hall, though the woman followed, nearly at her heels.

"But . . . Mr. O'Byrne instructed we stay in from danger until dawn."

How Maeve wished for a calm outside—such that it might explain her intent to leave the manor. But with sea breezes rattling the windows in the hall and sprays of rain upon the glass, there wasn't likely an explanation that would satisfy.

Perhaps truth mattered more.

She halted in the shadows of the upper floor hall, the generous line of windows backdropping them. "And what danger is this?"

"There's an ill wind that blows this day, milady."

"We're quite used to the sea wind on the ridge. And I'm forced to imagine what danger might befall me on my own estate, save for the unsavory nature of rumors spread without even the most loyal in service to the family Ashford to contradict them. I would ask you, Mrs. Finnegan, please do not obstruct me in leaving this manor. My place is at my husband's side."

"I meant no disrespect." The hint of a smile pressed Mrs. Finnegan's lips. "And I am most cheered in my heart to hear what you are about."

Taking Maeve's hand in hers as a mother might, the woman patted it in her palm. Truly, she could not account for the shift in the tone and manners. Mrs. Finnegan acted almost . . . proud. And how could that be, when the mere sight of Eoin O'Byrne could spark talk of freebooters and an almost-simultaneous locking of the silver pantry in the same breath?

"If you felt this way, why then did you remain silent on the very matter that resulted in this hastily bid marriage? Had you no care for truth and consequence when you did not stand up for us? We saved his life together—you and I. Or have you forgotten that?"

"I could not contradict the matter of that night, milady, because I do not believe your marriage hasty. Mr. O'Byrne is a mite brusque and coarse for a gentleman, but all the pomp and manners and titles in the land could not make up for what he *does* possess. I regret to say that your mother knew Mr. Cian's heart, and the coldness she saw in her elder son grieved her much. When she left us, she bid me to look after not him or his lordship, or even this estate. She bid me to look after you. Knowing you took the loss of Mr. George so hard—"

Maeve tore her eyes away, clamping them shut.

"But your brother's death was never your burden to repay. And not until that pirate out there did anyone step onto this estate who was worthy to stand as tall, as proud," she whispered. "And as brave, right beside you, my dear."

Maeve felt the merciful touch of the woman's palms take her chin in hand, and she opened her eyes.

"But he is an O'Byrne. A Catholic. Does it not give you pause that he may take up arms against England?"

"Then I would see wisdom in not having contradicted the rumors about that first night. You needed a champion, milady. That young pirate might not know it yet, but so does he."

"And if I said that I love him—despite his convictions and how they might differ from ours? What say you then?"

"Perhaps we change ours? We could stand something to shake us up a bit." Mrs. Finnegan waved her off as if unconcerned and stepped over to the shadows at the twist to the upper floor stairs. From the darkness she pulled a nautical lantern—oversize, of tin with razor-thin horn panels instead of glass, and a thick hook handle that curled around her palm.

"You found it in the silver closet."

"Where else would you put it, to keep it locked out of sight so no one would know what Mr. O'Byrne was about? He thinks he's shifty and sly when he must be. But I fear that boy hasn't met a skilled English housekeeper. We know all that occurs in our master's house. He'd best be remembering that fact."

The wind was punishing the leaded glass at her back, reminding Maeve that the storm wouldn't wait. And neither would ships at sea, looking for their port.

"Mrs. Finnegan, are you quite certain you know what you would be asking me to do?"

"You are Irish now, milady. And these are your people. If you wish to end this war between factions, it must start with you.

Go—light the lantern. Call the boats to shore. Peace is forged only aft it's gone through fire. And if it's more fire that will be brought to this estate, then we shall be ready for it."

The woman took her hand and curled Maeve's fingertips around the cool metal handle, transferring the weight of the lantern over to her.

"And so it's plainly known, I never said I disliked pirates. Only that I believed him to be one."

The gorse would welcome the storm, even if the people did not. Rain fell soft. Misting like dew over the fields of yellow. Maeve crossed the glen through it, sweeping through the stone gate and venturing up the rise with a single purpose in mind.

Eoin stood in the window of Castle Chryn, a rifle resting crosswise over his shoulder as he stared out to sea. He seemed to know she was there, for his stance eased as she approached.

"I asked ye kindly to stay inside." He finally turned, his cocked hat dripping raindrops off the front corner. "So naturally I've been waitin' for ye to defy me o'er the last hour."

Unaware that she was as yet so wholly predictable, Maeve stepped inside the ruins to the place they'd stood weeks ago—the very same window, in fact, where she'd unwittingly bared her heart to him.

She held out the lantern, its size requiring the bulk of both arms to lift it high.

"Mrs. Finnegan bid me to take a fire steel and chert—in case you'd not thought to bring them with." She smiled. By the looks of him, Eoin hadn't expected her to produce it. "She knew I'd hidden the lantern in the silver closet all this time. It was locked away, keeping our secret of that first night. Until it was needed again, of course."

"Well, I admit I didn' expect an Englishwoman who prays a

hole might open beneath my feet would be the one to encourage insurrection on yer estate."

Maeve set the lantern down at her feet. "You're wrong. She likes you very much. She'd just never admit it."

"An' the gesture is deeply felt, I assure ye." He lowered the rifle and held a hand out for her. "Come here."

She stepped over stones and gorse that had sprouted up between them, and he drew her close by his side. Before she could catch her breath or say another word, she knew what he watched.

Ships.

A half dozen at least, sails drifting like phantoms on the water. And if they were so close, the lantern light would signal them to shore. Every crash of surf against the cliff rocks or thunder clap might drown the sound of oars cutting water and men sailing skiffs to shore.

"Are they French?"

"French vessels an' arms, but those men are Irish. An' they mean to set this rebellion afire as planned." Eoin pointed the rifle down to the glen. "We don' need the lantern now."

Maeve saw them—trails of men carrying crates on their shoulders, cutting a silent path through the glen like ghosts from the sea. And out front, a man in an impressive naval coat and cocked hat was evident to be their leader.

He looked to the rise and tipped his head in a nod toward Eoin watching from the ruins, his rifle trained in their direction, and went on with his men.

"Who is that?"

"General Holt."

Maeve stared at Eoin. "You know him."

"Joseph. I do." He kept a keen eye on the flight of men and arms filtering through the glen. "What do they say—the enemy of yer enemy is a friend? France is at war with England, an' so they become the Irishman's consort. When the English put down riots after forcin' conscription of Irishmen for their milita, hundreds of Catholics were killed as a result. An' then the Crown set upon the Society of United Irishmen, to weed out leaders from the ranks, temptin' them out o' hidin' wit' violence so bloody no man could forget as long as he lives."

"What kind of violence?"

While Eoin wasn't one to collapse into emotions he fought to hold at bay, Maeve could see it upon his face. He trained the rifle on a line of men, allowing them to pass, with a brow as harsh and a glare as intense as any she'd seen.

"What kind of violence, Eoin?"

"It was in a church in Monkton Row, before the Hoche expedition. The English filled the pews with men, women, an' children, chained the doors, an' burned it to the ground with all souls inside."

Maeve bit her bottom lip over the emotion that such blackness drew from her. Eoin kept his gaze trained on the army, watching over the top of the rifle sight.

"And you . . . saw this occur?"

He shifted his glance to her then, words unnecessary to reveal what he had seen. And felt. And what no doubt still burned in his memory.

"Oh . . ."

"I was in a pub that night for a meetin' where the Hoche expedition was planned. With my father already dead it was put upon my shoulders to care after my mother an' two sisters. I went out that night at Wolfe's request."

"I just thought all of your family was gone after you said none were waiting. Where are they now?"

"They were among the dead—all Catholics, an' what was left o' the doorframes still chained from the outside. It was meant to draw a suspected leader out of hidin'. An' I swore a vow that day, that never again would a soul die for me. Not if I could conceive to stop it."

"And that is why you refuse drink?"

"Aye, love. That is why I refuse it. Because I will never again falter when one o' my own needs protectin'."

Daybreak continued to hide behind storm clouds. They'd have a lingering darkness on the day the rebellion would begin. But there was enough light to find a large, burly figure Maeve recognized, bringing up the tail of the group.

She gasped as Leary Ó Flannagáin cut through the morning shadows. "Do you see—?"

"He knows what he's about as long as I'm here. The rebels wouldn't dare attempt an attack on Ashford now."

"But you do not go with them?"

"I will not," he whispered, rifle trained on the leader of the line as they moved through the fields of yellow. "But nor will I turn them in. If they are peaceable, we let them pass, all the way to the mountains. Leary knows there's a line drawn at the castle, where this rifle will not allow any of them to threaten the lives here."

"But the fires on the estate . . . Why would you allow him to set foot here again knowing it was very likely he who set them?"

"He's no murderer to set fire to a family cottage of the man who's takin' delivery of arms an' command with Holt's unit."

"O'Malley is a leader in the ranks of fighting men too?"

Eoin nodded. "From the beginnin'. An' Ó Flannagáin would cut off his own arm before settin' fire to the estate now, knowin' it would alert the soldiers an' threaten the entire rebellion. He may wish to see me downed wit' musket shot, but never would he harm a chance to overthrow English rule. There has to be somethin' else to it. An' I mean to find out what."

"So what do we do?"

Eoin lowered the rifle after the men disappeared into the tangle of trees leading to the Wicklow Mountains.

"We watch, an' we wait."

TWENTY-EIGHT

PRESENT DAY
ASHFORD MANOR
COUNTY WICKLOW, IRELAND

Cassie turned circles around castle stones, skipping under the whisper of snowflakes floating over the ridge.

Making memories in the last days under an Irish autumn sky seemed as good a way as any to spend them. They'd been laughing and singing, exploring around the castle ruins, and Laine snapping photos on her phone while they took a breather outside. The sound of tires crunching gravel snagged her notice, and she looked up to the arbor of pear trees lining the rock wall.

A black sedan turned off the road. It lumbered up the drive, then came to a stop in front of the manor. It wasn't a car Laine recognized. A tourist must have taken a wrong turn.

She called out to Cassie to stay put at the castle, intent on meeting the lost soul across the path. Only, the one who'd driven here wasn't lost at all. The driver's side door opened and out stepped Jack Foley. He walked in Laine's direction, meeting her halfway.

"Jack . . . hello." Laine smiled, hoping she didn't look as awkward as she felt. "Do you want me to get Cormac for you? He's inside but I can—"

"No. Don' bother him. He's stayed away from the pub an' that tells me he needs some space." He shoved his hands in the pockets of a fisherman's jacket, taking in the glen, the castle, and the tucked-away manor. His inspection of the grounds appeared to have a purpose.

"It's nice here, isn't it? Not another view like this in all the world."

Cassie's delight abounded as she tipped her head up, opening her mouth to catch snowflakes on her tongue.

"It must have come as a surprise when Miss Dolly left all this to you."

"*Surprise* is one word fer it. I should've had a notion she'd do somethin' like this. Wish she was here now so I could give her a piece o' my mind, but then, Dolly'd have laughed in my face. Had that tough way about her. Didn' care what nobody thought—she was goin' to do exactly what she wanted. 'Tis why she never married. An' sat at the bar to drink her pint o' plain day after day. I think she wanted to show the regulars who was boss."

"You knew her though?"

"All Miss Dolly an' I ever talked about was one thing, an' that was the estate. She claimed the Byrnes an' Foleys have connections that go back to the earliest days of this house. An' some fanciful story about her grandparents havin' lived through the Rising, an' a Foley marryin' a Byrne from this house. I didn' believe it—every third person's named Foley or Byrne 'round here. Thought she was just a lonely old soul at the end o' the bar. But she had an eye for our piano, an' I gave her a name once of a shop I knew in Cork—after she said she didn' want any Dublin shops nosin' around the estate. I never asked why."

"But you didn't tell Cormac?"

"No. I didn' see anythin' to it. It was just drivin' pears to market once or twice a season. An' helpin' a lady care after her prized possession. I never wanted nothin' out o' it. Not this anyway."

"A Steinway might be a prized possession, but she had pianos on every floor of this house."

Jack sighed—a long, drifting exhale of understanding. "So that's why."

"I'm sorry?"

"Cormac. This manor. I thought maybe he was followin' after yer interest in it, but it makes sense now. The pianos are why he's refusin' to give it up so we can get back to life as normal."

"I'm afraid I don't understand. I know he plays the piano—or did once. But why would that cause Cormac to want to keep this place?"

"Because there's a piano shoved in a corner snug at the pub, an' he won't touch it. Brings back painful memories for him. 'Tis the same reason my younger son picked up an' left one day an' didn' come back—not even when his blessed mother died. 'Tis why both boys rarely see their sister. This family is haunted by past doin's. We're broken. Too broken to be fixin' with a few weeks at a castle. An' if Cormac is stayin' on here because he thinks it'll bring her back, he's wrong."

A rather pointed series of thoughts . . . Brokenness was something Laine hated to understand so completely. She swallowed hard, feeling the cold wind as it swept over the ridge, watching as it toyed with the hood on Cassie's jacket.

Oh. Mothers and children . . . "Her? Is that Cormac's mother?"

Jack nodded. "Aye. Juliette." He looked out at the sea. "She passed nigh an' almost ten years back now. Cancer. By then we were divorced. Quinn skirted off for his globe-trottin' an' couldn' see fit to come back an' say good-bye. Never could be tied down, that one. An' Keira was too young to understand what was happenin' wit' her family breakin' apart. So Cormac stepped up. Left his Trinity education to go to London. Did he tell ye that?"

"No. He didn't."

"Ah, but then he wouldn't. Doesn' think o' himself. Never has. He put his life on hold to care after his little sister. Got her to school every mornin'. Took his mother to her doctor's appointments. When she was too sick to come downstairs an' Keira was too heartbroken to leave her, he played piano for them both—the Richard Lipp. An' after she died, I brought it back here, for him. He never asked who. Or why. Just took it in the pub, shoved it in the corner, an' walked away."

"I didn't know. I mean, he told me he has a sister but not about the rest."

"Well, he's always been good at workin'. He's just not one for talkin' or livin' too much." Jack straightened his spine and cleared his throat. "He tried it once. An' when he came home to Dublin—an' Foley's pub—the girl he'd hoped to hang on to was long gone. I never did understand that."

If it was possible for Laine's heart to sink even more, it did right then. Cormac had said he understood something of how hard things were when Laine had adopted Cassie. But losing part of his own future in a similar way? He'd never mentioned a fiancée. Or helping to raise his sister.

Laine looked to the manor, imagined Cormac inside fixing things. Searching through boxes. Trying to do what was right by a woman their family had barely known. It was that kind of staying power she couldn't understand. What made one person stay, while another, with an equal heart beating in his chest, simply walked out?

"And that's why Quinn doesn't come home? Because he didn't when he had the chance?"

"I don' blame Quinn. That boy's always gone his own way. Pigheaded like his da. I couldn' have stopped him from leavin' any more than his ma."

"I think he's trying to make up for it now, with Ellie."

"That he is. An' we'll ease off the gas pedal wit' bristle between us in time. But there's no need wit' Cormac—he's ready to forgive yesterday. It's his way. He stayed even when his brother . . . an' then his da couldn' take it an' we left. That boy sat by a hospital bed an' held Juliette's hand, every day until the last. Problem is, now I don' think he's ready to let go."

"Mommy—I'm cold." Cassie trotted up between them, breaking the moment with cheeks as red as cherries, and tugged on her hand.

"Alright, honey." Laine wiped at tears that had collected under her lashes, trying to collect herself. "I'm sorry, Mr. Foley. I need to take her inside. But if you'd maybe like to join us?"

He shook his head. "Not now. 'Tis best left alone."

Of course. Fathers and sons . . . They were a complicated dynamic too, and with pasts that couldn't be sponged away in one visit to castle ruins. Maybe he'd had enough of memory lane at the moment, because he tipped his head and stepped toward his car.

Thinking that was it, Laine swept Cassie into her arms and headed for the manor's front steps.

"Miss?"

She stopped. Turned. And found deep-green eyes staring near through her with a surprising dose of care in them.

"I don' pretend to push into my sons' love lives. What they do is what they choose. An' Quinn runnin' off to get married on a whim is his way."

"Mr. Foley, my best friend is not a whim. Not to me. And definitely not to your son. As far as the rest of it, I—"

He raised a hand. "I meant no disrespect. Just to say I own to a lot o' the trouble here an' if I can, I'll make it right. Where Quinn is apt to run out like his old man, Cormac's exactly like his ma: he'll stay until the last note is played. That's why Dolly liked him, I think." Jack slid into the driver's seat. "An' if this estate is that important to him, then I won' stand in his way."

"Wouldn't you like to tell Cormac that?" The weight of an admission like that should come from father to son—not from her. "Come inside. Have a cup of tea and warm up."

"Another time, perhaps. But I wish ye well. An' ye can tell Cormac he's welcome an' wanted down at the pub anytime. I just came to tell 'im there's a key hangin' on a high-up hook in the larder here. Where the pear crates are kept? I don' know what that means exactly, but it seemed important to Miss Dolly that I knew it. An' I got to thinkin' it just might open a door ye both thought had been closed."

"Have you been in the larder yet?"

Cormac turned from searching through boxes on a wall of shelves back to her. "Uh, a big scary cellar used before there were refrigerators? No. Not terribly excited about that."

"Right. I left Cass upstairs with Deborah so we can go through it," Laine said, looking around the basement room with little light coming in from high-up windows. "Which way is it?"

"We don' have to do this now. We've got a little time before we need to leave, so why don't we wrap up an' look in tomorrow?"

"This can't wait. Or I don't think you'll want to wait."

Something piqued his interest. A little lift of the chin and twinkle in the eyes told her he was game. Cormac set his smart tablet on the shelf and pointed down a hall with a checked-tile floor and a row of doors on each side.

"I don' know what this is about, but the only scary cellar here is past the old service staff offices an' such. That way. At the end."

They strode down the corridor, thankfully with thin windows set near the ceiling that let in a little light. If not for them, they'd have been in pitch blackness. When they reached the end, Laine tried the old brass knob. It gave, and she pushed the door open.

Laine tugged a thin cord hanging from a bulb dangling from the ceiling, washing the space in light. There were a few worse-for-wear baskets, garden tools, stacks of empty pear crates, and a bucket of cleaning supplies. But other than that, the shelves were bare.

If anything was hiding here, they'd find it.

At least Miss Dolly thought to wire this room, or else we'd be bumpin' into the walls.

"Look high." Laine checked the shadowed corners.

Cormac flipped on his phone flashlight and checked the opposite side of the larder. "It might help if I knew what I'm looking for, Laine—other than cobwebs."

"We're looking for a key. It has to be old. Wrought iron or brass. It'll be hanging on a hook, high up if it's here."

"You mean like this?" Cormac pulled a key down from wherever he'd found it and turned it over in his palm. The thick wrought iron was rusty and worn, with a scrolling loop at the bow and a heavy plank at the tip. "How on earth did ye know that was there? Deborah said she's been in here a hundred times, and she never mentioned it."

"She probably didn't know about it."

"Then who did?"

She breathed in deep. *Out with it, Laine.*

"Jack stopped by."

"What? Why would he come here?"

"Because you haven't been to the pub in days, Cormac. I asked him to stay, but he said maybe another time. Before he left, he passed along a message for you from Dolly."

"For me?"

"Yeah. It seems she took a liking to you."

He raised a brow—as if he owned the monopoly on boyish good looks and it was high time someone noticed.

"Don't let it go to your head. Dolly made a point to tell Jack there was a key hanging on a hook down here, so it must have been important." She paused a few seconds. "I think it's his way of apologizing for fighting you on this."

"I know it is." Cormac smiled in the dim light and turned the key over in his palm. "An' we'll talk or we won't. But right now, I want to see where this goes."

Excited to solve this little mystery, they tried the key in doors along the corridor, nothing even close to a fit. They flew up the stairs. First to the upper story and down a window-lined hall. Trying doors. Smiling bigger when they failed with each one. And Cormac led her up the next flights, in the tighter spiral to the tower. They paused together, winded and eager, in front of an arched wooden door.

"Well? We've come this far. Try it." She brushed hair out of her face.

Cormac slid the key into the lock, and with a deep breath and a quick look into Laine's eyes, he turned it. Loud and scraping against storied metal, it gave. *Click*.

Hinges creaked as he opened the door. Cormac lowered his hand and paused. "After you."

A tower room opened before them—circular stone walls, a timbered vaulted ceiling rising to a near point at the top. A spear of daylight pierced through the wooden shutters on the room's lone window.

Cormac looked into the darkness. "Another reason electricity would have been good here."

"Yeah, maybe no lights but I guarantee you there's a spider or two. Have you lost your mind? I'm not going in there until you turn on your flashlight—or get out a can of Raid. That's bug spray in the States, in case you Irish boys haven't heard of it. Might be good to have some on hand from now on."

Cormac smiled, in that quiet way he often did when he

appreciated wit. "Good thing we Irish boys have heard o' bravery then." He walked in with his phone flashlight pointing at their feet.

Nothing blocked their path to the back wall. No boxes or lost wares. No furniture to speak of, save for what looked like an overly long desk hidden in the shadows.

"More books." He ran the flashlight beam across some dusty spines lined on the mantel. "And some sort o' leather case." Cormac swept the light above the hearth, to a painting of a woman with a remarkable presence—wearing a blue eighteenth-century gown, if Laine had to guess, cradling a basket of yellow wildflowers, and with the subtle paint strokes of kindness in her eyes—keeping watch over the shadows in the tower.

Laine backed up a half step. Why was the woman hidden in a room so far from everything else in the manor? There was only one other thing taking up space, like she was put here to protect it, if that didn't sound silly even inside her head.

"So, we have another paintin', books, an' a desk. Not bad for a day's work."

"A desk . . ." Laine glanced at the painting on the hearth, then at the desk standing against the opposite wall. She crossed the room and knelt before it, running her fingertips through the veil of dust on the rolltop. And her heart started beating faster.

"Cormac—I need more light."

"Yeah—the window should do it." He unhooked the shutters, pulling them wide, and sunlight flooded in. Streaks of gold illuminated the inlay of flowers detailing the desk's wooden legs, a sharp-cut rectangle body, and a looping inscription buried under dust on the front.

"What's it say?" He drew up to kneel at her side.

"'*To my beloved Maeve, Your Eoin,*'" she whispered, running a fingertip over the words.

"So, looks like we have another desk—a really beautiful one. A gift for a beloved Maeve. I wonder who she was."

"Cormac, this is no desk." Breathless, Laine released a rolltop that wasn't a rolltop at all. The fallboard creaked and she lifted slower, until black-and-white keys—yellowed with age—caught the light. Two perfectly rendered pears were inlaid on either end of the row of ivories, with ornate swirls and loops along the underside of the fallboard.

"Remember when Deborah said they didn't know where the seventh piano was?" Laine breathed out, feeling a little enchanted that what she'd thought was an old desk could hold such a secret.

Cormac ran a hand through his hair and exhaled, smiling wide. "Yeah, Laine."

"I think we just found it."

TWENTY-NINE

April 27, 1916
Merchants Quay
Dublin, Ireland
0715 Hours

Desperation had begun to befall the south side as they neared the River Liffey.

Issy watched as tenements were eaten up by fire and scores of civilians were sent careening from smoke and flames, spilling out to the mercy of turbulent streets. English soldiers had been rumored to have entered the slums on both sides of the river, tunneling through connected walls to gain positions against the rebel strongholds all the way up to North King Street.

Rebellion had never looked so without purpose, and so full of pain.

Sean held Issy's hand, tugging her along by the extension of her good arm. Levi trailed behind, having slung a wounded Rory over his shoulder. They'd moved through Portobello, slept in an abandoned grocer's in Warrenmount, and now were slow but sure in moving closer to the river . . . though it seemed near madness to continue on.

They were dodging soldiers, and luck would have to run out eventually.

"We must stop soon. He's bleedin' again," Levi said, breathless and slowing up, as Rory's feet had begun tripping and dragging like a rag doll behind them.

Sean slowed, tearing fabric from his shirt hem to press to the wound at Rory's collarbone. The action caused Rory to suck in a desperate, grating breath.

"Try putting pressure to it again."

Levi took the wad of fabric. "I can' do this to 'im."

Sean took heed, stopping them up by the side of a stone fence and a courtyard dotted with trees. Issy recognized the medieval façade of St. Audoen's Church standing guard behind, looming up like a silent protector as they took refuge in its shadow.

Rory gritted his teeth over a moan as Levi readjusted him against his shoulder, the wound from his collarbone bleeding tracks over both men's shirts.

Levi looked to his brother, shaking his head. "No more. I know he's the one who said he wanted to go on, but Rory can' now. He'll die if we attempt it."

Sean nodded. "I'll stay with him."

"Not on yer life, Brother."

Issy's heart lurched—the one thing she'd promised Honor was she'd return with Rory. They could not, knowing how serious the situation had become. Without going back and unable to go on, where was the stopping point?

"Perhaps we can go in this church? They'd hide us, wouldn't they?" Issy had asked it, only to have hope fade when she saw the O'Connell brothers exchange looks. "Oh . . . How foolish of me."

"The English are on our heels. 'Tis either a bullet or a court-martial waitin' if they catch us." Levi sighed into the truth, bracing a shoulder to the stone wall as he held Rory up. "Ye have to go to the north side. Two get out or none of us do."

"Ye think we have a chance if we go through Four Courts?" Sean scanned the streets around them.

"The Ha'penny Bridge is overrun. An' there's fierce fightin' 'round the Four Courts, but the ICA should still be tryin' to hold Richmond Bridge. Killian Brent is leadin' a unit out that way. Tell him yer my brother an' have Issy show off her camera. He'll remember her. Said she had a bonny face." Levi shifted his gaze away from her over the unintended remark. "'Tis a risk, but ye might make it if ye try."

The line of Sean's jaw tensed as he calculated the risk of going on versus the pain of leaving two behind. He nodded a moment later, resolute it seemed, but then turned to her. "What do ye want to do?"

Shock must have felt different than what they'd been running through all night as it swept Issy anew the instant he asked her to render the final decision.

"Ye said ye needed to get back to the GPO, to help Honor. I want this to be yer decision too. So we'll go if that's still what ye truly want."

"But you could be killed, Sean—we both could."

"Neither the soldiers nor the rebels will want to direct fire at a man of the cloth. The sun's comin' up sure. There'll be enough light for them to see the collar an' leave us be. So it's go on or stay behind. Either way, I'll honor yer choice."

Something told her the selection of words held a deeper meaning than running across a bridge. Was she content to trust him—with everything, as the world fell to ash on all sides—or would she stay behind, where love was safe and risk was far less severe?

Death could be sure in either place, but her heart could be content in only one.

Sean stared back in her eyes, the blue bright despite the clinging of early morning shadows around them. Waiting. Painfully patient, as was his way whenever something concerned the inner workings of her heart.

"You'll be okay?" she asked Rory, wishing there was any other way.

"It's like that nick in your arm—a mere nuisance to a rebel," Rory bit out, pain draining him back against the stone wall. "Tell Honor I'll just be a few steps behind you."

Issy gripped her brother's hand, squeezing tight. "And Mother and Father? What shall I tell them?"

"That I'm sorry," he whispered. "And I hope to heaven Gard comes home."

Tears trailing down her face, she nodded.

"We're all coming home. I promised Honor that. You'll be but a few steps behind us."

Rory smiled at the vow—the Byrne constitution refusing to yield. She dotted a light kiss to his cheek for it.

Issy nodded to Sean, putting on a brave face, though instinct warned her it could be the last time she'd see Rory alive. She refused to believe it.

"We go." She sealed their fate.

"Take this?" Levi held out a pistol. "I know ye won't use it, but I'd feel better if ye had it for looks just the same."

"I held one on a man once already."

"But ye didn't even fire it, Sean. There's a difference. We both know who pulled the trigger on Corley."

"'Tis enough bloodshed for a lifetime." Sean sighed. "Give me a moment, an' I'll see if ye can have sanctuary inside here. They may open doors to a vicar. Prayer an' God willin' a physician are inside . . . Should be good for somethin' before I leave ye here, yeah?"

Issy would have bid Sean to take the weapon even to walk up to the church doors, seeing as he'd be out of sight. But she scolded herself inside because they each knew the measure of the man before them. Not a one could have asked him to be less than who God had made him to be.

It was clear he'd never pick up a pistol again.

"One minute. Then we make our run." Sean squeezed her hand. "Together."

They watched him slip around the stone fence to the courtyard beyond.

The rain had stopped long ago. And something was on fire close by—ash and soot tinged the air with a choking haze of it. Issy lowered her face, covering Rory's exposed side with her jacket so he wouldn't have to breathe it in.

"I'm sorry, Issy," Levi whispered into the cool morning air, through the distant booms of artillery fire echoing across the skies.

She looked up, still shielding Rory's face as best she could. "What?"

"'Tis wretched timin', but I owe ye that. I should not have said I loved ye when I didn'. An' then left ye—not like that. I was selfish, an' brash . . . an' hurt ye because of it. An' all the while Sean loved ye more than life. That means somethin'. If we're taught anythin' after all this madness, it should be to fight for the deepest convictions we hold. He's prepared to do that for ye in a way I never could."

For the daring and the dashing, the smiles Issy had always thought she so wanted from Levi O'Connell, she realized that his simple "I'm sorry" meant more. It confirmed what she'd hoped, that Sean still might return the affections he'd once professed—the same she could no longer deny.

"An' for what happened at the bridge. It changes things, yeah? I'd pulled many triggers on soldiers while at the Green. I never saw one fall though—not right in front o' me."

"We're all changed now. And you couldn't have stopped it, Levi. No one could. We tried. And I'll forever be in your debt for saving our lives."

Issy looked back, pain stabbing in the pit of her stomach when she thought of those moments on the bridge, when it seemed as though none of them would walk away.

"Don' tell him I said so." Levi surrendered a deep smile as Sean trotted around the corner of the fence again. "But he's always been the better O'Connell, an' he'll see ye out o' this. Rory an' I will hold back fire on the bridge so ye can get across, if it's the last thing we do."

Sean ran up to them, winded but safe. "They'll hold ye. Can' promise that the soldiers won' interfere at some point, but 'tis a chance anyway to hide inside."

"A chance we'll take. Gratefully." Levi gripped his brother's hand tight. "After we see ye duck an' take that bridge."

Issy couldn't look back . . . Not as fires blazed their world to ash . . . Not as bullets chased them . . . Not as they left Rory and Levi behind.

Sean covered her with the shield of his back as they ping-ponged from street corners to barricades, racing over the stretch of bridge. The ICA had endured heavy losses as soldiers advanced in a bloody push, but Killian Brent and the dwindling ranks of rebels still held the Four Courts—for the moment, at least—and let them through.

All the while, the Kodak remained stowed in Issy's jacket.

Even as Sean led her north and they came upon the disaster of Sackville Street. Even as Clerys department store was engulfed in flames so intense, the heat melted the glass windows like water crying down scorched walls. Even as bodies of men in ICA uniforms and English soldiers mingled together in the streets.

Issy watched, horrified, as the block surrounding Jack Foley's was eaten up by walls of roaring flames. The camera lens remained closed as they were hurried into the back doors of the GPO.

No photos. No memories.

She never again wanted to see the scene of Dublin's fiery death.

APRIL 28, 1916
10/11 SACKVILLE STREET LOWER
DUBLIN, IRELAND
0100 HOURS

Desks shook and plaster fell from the ceiling as artillery fire continued pounding the GPO's exterior walls. A pungent mix of fire and cordite clung to the air. Voices chattered down the first-floor hall, unintelligible but frenzied, though few remained in the offices.

"I don' think it can hold much longer." Sean looked up as they huddled on the floor in a back office. "Appears we may be runnin' again."

"The *Irish Times* building is completely gone, as is Clerys and the Imperial Hotel. Winnie said everyone is evacuating to Moore Street by noon. Troops are advancing too quickly up Henry Street, so Pearse wants all out in the event fire spreads this far."

"We got in, an' everybody now wants out."

"Do you? Connolly took a bullet to the ankle—it's injured him too badly to be moved and Winnie's refused to leave him. I imagine she'll stay on as long as Pearse does, so I suppose we go when they do. Or with the waves of people evacuating at first light?"

Issy paused. Thinking. Fear turning knots in her stomach as artillery blasts cut the streets in two on all sides.

"Do you think if we try to go, the soldiers will come for us . . . after what happened on the bridge?"

"Couldn' say. But a dead officer means an explanation is goin' to be demanded by someone. They'll come, I suspect, if they catch up to yer brother an' mine. But I'll tell the truth, whatever the outcome."

Pictures rattled then, the walls trembling in groans at their backs. Sean slipped an arm around her as another series of blasts pierced the darkness, holding tight until the worst passed by.

"Who would have known this could be worse than the streets around St. Audoen's? Or that Honor would have fled back across Sackville, battling the fire around Jack Foley's, and we couldn't even cross the tramlines to go help her?"

"I trust God to watch over us. Honor an' our brothers too." Sean's voice was strong in the darkness. "Especially now that it looks as though Dublin will fall."

"The leader of all this, who hasn't fired a single bullet himself, won't relent even as the walls burn down around us. But I can't be surprised. That's what Winnie said the first day I was here. That Pearse and the rest of the leaders knew it was a battle they couldn't hope to win but went through with it anyway. What do you suppose that means, when a man feels something so deeply that he's willing to risk anything—including innocent lives—for his chance to attain it?"

"I suppose in the case of freedom, the chance just to taste it would be enough for some."

"Is that Pearse then? Do you think him an uncaring bloodthirst of a man, as long as he might get what he wanted in the end? Or is there compassion buried somewhere for the people dying in the streets? I can't make sense of it."

"I don' believe war is ever that black an' white. An' I don' believe he wanted anyone to die. 'Tis a great divide between bein' prepared to die yerself an' watchin' someone else have the same taken from them without choice. But he's still here, isn't he? Even as he's ordered everyone else to begin evacuations. That says somethin'. What other truth can we know right now?"

Issy pushed back thoughts of the cruel twists of fate surrounding them and eased into the crook of Sean's shoulder, resting her head upon it. He braced his arms around her as they sat, quiet for long moments, listening to the cadence of war outside.

"Levi said you love me still." Issy held her breath when he tensed against her. "Is that true?"

"As ye said, some convictions die hard," he said, the admission heavy in the darkness.

Issy turned, looking up. His face was so close she could feel his breath against her lips. She reached a hand up to his chin, a surprised smile overtaking her when she felt the prickle of an unshaven jaw against her palm. "Where is that straight razor I loaned you?"

He stared back, allowing her the liberty. Waiting. Still holding back. "'Tis in my pocket."

"Well, you should use it sometime."

"Like ye did? Who's yer barber anyway?" Sean flicked a wisp of chopped hair out of her face and smiled too—a beautiful, pain-wracked smile that said even if time was short, he'd not shy away from the truth.

Not anymore.

"I've loved ye always, Issy-Girl," he whispered, slow and steady. "Yer my conviction."

The many weeks that had slipped by since that day at the castle had seemed such a waste before. But in that moment, no more words were left to say. No apologies or explanations to hear from either side. Just the drumming of Issy's heartbeat as her best friend crossed the breath's distance between them and swept his lips over hers. They held on, clinging, safe, abiding with one another as the world rained fire outside.

"Vicar?"

Issy jumped back as a nurse appeared at the door.

"I'm sorry, Vicar. But there's a Volunteer in back—he's askin' for a priest but all evacuated before nightfall." She turned her eyes away, having broken the moment. "He won' last the hour, an' he's needin' prayer."

Sean pressed a kiss to Issy's brow, then gave a pointed look. "Stay down?"

She nodded.

"I'll be back." He rose and hurried down the hall to the back offices where rebels still bled.

Issy closed her eyes, ghosting fingers over the place where Sean's lips had been. Smiling inside. Praying they lived—that fate would not be so cruel to have brought them together now, only to rip them apart again.

The sound of a rustle in an office drew her attention across the hall. Curious, she looked up, for so few were left in the recesses of the battered building.

A man struck a match and lit a lantern wick, placing a glass hurricane over the flame. He pulled out a chair and slowly, as if weary and worn, fell into it. The glow illuminated his features: a clean-shaven face. Strong brow. Passion still flickering in the eyes. His shirt collar lay undone and the tie dangled around his neck, the weight of Ireland resting squarely upon his shoulders.

Pádraig Pearse hunched his shoulders over the desk, a book open before him.

Issy's breath escaped, for she recognized it—the book she'd left from the first day at the GPO: the Bible she'd tucked into her own pack. Since running a dispatch and watching Dublin crumble to pieces around them, she'd completely forgotten it had been left there.

He must have found it. And as if he'd listened to the conversation she'd had with Sean but moments before, the rebel leader fell into the war-tangled trench between conviction and sacrifice, hope and despair, like she'd never seen set upon another soul.

Was it wrong to watch such a private battle? Should she turn her eyes from a man in anguish, with fingers laced in such fervent prayer that his knuckles knotted white and his brow burrowed upon them?

Whatever was happening, Issy couldn't judge. She'd worry about film and story and justice later. In that moment a still, small voice whispered to her heart, giving her freedom to record the moment as it was, in three whispered words:

"Tell the truth."

She pulled up to her knees, reaching for her Kodak on the desk. Issy pulled the lens out. Silently turning. Adjusting. Sharpening the anguish until it was as real and raw as the man sitting at the desk. And before their world shook again, she eased her thumb over the shutter . . .

Click.

Another photo.

Another moment history would never see again.

THIRTY

June 22, 1798
Ashford Manor
County Wicklow, Ireland

The sound of boots thundering up the stairs startled Maeve from sleep.

By the time their chamber door opened and shut, she'd sat up in bed.

They hadn't slept well for weeks, what with soldiers engaging in skirmishes along the road to Dublin and chasing rebels back into the mountains. And with the horrifying rumors of loyalists meeting a gristly end by mobs with pikes and torches, all estates were on edge. When they could manage a few precious hours for sleep, it was seized upon, with the understanding that they might wake at a moment's notice.

Eoin charged in and moved in haste about the room, putting things in his pockets. He was already dressed in shirt and trousers but pulled on a waistcoat.

Maeve immediately glanced at the window. It was barely dawn by the looks of the light beyond the shutters. "Eoin? What is it?"

He stole away to the wardrobe, pulled out her leather pierrot and a round gown of wine linen, and tossed both upon the coverlet. "Dress quickly, love." He retrieved a pistol from the top bureau drawer and checked it for load. "I've already saddled Éire. We must go."

Maeve obeyed, knowing not to question him when he made a request of such an urgent nature. Relying on his judgment could be a matter of life and death, so she decided to forgo stays for the ease of haste, and stepped into her dress directly over her chemise.

Eoin paused at the window, easing the shutter open enough to watch through a thin line against the glass. His jaw was sharp and eyes focused, as if he could see a threat walking across the glen.

That kind of silent vigilance quickened her hands. "What is it?"

"Tenant farms burned beyond the crossroads—all the cottages gone past the east field border. An' the village."

"Attacked?" Maeve fumbled with the hooks at the front of her bodice as she quickened her pace, somehow not expecting him to say that.

"The rebel force was defeated at Vinegar Hill just yesterday—a last stand for the United Irishmen, it seems. It took time for dispatch to get north from Enniscorthy, but by then it was too late. Appears the whole of Wexford was surrounded, 'tis said by English numberin' in the thousands."

"*Judas* . . . And one would have thought they weren't fighting a war with France just now, to have so many men brought to the island to put a rebellion down."

"'Tis not goin' to stop there, I'm afraid. It was rumored villagers in Wicklow were harborin' rebels from the stand at Wexford, they who were retreatin' to join up with Holt in the mountains. The village was set upon in reprisal."

"How many killed? Please say none of the children were harmed." She buttoned the pierrot just halfway before moving on. She held her breath, waiting for dread to follow.

"Can't say. But scores of Irish are felled by musket an' artillery fire. Grain stores torched an' villagers trampled under soldiers' boots. 'Tis said cottages are still burnin'. By the time we get there, they may well be burnt to the ground. But we can go to save as many as we can, an' sanctuary off the main road—at Wicklow Chapel."

She pulled stockings on and boots, her heart sinking. Their lovely little chapel with the view of the sea . . . Only weeks before it had played host to their wedding and had harbored hope for a peaceful future. Now the anguished would fill its walls while Wicklow burned around them.

Maeve rose from the side of the bed, knowing what the news would mean to Eoin. She crossed the room to where he still stood. His gaze was transfixed, rendering him lost on some distant point beyond the glass so he didn't even notice her until she placed a tentative hand upon his arm. "Eoin?"

He stirred. Turned his gaze down to her.

All that Maeve had imagined might exist in his memory stared back in one tortured look. She didn't understand it, save that pain and loss must have replayed so fervently in his mind. He gazed at her with eyes intense and a brow furrowed in a dangerous manner. That look was dark and deadly—so unlike the man she'd come to know in all these months together at the estate. Whatever his intentions, something had stoked the passion of his hatred for the English and she feared, without an ability to ease it.

"Eoin . . . What is it?"

He started, then stopped. Swallowed emotion and started again. "I love ye. I need ye to know that. I didn' marry ye fer any other reason. Yer why I stayed, from the first night."

"No one could make you do something you did not set your mind upon, my love. That I know with assurance." She swept her arms around him, holding on. "I was tumbling into oblivion before I found you in that field. So when you said you saved me that night, it was true. You made me believe that the land of Castle

Chryn—and Ireland itself—will not bleed for naught. And it will not bleed forever. I have hope that we will one day forge peace in this place."

Eoin's gaze was marked by tenderness in a flash, but it seemed only for her. He was kind but just. Strong but, in many ways, reckless. And all of it seemed to show upon his face in that moment he bestowed her with one of those hard-won smiles she'd first longed to receive from him.

"I'm but sorry we couldn't stay in this tower as ye wished. Seems our world is determined to war with itself no matter what we do."

"I care not for a tower—I care for you. So if we must go to Belfast or flee to South Wicklow when this is over, then I'll go. I know it tortures you to think of your people in harm's way, so we will go to our friends and tenants this day. We will renew the New Year's promise that you and I made to them. Does that ease your heart at all?"

He nodded, but with a shade of vulnerability in his eyes that said, *"Not again."*

Not women and children. No more death to the innocent. It was as if anger radiated from every nerve in his body—righteous anger over death that carried no recompense after. Cottages had already been burnt to the ground and lives shattered for weeks since the fighting began, until the soil had turned blood red on all points around the estate grounds.

Now the battle had come for them.

Maeve pressed her palms to Eoin's jaw, looking him full in the face. She kissed him—a soft, willful moment of solidarity that said whatever would befall them, they would be together.

She drew back and took in a steadying breath. "And what of Ashford? Please tell me the truth. Will rebels come here to fell the loyalist masters?"

"Jack Foley ran the dispatch north from Wexford—'tis Cian

who took it at the crossroads. The English believe there are no rebels on this estate. An' as the rebel armies know I've wed the mistress at Ashford, we haven't anythin' to fear concernin' destruction upon this house. Cian will stay on here with his lordship an' hold the manor while we go to the tenants."

Maeve crossed the room, tore open the drawer in the bedside table, and slipped her dagger and sheath down into her riding boot. She stood tall before him, hands fixed on her hips. "Then I am ready. We show them The O'Byrne—two now, instead of one—will follow the conviction to save lives instead of taking them."

Maeve held the reins and Eoin kept a pistol drawn at his side as they followed the great plumes of black billowing into the sky.

It was safer to go on one horse, so he'd pulled her up crossways in front of him, holding Maeve's back so close, his cocked hat bumped the side of her head as Éire took them down the road to the village.

They passed former cottages reduced to shells of stone and ash, with smoke still rising against the rain. The hills no longer boasted great ridges of green or wildflower beds of yellow and violet. Now the earth was churned in violent trails, where wheel ruts from wagons and artillery cut the rocky ridges as though they'd been readied for some odd kind of planting. They rode around carcasses of sheep strewn in the road . . . Passed overturned wagons . . . Traversed the fields past barns, trees, and even rock walls—all scorched and crumbling by the path cut by a wave of advancing soldiers, thousands thick.

Though the wind blew and rain cried from the sky, smoke lingered in a haze as they neared the village row.

"Keep an eye for uniforms," Eoin whispered at her ear.

While Maeve couldn't look back at him, the rigid feel of his chest behind and arm around her waist said his was a soldier's caution. He was silent as they neared the rise that led to the village, the pistol balanced on his thigh as if itching to be used.

The rise opened to carnage.

The earthy smell of fire eating wood and the stifling haze of smoke thickened the air.

The grain stores were gone, just as Eoin had said. Building after building lay exposed. The milliner shops and pubs burned down to their foundations. Cobblestone streets were littered with grain and lost wares—buckets, ladders, rakes—as if the people had tried to defy the burning and pillaging with mere workmen's tools.

And then . . . bodies.

Through the smoke emerged bodies of men and women alike, facedown and crumpled in the mud. Their clothes were marked with blood and soot, the hues dulled by the rain.

"Don't look," he whispered against her ear. "Keep yer eyes set out ahead."

Eoin may have wished to shield her from it, but the sight wasn't what had shocked Maeve the most. It was the fact that besides a ghost horse sweeping over a distant rise without rider, and a flock of guinea hens that had survived the raid, not a living creature stirred in the once-vibrant village square.

It was as if an entire town was just . . . gone.

They swept through, chasing wheel ruts in the landscape, dodging abandoned bodies and wheel-broken artillery left behind, until they reached the bend in the road that carved along the coast. And there, tucked in the hollow between sky and cliff and sea, was their little chapel—standing firm, no smoke rising.

The only firelight that glowed was from candlelight illuminating stained-glass windows.

No uniforms were about. No armies encamped that Maeve

could see, yet there was also no sign of villagers who may have taken up sanctuary either. The lack of horses or wagons parked outside seemed an oddity if the chapel was full of sheltering townsfolk.

Maeve eased up on the reins, slowing Éire to a walk.

A thin fog toyed with the path, drifting in and out, as if playing its own game. They moved through it, entering carved-iron cemetery gates. The summer grasses were high and the trees weighted by rain, forming a soft canopy over their heads. Blue-gray-capped chaffinch flew about the trees, chirping in the mist. Gravestones dotted the landscape on both sides—some crude lumps of stone, others elaborate with angel wings or the effigy of Christ carved at the top.

All else was silent but the rain and the birds and the gentle *clip-clop* of Éire's hooves—as if the landscape itself was holding its breath.

She swallowed hard, finding the greeting ominous rather than encouraging. "Perhaps we should go back."

"'Tis all right. We're almost there." Eoin ducked with her as they moved under a low branch.

When they rode up to the side door, he leapt down, then reached for her.

Maeve slid out of the saddle with his hands bracing her waist, boots hitting the ground. Eoin paused to look down on her—not wasting time but not letting go either. She took it as a mark of solidarity that he squeezed her waist and pressed a quick kiss to her lips. "Stay behind me."

She nodded and Eoin raised his pistol, taking large strides but moving as one cautioned. They proceeded to the side door that opened to the chapel sanctuary—heavy oak, rounded on top, and hinged in thick iron.

Eoin gripped the door handle, pushing at the wrist.

Relief washed over Maeve as the door gave easily and opened wide. The sight of villagers came into focus in the dim light.

Brigid hovered in a nearby pew, daughters at her side. There, too, was young Jack Foley, soot-covered and hair caked with mud but unscathed. As face after face came into view, Maeve's heart lightened to see so many of the village children alive and unharmed—she hadn't allowed herself to hope they'd been so fortunate as to have survived the brutal raid in the village.

Maeve swept in, running to the children, then kneeling before them to pat their faces and kiss little hands. She hugged Brigid and the girls, reassuring all that they would be looked after until Brennan returned. They would rebuild every cottage on the estate. And Eoin would see that the grain stores were built back up. They'd restore and redeem all that had been lost. And for those who had sacrificed a loved one, none would be sequestered to an unmarked grave.

These promises she made, from person to person, until a flash of red caught her eye. And then another, sweeping behind rows of soiled linen shirts and caps. Her breathing quickened when the distinct reflection of metal turned from one bayonet into many, and the aisles surrounding pews were flooded with English uniforms.

And rifles.

And there was nothing they could do to stop it.

A pit formed in her stomach and Maeve began backing up, then turned to the spot where she'd left Eoin. He remained fixed in the doorway, daylight illuminating a halo around him.

"What is this?"

Eoin's eyes said he was sorry. Why, she didn't understand.

"I hereby surrender." He reached out, turned his pistol butt forward, and handed it to an officer who'd swept up the aisle. The villagers remained silent—save for the fearful whimpering of little ones and muffled cries from women in the back of the chapel.

"Eoin?" she whispered, fear flogging her from the inside out.

The unmistakable metal-on-metal *clink* echoed loud as the officer held out irons, and a soldier affixed the weight of iron shackles at his wrists.

"No . . . Please." Maeve's cries overtook her as soldiers surrounded Eoin, bayonets escorting him back outside.

In a moment of sheer terror when she thought they'd been left without ally, horses approached. Relief flooded her as she saw her brother dismount at the cemetery gates—a champion who would speak for them.

Maeve fled down the path, meeting him. "Cian? You are magistrate," she cried, gripping his forearm, glancing from him to the soldiers. "Please tell them! Eoin never took up arms. I'd swear it. He refused to fight. He's only here to care for the tenants."

"That is not the only reason he's here. This man was seen organizing the delivery of arms at the cove of Castle Chryn. And he was named as a conspirator for a foiled attack of Ashford Manor on Christmas Eve. It is for these crimes against the Crown—and for involvement in the Hoche affair—that The O'Byrne is now under arrest."

Maeve lifted her palm from him, as if his touch might burn her skin. She turned back to the villagers, who'd spilled half from the church onto the cobblestone path leading to it.

"No man here would dare speak against the one who has saved them ruin. Let him stand and be known," she accused, blasting the officer. "What witness accuses this man?"

The officer flitted a glance to Cian, then back to her. "Master Cian Ashford, milady." He tipped his head, odd civility for the war he'd just made upon an entire village. "The accused will be transferred to Provost Prison to await trial. You may inquire after his fate there. Good day, milady."

Anguish swept over Maeve as she realized what had happened.

Those last moments in the tower room . . . the tortured look and the embrace . . . Her husband wasn't reliving past pain. He'd known what was coming and was saying good-bye.

Soldiers hovered with bayonets at the ready. She walked to Eoin, then stopped before him—wishing she could rebuke him for being so frightfully honorable. But the words wouldn't come. Only tears.

"Do ye remember what I told ye, that day we stood in the tower together?"

Their conversation before he'd showed her the pears . . . His words of encouragement flooded her heart.

She nodded. "I remember."

"Then ye know what task is put upon yer shoulders. The estate is yers. Show them yer their mistress. Ye can do it."

Maeve leaned up on her toes, whispered a few precious words in his ear before pressing a kiss to his lips . . . and let him go.

Eoin stared back for the first few steps and she nodded, standing alone, helpless and broken, but willing herself to show him none of it. Her world turned in slow motion as the soldiers marched him back through the cemetery gates, to a circle of soldiers on horseback who would escort him away.

The bayonets and redcoat owners disappeared over the rise, and she was left with the flutter of wings in the trees, the gentle cadence of rain hitting headstones . . . and rage.

Blood boiled through Maeve's veins, emboldening her as she turned to face her brother. "Have you no honor at all? How could you do it?"

"I did nothing, Sister. It was his decision."

He was matter-of-fact. Cold. As unfeeling as Mrs. Finnegan had warned her.

A man's life was at stake and he'd treated it as a business transaction. Why hadn't she seen it before?

"The O'Byrne was the price the English demanded to save these people . . . to save *you*. I put it to him when the dispatch came through. He could walk away and save his life, or surrender it for all of yours. Submission was the only upright thing that piece of filth has ever done. Now get on your horse, dear sister, and we shall return home—where I will relay none of this blackness to our father. And from there, we will return to England and forget this godforsaken island exists."

Maeve turned, finding the eyes of the villagers upon them.

They watched in silence along the garden path, though she thought she read as much defiance in their eyes. Young Jack Foley had stepped forward, as if ready to spring.

"And what about them?" She turned back to Cian.

"They shall receive what is owed to them."

And that, she hadn't far to guess, would involve the locking of doors and burning of a chapel to the ground had he his way.

"If you knew who Eoin was, why did you force a marriage between us? You certainly did not care after my reputation."

"George was gunned down like a dog in the road. Mother contracted a deadly fever sickness from this filthy breed. Fire was set upon the estate. And still, thus did not convince you—nor Father—of the vile nature of this land."

Dread sank in. "You did this?"

"Don't sound as if any great crime has been undertaken. Our former stablemaster was only to create a gentle concern on Christmas night—a campfire or two. Just enough to encourage Father to get on a boat to England for good. But Ó Flannagáin deviated with his aims for a grand rebellion, indeed setting fires on the estate but only to fell witnesses of his original intentions. It was when I received your letter that I returned straightaway, had Ó Flannagáin arrested, and learned that a true insurrectionist had infiltrated my father's home. I knew then if The O'Byrne were to marry you, he would not leave. Not before I could negotiate the terms of his surrender in exchange for our loyalty to the king."

"I might wonder if our former stablemaster confirmed his plan to see your sister and father put in a grave Christmas night as well?"

"That is of no consequence now."

"How is it not?"

"As he was hanged for treason against the Crown. But enough of this insolence. You are safe, and we are finally bid to leave this island to rot."

Cian paused, staring down his hawk nose, an arrogance permeating the very air between them. He slithered a hand around her wrist in a none-too-subtle attempt to pull her into submission. "Do not challenge me, Maeve. Mount your horse—*now*."

Ripping her wrist from him caused Maeve to lose her balance, sending her to the ground on her backside. Cian reached for her with furious hands, pulling her by the arms. The miscalculation cost him dear, as she unsheathed the dagger from her boot and sliced the air, cutting a wide gash through the robin's egg silk of his sleeve.

"You may return to England as you please, dear brother. But I bid you never to set foot upon Ashford land again." She held the dagger in defiance as she climbed to standing again. "Or I shall finish what the rebels started, one cut at a time."

"Have you gone completely mad?" he blasted, fingers squeezing sliced flesh. "You would actually defend these . . . these *Irish*? Mother would weep to see how far you've fallen!"

"I take solace in the fact that any fall of mine shall never be as far as yours on this day. I am Irish. I am an O'Byrne. And here I will remain."

Maeve stood firm, breaths rocking in and out as she watched Cian stare back in disbelief. Even as he mounted his horse, bleeding through his coat, and swept off on the road to the sea, she refused to move, wanting the last thing he saw to be an O'Byrne standing in defiance before him.

Jack approached, stopping at her side, tucking a pistol in his belt. She looked to him, a profile of one young but exceeding in strength beyond his years.

"Come, milady." He offered his arm. "'Tis our promise to The O'Byrne that we'd see ye safely home."

Maeve sheathed the dagger in her boot and climbed up into Éire's saddle. But this journey they'd take slowly, one step at a time all the way to the castle ruins, for an entire village followed behind.

THIRTY-ONE

PRESENT DAY
ASHFORD MANOR
COUNTY WICKLOW, IRELAND

"This is a special piece, Cormac."

"How special, would ye say?" He ran a hand over the back of his neck, like disbelief was gripping in a good way.

"Well, it's not a modern piano by any stretch." She stroked the keyboard. "There would be eighty-eight keys, right?"

Cormac nodded. "Right."

"And this row is much smaller. Meaning, older. I really think this is a pianoforte—made before modern pianos." Laine leaned back, lowered her hands. "That'd put it, I don't know . . . late 1700s maybe? And between the inlay, the woodwork, and the custom engraving on the front, I'd say it's a good possibility this should be in a museum, instead of a tower in an old manor by the sea."

"An' with all that, what would it sound like if we played it?" he teased.

"Play it? I don't want to touch it. Not until we get a professional out here. This might be worth the whole manor." Laine moved around to the side, still kneeling, following her gaze along the length of the inlay and blowing dust off the wood. She leaned back, bracing her hands at her hips while she thought things through.

"We've been all over this manor. None of the rooms had intentionality like this one does. There's no storage or broken furniture. Just a few carefully placed items. And the pianoforte isn't even pulled out from the wall to slip a dust cover over it when it's near priceless. Why?"

"We've got a row of books. Big surprise wit' this place," Cormac said from behind, running his finger along the line of spines. He pulled one out, looked in the front cover. "George Ashford. I suppose we'll have to find out who he was."

Laine stood and joined him across the room. "Looks like a Bible on the end. More German poetry. Novels. But these are older, Cormac. I don't know what to make of this—the painting either. I think I need to call my father. We might be in over our heads a little here."

He reached over her shoulder and exchanged the book for a leather case on the mantel. "An' what's this?"

"Early Kodak, I'd bet. These cameras aren't really worth a whole lot, but they are a novelty. Kind of fun. You see them a lot in antique stores in America, that's for sure."

He put it back, then drifted back to the pianoforte. "So we have an old camera—not really worth much. Another stack of books we can add to the crate in the library. A rather remarkable painting, an' Miss Dolly's lost pianoforte . . . That should be in a museum. Right. That makes all kind o' sense."

"Well, how do we know this was lost? She told Jack about the key."

"Why all the secrecy then? Miss Dolly can't have wanted to hoard a piece of art up in a tower, keepin' it to herself for decades. For what? Just to have it?"

"Well, Mr. O'Brien certainly didn't know about it, and he's come to Ashford to tune the Steinway for years. Maybe Dolly didn't want to let something go, so she just held on in secret. Could be simple as that."

Cormac looked her in the eyes, softening his tone. "I could believe somethin' like that is true. Wonder what we might need to let go."

A lot. Too much? Why can't I tell you what I want?

Laine eased backward a step, bumping the pianoforte against the stone. She yelped when something crashed down to the hardwood and slammed her eyes closed for a split second. She did *not* just break something priceless off the antique. "I'm so sorry . . ."

"'Tis alright." Cormac stooped down. "I don' think it was the piano. But looks like somethin' was wedged in behind it an' ye just bumped it free."

A stone wrapped in yellowed linen lay in the middle of the floor beneath the pianoforte's carved legs, next to an envelope that had spilled a line of postcards from its insides in a haphazard fan against the hardwood. The images were sepia—so old it was difficult to make out what they were.

Cormac reached for them and sat back on the floor. Laine scooted on the floor next to him, looking over his shoulder. One image showed men carrying what looked like thick pipes across a street. Another, a man standing before a crowd, reading from an unfurled paper in his hands. They wore early twentieth-century clothing—ladies in hats and Gibson-girl hairstyles and men in uniforms, carrying rifles. The next, a strange image of a broken-down store, with hats and shredded fabric and some kind of furniture barricade in a street.

Cormac flipped through the small stack, and she felt his shoulder muscles tense at an image of a man seated at a desk, his head bent over an open book. "Laine . . . I don't know if we should be touching these either," he breathed out, holding the images in his open palms to avoid fingermarking the edges of the exposure. "If these are what they look like, I, uh . . . I think we need to make that call to yer father. Today, if ye don' mind."

"Okay." She nodded.

"We might need some help, sooner rather than later. An', uh, no word o' this outside o' Deborah. Not just yet. Let's keep this between us, yeah?"

It was the oddest yet most beautiful moment Laine could have imagined. The two of them sitting on the floor in a dusty tower room, barely breathing as they spread old photos on the floor around them. Never guessing that the reclusive Dolly Byrne had hidden treasures that meant more than a manor did to one family.

If the find was what they thought, it belonged to Ireland.

Cormac reached out and took her hand. That soft and simple. Quiet. And private, the poignant moment shared just between them, even when his fingertips trembled a shade.

"That can't be Pearse, leader of the 1916 Rising, can it?"

"Ye know yer Irish history."

"I read enough to recognize this. And Ellie and I toured the GPO, you know. History nerd that I am. Maybe these are commemorative postcards or something to mark the centennial?"

"They're not machine printed though."

"No. I agree. They're not."

"Laine, I think these two at least could be from inside the GPO itself. An' this one? I've seen the doctored photos of surrender, cuttin' out Elizabeth O'Farrell—ye learn about that in school here. But this is from a position on the other side, where ye can really see her face. If these are authentic . . . they might be some o' the only photographs o' Pearse from inside the Rising itself. I mean, the only photographs the world might ever have o' him in this way. It's a little . . . overwhelmin', I gotta admit. I'm tryin' to breathe over here."

Laine squeezed his hand before letting go to turn her attention to the linen and rock piled on the floor. "And what about the other thing? It's a rock . . . No, a brick. Is there something in it?"

Cormac leaned down, eye to eye with an oblong round of melted metal lodged in the center. “I think it’s a bullet.” He took a deep breath and rocked back on his heels. “Good Lord, Laine. What on earth have ye found?”

THIRTY-TWO

April 29, 1916
Moore Street
Dublin, Ireland
1530 Hours

Dublin held its collective breath.

Sean and Issy stood behind an iron garden gate, awaiting confirmation of the rumor that had filtered up from the leaders' temporary haven at 16 Moore Street: Pádraig Pearse's unconditional surrender was to follow shortly.

With English soldiers barricading corners along the smoldering remains of Sackville, a garrison of some three hundred rebels strong had been forced to flee the GPO under cover of night, with leader Michael O'Rahilly carving a diversionary charge into the cobblestoned nightmare of Moore Street. Rebels and citizens alike were felled under a hail of machine gun fire, their bodies left in full view through the night. Brick buildings pushed up against the retreat on both sides, leaving no choice but for the rebels to tunnel through the interior walls of terraced homes lining the route.

Sean and Issy had found respite through the steady assault, huddling under a porch in a walled garden, finding potatoes and green onions in a nearby grocer's to fill their aching stomachs that morning. And it was past midday when the last haze of smoke began to fade into clear skies and the rebels watched in disbelief as nurse Elizabeth O'Farrell marched the length of Moore Street under cover of a white flag.

Now it was said she'd return, braving the walk again, and deliver Pádraig Pearse himself to General Lowe and his garrison of English troops swarming the corner of Parnell Street.

"Keep watchin' down in the direction of Plunkett's Poultry Shop. He'll step out there if he's goin' to at all." Sean stood just behind her shoulder.

"Winnie is still inside with Connolly, but there's a group in the home next door that whispers it's true—the leaders are negotiating a surrender. Evidently Pearse watched as three aged citizens were gunned down in the madness last night. They fell dead at his feet and he hasn't recovered. It's as if that made the decision for him, that no more of Ireland's innocents will die for this."

"An' we must pray then that no death will come wit' a surrender either. That it will all stop right here."

Issy gripped her camera, holding it down in front of her torso, fixing the lens for a sharp image through the sunlight. Rebels watched and waited. A slight breeze twirled a crumpled piece of paper along the sidewalk, its edge seared black.

"Look, Issy. There." A sigh escaped Sean's lips as he pointed down Moore Street. "Pádraig Pearse. What do ye know—he really does have a sword."

Issy would have smiled, remembering Sean's mocking about Pearse's cane that night at the Abbey Theatre. But nothing could lighten such a sober moment as the president of the Provisional Government of the Irish Republic stepped out on the sidewalk. With Elizabeth O'Farrell at his side, they walked with confident steps, Pearse in full military hat and coat, brandishing the sword at his side.

It occurred quickly on the corner, the handing over of Pearse's sword, pistol, and ammunition into the waiting hands of General Lowe.

Click.

Issy breathed deep, emotions spent as she'd eased her thumb over the shutter. Then in knowing what must come next.

The camera had become a beloved friend by then—a truth teller of their last several days—and she couldn't bear to part with it. Even so, Issy slid the mechanism into place with careful hands and placed the Kodak back into the safety of the leather case.

She ran her fingertips over it as Pearse was led away and dismay descended upon the crowd of rebels lining the street. Soldiers marched down the sidewalks and rebels raised hands in the air—their abandoned dream laid bare on the bloodstained sidewalk.

"Here." She turned away from the action on the street to face Sean. "Take it."

"What?"

"The English will move quickly. They'll arrest anyone in the vicinity. And before you argue that they wouldn't dare take a woman, know that they will if she's been seen running a dispatch for the rebels and took a sniper's bullet to the arm. I'll try, but I can't hope to explain away all of that. As a member of clergy, they're more likely to let you go free. With you, this camera has a chance at survival. With me—none."

"I'm not leavin'! Yer mad if ye think I'd do that now."

"But you must. You know as well as I that they'd never allow me to keep it. Whatever it has seen will be destroyed the moment they get their hands on it. And that I couldn't allow." Issy pressed the seal-leather case, now scarred and battle worn, into his hands. She covered his fingertips with her palms and squeezed. "Go. Take it and hide it away—you know where. In my favorite place other than the castle ruins. I'll find it."

"Issy . . . I can'. Please don' ask it of me."

"You once said I could ask anything of you—remember?" Issy whispered, leaning up to whisper an "I love you" against his lips. "You're my conviction too. And I'll see you after. I promise."

Soldiers invaded the terrace, nearly tearing the gate from its hinges as they swarmed the garden. She winced as soldiers yanked her arm, staring back in the vicar's eyes, willing him to stand down as handcuffs shackled her wrists and to guard the treasure under his clerical coat.

Never had a sunny afternoon felt so cold as Issy was forced to march with the group of rebels out to the remains of Sackville Street, leaving everything in her world behind.

May 8, 1916
Kilmainham Gaol
Dublin, Ireland

Dawn sketched a crosshatch design through the window of Issy's cell on another day death woke her.

For three days the executioners' guns had gone silent, and she'd hoped it was over. But the deafening crack jolted her awake again and she'd flown to the window, seeing the same prison wall that blocked her view of the Stonebreakers Yard. Even with the reams of sunlight, the soiled linen shirt and herringbone wool trousers she'd worn since her arrest ten days earlier offered little warmth against the damp air. She paced to stir what heat she could—arms drawn in at the waist she marched in her cell, from one brick wall a few steps to the other.

The metal-on-metal *clink* of an unlocking bolt roused her.

In haste she turned to the cell door as the hinges creaked. Her heart thundered as the door swung open, sunlight from the corridor flooding inside. In the threshold stood a figure dressed in black. She had to blink—twice—to realize it was not an apparition of death come to claim her, but the very real person of Sean O'Connell who'd stepped in.

He paused just inside the door, whispering an inaudible something to a soldier posted on the edge of the shadows. Whatever passed between them, the guard acquiesced, bolting the door to leave them a precious few moments alone.

"Lady Isolde Byrne." He gave a priestly bow of the head. "I've come to see to yer spiritual needs."

Leave it to Sean to hold formalities at a time like that.

Even with brown hair mussed like he'd run his hand through it and his eyes reading as if he hadn't slept in days, Issy chastened herself not to find a world of comfort in his presence. But she failed, throwing herself into the haven of his arms.

"Don't you dare presume to 'Lady Isolde' me ever again," Issy whispered and held on, gripping the lifeline of his shoulders, even with pain in her arm still lingering. "Just know, I'd give anything to kiss you right now for not leaving me alone in here."

"*Shhh* . . . We must watch what we say, Issy." Though Sean's voice hitched as he whispered against her ear, he seemed as relieved as she was to be standing in the cell.

Sean eased back and scanned the space in a slow, earnest survey. There wasn't much to see but brick wall and dingy brick wall. Cot with a musty, sagging pallet. And a barred window that allowed in more cold than light. Issy's cheeks burned when Sean's gaze fell and then lingered over the crudeness of a sanitation bucket in the corner. He turned back, restoring her dignity in the pretense that he hadn't seen it—though they both knew he had.

"'Tis no better than a rain-sodden trench in the Green. I'd hoped for better, seein' as they're keepin' women on here. Ye an' that blasted camera are in a right fix."

"We've all been in a fix since Easter, Sean."

"I know . . . but I was meanin' *you*, Issy."

"A fix? Is that what we've taken to calling prison these days? How civilized. It sounds so much better the way you men of the cloth put it, like I'm simply away on holiday." Humor and wit, she wagered they'd keep her sane if anything could. "But is that why you've come, to tell me I'm in a spot of trouble?"

"That much I knew. But I'm doin' my best to see about gettin' ye out."

Issy tucked a loose wave of hair behind her ear, pushing away thoughts of what she must look like with a boyish cut clipped at the chin, gunpowder under her fingernails, and bloodstained clothes. She melted down to the cot and nudged over a shade, giving him room beside her. Sean sat, understanding what she meant without her saying a word. He reached for her hand and held it, out of the eyeshot of prying guards.

"The guns this morning, Sean. Dare I ask who it was?"

"Éamonn Ceannt, Seán Heuston, Con Colbert." Sean stared at the stones in the floor. "An' Michael."

"Mallin?"

He nodded. Once, on an apologetic close of his eyes.

"I wish we could stop this now. It's too terrible for words. To think of everyone who's lost someone dear . . ." Issy couldn't finish the thought.

"I know what yer thinkin'. 'Tis alright. They're alive. Saw Levi yesterday." Sean leaned in, the faint shadow of understanding manifest in his whisper. He could always read her that easily, enough to guess what she was thinking.

Alive. That was enough for the moment, to check one name off their list of worries. She straightened up, her spine poker still. "And my brother?"

"Housed in the gymnasium at Richmond Barracks, wit' most

o' the others. Rory's still fightin' the gunshot wound, but he'll mend."

She exhaled, a grateful breath. "Does Honor know?"

"That her fiancé is languishin' in a makeshift English prison? She does, God bless her. But the soldiers won' arrest a woman bein' wit' child. Right now she's a humble Irish citizen helpin' her family rebuild the block 'round their pub. She'll not draw any notice outside o' that."

"And what of Francis Skeffington? When innocent journalists are gunned down in cold blood or the lives of bricklayers are threatened for the cover-up, that's of note."

"Aye, but the English have arrested thousands of Sinn Féiners—even the rumored ones. No matter that most had nothin' to do wit' this blackness. Scores o' women in the lot wit' ye, though the English won't claim barbarism enough to actually send one to the guns. I'd wager ye Winnie an' Countess Markievicz pose an interestin' problem for 'em. Quite the group, ye titled ladies."

Sean tried to force a smile in reference to Issy's pedigree, but his brow tightened, the shadows of his face taking a grim turn.

"Public opinion hasn't stopped Blackader from holdin' his court-martials. Not even allowin' a defense for the accused before sentences are carried out." He shook his head, like it was all a waste—a shame what atrocities men could inflict on one another. "The Crown wants this all put down so they can get back to the task at hand."

"A task is it then, this Great War? What does it matter whether men bleed in a trench in France or right outside these walls? I see no difference."

"'Tis over for Ireland. At least now. Pearse is dead. Plunkett. MacDonagh an' Clarke too. An' no matter how bad he's busted up, Connolly isn't likely to escape the guns. Under guard at Dublin Castle, but 'tis rumored he's next. Every man who signed the Proclamation penned it in blood, an' the Crown's come to collect payment."

Issy exhaled, the wind socked right out of her gut. "I'd heard the news in here, but I could scarcely believe it until now."

"'Tis rumored Pearse whistled when they led him out o' his cell. Like he knew it would end this way from the start an' still went through with it all, just as ye said."

Issy neither confirmed nor denied his comment owned a grain of truth. She didn't tell Sean what she'd witnessed from inside the GPO that night . . . what her camera lens had recorded of the enigmatic rebel leader the last night before they'd been forced to abandon the rebel post.

"And my camera?"

"Put up safe, just as ye asked."

"Then I thank you for coming here. The news is wretched, but it's far better than the not knowing at all. At least this way I can breathe again."

"'Tis not the only reason I'm here." Sean didn't return any warmth in the sentiment, and that wasn't like him at all. "Rory an' Levi are set for court-martial today."

"Court-martial?" Issy searched his face for a denial.

Sorrow etched his brow without a trace of hiding. If they were sentenced and transferred to Kilmainham Gaol, it meant execution. Or further transfer for hard time in a Welsh penal colony, which could be as deadly of a sentence in the end. Either way, they'd lose them.

"A witness has come forward claimin' he saw one of 'em pull the trigger on an officer—Corley. Neither's givin' the other up, so it doesn' matter they weren't signees o' the Proclamation. Unless we can come up with a witness to state the opposite—which they won' do, bein' soldiers—they'll be found guilty."

"This is because of what we saw, isn't it? The night Skeffington was killed. The English want to silence any witnesses."

Sean tossed a quick glance over his shoulder, inspecting the closed door as he dropped his voice even lower. "I can' talk about that now. But I'll be allowed to pray wit' them before the trial. So if ye want me to tell them anythin' . . ." He swallowed hard with eyes fixed on hers. "Anythin' at all, I swear I'll do it for ye."

A thousand words died on her tongue.

Silence cut the cell in two, amplifying the *drip-drop* of water bleeding down from the ceiling in the corner.

"I don't know what to say, Sean. For Honor to lose Rory now, when he could have had his revenge but chose not to? And Levi saved us all on that bridge. This can't be the end, can it?"

"I pray not. I said if I could help ye, I'd do anythin'. Looks like 'tis time to test that vow." He hooked his index finger under a wisp of hair that had freed itself at her temple, finding a place of remembrance between them. He was slow and intentional in brushing her hair back, like he'd done so tenderly once, in the beauty of an empty sanctuary.

The door clanged again, the sound of unlocking bolts jarring them out of the innocence of the past.

"Vicar?" the guard barked. "A word."

Sean stood, the void he'd left next to her cold as death. And she'd not said good-bye. Not properly. Not the way she needed to, if this was the last time . . .

"No, wait—" Issy cried out, unable to let him go.

"Hold on to this." He offered a Bible she hadn't realized he'd brought, the beauty of worn black leather extended to her. How he'd rescued it from the GPO she hadn't a clue. "I'll be back. I promise."

The contrast of gunpowder that still darkened the underside of her nails seemed so foul against the Book. But she took it in hand. Carefully. Humbly. As if it were made of something so pure that not even the tarnish of her hands could manage to soil its beauty.

Issy watched sunlight swallow Sean back into the corridor, and darkness fell again as her cell door clanged shut. The sound of bootfalls echoed in the hall . . . and she was alone again.

She gripped the Bible in her palms: paper and ink and cracked leather her lifeline. With hands shaking, gut lurching, untapped courage bubbling its way to the surface, she ran her fingertips over the pages.

One was marked with a slight rise of paper wedged close to the binding. Issy split the Bible at it and found the tender reminder that she wasn't alone. Folded inside a scrap of paper, Sean had tucked in a lock of cinnamon hair she hadn't even known he'd saved and two words penned in Gaelic: *Tá súil.*

Hope.

The unlocking of bolts jarred her from her tears.

Sean reemerged in the open cell door, standing in the space where sunlight pierced shadow.

"It seems God smiles upon ye, Issy-Girl. Yer free to go," he said, his smile victorious. "I'm to stay on at Kilmainham, if we want to be doin' anythin' about helpin' our brothers when they get here."

"But how?"

"Seems a witness has come forward, ready to tell the truth."

THIRTY-THREE

August 4, 1798
Ashford Manor
County Wicklow, Ireland

It was a crisp morning, with mist that clung to the hills and hollows, though morning sun was fast burning it off in the fields.

Maeve looked up from her planting as a rider approached.

Stilling the spade in the ground, she stood, dusting soil from her hands. It wasn't seemly for an estate mistress to be about with dirt smudges on her face and hair mussed as the wind pulled waves from her kerchief, but she supposed it would have to matter not. Maeve was estate steward, and she supposed she'd be the one to plow into the earth when the occasion called for it.

She held her palm up to her brow, squinting through the sunshine as Jack Foley slowed before her.

"What say you?" Bracing hands at her hips, she stood to the side so he might see the plant rows beyond the rock wall. "Have we made progress then?"

Maeve offered a smile for the young man, grateful that their estate had such a devoted groom. He'd been an incredible help in the last many weeks since Eoin's arrest.

"In no doubt, milady."

"And has my father sent you upon another mission to persuade me against cultivating pears on this property? Because if that is the case, I'd admonish him to cease meddling. We shall have our own pears grown in Ashford soil before he knows it."

"'Tis not on account of his lordship that I've come."

"Oh?" She sensed his apprehension.

Her heart best faster in reply.

"Is there another reason?" Maeve left the tools in the earth and walked around to a gate-break in the fence, meeting him at the side of the road. Jack slipped out of the saddle and took off his tricorne, holding it and the reins loose in his hand as he walked to her side. He stopped to retrieve a sealed missive from the inside pocket of his waistcoat and held it out to her.

The front was inked with *Maeve* in looping script.

"From Provost Prison, milady."

No . . . Not Provost.

The last she'd been privy, Eoin was to be tried for treason. They'd been waiting for a missive with the trial date each day since. She dreaded the wait but judged that must have been it. They'd go to Dublin, and there they would fight for his freedom.

"Aye. 'Tis yer response from The O'Byrne. He said on account of what ye last told him at Wicklow Chapel that day."

Taking it in a shaking hand, she nodded. Maeve lifted a fingernail under the wax seal and broke it. She unfolded the missive, reading:

> If a boy . . . name him George.
>
> Always—my love,
>
> Eoin

Maeve whirled around. Pain punished her for feeling so deeply, stinging her eyes so she could scarcely breathe.

"He bid me to put this into yer hand, milady . . . after. Said I wasn't to allow ye to come. No matter what, I was to keep ye from Dublin. 'Twas his express wish, he said, as not to cause ye distress in the watchin'."

"The watching of what?" she cried out, the pain more than she could bear. "Of what, Mr. Foley?"

Maeve covered her mouth with a trembling hand and nodded as if she understood, though her heart didn't. Couldn't. She stumbled to the stone wall, catching it as she slid her knees down into the tilled earth beneath her feet.

Jack was at her side in an instant, all thumbs as he tried to hold her steady.

She'd been denying the facing of it for weeks. Her husband had been tried and executed . . . and she felt her life had ended too. Eoin would have a son or daughter in the spring. And for the life of her, she couldn't fathom their child growing up without its father there to see even one day of it.

"When?" she sobbed.

"The gavel came down yesterday. An' then the other . . .'Twas at dawn, milady."

"Were you there?"

He nodded, and the dearest action of tears glazing his eyes meant he shared the pain, because he, too, cared for such an honorable man.

The familiarity of the rock wall drew Maeve back to the precious row of seedlings—their dream together forged by his own hands—that she'd been planting along the road. She stood, walked to it, the field welcoming her with a measure of peace she hadn't expected.

Covered in late-summer gorse so bright it shone as though the ridge to the castle had been fashioned upon hills of gold mixed with God's green. In the land was not death. It was life and beauty and something that had the power to outlast all of them.

She folded the letter with careful hands, tucked it in the inside pocket of her gown, then brushed a palm to her growing middle as she tried to calm her breathing.

"Mr. Foley, I wonder if I might ask a favor of you." Maeve turned, wiping away tears with the back of her palm.

His face softened. "A favor, milady? Anythin'."

"His lordship and I find that we have need of a head gardener at the estate. Mr. O'Malley shall be shouldering many of my duties in the months ahead. But I know Mr. O'Byrne would be most aggrieved were his wife to fall into her hardheaded ways and insist upon planting pear trees the length of the road of her own volition. So if you are agreeable, sir, to work alongside a Protestant mistress, I believe I could use some help to keep a promise I made to my husband."

"Of course. It'd be an honor, milady." The hint of a smile spread across his face. "A great honor." He tied up his horse and came alongside. Maeve handed him a shovel leaning against the rock wall.

"Somethin' I believe, milady, is that the Foleys an' the O'Byrnes will always be friends. As long as there's this land to care after, our kin will pledge to work alongside its mistress."

From winter's tears covering the field, to the sight of gorse and summer sun now painting the hills golden, Maeve wanted to feel every moment they'd lived in that place. She took her mattock, tilling it into the earth from the rise where she and Eoin had first met, and thanked God that death had no victory—not if the faithful lived, and lived well.

"Come then, Jack. We have much work to do to see about making peace grow."

March 27, 1799
Ashford Manor
County Wicklow, Ireland

The sea lay still far out on the horizon but fought the cliffs, smashing into the cove with foam and waves just as it always had. The wind billowed Maeve's skirt about her legs and whipped her hair about her shoulders as she looked out from the rise.

There was talk the Irish parliament would be abolished as reprisal for the attempted rebellion. But even if they were to be ruled directly from London, Maeve still believed the estate would live on.

She thought of it every time she rode past the cottage at the crossroads. Or visited Eoin's grave at Wicklow Chapel. Maeve watched as smoke curled from the chimneys of newly built cottages dotting the Ashford land. Sheep grazed beyond the rock-wall borders of the castle ruins. And they'd have seasons to go before they could hope for a worthy yield of pears, but she could wait.

Peace was worth the patience.

One day Ireland would be free, and that was worth the wait too. And though she may not see it, Maeve knew the expanse of the sea, and the land, and the crumbling castle ruins would.

"Maeve? What has you all the way out here?"

She turned, the kindly voice of a concerned father welcome behind her.

"Papa," she acknowledged him when he stopped at her side, looking out over the same view as she. "There is much to be done and I fear there are not enough hours in the day to accomplish all that I've set my mind to."

Lord Chryn studied her for a breath, then nodded.

His shirtsleeves billowed in the sea wind, the linen fighting to come unrolled from his wrists. His undone waistcoat and the contentment upon his face said he'd been at work too. At work, and restored to high spirits because of it.

"We have much to do, I agree. But for now, young Foley is seeing to the horses." He pulled a timepiece from his vest and popped the gold cover to check the face beyond. "And it is past a proper dinnertime for all of us."

"Who said we should desire to be the least bit proper?"

"Certainly not you, my dear. But I believe you are wanted back at the manor. Young master is fussing about, and Mrs. Finnegan bid me to fetch the 'pirate's wife' back to see to her maternal duties . . . or some such grouse." He broke into a laugh at their housekeeper's antics.

How Eoin must have smiled at that.

"I'll return just now." Maeve smiled too, lifting her skirt over the field grass. "The last thing I should want to do is to cause a mutiny amongst our most devoted staff. Or miss a moment of telling Eoin George how much a part of both his mama and papa he is—lateness aside."

Lord Chryn of Ashford Manor took her elbow, the way he used to do when a father would lead his daughter into a room—as if pride and affection and forgiveness had never been in question.

They passed the stables in a slow climb up the rise, as shadows began to fall.

"Do you mind terribly that Cian will not return to us?" She watched for concern and truth in his profile. "You must feel troubled that your only son remains so far away."

"England was Cian's choice. And Ireland ours. I do not regret staying here with your mother and George. But it is for the living—who, I must say, I am particularly proud to escort across her land—that I wish to remain. Our very land set upon with fire, not from Anglo-Irish tensions, but from greed and prejudice of my own son. It was you and Mr. O'Byrne who showed me that. And if you'll forgive a foolish old man, I'd pledge to defend your land for the remainder of my days."

"My land, you say?" She laughed. "I thought of it as family land, but never mine alone. Cian is heir apparent. We both know that. I'm content to work it but not need it in name."

"I like the old Irish way of inheritance—it goes to he or she deemed worthy. Peerage laws are muddled between England and those whose titles originated on these shores, especially those with condition in the original patent. It may be rare, but I'll fight to ensure this land and title goes to my grandson, by way of his mama."

"And if Cian goes to parliament to fight that?"

"Then he shall lose." He paused, shaking his head against ill tidings. "A delivery arrived today."

The abrupt shift in conversation slowed her steps. "Oh? No pears lost upon the ocean, I trust."

"No, Daughter. We'll have our own pears in but a few seasons. And those we can wait for."

"Then what is it?"

"A pianoforte . . ." He turned to her as she slowed to a stop.

"A pianoforte—for whom?"

"A wedding gift, it said in the missive."

"Oh . . ." She breathed out, emotion catching her with eyes that glazed in a flash. "Eoin said he'd purchased something. I'd forgotten all about it."

"It was addressed simply to 'The O'Byrne' of County Wicklow. The villagers brought it to our door. Because this is how they've known you. And now, it is who you are. I believed once that The O'Byrne would take over this estate, and I still believe that is true, because *she* has."

Maeve looked from him to the span of leaded glass at the far end of the manor, the music room that had once been so alive but had lost its music since George's death. Eoin had known it, and he wanted her to hear music once again.

"I think for now, it should go in the music room. And for each O'Byrne and Ashford bloodline born to this house, if they so choose, we shall buy another. Until we're so full of music . . . ," she whispered, loving the way the glow of candlelight through the music room windows cut the fall of darkness, setting the castle ruins with a slight shimmer under the twilight sky, "that we must utilize space in the tower. Not because we're hiding away from peace and joy in this place, but because we've no room left to hold all of it that we possess."

THIRTY-FOUR

PRESENT DAY
ASHFORD MANOR
COUNTY WICKLOW, IRELAND

Slate-and-blue ash painted the sky in stormy sweeps of color that blurred the horizon line where sky met sea. Ellie sat atop one of the fallen stones on the castle rise, her back to Laine, lost in the view.

Laine walked up and slipped a quilt around her friend's shoulders. Ellie stirred, turning with a hand to catch her rain jacket hood against the wind.

"Hi." Laine held out a thermos to Ellie. "Coffee. Want?"

"You know I do. Sit." Ellie edged over, giving them side-by-side views and Laine half of the patchwork quilt. "Quinn wouldn't like me being out in this weather, but he's helping finish up inside. Making last-minute notes for the curators on the miracle find."

Laine poured a cup, then handed it to her.

"It's hard to believe so much has happened—will happen, really. If the photos are authenticated, I imagine it will be some kind of media circus when word leaks out to the international press. We found Dolly's family history tucked in front of the Bible from the tower room, along with newspaper articles about the *Irish Times*' first female photojournalist—an Issy O'Connell of Ashford Manor. Cormac might not like the spotlight, but I'd say after all that, he'd better get used to it."

"And at least he and Quinn have something in common to work toward. Lainey, that's all I wanted for my husband—a bridge between them. The rest will come in time, but at least it's a start."

And for Cormac too. He deserves peace in all this.

They sat sipping. Listening. Looking. Sometimes friendship was as simple as a thermos of French-press coffee and the sea stretched before them. It was just . . . silence. And *time*—as long as it took to nestle the moment into their hearts.

In these quiet moments, time became the most valuable thing they shared.

"I need to go home, Laine." Ellie looked down, twirling coffee in her cup.

"I thought you might say that. I know all this has delayed it. And Christmas will be here before we know it." She tossed Ellie a smile that said, *"I can still read your thoughts."* "I saw the packed suitcases in the loft. So, you leave for France soon?"

"Nope." Ellie shook her head, still staring out over the sea. "I mean *home*."

"Oh. All the way home . . . to Michigan."

"I'm going to need more treatment that Quinn thinks would be better to receive in the States. And to be honest, I want to see Grandma Vi's cottage again. It's been too long. I think my memories will bring me comfort, to be where I know I've been loved. So Quinn and I agreed—Christmas we spend in France with his family. Then we start our new year back at home. My first home."

"But you're not abandoning the dreams of restoring The Sleeping Beauty?"

"Are you kidding? Never. That castle's in my blood. Quinn's too—even if he pretends to hate it, I know he's as committed to bringing it back to life as I am. But there's something about dreams that don't need castle ruins or fairy-tale endings to make life beautiful. We can still have the happy while we stand up to the sad."

Ellie wrapped a finger around the knotted end of the wine-colored pin-dot scarf covering her crown, holding it down from the wind's playfulness. It was her favorite—the first gift Quinn had given her, the one Laine never saw her without. "Right now my dream is Quinn strumming his guitar in my chemo room until I fall asleep. It's the way he can make me laugh when all I want to do is cry. And stop fighting because this is so hard. And Quinn wanting to hold my hand through it all. And telling me I'm beautiful when I know surgery scars and chemo-sick are not the least bit cute.

"I'm learning that's marriage. At least it's the kind of marriage I want. And I know I once said that our fairy tale is on hold for a while, but I don't think that's true now. *This* is the fairy tale. We're living it."

"Fairy tales were never really about a perfect end to a story. It's the day-by-day living it that counts. I like that scenario better anyway. At least it's real."

Ellie turned, with the deepest of sighs her friend had ever doled out, and stared back with glassy eyes. "Something like that. And I wanted to tell you . . . That's why I know you're going to be okay too."

"Okay with going home?"

"No, Laine. I mean *you*. And Cassie. You're both going to be okay."

Laine looked down for a moment, staring into her palms. "How long have you known?"

"I called your mom a few months back, when you stopped posting on social media and texts kept getting shorter, and the time between them longer." Ellie leaned into her side. "I was worried. Mother hen kind of stuff, you know."

"And classic for my mother. She has one daughter incarcerated and is fast working on covering up the failed marriage of the other. I shudder to think what she has to say at the country club."

"Try not to be hard on her. I dragged it out of her. And funny enough, I don't think she was aiming for the moral high ground on this one. She said if you showed up in France, to tell you she was sorry to have been the one who spilled."

"Oh, Ellie. I'm just sorry I didn't say something sooner. But you had your whole world going on in France, and then with losing Grandma Vi, I didn't want to cast a dark cloud over your wedding. And then everything after . . . You didn't need to shoulder my problems too."

"It's okay. I understand. I didn't tell you about my cancer right away, did I? Sometimes the truth just feels farther away the less we talk about it. And for the record, I think you should know Cormac barely made it through the wedding before he'd stopped his new sister-in-law to ask about the blonde stunner across the chapel." She winked. "My words, not his."

"What?"

Ellie's laugh faded and she squirmed at Laine's side. She finally turned and made eye contact. "Oh. Right. I guess I just assumed you and he were . . ."

"You mean Cormac knew? But you said you told him I was married."

"*Was* married. And all I said was I told him about Evan—that's leaving it open to interpretation."

"Interpretation? That's my life you're talking about." Laine stood, feeling a pit forming in her stomach. "I can't believe it. All this time . . ."

The memory of the night in the estate house kitchen after the wedding . . . On their walk through Dublin's streets that first night . . . When Cassie had awoken in the loft and he'd made grilled cheese sandwiches at two a.m. . . . And when he accepted her little girl's hand on the front steps of Ashford Manor . . . And in the salon—before they ever got to the church.

Cormac knew. *Everything.*

For the life of her, Laine could think of only one thing to do. "Do you think Quinn's ready to go?"

Ellie shifted alongside her. "Probably. Why?"

"Because I need a ride back to the pub. Now."

"Which snug?" Laine nearly took the bell off the top of the pub's front door she slammed it so hard.

About to sign for a package, Cormac looked up from the bar, the deliveryman also taking notice as she stormed in. Both stared back in unison, along with the gathering of locals along the pub's stool-lined bar. Brows lifted, and a few chuckles were barely restrained behind curious smiles.

She stood before Cormac, uncaring if they thought her a fool or not. She'd stare him down as long as necessary.

"Laine." Cormac clicked the pen with his thumb. "I thought you were stayin' out at Ashford today."

"I said which snug, Cormac Foley? Men's or ladies'—because we're going in one. You choose. And think carefully, because the girls at the bar over there might have to breathe in a paper bag if you go in their sacred closet."

Cormac scrawled a quick signature to the clipboard in his hand and ducked under the amused stare of the deliveryman as he hurried his way around the bar. "So ye need to talk, yeah?"

Laine kept a firm connection with those Foley greens, barely blinking, daring him to question how serious she was.

"Right. Yer mad. Uh . . . We should talk then." He looked nervous. Sounded nervous. And if Laine wasn't so lit, she might have been too. "The men's will do fine."

Laine cut her glare to the row of sweater vests, daring any one of them to squeak a word of protest. They gripped pint glasses in steady hands. One took a gulping drink, like a popcorn eater at a movie premiere. The rest—properly intrigued and terrified in equal measure—stared back while they waited for whatever was poised to happen next.

The gent leading the pack nodded, lifting his glass. "As ye like, miss."

"After you." Cormac cleared his throat and held an arm out, fast-ushering her to the snug at the end of the bar with a hand at the small of her back. "We'll just be a moment, chaps." He eased the door closed behind them.

"I don' know what's happened to kick-start yer temper, but . . ."

Laine had never fist-grabbed a man's shirt in her life. She'd seen it in the movies a hundred times—no idea how they made it look real. But the instant Cormac turned around, her decision was made. Buttons, seam, and all—she twisted them in her hand, pulled him down, and slammed her mouth to his.

No words. No talk. No explanation—Laine just wanted his arms around her with her back pressed up against the piano, and a moment of Irish snug-snogging that was long overdue. She held him there, happy to drown inside walls of polished wood and glass, with every bit of a world outside those four tiny walls duly forgotten.

And oh, did Irish boys know how to kiss.

Cormac kept his arms around her but drew back, enough so they wouldn't bump foreheads in the confined space. "So . . . what yer sayin' is . . . ye really didn' want to talk." He took a solid two breaths to catch up. "Yer not mad, actually. Is this you, not mad?"

"This is me." She smiled, a little brashness having fast melted with the heat of that kiss. "Officially not mad."

"Right. Good." Cormac nodded into the line they'd just crossed. He smiled back. Offered a tip of the brow and another brush of his lips to hers. "Ye may not be Irish, but ye've got the temper to match.

I think ye just impressed the whole o' the dinin' room out there, an' that's sayin' somethin'."

"You knew? Even before I told you at the church?"

Cormac eased back from the breathlessness of the moment, still holding her but only just, hands lingering at her waist. "Yeah. I did." He looked at her with a brow furrowed into the truth. "Didn' last until the receivin' line before I cornered Ellie. I think I remembered to say 'Congratulations' to the bride in there somewhere, but I had to ask who in the world ye were."

"You've known since the wedding and you didn't say anything? And Ellie, too, so I'd have to assume Quinn does. Here I was thinking I'd kept this big secret and everyone already knew."

"I'm sorry. Ellie believed so strongly that it was yer story to tell an' yer decision who ye'd let in. It wasn' meant to be a secret unless ye wanted it to be. An' believe me—that day in the salon? I thought it might kill me if I didn' say somethin' soon. But then ye told me on yer own, an' I knew that was hard for ye. An' then all o' this happened so fast, from markets an' piano shops to findin' Dolly's lost treasure. I couldn' think straight."

The thought of Cormac at the wedding, hiding awkwardness behind a confident smile and a sleek suit . . . or struggling in an old piano alcove because he only wanted to have honesty between them—it shouldn't have warmed her so much. But it did. In a way Laine hadn't expected or sought. And in a way that made standing inches away from him in a crowded little Irish snug suddenly feel like she'd found home somehow.

She didn't dare hope beyond this moment.

"When Cassie reached for your hand at the castle ruins that day . . . and when you looked at me across that salon . . . I thought it couldn't be true that you might see us that way. Because I thought no one else knew what had happened. That Evan left us. Left *me*. That he didn't want a child who wasn't his own. Even if we could make her ours in home and name—he didn't want us in heart. It might be wrong, but I felt ashamed because I'd failed so badly."

He pressed in closer, eyes locked on hers. "This was not yer failure."

"But it felt like it. It *feels* like it is."

"Ellie told me that night after the weddin' how you gave up everything to adopt Cassie. Ye lost yer job to take her to doctor's appointments. Lost yer home. Even yer marriage when it came to it. She just wanted to give ye space to heal, an' to trust again in yer own time. God knows I wanted to do the same. From the first night ye walked through the kitchen in those socks, I was a goner."

Laine shook her head, failing to hold tears at bay. She used her palms to swipe at a drop that had drifted from her bottom lashes. "I'm a mess, Cormac."

"We're all a mess. 'Tis no secret. It's just that some of us are better at hidin' it."

"I thought I was hiding it."

"But I don' want ye to. Don' ye think I've been a mess out there in that pub, grindin' through the kitchen by day an' the books at night, wit' nothin' to care about anymore? I'll always honor my da. My brother an' sister. An' our ma's memory. But that's why the castle means so much—an' the days I spent there wit' ye an' Cass somethin' I'll never forget. Ye woke me up, Laine, when all I'd been doin' was sleepin' through life."

"Putting one foot in front of the other is all I can manage right now."

"An' if I can manage that wit' ye? I know my own mind. What if I'm standin' here in front o' ye, tellin' ye I won't leave?"

"I'm still figuring this out with a daughter who's healing too—and we might always be. But I won't let her down. She's the best of me. You couldn't mean you're willing to take on all of that."

"Do ye hear what yer sayin'? Laine—may God make me so

lucky a man." He swept his fingers over the wave of hair that had fallen over her brow. "Some people don' leave."

"And some do."

Both of his hands, palms gentle, touch soft, claimed either side of her face, renewing everything her heart had once buried. "Yes, but not . . . *me*."

THIRTY-FIVE

May 9, 1916
Castle Chryn
County Wicklow, Ireland

Issy leaned into the ruins of the windowsill at Castle Chryn, holding a hand to the cropped hair at her nape as she looked out over the Irish Sea.

Even a day before, she'd stood in a cell at Kilmainham Gaol, wondering whether she'd ever see her beloved ruins again. It was strange to be back as so much had changed in so short a time, standing where ancient stones drew an outline against the early morning sky and the sea crashed the rocks in as vast and blue and heart-stirring a manner as she remembered.

"I thought I'd find ye here."

Issy turned, breath arrested to see Sean standing there—whole and alive and just as free as she—smiling in the sunshine. She bounded from the window the few steps over grass and patches of wild aiteann flowers, until she was safe in his arms.

"So it's true? They let me go, and Levi and Rory too, all because of you?"

Emotion seemed to pause his reply. He held on as fiercely as she did, standing as the sea wind drifted around them.

"They let ye go because of *you*, Issy."

She leaned back, knowing it was nothing she'd done for the soldiers to allow him back in her cell and, without ceremony, to push them out of Kilmainham Gaol.

"I don't understand. Who was the witness?"

"I have a gift for ye." Sean pulled an envelope from the inside pocket of his jacket.

Issy took it in hand—a single envelope no bigger than a postcard, date-stamped and tied in the familiar twine she was used to receiving from a camera studio.

"However did you manage it, with so many shops damaged?"

"Ah, had to go into Wexford to find one that could develop the film on a moment's notice. Smart, my girl, to know it could save us from this messy affair."

The photos from the heart of the rebellion were there, real and untouched, and in her hands.

She swept through the postcard-size memories . . . From the start, of the day the GPO was taken. Of Pearse reading the Proclamation. From Clerys on Sackville Street, to Grafton, to trenches in the Green. And the poignant image of Pearse that last night at the GPO, and the fateful surrender, as he stood alongside nurse Elizabeth O'Farrell and handed over his sword, pistol, and ammunition.

And the last . . . a shot of castle ruins and sea and sky.

"I never told you how to work it, but you still took the last shot."

"I've seen ye do it a hundred times. An' I needed one last photo to finish out the roll. What better than to capture yer favorite place in hopes I could save a memory ye might have missed?"

Realizing all were not accounted for—perhaps the most important ones of the ten were missing. Her heart beat faster. Did those photos not come out?

"There are three missing?"

"Aye. The three the English wouldn' let me keep. They didn' know about the rest o' course, an' I'd have never turned them over anyway. Ye secured yer own release when ye snapped photos o' Skeffy's arrest at Portobello Bridge, o' the executions at the barracks, an' as Lieutenant Corley held what he believed were unarmed bricklayers at gunpoint."

"But . . . how did you know? I didn't tell anyone I took the photos."

"Issy, I know yer mind as well as yer heart by now. An' I felt that lens turnin' when I put my arm around ye on Portobello Bridge. I knew even if Corley's bullet hit me, ye'd still have proof in a photo that might save ye in the end. I was bettin' on it, an' I was right."

"You and your bets." She smiled, thinking how well he knew her. "I'd speak to you about that particular vice had it not saved us this time. Yet with all of the talk of convictions, you were forced to break the one most important to you. I never thought I'd live to see the day when you'd hold a pistol to another man."

"Well, 'tis not really takin' up arms if it wasn't loaded."

"Not loaded . . ." Issy shook her head, disbelieving at first that any man could be so brave as to challenge an officer with an unloaded gun. But then, after everything, could she question that such a man existed save for Sean?

"I was able to smuggle my camera in with the tools because they were none the wiser to a small leather case tucked in a wheelbarrow. But how on earth did Levi end up with a pistol to fire back on Corley?"

"No one thought to search the vicar at the barracks gate."

"You gave it to Levi as we fled away, but you didn't give Rory one?"

He shook his head. "No. I couldn' allow him to kill Corley. Self-defense is one thing—cold-blooded murder is another. I don' make excuses for what my brother did, but he saved us, he an' Rory both, for jumpin' across to take that bullet to himself."

"What about the soldiers on the bridge that day? You said

someone accused either Rory or Levi of murder, but neither would give each other up."

"One o' the soldiers was killed at Four Courts sometime after we went through. An' the other . . . He backed down when presented wit' the photos. Couldn't say anythin' sure but that Corley shot first an' a bullet got him after. Without clear evidence to conflict with yer photos, the court marshal was forced to conclude that it could have been a sniper that felled the lieutenant."

"And they let Rory and Levi go as a result."

"That, an' on account o' the string of executions at Kilmainham lit a fury among the Irish people. The Crown had no choice but to begin openin' cell doors all over Dublin. So Levi an' Rory are free wit' ye. I'm just sorry we've had a more tragic end than anyone bargained, an' an independent Ireland seems that further away."

"I wonder if we're freer here than we realize." Issy looked around them, gazing out over the Irish Sea and the span of stones that had stood for generations.

"I admit I misjudged Rory. He'd planned to take Corley down, but not by shootin' him. I'm proud he used his wits that day instead o' his gun. We didn't even know he'd taken the bricks wit' the bullet evidence, hopin' to use that instead. I still don' know how he managed holdin' on to 'em when he could scarcely walk. But one, I'll keep. An' when the time is right an' the story is known, I'll make sure 'tis sent back to Skeffy's widow wit' a full account o' what happened. She's owed the truth for the sacrifice o' her husband."

"And the other?"

"I propose we hold it back—save it until a day such that Ireland is free an' the world is ready for the truth. Rory will be around to marry Honor an' run Foley's pub with her family. The extra brick has everythin' to do wit' that."

"They've already come to see you to set a date then?"

He laughed—a bright, beautiful, oh-so-familiar laugh that Issy felt at home just in hearing it again.

"The instant Rory walked free." He reached down, betting that her heart would still accept it if he laced fingers with hers. "Isn't it curious that nearly the whole o' Sackville Street burnt to the ground, save for the front room o' a pub an' its near-ancient snugs, where generations o' marriages have been brokered an' life stories told. They talked about *Aisling* if they have a daughter, because it means 'dream' in Gaelic. Maybe 'tis what all this is for . . . a dream Ireland can cling to."

On a whim Issy turned, inspiration capturing her with an idea. She pressed up against his chest, holding the photos between them, fanning them like a deck of cards.

"Let's put these away. The brick too. Let's hold them back, as you say, until Ireland is ready. They can find a haven here at Ashford, under careful watch of the castle ruins. After the war and Gard comes home. My parents' anger will cool toward Rory—and me—now that they know it's over. We're safe. And who knows? Maybe I'll push my way into the *Irish Times* building like I did at the GPO and tell them they need to hire me. I'll be a working woman with real experience, and they cannot deny me the camera then."

"I think, Issy-Girl, there is only one thing that would find me agreein'." He looked over the images, careful to select the final one he'd snapped in the roll.

"I want this one." He pulled the photo of the castle from the stack. "I think I'd like to ask that it always hang in Foley's snug, where marriages are brokered an' life stories are told. It could stand as a symbol that the Byrnes an' Foleys will always have a bond."

He slipped to his knee . . . kneeling and asking and her heart was bursting.

"Lady Isolde Byrne, my wish is for that bond to extend to the

O'Connells, if ye would say yes this time an' do a humble vicar the honor o' becomin' one?"

The castle stood witness as Issy shouted a yes over the call of the sea wind on the rise, and Sean lifted her into his arms to twirl her around.

The crumbling walls recorded another story in the place where Issy had captured images of wildflowers in bloom . . . where the sea lived on . . . where the pear trees' symbol of peace would always grow . . . and with the ardent hope that one day, a future generation might write a freedom story of their own.

One day, Ireland would be free.

EPILOGUE

Present Day
Ashford Manor
County Wicklow, Ireland

Dolly's secrets may well have slept for decades, but time had grown wings since they'd opened the tower room. A flurry of activity followed, with reporters and historians and government officials descending upon Ashford Manor in droves. It seemed the last days Laine and Cormac had spent together were with the whole of Dublin right beside them.

Memories of a few blissful moments alone in a snug and the hopeful conversation that followed had been eclipsed by it all. And now it seemed Cormac's future would stretch beyond the polished wood walls of a Dublin pub and welcome travelers to an estate that had as much historical meaning to Ireland as nearly any before it.

Laine ran her fingertips over the delicate petals of the yellow wildflowers that grew around the castle walls, feeling the stems' prickle beneath her skin. Soft and strong at the same time—they were perfect for blanketing the glen beneath the mountains and taming the wilds of the winter landscape along the sea cliffs.

That was how she'd choose to remember Ireland—wild and free, and full of everything that said a new life was possible, if you were willing to fight for it.

"Quinn said they're ready to go to the airport. Sent me to fetch ye."

Laine half turned, seeing Cormac out of the corner of her eye. "I'll just be a minute. I wanted one last look." She knelt, trying to pluck a stem without thorns pricking her fingertips. "What are these? I've been admiring them since the first time Ellie and I walked the road to the estate. They sprouted up between the pear trees in the glen."

"Irish aiteann—yellow gorse. They spread like wildfire an' bloom on the rise all around the castle. Over the whole estate, really. Cassie here's been tellin' me how she'd like to come back an' see 'em. Maybe when the pears are ready for harvestin'."

Laine turned around then, not noticing that Cassie had left Ellie at the car and walked up the rise with Cormac. "You didn't say anything about wanting that, honey. Maybe we can come back."

Laine looked up to Cormac, brushing her hair back as she squinted in the sunlight. "When will they bloom again?"

"Gorse can bloom all year."

"Even in winter?"

"Some things can, yeah. When everythin' else is supposed to have died out, ye find somethin' can grow where ye didn't expect it. Ye probably thought this was a castle in winter without any color to it. But 'tis as open an invitation as I can make without sayin' outright that I love ye. An' I can't let ye two go without a fight."

Laine stood on instinct. She'd have gripped the side of the castle wall if it hadn't been obvious that the mention of a certain word nearly shocked her out of her shoes. Cormac read her though, smiling down at Cassie before releasing her hand.

He took a slow, marked step forward through the gorse. "I should probably tell ye that Cassie an' I had a meetin' down at the pub, before we came over to the castle. We came to a deal in the snug—traditional place marriages have been brokered for the last two hundred years. She didn' seal it with the traditional pint, mind. But 'tis bindin' no less. We shook hands an' everythin'. The gents at the bar witnessed it, so there's no goin' back if we want to save face at Foley's from now on."

"Cormac, we're supposed to go back to Michigan. To go home with Ellie and Quinn. They've said Cassie and I can stay at their cottage until we figure things out. So, that was the plan."

"I know that, an' I'm not askin' for anythin' yer not ready to give. Healin' an' trustin' take time. But I needed to tell ye that I can' let ye get on that plane unless I know I'll get to keep the promise I made to Cassie here. Because she wants a daddy, Laine." He paused. "An' God knows I want both o' ye too."

He waited. So did she, disbelieving he'd actually said what was bursting inside her too.

"Please don' make me have to sell a single pear to that old codger at the English Market. Without ye there to negotiate a right price, I'll get fleeced."

The wind whistled around the castle walls, tossing Laine's short hair with a reminder of all that lay around them. Centuries of story that breathed and lived on through the generations. It was the most incredible thing to somehow feel it, that there was a fairy tale at work—one where battles and rising up became the focus of the story, instead of anything less.

"I remember what you said that first night in Dublin." She eased a step closer. Laine held out her hand to Cassie, taking her along, step by little step until they stopped before him. And with intention she knew he'd understand, she took his hand, inviting him into the sacred space of a wounded woman's affections, and let him enter a door she'd thought might be forever locked.

"I said a lot o' things between us."

"You said Ireland has a million stories . . . and if you stay long enough, you learn them all."

Cormac nodded as she rose on her toes, placing her lips a breath from his.

"I did say that."

"Then we accept," she whispered, then drifted a soft kiss across his lips to seal it. "We want to learn them all with you, Cormac Foley."

"There's an old sayin' around Ireland that when gorse is out o' bloom, kissin' is out o' fashion."

"Is that so?" Laine arched her eyebrow.

The flowers of Ireland were hearty but beautiful—so much the definition of where their journey had taken them. Laine stooped to pick one. She turned to Cassie, and being ever careful that thorns wouldn't touch skin, she swept the flower behind her daughter's ear.

They stood in the shadow of Castle Chryn, where the rise always allowed something new to grow, and Cassie reached out, taking a hand from each of them.

Cormac smiled. "Good thing I've got all year wit' my girls to prove that wrong."

AUTHOR'S NOTE

Dublin and I officially met as the Christ Church Cathedral bells chimed, lulling me awake on my first morning in Ireland.

I leaned into the windowsill of our hotel room, warmed my hands around a cup of Irish breakfast tea, and closed my eyes, listening to the same melodic greeting that travelers have heard for over a thousand years. Though the characters in this Lost Castle novel chose a most inopportune time to come alive (a red-eye, transatlantic flight to Dublin), I still believe the magic of this journey began on that first morning of our family's research trip to Ireland.

From the moment our plane touched down on Irish soil and a cabdriver drove us through the quiet, predawn city streets to our hotel, I sensed a story building. Like the best Irish cabbies do, he expertly angled roundabouts while schooling his American travelers on three things: the merits of a pint of Guinness per day, telling stories about the Easter Rising, and sharing pride in the Republic of Ireland—in that order.

On our family's first days in Dublin, we unknowingly walked the exact steps as the characters in this story. We have video footage of walking the length of O'Connell Street—passing the GPO in the spot where Pádraig Pearse read the Proclamation on April 24, 1916 . . . We walked past what was once Clerys department store—a structure rebuilt years after the original burned down in the 1916 Rising . . . We crossed the O'Connell bridge in the spot Issy would have made her daring run, dodging sniper fire to get a dispatch to the rebels . . . Our sons played American football on the very ground where Irish rebels may have dug their trenches at St. Stephen's Green . . . We, too, drifted into a back pew of St. Audoen's Church one rainy night . . . And we even ate our first Irish meal in the Grand Central Pub at 10/11 O'Connell Street Lower—the exact city block where one day Jack Foley's fictional pub would be located.

This is the first time I've had the opportunity to walk in the footsteps of history so closely and then build a story crafted specifically after the experience. To explore the setting with my own senses, to hear the voices of the people, to feel the richness of the earth beneath my boots and smell the salty sea air—the beauty and legacy of the land made Laine's story come alive in a way that hit with a soul-deep familiarity.

At its core, *Castle on the Rise* is a story of rebellion—not just the fight for freedom of the Republic of Ireland, but the rebel spirit that arises in each of us as we weather the battles in our own lives. The characters in this novel display courage and resilience when the worst happens and the fairy-tale story begins to crumble. Instead of lamenting what "should have been," they dig their heels in the dirt and, with conviction, anchor themselves to the one thing that will see them rise: faith.

Inspired by revolutions in both the United States and France, Irish rebellions sparked in 1798 and again in 1803—but were quickly put down by the English. With the outbreak of World War I, however, England's attentions were so diverted it seemed Ireland was primed to try again.

By spring of 1916, increased radicalization had formed among factions of the Irish Volunteers, the Irish Citizen Army (ICA), the Irish Republican Brotherhood (IRB), and a smaller network of organizations such as *Na Fianna Éireann* and *Cumann na mBan*—the latter being a women's military organization formed alongside the men's Irish Volunteers. It was here that leaders emerged, drafting and signing the Proclamation declaring an independent Irish Republic. Among the signees were Thomas Clarke, Seán MacDiarmada, Thomas MacDonagh, Éamonn Ceannt, Joseph Plunkett, James Connolly, and Pádraig Pearse—who was named leader of the Provisional Government.

All signees of the Proclamation—as leaders of the Rising—were among those executed at Kilmainham Gaol prison between May 3 and 12, 1916.

The fight for an independent Republic of Ireland features a strong history of women as well—this story could not be told without their inclusion. Names like Maria Winifred "Winnie" Carney, Elizabeth O'Farrell, Julia Grenan, Lily Kempson, Mary Hyland, and Constance Georgine Markievicz (whom history knows as Countess Markievicz) have now become synonymous with the major Irish Rebellions. Emerging organizations like the *Cumann na mBan*—Irishwomen's Council in English—included suffragists, nationalists, unionists, socialists, and Irish independence activists as some of their distinctions. And while this book makes no political statement on which side of history the Rising leaders belong, we include their involvement through the lens of experiences of the fictional characters Maeve Ashford and Issy Byrne, who not only fought alongside the men but also championed equal rights for Irishmen and Irishwomen—Protestant and Catholic alike.

Though there is no evidence that James Connolly's adjutant, Winnie Carney, contributed to the bulletin Pearse wrote and issued as the *Irish War News*, the rebel-printed newspaper released only one edition—on Tuesday, April 25, 1916. Thought to include fact and fiction (from a decidedly rebel point of view), the paper did present news to account for the first twenty-four hours of fighting. As newspapers printed accounts after the dust cleared on April 30, 1916 (with staged photographs thereafter), they underscored the lack of both accurate reporting and photojournalism from inside the ranks of the Rising itself.

Though I've taken fictional liberties to invent sites such as Ashford Manor and Castle Chryn in County Wicklow, Portobello Church in Dublin's Portobello Quay, and the figure of English lieutenant Corley, the executions of Irish writer and pacifist Francis Sheehy-Skeffington, along with journalists Thomas Dickson and Patrick MacIntyre, did occur by order of real-life Captain John Bowen-Colthurst. The executions and subsequent cover-up at Portobello Barracks sent shockwaves through the population of Dublin. Bowen-Colthurst was later tried and found guilty of murder, though insane.

While the "bricklayers" in our story were also figments of this author's imagination, there are factual accounts of bricklayers who were brought in to cover up the evidence of murder. A bullet lodged in a half-brick piece was saved by one of those bricklayers and in 1935, through a member of the clergy, was sent to Francis Sheehy-Skeffington's widow with a note authenticating its survival.

Hanna Sheehy-Skeffington donated the brick to the National Museum of Ireland in 1937, where it remains a piece of the museum's permanent collection.

Though many facts are recorded—and even more myths have emerged—history alone knows the full path that led to the Republic of Ireland. Even as bloody battles would continue to the establishment of the Irish Free State (1921–1922) and Republic of Ireland (1949), and sectarian violence would last for decades beyond, it is firsthand accounts and artifacts like the photo of Pearse's surrender (with nurse Elizabeth O'Farrell curiously edited out) or the Skeffington brick that seek to tell the full story.

As Cormac Foley so rightly put it: *"Ireland has a million pasts an' even more stories. Ye stay long enough . . . ye learn them all."*

ACKNOWLEDGMENTS

It's no surprise when I tell friends that my favorite part of the writing process comes before I ever pick up a pen—it's in the research where a story is born.

From poring over newspaper articles for the centennial of the Easter Rising, to researching maps of Dublin and the vast coastal areas of County Wicklow, to conversing with curators and guides at Trinity College Dublin, Muckross House (County Kerry), Blarney Castle and Gardens (County Cork), and Ross Castle (County Kerry) . . . researching the history of the Republic of Ireland has become one of the most incredible experiences of my life.

Thank you to the dedicated, the fascinated, and the inspired . . . by history.

To my publishing family—who know this writer-gal had to fight for this story—I extend my most ardent appreciation: Amanda Bostic, Kristen Golden, Allison Carter, Jodi Hughes, Kristen Ingebretson, and Julee Schwarzburg—especially for your brilliant commentary as we carved down this story, line by line. To Becky Monds: Thank you for the time you gave for the crafting of this story and for showing me how exceptional some souls can be at genuinely loving and supporting others. To the dear Katherine Reay, Sarah Ladd, Beth Vogt, Allen Arnold, Maggie Walker, Sharon Tavera, and especially Rachelle Gardner—agent extraordinaire and very, very patient friend—I owe you all a debt of faithful friendship during the writing of this story that will be my pleasure to one day repay.

To Dr. Ray Wallace, chancellor at Indiana University Southeast, I extend a researcher's most enthusiastic *thank you*! For the offer of your time and expertise in exploring Dublin's vast history, your aid in pinpointing locations of camera studios that existed during the Rising, and the loan of a truly remarkable 3A Autographic Kodak Special camera—Issy's exact 1916 model!—I remain grateful. This story came to life in part because of your firsthand accounts of the Irish life.

In addition to the authentic names I picked out of 1911 Irish census records—Eoin (O-in), Maeve (MAYV), Honor, and Sean—a special thanks also goes to readers who helped name characters in this book: Sharon T. in honor of her beloved grandmother, *Dolly*; Somer N. and her daughter, *Cassie*, for lending her name to this strong little character; dear friend Eileen P. for allowing me to borrow her family name *McGinn* for the fiery Honor; Caryl K. for choosing *Aisling* (ASH-ling) as the name for the dream of Honor and Rory's future; Sarah O'Malley, who pointed me to *Cian* (KEE-in); and for *Deborah*—an incredible lady who served our family a much-needed meal at Blarney Castle and Gardens on one chilly day of research in Ireland. You warmed us with your conversation and smiles, and we were delighted to name this character for you.

To Dr. Richard and Jeannie Chryn: While I couldn't buy you the castle you've always wanted, I could build one in a story world. Much love to you both!

For every story ever penned to paper, an author has had those who believe in him or her, supporting from the critical place behind the scenes. To Lindy Wedge and Jennifer Thompson—what would Dad think of all we've seen and done? Thank you for your love and support. To Jeremy Cambron—I get to walk this writing road because of you. I love you. And to Brady, Carson, and Colt—I am most proud to have been involved in the creation of you.

To my Savior, Redeemer, King, and best friend: the reason I have to dig my heels in the dirt and rise to battle *anything* is all because of You.

Kristy

DISCUSSION QUESTIONS

1. Laine and Cormac's journey together begins on somewhat rocky ground, with brokenness on both sides of their family tree. How does Laine's reluctance to step back into love—especially when she wasn't expecting to—impact her ability to heal from past hurts? Is their ability to accept each other's broken past what helps them move on?
2. Eoin originally comes to the Ashford estate to stop more innocent lives from being lost—including Maeve and her father—on Christmas Eve. Yet as he and Maeve begin to envision a peaceful future together, he doesn't stop rebellion leaders from transferring arms through the castle cove. How did Maeve honor her husband's convictions while still holding on to her own? Can we stand firm and support someone we love, especially when they hold beliefs opposite of ours?
3. Issy's journey from her unrequited love of Levi to the steadfast, more authentic love of Sean anchors her through the midst of Ireland's turbulent Easter week of 1916. How did her view of love—and life—change over the course of the Rising? How did her faith in God, and in Sean, serve as a stronghold to keep battling for those she loved?

4. *Castle on the Rise* opens with Ellie and Quinn's chapel wedding, though their fairy-tale ending is called into question almost immediately. How do Laine and Cormac support their loved ones when life doesn't work out as they'd originally planned? How does Laine come to view similar circumstances surrounding an unwanted divorce and Cassie's adoption?
5. Issy's view of women in society might be considered revolutionary for the era in which she lived. How did her bravery to enter a vocation largely held by men show dedication to her passion for photography? What other women in the 1916 Rising stepped up to lead in areas where they hadn't been represented before?
6. Did Maeve abandon her love for music after George's death, or did she allow it to be hidden so her father could endure his grief? In what ways was Eoin able to encourage her back to the things she once loved? Can we still hold onto a passion when life doesn't turn out as planned?
7. History refers to the fighting men and women in Ireland's rebellions as "rebels." Given the scope of destruction in the aftermath of both the 1798 and 1916 rebellions, do you think their fight for freedom was justified? Why or why not?
8. *Castle on the Rise* weaves three storylines in different eras into the long history of Ireland's dream of freedom—all with hints of a "rebel spirit" as an undercurrent. How did Ellie and Quinn, Laine and Cormac, Issy and Sean, Maeve and Eoin, and even Rory and Honor overcome the obstacles in front of them in order to battle for hope, healing, and a future?

DON'T MISS THESE OTHER FABULOUS NOVELS BY KRISTY CAMBRON!

"A vivid and romantic rendering of circus life in the Jazz Age."
—*USA TODAY*, *Happy Ever After*

"Prepare to be amazed by *The Illusionist's Apprentice*."
—Greer Macallister, bestselling author of *The Magician's Lie* and *Girl in Disguise*

Available in print, e-book, and audio!

ABOUT THE AUTHOR

Photo by Whitney Neal Photography

Kristy Cambron fancies life as a vintage-inspired storyteller. Her novels have been named to *Library Journal Reviews*' list of Best Books of 2014 and 2015 and have received nominations for *RT* Reviewers' Choice Awards Best Inspirational Book of 2014 and 2015, as well as INSPY Award nominations in 2015 and 2017. Kristy holds a degree in art history from Indiana University and lives in Indiana with her husband and three basketball-loving sons.

Website: www.kristycambron.com
Instagram: KristyCambron
Facebook: KCambronAuthor
Twitter: @KCambronAuthor
Pinterest: KCambronAuthor